S   in
h   or
u   n't
h   k.

Tease me? Please me?
Please. Let me please you.
Tonight, I believe I will dream of your
mouth.

Until next time,
Nick

Heartfelt Applause for the Romances of Geralyn Dawson

SIZZLE ALL DAY

THE BAD LUCK WEDDING CAKE

"Fast and captivating from start to finish. This humorous story is as delicious as one of [the heroine's] cakes!"

—*Rendezvous*

"A delicious gourmet delight! A seven-course reading experience."

—*Affaire de Coeur*

"This funny, fast-paced romance is a joy to read. Geralyn Dawson has written a laugh-out-loud tale with a few tears and a big sigh at the end. Another keeper."

—*Romantic Times*

"Warm and delicious enough to satisfy the sweet tooth of any reader. Geralyn Dawson leaves me hungry for more!"

—Teresa Medeiros, author of *The Bride and the Beast*

SIMMER ALL NIGHT

"Delightfully spicy—perfect to warm up a cold winter's night."

—Christina Dodd, author of *Rules of Surrender*

"A romance buoyed by lively characters and Southern lore. Dawson sustains readers' attention with her humorous dialogue and colorful narration."

—*Publishers Weekly*

"Once again, Geralyn Dawson has come up with a winner. Great verbal sparring, delightfully funny at times and also extremely touching."

—*Romantic Times*

"*Simmer All Night* is an entertaining blend of a western romance with a Victorian romance. The mix works as the characters imbue a special jocular charm into the story line. Geralyn Dawson shows she is a gourmet chef who serves simmering hot Texas chili with a cup of tea."

—*Painted Rock Reviews*

"*Simmer All Night* is a wonderful, delightful, and gratifying book that is not to be missed."

—*Denver Rocky Mountain News*

Also by Geralyn Dawson

The Wedding Raffle
The Wedding Ransom
The Bad Luck Wedding Cake
The Kissing Star
Simmer All Night
Sizzle All Day
The Bad Luck Wedding Night

Published by POCKET BOOKS

GERALYN DAWSON

The Bad Luck Wedding Night

SONNET BOOKS

New York London Toronto Sydney Singapore

An *Original* Publication of POCKET BOOKS

A Sonnet Book published by
POCKET BOOKS, a division of Simon & Schuster, Inc.
1230 Avenue of the Americas, New York, NY 10020

Copyright © 2001 by Geralyn Dawson Williams

ISBN: 0-671-03449-9

First Sonnet Books printing April 2001

10 9 8 7 6 5 4 3 2 1

SONNET BOOKS and colophon are trademarks of
Simon & Schuster, Inc.

Front cover illustration by Ben Perini

Printed in the U.S.A.

For
Andrew Hobbs
with thanks for the title
and
Steve Williams
for your love and support

The Bad Luck Wedding Night

*It's bad luck to marry in May, on Friday, or on an
odd-numbered day, especially the Thirteenth.*

~1~

Friday, May 13
Fort Worth, Texas 1877

In the two-room honeymoon suite at the Blackstone Hotel, Sarah Ross extended her left arm, wiggled her fingers, and smiled with delight as the
lamplight glistened off the shiny gold band. "Mrs.
Nicholas Ross," she murmured with a sigh. "Sarah
Ross. Mr. and Mrs. Nicholas Ross."

Happiness bubbled up inside her as she clutched
her ring hand to her chest and twirled around. Her
wedding gown billowed in a cloud of satin and lace,
and she laughed aloud. She was gleefully, joyously,
jubilantly in love with being in love. "Oh, Abby.
Wasn't the wedding wonderful?"

Sarah's best friend, Abigail Reese, smiled dreamily and nodded. "It was a fairy tale. Everything about
it. Your wedding was without a doubt the most spectacular this town has ever seen."

"That's sweet of you to say."

"It's true, though. The flowers especially were
divine. Whatever gave you the idea to give miniature

rose bouquets to all the little girls in the congregation?"

"They were perfect, weren't they?" Beaming, Sarah kicked off a slipper. "I believe now more than ever that a wedding should be enjoyed by both family and guests. The perfect wedding should create warm memories that will linger in the minds of all who attend—not just the bride and groom. The bouquets were part of my effort to make those memories."

"You accomplished that." Abby brought her own bridesmaid bouquet up to her face and inhaled the sweet scent of roses. "Did you hear all the squeals?"

"I did."

"And so did the girls' parents and the other guests. Sarah, those sounds of delight were as much a part of the wedding music as the songs the organist played." Abby sighed and set down her bouquet. "Plus they perfumed the church and enhanced its beauty."

"St. Paul's is lovely, but a bit dark. All that yellow helped make it bright and cheerful inside, but more important, the flowers made each girl feel like a bridesmaid. They'll have fond memories of my wedding for years to come. Now the boys might have preferred something other than the little wish boxes we passed out, but I think they'll put them to good use. Tommy Wilson said he wished his way out of church during the ceremony."

She smiled slyly as she kicked off her second shoe and added, "While the girls dreamed of their own wedding day, the boys wished themselves far away."

Abby laughed. "But they were quiet."

"They were quiet." Sarah wiggled her toes. "And their parents enjoyed the ceremony."

"You have a special talent," Abby said, staring wistfully into the future. "I hope someday you'll help me plan my wedding."

"Of course I'll help. I'll be honored to do so." She clasped her friend's hands and gave them a squeeze. "And I hope that stubborn Jerry Johnson quits piddling around and asks for your hand soon. Wouldn't it be lovely to do a Christmas season wedding? I have lovely ideas about poinsettias."

"Christmas! Maybe Christmas two years from now. My papa is different from your mother, Sarah. He thinks sixteen is too young to marry."

Sarah wrinkled her nose. "I never told you this, but my mama tried to convince us to delay the wedding until I turn seventeen in August, but Nick and I didn't want to wait. May weather is so much more pleasant for wedding festivities, and besides, I can't wait to move into the house Nick has built for us. I can't wait to put all our beautiful wedding gifts to use. Did you see the silver service the Washingtons sent?"

"I did. I love the curlicues on the end of the handles."

"I do, too. I intend to display it atop the teacart my aunt and uncle gave us."

"It'll be beautiful. Just like the wedding and just like the bride." Abby beamed a teasing smile Sarah's way and added, "Nick looked poleaxed when you started down the aisle on your uncle's arm."

Dreamily, Sarah recalled the moment. "He was the one who looked beautiful. That thick dark hair and those brilliant blue eyes. Oh, Abby, when he smiles at me I feel a flutter all the way to my toes."

"Sometimes when he smiles at you, his eyes get a wicked gleam in them. I'll never forget how at your piano recital last month he slouched against the wall with his arms folded. He never once looked away from you, and when you finished your piece, he straightened up and clapped real slow."

Sarah sighed breathlessly. "Then he winked at me."

"And you blushed pink as your dress. Wilhemina Peters leaned over to my mama and said, 'John Simpson must be rolling over in his grave at the notion of his little girl with that boy. Nicholas Ross is a devil in denim.'"

Sarah sniffed. "My papa would have liked Nick. He's no devil. He may look a little dangerous since he's so tall and broad for a man of eighteen, but he's really sweet and kind and gentle."

"Maybe she meant devil in a good way," Abby reassured her. "But it's good that he's gentle with you. That will make tonight easier."

Both girls' gazes traveled toward the tall poster bed partially visible through the half-opened doorway into the suite's second room. Sarah's stomach took a nervous roll.

Tonight. The bedding. Though she'd managed to avoid dwelling on It during the festivities, the subject had hovered at the edge of her mind all day. She couldn't ignore It any longer. Not since her mother had sent her up to the room to prepare for her new husband's arrival.

Sarah sank into a chair and shut her eyes. She loved Nick. She really, truly did. But all in all, she'd rather crawl under the bed and hide than crawl into it with Nick.

Abby cleared her throat. "Did your mama have a talk with you about It? Did she tell you what to expect? I've been dying to know, Sarah."

Sarah swallowed a little moan. "Yes, she spoke with me, although I almost wish she hadn't. You know this isn't the first time we've discussed It. I've told you what she said in the past. What she had to add today was ... well ... just a little more detailed."

Eyes going round and wide, Abby sat on the sofa across from Sarah. "You mean she didn't take it back? All the previous talk was true? She didn't say it to scare you off from acting loose?"

"It's all true," Sarah said glumly. "And I hate to tell you, but according to the new information she told me today ... well ... It is even worse than we thought."

"No! You mean the part about the tongue is true?"

Sarah felt the warmth of a blush steal up her throat. "Uh, actually, I know about that myself. That part is kinda nice."

If possible, Abby's eyes went even rounder. "Why, Sarah Simpson. Or, I should say, Sarah Ross. You let Nick use his tongue? Before you were married?"

"Technically, it was a kiss. Mama always said kisses were allowed with a fiancé. Besides, sometimes he gets all het up and the Scot comes out in his voice. The sound of it makes me go all soft and ... willing."

"But still . . ." Abby leaned forward, her eyes bright. "His tongue? And you liked it?"

Embarrassed now, Sarah nodded.

Abby waited. When her friend failed to elaborate, she said, "Well. Maybe you'll like the rest of it, too." After a moment's pause, she asked, "What *is* the rest?"

Sarah wasn't certain how much she should say. Mama told her a lady didn't discuss the private side of marriage, not even with her husband, except to prepare her own daughter when the time came. But she and Abby had always shared secrets, and if Abby learned the truth now she'd have enough time to get used to the idea before she herself married.

Sarah thought that would be a good thing. She certainly wished she'd had more than one day to prepare herself. She might not be so scared in that case.

She cleared her throat. "Remember last year she told me how men sometimes want to pinch and pull at women's bosoms?"

"Yes, and I know that's true because one time not long ago my papa wasn't paying attention, and he took a wrong turn on the way home from church and we drove through Hell's Half Acre. I saw a man with his hands on a painted lady's breasts."

"Well," Sarah said, wincing, "according to what Mama told me this morning, men like to do more than touch. Mama says that sometimes men act like babies and suck on them."

Abigail's mouth dropped open. "No."

"Uh-huh. And that's not the worst of it." Sarah drew a deep breath, then exhaled with a sigh. Frowning, she leaned forward and crooked a finger, gesturing her friend to come closer. Then she whispered, "Mama says his tallywhacker will turn into a Rod of Steel, and he'll want to put it between my legs and ram it into me until I bleed."

Abigail responded with a horrified gasp. "What?"

"I know." Sarah's stomach took another roll. "It's awful. She says it hurts, but it's a woman's lot in life, and the reward is children, which makes it worth the pain. And, she said maybe I'll be lucky and have a considerate husband who will get it over with fast."

Eyes glazed with shock, Abby slumped back

against the sofa. "Oh my. A Rod of Steel. Oh my. Do you believe her?"

Sarah swallowed the sudden lump in her throat. "My mother doesn't lie."

The two girls sat quietly for a time, pondering the mystery. Finally Sarah said, "I've tried to be sensible about this. If it's as bad for every woman as it was for my mother, the human race would have died out long ago. Men might be stronger and physically able to force their desires on women, but we have the advantage of our superior intelligence."

"That is true," Abby said, her yellow hair ribbon swinging as she nodded in agreement.

"So, if It is *that* awful, surely women would have figured out a way to avoid It long ago. Or make It better, anyway."

"I think some women actually like It," Abby declared. "How else could one explain mistresses? Soiled doves might be forced into the life by circumstance, but from what I've heard while eavesdropping on Mother's quilting circle, some women actually choose to have affairs with men. They must like to do It."

"True." Sarah sighed. Actually, she had considered that notion herself. Her stomach almost always got fluttery when Nick kissed her, and once after they'd been kissing for a long time, he'd pulled away groaning and said she was wicked. She'd certainly felt wicked at the time. Hesitantly, she put her question to her friend. "Maybe I'm an evil woman, too, and I just don't know it."

"You're not evil, Sarah, although in this one case it might be better if you were." Abby stood and paced the room, pausing beside the wardrobe where Sarah's veil hung like a lace waterfall. She fingered the seed pearls at the crown and gave a nervous little laugh. "All of a sudden I'm glad Jerry is stubborn, and my papa won't permit me to marry anytime soon."

"All of a sudden, I wish I were still a fiancée, not a bride. I adored being a fiancée."

Abby stepped away from the veil and crossed the room to sit beside her friend. Taking Sarah's hand in hers, she said, "Are you certain you want to go through with this? Do you have to do It? Is it a law or something? Maybe you could talk Nicholas into playing chess instead. You said he loves to play chess."

"I get the feeling he's gonna love doing It more," Sarah replied, recalling the hardness she'd felt against her when he'd tongue-kissed her senseless at her front door after walking her home last night. For a minute she'd wondered if he carried a pistol in his pocket, then she'd realized it must have been his Rod of Steel.

Sarah wanted to bury her head in her hands and shudder and shake. Instead, she lifted her chin and squared her shoulders. "It will be fine. I'll be fine. I love our new home, and I can't wait to arrange all the pretty gifts we received. I look forward to cooking for Nick—he loves my molasses cookies—and I'll plant roses by the front door and wash our clothes on Mondays, and we'll attend the Literary Society meetings on the third Thursday of every month. I want to do all those things. I look forward to doing all those things. We'll have a happy life, Nick and I, and someday we'll have children. I vowed to be his wife for better or worse. I keep my word, Abby. I won't deny him his husbandly rights."

"Oh, Sarah, you are much braver than I."

Sarah squared her shoulders and spoke in a martyred tone. "No, I'm a wife now, and I will accept my lot as such. Besides, Nick has always been a considerate man. Maybe I'll be lucky and he'll be quick about it."

Nicholas Ross wondered if acute sexual frustration could make a man ill. Considering he'd been walking around with his wick constantly lit for weeks now, he was in trouble if that were the case.

Thank God it was almost time to take the cure, and Sarah was certainly the cure for everything that ailed him.

Nick grinned at the thought. Actually, he'd grinned at just about anything and everything today. For the first time in a long time, he was happy. He had a family again.

Family meant the world to Nick. Two years ago, through a combination of his own hardheadedness and the capriciousness of fate, he had lost the family of his heart, the family had taken him in as an infant and raised him as their own. The one dark cloud in the sunny sky of this special day was the fact that his Scottish loved ones had to watch him wed from their places in heaven.

The thought sent a pang of emotion through him that he swiftly suppressed. He wouldn't think of sad things now; he'd turn his thoughts to merrier matters. He'd think about his bride.

Nick glanced at his pocket watch. Her mother had asked him to give Sarah an hour, and he still had twenty minutes left to wait. He could wait twenty minutes. Barely. He'd wanted Sarah since the moment he'd laid eyes on her.

She sparkled. She was blond, with rich, whiskey-brown eyes and a ready smile and laugh that warmed him from the inside out. Most men would call her pretty rather than beautiful. Most men would prefer a few more curves on her thin, relatively straight figure. But to Nick, Sarah was perfect, and he'd challenge anyone who claimed that Fort Worth had ever seen a more beautiful bride.

He wondered what she'd wear to greet him this evening. He had fantasized her in a filmy, Greek-goddess gown with one shoulder bare and tantalizing shadows visible beneath the clinging ivory silk. He would open the door and she'd smile invitingly, lifting her arms and beckoning him toward her.

Or, maybe she'd smile, then reach up and release the clasp at her shoulder and the gown would slip, slowly revealing the breathtaking beauty of milky skin and pink-tipped breasts and . . .

A spattering of laughter from the wedding reception guests still gathered in the hotel ballroom shook him from his fantasy. One side of his mouth twisted in a rueful grin. Knowing Miss Modest Sarah, he'd find her wrapped in flannel.

Sarah wasn't one to flaunt her femininity. Indeed, when it came to romance, the girl was downright shy. It had taken him two full weeks of determined pursuit to coax her into letting him kiss her the way he desired. As a result, Nick found himself a wee bit apprehensive about the wedding night to come.

Not that he was complaining. A man valued virtue in a bride. Besides, judging by the way she had taken to his kisses, once she got over being shy, Sarah worked up a fine enthusiasm toward the activity.

His task tonight would be helping her past her shyness. He prayed he had the patience to do the job properly.

A hand clapped him on the back. "Well, son," boomed Sarah's uncle's voice. "This is the first time I've found you alone since the wife and I arrived in town from Galveston. How about we take a short walk outside?"

All in all, Nick would rather have his teeth pulled out one by one than take this particular walk. He knew he had to do it, though. With Sarah's father dead for a decade, her uncle was her closest male relative. Nick hadn't expected to avoid the *Hurt our little girl and I'll kill you* conversation entirely. Hoped, yes. But not expected.

Outside the Blackstone Hotel, streaks of scarlet, orange, and gold painted the western sky. Wagons rattled up Main Street, while from the direction of Hell's Half Acre came the tinny sound of piano music and an occasional raucous shout that heralded the beginnings of a hell-raisin' Saturday night.

Nick resisted the urge to tug at his collar. "It is a beautiful evening."

"Yes, and I trust it will stay that way." Michael Banks opened his suit coat and removed a cigar from an inner pocket. After going through the ritual of lighting it, he blew out a pair of smoke rings and said, "You have a challenge ahead of you, son. I hate to say it, but the girl is spoiled."

Nick immediately jumped to her defense. "She's high-spirited."

"That, too. Make no mistake, I love her like she's my own, but the girl has suffered from not having a father around. Not that her mother didn't do her best, but Sarah was a willful child and my sister never learned how to say no. Take an old man's advice, young Nick, and teach her the meaning of the word from the git-go. Otherwise, you'll pay for it for the rest of your life."

Nick relaxed a bit with the unexpected direction the conversation had taken. It turned out he relaxed too soon.

Banks blew a puff of ratafia-scented smoke his way, then abruptly demanded. "Who are your people?"

Now Nick gave in to the urge to pull at his collar. "My people, sir?"

"Your family. The Rosses. My sister says you claim to be a Scot, but she mentioned some confusion about English parents, too. While I don't hold a man's character hostage to his family background, I do consider it something important to know. So, tell me about your family, Mr. Ross. Who is your father?"

Nick bristled at the older man's words. He refused to ruin this happy day with talk of his sire. "I'd rather not."

After two more puffs on the cigar, Banks asked, "What are you hiding?"

"Not a blessed thing. Sarah knows of my past. She has a right to know." Left unsaid was the charge that her uncle didn't share that right.

It didn't deter Michael Banks. "I understand you purchased the Seven-F Ranch just last month. You have family money?"

Nick sidestepped the question and attempted to guide the conversation in another direction. "I promised Sarah we'd live within a half day's ride from her mother. Since it's been just her and Mrs. Simpson for so long, Sarah is worried about leaving her mother alone in the house. In fact, we asked if she'd want to move out to the ranch with us, but she declined. Mrs. Simpson has worked hard to establish her private school, and she loves teaching. Although, after the way those McBride children acted at the wedding today, I am inclined to wonder why. Now I know why townspeople refer to them as the McBride Menaces."

Sarah's uncle didn't take the bait. "I understand there's no mortgage on your land. What did you do, Ross, rob a stage or two?"

Nick smiled grimly. "I have my own money."

"From what source?"

Nosy old fellow. Nick wanted to tell him to go to the devil. But because he understood the man's need to protect Sarah, Nick sighed heavily and surrendered. "All right, Mr. Banks. I'll speak of my family skeletons once, then never again. Two years ago, I discovered my parents had lied about the circumstances of my birth. I learned I wasn't their son, but the third son of an English marquess and his wife. It seems I was conceived during a time Lord and Lady Weston were experiencing trouble in their marriage."

"Oh," commented Banks. "You're a bastard."

"No, apparently not. Lady Weston swore I was her husband's get, though he believed she lied and hated me because of that. He knew she'd had a lover during the significant time. When within months of my birth it became clear he wouldn't accept me, and since Weston already had an heir and a spare, she sent me to Scotland to be reared by distant cousins of her husband, thinking it was better for a child to live in a home where he was loved by both parents than in a home where he was hated by his father."

"And was this a good choice?"

Nick hesitated as he once again felt the absence of the Ross family on his wedding day. Quietly he said, "An excellent choice. My greatest regret is that I forgot that for a time."

"My niece mentioned you recently learned your family was killed in an accident. Was this your English family, your birth parents and brothers?"

Nick didn't respond. Instead, he focused on the amusing sight of the older two McBride Menaces. They had abandoned all regard for the state of their clothing and lay flat on the sidewalk in front of the hotel, using their miniature rose bouquets to guide a trio of doodlebugs in the direction they desired. His bride's uncle shifted his gaze from Nick to the girls, then back to Nick again. "You inherited money from your father?" he pressed.

" 'Tis my Scots family who died." Frustration flared like a match. "Is there no question you winna ask? Lord Weston pays me a remittance to stay away from England. I dinna use it if I can help it, so it has added up over time. I bought the ranch with those funds." He made a show of checking his pocket watch, then added, "You'll have to excuse me, sir. My bride is waiting and I'm anxious to join her. It is, after all, our wedding night."

Banks scowled. "Oh, I remember, all right, and there is something I hope you remember, too." He tossed his cigar to the ground, then mashed it under the toe of his boot. "Hurt Sarah and I'll kill you."

Finally the message he'd expected. "Your niece is safe with me, sir. You have my word on it. I'll treat her like a queen."

Sarah felt like a sacrificial lamb all gussied up and ready for the slaughter. She'd been bathed and brushed, powdered and perfumed, and left alone with her teary-eyed mother's words of wisdom ringing in her ears. "Remember, dear, marital relations are like menstrual cramps. Sometimes a swallow or two of brandy makes all the difference."

The words ran around and around in her mind as her finger idly traced the pattern of sharp edges and valleys cut in the crystal brandy decanter. She wished now that she'd asked her mother some of the questions that continued to plague her as time for the bedding approached. But Sarah's aunt had accompanied her mother and stayed in the room until the very end. She'd been too embarrassed to ask in front of Aunt Lena. Now she was left to figure it out for herself.

Or wait for Nick to show her.

Sarah shut her eyes and groaned. Why had she compared It to menstrual cramps? Sarah knew her mother had loved her father, and one time when she'd talked to her daughter about the private side of marriage, she'd even admitted she liked to be kissed.

Sarah liked to be kissed, too. She liked it very much. And hadn't she always been a lot like her mother? Didn't they have the same tastes in everything, from food to fashion to furniture? Hadn't they agreed on the choices for the wedding arrangements, from the flowers to the music to the gown and everything in between? The only time they'd differed in their opinion was when the time came to choose her nightgown for tonight. Sarah had pictured flowing white that bared one shoulder, the design right out of Greek mythology. Her mother recommended high-necked, long-sleeved, floral-sprigged flannel. They'd settled on emerald satin and lace and lots of it.

Could it be a physical thing? Sarah wondered. Were some women physically more suited to It than others? Maybe that's why her mother never remarried after her father's death. Heaven knows, it wasn't for lack of admirers. Maybe her mother wasn't built to bed a man comfortably.

If so, the usual similarities between mother and daughter didn't bode well for the night's upcoming event.

Her mother's voice floated through her mind. *A woman's lot. Rod of Steel. Like menstrual cramps.*

Sarah shuddered, yanked out the stopper, and took a swig of brandy straight from the decanter.

Fire scorched down her throat to her stomach. Her eyes widened and watered. She coughed, then gasped a breath. "Mama thinks this will *help?*"

Heavens. Sexual intercourse must really be awful.

As that thought flashed through her mind, a knock sounded at the door. Nick's voice called, "Sarah?"

Panic rose like a tidal wave within her. Sarah literally bit her tongue. Pain. Blood. A ramming Rod of Steel.

"Sarah? May I come in?"

She took a deep breath and shouted, "No!"

*N*ick thought he must have misheard her. He rapped on the door again. "Lass?"

"You can't come in, Nick."

His mouth lifted in a slow, crooked smile, and he checked the corridor to confirm their privacy before answering, "Don't rush to get dressed on my account."

He heard a gurgling sound and he frowned. Was she choking? He tried the door. Locked. He fished in his pocket and removed the brass room key he'd obtained from the desk downstairs, then slipped it into the lock and twisted. Metal clicked. Nick turned the knob and stepped inside the honeymoon suite.

He saw a streak of emerald green disappear into the second room. "Sarah, are you all right?"

"Y-y-yes."

She didn't sound all right.

"Did you eat something that went down the wrong way?"

"N-n-n-o. I'm fine."

Nick's mouth settled in a grim line. Judging by the quaver to her voice, he had his doubts about that. He glanced around the simple suite's sitting room, spied the open brandy decanter, and mentally cursed. He should have resisted this silly tradition of having mothers and aunts and best friends—that silly Abigail Reese was an agitator—help prepare a bride for her wedding night. Now Sarah was all worked up and nervous. Better that he and she had come upstairs together and let the passion of the moment carry them away.

He slipped the bottle of sweet wine he'd thought his bride would prefer into the waiting ice bucket, then poured himself two fingers of the brandy she'd left out. He tossed it back like the worst rotgut whisky before turning to face the bedroom.

"Sarah, I'm coming in," he called as he approached the doorway between the sitting room and the bedroom. He was two steps away when she slammed the door between them shut.

Nick raked his fingers through his hair. "She's a virgin, remember," he muttered. An obviously reluctant virgin.

And he had no experience with virgins.

Damnation. He dragged his hand along his jawline. He'd known she might be skittish, but he hadn't expected slamming doors. Maybe he should have seen it coming. Sarah was an intriguing, appealing combination of innocence and passion, a rosebud on the brink of first bloom.

Considering her youth, it probably would have been better not to rush toward a wedding as quickly as they had. As much as Nick wanted her in his bed, he could have waited. Indeed, he wasn't exactly certain how he'd ended up engaged. Back in January, Sarah and her mother had been helping Trace McBride oversee the birthday party arrangements for one of his daughters. Sarah had asked Nick to entertain the children with Scottish folktales, and before the night was over, the conversation had gone from fairy spells to wedding bells.

From the beginning, Sarah had had her heart set on a May wedding, and as hungry as he was for her, he hadn't seen how hurrying things along would hurt. Now, though, he had a better view of the troubles that lay ahead.

Starting with the paneled oak door in front of his face.

As Nick reached for the brass doorknob, it turned and the door inched open. He all but swallowed his tongue at the sight that met his eyes.

Sarah's unbound hair cascaded like a golden waterfall upon a field of emerald green. Her dressing gown hid everything, promised everything, and set Nick's heart beating faster. She licked her full, Cupid's-bow lips before gazing up at him through thick, curling lashes that framed solemn eyes the color of the finest Highland malt.

"Would you like to play a game of chess, Nicholas?"

He wanted to throw back his head and howl.

Instead, he cleared his throat. "Chess?"

"We haven't played a game in two weeks."

To his mind, all they'd been doing was playing games. He decided to speak to her honestly. "Sarah, it's our wedding night. Couples don't ordinarily play chess on their wedding night."

"But we're not an ordinary couple, are we?" she asked hopefully.

He had to laugh at that. "Come here, lass."

Nick took her hand and stepped past her into the bedroom, forcing himself to ignore the fact that she'd planted her feet like roots in a pecan orchard as he dragged her toward the bed.

"I'm not sleepy, Nick. If chess doesn't appeal, we could play something else. Cards, maybe?"

"Five-card strip poker would work."

"Pardon me?"

"Sarah, sit down, please." He guided her up against the bed, then gave her a gentle push. She sat on the edge of the mattress and gripped it hard. He hunkered down in front of her so that their eyes were level. "At first I thought it was simply embarrassment, but now I suspect it's more than that. Are you afraid of me?"

She blinked once. "No."

"But you're afraid of something."

"Yes."

"What is it?"

She nibbled at her lower lip. "It."

He waited for her to complete her sentence, but it soon became apparent that she had already finished. "It?"

She shut her eyes and sighed. "It's the idea of steel that bothers me. I've always thought more along the lines of a noodle, so you can see how this takes some adjustment."

Nick rocked back on his heels. She'd lost him entirely. "Sarah, I don't understand."

"I'm not being rational, am I?" She opened her eyes and looked at him then, her gaze both wary and pleading. "Be patient with me, Nick. I think I was so involved with the wedding and all the arrangements that I didn't take time to consider what is supposed to happen afterward. Now that the time is upon me, I'm a little bit . . . no, I'm a lot concerned. You see, I've always been a baby where pain is concerned."

Pain. *Ah hah. It's the virginity problem.*

Nick slowly stood, then took a seat beside her. He wished he knew just what to say to reassure her, but he'd never been with a virgin before, so he wasn't entirely certain what to expect. He linked his fingers through hers and tried to distract her. "It was a nice wedding."

Immediately her face brightened. "Wasn't it? Almost everything turned out like I planned. Except for the cake. I know Mr. Spooner did his best, but I do wish Fort Worth had a more skilled professional baker. I know our guests had a good time. Did you see those McBride girls dancing with their daddy, all three at once? I know that folks here in town don't consider Mr. McBride respectable since he owns a saloon in Hell's Half Acre, but no one can deny that he's a wonderful father to those girls. Not even Wilhemina Peters. Did you notice that hat she was wearing? What would possess a woman to—"

Nick kissed her. It was the best way he knew to hush her babbling, and when she melted in his arms, he realized this might be the best way to get past the first-time jitters. Experience had taught him that once he managed to breach her defenses, Sarah caught fire faster than tinder. The trick was not to give her time to think.

So Nick put his best effort into the kiss, which in return stoked the fires of his own hunger. He kissed her deeply, his tongue seeking, exploring, demanding. She tasted of brandy and promise, and the sweetness of it exploded through his senses. The taste combined with the heady, intoxicating scent of arousal that permeated the air and interfered with reason, leaving him vulnerable to the driving force of his own instincts.

She was his wife. Legally and morally. Nothing stood in the way of making her his mate. Nothing but the thin barrier of flesh that was her final defense.

Nick knew a fierce, primal urge to conquer, to claim, and he had to fight for the will to slow down.

He lay her back against the mattress, and the whispered sound of his name on her lips shuddered through him. A haze of desire surrounded him, thicker and hungrier than any he'd known before. He tugged at the belt of her dressing gown until the knot slipped free and emerald lace slid away to reveal a neckline that plunged to a deep vee between the perfect mounds of her breasts.

Nick gritted his teeth against a groan. *Slow down. Don't scare her. Get control of yourself. Slow down before you go off like a virgin yourself.*

He swallowed hard, then reached for the trailing edge of a silver satin ribbon. With one slow tug, the bow disappeared, fabric parted, and skin was revealed.

"Sarah," he said hoarsely. Her breasts were exquisite: high and gently rounded and crested by nipples that were pert and pink and perfect. Without stopping to think, he lowered his head and licked first one proud tip, then the other.

Her quick gasp filled her lungs with air and lifted her toward him. Nick took it as an invitation, whether she meant it as one or not. He knew he had to taste her or die.

He took her in his mouth and began to suckle, stroking his rough tongue across the downy texture of her nipple. Hazy heat gathered force within him, spiraling downward, filling his loins to near bursting.

Even as he realized she'd gone stiff in his arms.

"What are you doing?" she demanded, her voice a reedy squeak as she pushed against his shoulders. "Nick, stop it!"

Silently groaning, Nick released her and looked up. Her eyes were wide and stormy, her color high. He struggled to ignore the pounding of his heart and the twisting ache in his loins as he forced a smile and soothed her. "Relax, lass. 'Tis all right. All is well. I'll slow down. It may kill me, but I'll slow down."

She flattened her palms against his chest and shoved. "I didn't say slow down. I said stop."

"Stop?"

"Yes, stop!"

Damnation. Grimacing, Nick rolled over onto his back and counted to ten as he tried to catch his breath. The lass was work. He bent one knee, then reached down and adjusted his trousers, which at the moment felt at least ten sizes too small. At that, his bride let out another affronted gasp, and this time he rolled his eyes before flinging his arm up to cover them.

He heard her scramble and assumed she was setting her nightgown to rights. His main concern at the moment, however, was wrestling his raging body back under control.

A full minute passed while the only sound in the room was the ragged noise of his breathing and the nervous scratch of Sarah's nails against the bed coverings. Then she surprised him by asking, "That was wrong of me, wasn't it?"

He cocked one eye open and peered out from beneath his arm.

She held her arms crossed over her chest and wore both a sickly smile and an apple blush. "Mama told me that might happen, but it took me by surprise. I guess I didn't really believe . . ."

When her voice trailed off, Nick sighed. Maybe he *should* give her more time. "Are you still ready for a chess match?"

After a wistful gaze toward the game table in one corner of the room, she shook her head. Swallowing bravely, she declared, "No, I must do my duty."

Damnation. He'd married a martyr.

It did not bode well for the immediate future. "Sarah, this might be easier if you'd take a different approach. Lovemaking need not be a 'duty.'"

Hope shone in the whisky eyes she turned his way. "I thought we had to do It. I thought it was a rule. Do you not want to do It, either?"

"Of course I want to do it. I'm a healthy, eighteen-year-old man. I *always* want to do it."

"Oh."

He was trying to be patient and understanding, but the fact was, her crestfallen expression annoyed him. Were all virgins this ridiculous, or was he just lucky?

She plucked at a loose thread on the counterpane. "So I guess that means you've done It before?"

"What kind of question is that? You're not supposed to ask me about the women I've had."

Her chin came up. "Well, how should I know that? Where's the book of rules? Someone forgot to give it to me. All I know is what my mother told me, and in all honesty I found it less than encouraging. The entire business seems messy and embarrassing. Unnatural."

"Unnatural!" Nick wanted to take her and shake her. But since he wanted to take her more, he forced himself to stay calm. "Sarah, sex is the most natural thing in the world. What's *un*natural is how you're acting about it. I dinna know what your mother told you, but sex is wonderful. It is fantastic. It is the best thing in the whole world. Sarah, you'll think you've died and gone to heaven."

"I will?"

"Trust me."

Her somber regard told him he asked for a lot. As she slipped into her dressing gown, rose from the bed, and crossed the room to gaze outside the window, Nick was reminded that this marriage of theirs was being built on shaky ground. She didn't trust him, that much was obvious. And to be honest, Nick wasn't certain she loved him all that deeply, either. He thought it more likely that Sarah Simpson Ross was in love with the idea of love. And weddings. The girl truly loved all the preparations that went along with weddings.

Obviously, that attraction didn't extend to the wedding night.

Hence, the current problem. The idea of the wedding night was what had made him listen when she brought up the idea of a wedding to begin with. He'd married her because his body craved hers like a child craves candy, and because Sarah could give him the treasure he'd lost—a family.

He missed his family desperately. He missed belonging. When he'd stormed away from Rowanclere Castle upon learning he wasn't John and Fiona Ross's blood son but the unwanted offspring of the third marquess of Weston, he had yet to realize the value of what he was throwing away. Two years of being alone had taught him the lesson, though not until it was too late. Now the Rosses were dead, and the only family he had was the one born this day at the altar of St. Paul's church.

So he'd damned well better take good care of this brand-new family tonight. He'd damned well better take good care of Sarah.

"Sarah, come back to bed. I give you my word I will do my very best to make our loving good for you."

"Do you think we'll have a happy marriage, Nick?"

"I do," he replied, believing it. If they could just get it started.

"You've been good to me so far, letting me plan the wedding of my dreams, buying property near town so I can still be close to my mama and my friends. I know you're a good man at heart. All your actions have proven it. It's just that . . . well . . ." She turned to face him. "I'm afraid."

" 'Tis nothing to be afraid of, lass. I promise. I won't hurt you." He held out his hand to her. "Come here. Be my wife."

She took two steps toward him, then stopped. "I like the kissing part."

"I know. I shall do extra kissing."

"That's considerate. Thank you. I was hoping you'd be a considerate . . . um . . ."

"Lover," he supplied, his mouth lifting in a grin as he began to relax and get back into the spirit of things. "I promise I'll be a very, very considerate lover."

With that, he pulled her into his arms and took her mouth in a long, deep kiss. He kissed her breathless. He kissed her senseless. He kissed her until she moaned with need. Then and only then did he reach for the fastenings on her gown and leisurely strip her naked.

Beautiful. So very beautiful. Now Nick was the one who went breathless, his mouth bone-dry. His gaze swept over her, lingering on the triangle of golden curls at the juncture of her thighs.

His erection was as hard as the ancient stone walls of Glencoultran Castle. It took every bit of his self-control not to turn it loose on her right there and then.

Slow . . . slow . . . slow. The words drummed like a mantra through his mind. His fingers fanned out and he circled her nipple with the palm of his hand for what seemed like forever until she melted against him. Her whimpers of pleasure encouraged him and stoked the fire of his own desire.

Nick groaned low in his throat. He badly wanted to replace his hand with his mouth, but having suffered the consequences of that once already tonight, he resisted. He would seduce her with the touch of his hands alone and save the tasting for later.

He battled against the urgent demand for release throbbing in his loins as he skimmed his hand across the silken skin of her belly and lower, over soft curls and delicate flesh. The scent of arousal perfumed the air, and she stirred restlessly, needily. He slipped his hand between her thighs and found her hot and damp.

But far from ready.

She froze like a corpse. "What are you doing?"

Damnation, not again. She tried to wriggle away from him, but Nick restrained her, panting, "Sarah, stay with me here. Trust me."

"But you have your finger . . . you're not supposed to use your finger. You're supposed to use your Rod of Steel."

Rod of Steel? Did she mean . . . ? Good Lord.

"I know what I'm supposed to do," Nick snapped. "Relax. You'll like this."

"Like it? Are you crazy?"

"I'm beginning to think so, aye." The girl truly knew how to kill a passionate mood. "You have to trust me."

"I'm trying, but . . . oh."

He dragged his finger out of her tight, hot sheath, then slowly slid it back in, stretching her, working her, readying a way for him. It was killing him. His body was telling him to climb on and have at it. His mind knew that way lay disaster.

Right now it was a toss-up which part of him would win.

She'd gone still again, her eyes squeezed shut, and Nick took the opportunity to rid himself of his trousers. He saw her mouth begin to move, and as he leaned down to kiss her, he made sense of her soft murmuring.

"Now I lay me down to sleep, I pray the Lord my soul to keep. If I should die before—"

"Praying?" he snapped, jerking away from her and rising up, straddling her hips. "You're praying?"

She didn't answer. She'd opened her eyes. They were round and wide and gazing in horror at his manhood.

Nick felt himself start to shrink. His tongue returned to the language of his youth. "Halie blude. What hae ye done to me?"

"Th-the-the Rod of Steel," she stammered out, locking her ankles. "It frightens me."

Passion of a different type burned through Nick's blood. "Well, ye need nae worry. He's nae match for the Evil Eye. Ye should just go ahead and emasculate me. Cut him off and be done with it. And to think whorehouses charge a premium for virgins! Some men must be gluttons for punishment."

In one smooth motion, Nick rolled off the bed. As he bent to retrieve his clothing from the floor, Sarah sat up and grabbed his wrist. "No, Nick. I'm sorry. Please, come back to bed. I trust you. I do. I want to be your wife."

Nick stared down at the slim, graceful fingers encircling his arm. It was the first time she'd touched him of her own volition since he'd entered the room, and like a dog to a bone, he snapped to attention. The instinct to mate gnawed at him. He gritted his teeth and hung onto his patience by a thread "Ye must mean it this time, Sarah. If I come to ye again, I'll not have it in me to leave."

She sounded as if she had a noose around her neck as she responded, "I understand."

Nick's doubts drowned beneath a tidal wave of lust when she slowly, deliberately released her ankles and spread her legs.

He joined her in their marriage bed and positioned himself above her. He knew he should wait, knew he should lull her with his kisses first, again, but at the first sweet, soft brush of her mound against the blunt head of his erection, he couldn't help but ease inside her.

Sarah flinched.

"It's all right, lass," he soothed, wanting desperately to believe it. She was tight and dry and the going was rough, but she felt so good, pure heaven on earth. Need was a raging beast inside him. Over the roaring in his ears, he heard her whimpers. He gritted his teeth, seeking the last vestiges of his control to take it slow. Seeking, but not finding. "Ah, Sarah, I've got to . . . I canna stop."

He bumped against the barrier. It failed to give. He flexed his hips, increasing the pressure. Her whimpers escalated to cries. The obstacle held strong.

Panic joined the passion barreling through him. He was hurting her. He'd promised he wouldn't. But he couldn't slow down. He couldn't stop.

His climax was upon him.

Nick yanked from her body just as she began to scream and his seed began to spurt.

Waves of exquisite sensation crashed over him. He shuddered, but not with pleasure. He'd gone off before he'd even breeched her innocence to the music of her screams.

It was by far the most humiliating moment of his life.

She lay by his side, not touching him. Without speaking. A single thought kept running through Sarah's head: *Mama was right.*

The private side of marriage was painful and distasteful and downright messy. It burned her, made her so sore. She wanted to get up and wash. How could she bear to go through this again? How often would he truly wish to do It? That was one question she'd never thought to ask her mother.

She certainly wasn't going to ask Nick. In fact, she might never speak to him again. He'd said she'd think she had died and gone to heaven. Under her breath, she said, "You had half of it right, anyway."

"What?"

"Nothing."

Silence settled between them like an unwelcome guest. Sarah didn't know what to do. What was proper etiquette between a husband and wife following the folly of the marriage bed? It was yet another question she'd not known to ask.

Finally, Nick took care of that problem. Heedless of his nakedness, he climbed from the bed and crossed the room to the wardrobe where a change of clothing hung. Though she didn't intend to look, her gaze strayed to his backside. She fleetingly wondered how those firm, sculpted muscles would feel to the touch, and wished she'd explored the answer to that when she'd had the chance.

When she realized the direction her thoughts had taken, she choked and coughed.

Fastening his trousers, Nick glanced over his shoulder. "You all right?"

"Um, yes."

He removed a shirt from the cabinet and slipped it on. "I'm hungry. I thought I would go down to the dining room and order something to bring up. Is a sandwich all right with you?"

Sarah didn't want a sandwich, but she did want a few moments alone. She guessed that might be what Nick wanted, too. "That's fine."

He finished dressing without further talk, then headed for the door. There he paused. He raked his fingers through his hair, then addressed her without looking at her. "Sarah, I am sorry. It will be better next time."

Then he was gone and Sarah darted from the bed in a rush to wash and dress before he returned, the words "next time" echoing through her brain like a death knell.

Nick took longer downstairs than she expected, so she had time to fix her hair and bolt back another fortifying two sips of brandy. She wasn't certain if the liquor had made It any easier or not, but under the circumstances, if Nick wanted to do It again, better safe than sorry. She decided to keep the bottle close.

As it turned out, nothing would have prepared her for what happened next. Her husband returned to their room a pale, shaky imitation of the man who had walked out half an hour earlier. Shocked by his appearance, she said, "Nick, what is it? What happened?"

His deep blue eyes were dazed and glassy as he lifted the sheet of paper he held in his hand. "A letter arrived for me at the rooming house. The Widow Larkin sent it over. It is from England. From my father. My brothers were racing horses. There was an accident. Both of them. They're dead."

"Your brothers? Oh, Nick. I'm so sorry. Were you close?"

He shook his head. "I never met them. They were my only brothers and I never even met them. He wouldn't allow it."

Compassion swept through Sarah. "That's terrible. I understand why you're upset."

"No, you don't. Think about it, Sarah. My father is the Marquess of Weston. His eldest son is the Earl of Innsbruck. Sarah, that's me. I'm now legally my father's heir. We must depart for London immediately."

"What?"

"It's true, lass. I'm an earl. Lord Innsbruck. And you, Sarah, are Lady Innsbruck. You are my countess."

The brandy bottle slipped from her hands and fell to the floor with a resounding crash.

It's bad luck to change your bridal clothes before nightfall.

~3~

"**I** won't go." Sarah repeated her assertion for the fifteenth time in the past fifteen minutes. She was dressed and perched primly on the settee in the sitting room while Nick paced the room. "It's not what we agreed. We have a nice house waiting for us to make it a home with all our pretty wedding gifts."

He halted in midstep and faced her, scowling. "Sarah, I am the Earl of Innsbruck. I own a townhouse in London, a castle in Scotland, and an estate in Surrey the size of Tarrant County. The manor house is huge and filled with enough pretties to keep you dusting for a month. You could fit every wedding gift you received in the china closet."

"I don't care." Her lips pursed petulantly, she brushed an imaginary speck of dust off her sky-blue skirt. "I don't want to live there. I want to live in Fort Worth. My mother is here."

"Your mother can come with us. She'll like London. She can attend the theater every night if she wishes."

"My mother won't leave Texas and neither will I. This is our home, Nick. We have roots here. We have family here."

"Well, I don't! My family is in England. I have three sisters and a father who want me back."

"That brings up the question of why they let you go in the first place. I'm sorry, but I have no desire to claim as relatives people who abandon a family member with no more than a flicker of conscience. Frankly, I'm surprised you can."

Fire flared in his eyes. "It is so easy for you, is it not? Only someone who has never been alone, who has never suffered a moment's doubt about belonging, could stand there and say what you just said. Lass, you are so spoiled you stink."

She gasped and shoved herself to her feet. "How dare you!"

"How dare *I?*" Nick braced his hands on his hips. "What about the vows you took this afternoon? Whatever happened to 'Wither thou goest, I will go'?"

She folded her arms and stuck out her chin. "You promised to 'goest' to a ranch just outside of town!"

"I didn't know my brothers were going to collide their horses and kill themselves when I said it."

"That doesn't change the fact that you want to go back on your promise. Just like you did a little bit ago." Sarah gave her head a toss and her golden hair went flying. "Your word, Nicholas Ross, is no good. You're a liar."

"Now wait just one minute."

"You promised not to hurt me." Now it was Sarah's turn to pace, and she did so while waving her arms about theatrically. "You promised not to hurt me, but you *did* when you took my virginity, and you *are* trying to break your word about staying in Fort Worth."

He muttered something beneath his breath, then snapped, "You're still a virgin, Sarah. I did not break your maidenhead. 'Tis as hard as your head. As far as hurting you goes, I apologize. Perhaps I could have done better. However, your lack of cooperation didn't help the situation at all."

She stopped short and brought her hands to her chest. "Are you attempting to lay the blame on me?"

"I'm not laying anything—certainly not you. And 'tis my wedding night, too. Who the hell would have believed *that?*"

"Don't you curse at me."

"You are lucky I dinna do worse."

"Is that a threat, sir?"

"That, Lady Innsbruck, is a promise."

With that, Sarah burst into tears. Nothing was going right. Everything was a mess. Nothing was turning out as she had planned. As Nick stabbed his fingers through his hair, she whirled around, threw herself down on the settee, buried her head in her arms, and sobbed. So wrapped up was she in her misery, she didn't notice he'd taken a seat beside her until he pulled her into his arms.

"Shush, now, lass. Dinna cry. 'Tis all right. Everything will be all right. Shush, now."

"I . . . I . . . I don't want to live in England!" she wailed against his shoulder.

"I ken. Perhaps we will not be required to live there. I dinna know the rules, Sarah. I simply know we must make the trip to Hunterbourne Manor to find out."

"But I don't want to go to your father's manor house. I want to stay here and crochet doilies for our

35

tables and hang pictures and plant daisies in clay pots on the front porch. I love daisies."

"Aye, Sarah, I ken. Except the part about crocheting, that is. I wasn't aware you could crochet."

That surprised a little laugh out of her, and the atmosphere between them eased. He drew back, putting space between them, then tugged a handkerchief from his pocket and attended to her tears. He followed each dab of the square of white linen against her cheek with a kiss, and Sarah felt her defenses melt with each gentle brush of his lips.

Nick truly was a good man. He was honorable. She needed to remember that. It wasn't right of her to hold the marriage bed business against him. He was just a man, after all, and like any man, he wanted It. Like her mother said, putting up with It was a woman's lot in life. As far as this circumstance of his brothers' dying went, he certainly hadn't planned that. She wasn't being fair.

Sarah sniffed, then said, "I'm sorry, too, Nick. I know you're not a liar."

His smile was both tender and bittersweet as he leaned forward and kissed her forehead. "We will work it out. Dinna worry. Now, it has been a long day. Let's lie down and take a wee nap. I want to hold you, Sarah. That's all, I promise. Just a wee cuddling. I will snore in your ear and perhaps when I awake, I will ken what to do about all of this. I have found it happens that way sometimes. I will go to sleep with a problem on my mind, and when I wake up, I have the solution."

Sarah agreed with little hesitation. She did enjoy being in his arms, and she wasn't worried he'd take advantage of her. Nick wasn't one for sneak attacks.

A few minutes later, they crawled into bed fully

clothed. Despite the trauma that occurred last time they'd stretched out on this mattress, Sarah relaxed right away. She drifted off to sleep cradled in his arms, cushioned by the warmth of his body and blanketed by his spicy, masculine scent that had grown so familiar so quickly and both curled her toes and made her feel safe.

Half an hour later, she was awakened by a man's bellow and a knock on the door. "Nicholas Ross, you sonofabitch. Open this damned door! Open this door, you fornicating bastard, so I can by God kill you!"

It was, by far, the rudest awakening of Sarah's entire life.

Damnation, what now? Nick rolled out of bed and headed for the door. He didn't recognize the voice, but that didn't really matter. Whoever was there would pay for interrupting Nick's wedding night.

Such as it was.

"This had better be good," he warned as he cracked the door open.

He'd never seen the man before in his life.

Whoever he was, he was older than Nick by thirty years or more. He wore a banker's suit and a furious scowl, and his gunmetal-colored eyes shot bullets. Nick caught himself before he could glance down toward his heart to check for wounds. "Do I know you?"

"If we'd met before, you'd already be dead," the man ground out through gritted teeth.

"Sir, I do not know what this is all about, but you are interrupting my honeymoon."

"Well, that's your bad luck, isn't it?"

Nick couldn't argue with that. From the moment

he'd knocked on the hotel room door, this had been one bad-luck-filled wedding night. Now what?

He got his first hint when the man pushed against the door and barreled past Nick into the hotel suite, dragging a young woman behind him.

"Susan?" Nick asked.

Susan Harris was a pretty, petite woman with dark hair, lush curves, and a normally ready, winning smile. She lived up in Birdville, northeast of Fort Worth, where her father was the preacher at the Baptist church. Today her expression showed no sign of a smile, and suddenly Nick had a bad feeling about what had brought her to town.

He had met her shortly after his arrival in Fort Worth. She'd made the trip into the town's tenderloin district with members of her father's church for the purpose of saving souls. Instead, she'd been intrigued. At twenty-two, she chaffed at her "preacher's daughter" bonds, and at least twice that Nick knew of, that streak of wildness inside her had led her into trouble in the dens of sin that made up Fort Worth's Hell's Half Acre.

And Nick was grateful for it. If not for Susan, he'd be dead right now. When a murderous thief attacked Nick in a dark Ft. Worth alley one harsh, rainy night last winter, she and a fellow named Tom Sheldon had intervened and rescued him. Nick still wondered how a Baptist preacher's daughter came to handle a knife so well.

Now the man who Nick deduced to be Reverend Harris flung his daughter down onto the sitting room settee.

"Wait just one minute," Nick snapped, taking a protective step toward the young woman.

Warning flashed in her eyes and she gave her

head a slight shake. In the periphery of his vision, Nick noted that Sarah had come to stand in the doorway between the suite's two rooms. After that, his entire focus remained centered on the preacher. The fellow looked angry enough to chew nails.

"The devil has worked his evil and stolen my daughter from the bosom of her loving family." Pointing an accusing finger at Susan, he continued, "In order to protect my other children from her wickedness, I hereby cast her out. As her partner in sin, you are now responsible for her. Her and the devil's spawn she carries."

Nick's stomach sank. Prickles of unease crawled up his spine like a thousand spiders. "Pardon me?"

"The girl is increasing!" the preacher shouted. "She's two months along and she claims the child is yours."

Everything within Nick froze.

Susan watched him, her gaze both proud and pleading. Nick's gaze flicked to the doorway where his bride stood like a statue, her complexion gone pale, her eyes wide and stricken. *Damnation.*

Nick fastened his stare on Sarah, silently pleading for her patience. She visibly flinched.

"Well? What say you?" demanded the preacher. "Do you deny it?"

Nick didn't see how he had a choice. She'd saved his life and he's sworn an oath to protect her in return.

Sarah wouldn't like it. She'd be hurt and embarrassed. Dread dribbled over Nick like sticky, warm molasses.

Well, she'd simply have to understand. Susan was in trouble and at the moment, Nick was the only one who could help her.

He cleared his throat in an effort to dislodge the noose around his neck and said, "No, I won't deny it."

The door between the sitting room and suite closed with a quiet *snick*. To Nick, it sounded as loud as a gunshot.

Midmorning sunshine glistened off storefront windows downtown as Sarah made her way toward the Texas and Pacific Railroad depot. A gentle breeze blew from the south, foretelling the approach of yet another cattle drive along the Chisholm Trail. Judging from the sting of manure on the breeze, they could expect the first of the herd to thunder down Main Street before noon. While Sarah didn't begrudge the drives that brought such prosperity to Fort Worth, she wished the trail took a path around town rather than directly through it.

Of course, she could wish all she wanted, but it would do her no good. Hadn't she learned that lesson the hard way where her so-called marriage was concerned?

She wished she could turn back the clock to this time yesterday, to before the moment when she'd stood at the altar and pledged herself to a man who'd betrayed her.

The news was already all over town. She'd been humiliated down to her soul. She wondered if she'd ever be able to hold her head up in public again. Leaving her room this morning and facing the curious stares of Fort Worth society had been the most difficult thing she'd ever done.

But she had done it. She had left the hotel and shown herself in public despite her mother's advice.

Advice given at daybreak when her mother came knocking at her hotel room door, shortly after receiving word that her newlywed daughter had thrown her new husband and his pregnant mistress out of the Blackstone Hotel.

Last night after Reverend Harris's departed the bridal suite, Nick had barged into the bedroom and insisted he wasn't the father of Susan Harris's child. He'd paced the room and told a vague, convoluted tale of debts and oaths and promises, and he'd asked for Sarah's trust despite withholding certain salient facts—such as the real father's name. That, he said, could come only from Susan.

He'd spoken with such passion that Sarah had been inclined to believe him, even in the face of Susan Harris's refusal to confirm his claim. The way the woman had placed her hand protectively over her womb told Sarah more than mere words.

Then, before she had quite made up her mind, the vitriolic sound of Reverend Harris's preaching had risen from the street in front of the Blackstone Hotel. He'd said mean and evil things about Nick and his daughter. He'd made Sarah look like a fool. The betrayed bride. The object of pity. That she couldn't abide.

Her humiliation before the people of Fort Worth complete, no longer willing to listen to Nick or believe in him, she'd banished him from their room, then spent the rest of the night crying into her pillow.

Now, though, it was morning. The nightmare of a wedding night was behind her and the rest of her life stretched before her.

A life without Nick.

It had to be that way. Shortly after dawn, Sarah had decided to take the failure of her wedding night as an omen. This marriage between her and Nick was not meant to be. When he departed on this morning's train, he'd be leaving without her. She was simply going to tell him good-bye.

Probably.

Sarah reached the station just as a train whistle blew. She glanced up at the clock on the wall. Nine fifty-five. Five minutes to departure. She drew a deep breath, squared her shoulders, blinked back her tears, and entered the depot. Nick was waiting for her.

He looked tired. He, apparently, had slept no more than she.

"Hello, lass."

She nodded. "Nick. Or should I say, Lord Ross?"

"Nae. 'Tis actually Lord Innsbruck." He shoved his hands in his pants pockets and rolled back on his heels, eyeing her intently. "I'd rather be simply your Nick."

Swallowing hard, Sarah looked away.

Nick's voice was raspy as he said softly, "Come with me, Sarah."

Sarah blinked back more tears. "Stay with me, Nick."

His eyes closed. "Damnation."

"Yes." Then, thinking, *What's one more scandal among many?* she added, "Damnation."

Surprise and a measure of shock lit the gleaming blue eyes that jerked toward her. Then Nick's mouth twisted in a rueful grin. "Ah, lass. 'Tis sorry I am it has worked out this way. I think under other circumstances we could have had a fine life."

She felt a sob well up in her throat. "I agree."

"Is it over now, Sarah? Are we to be free of one another?"

She swallowed hard. "I guess so."

His expression sobered. The train whistle blew. Nick heaved a sigh and said, "Fine then, I'll consider the question settled. You can send the annulment papers to me at Hunterbourne."

"All right." Bravely she held out her hand. "Good luck, Nick."

He eyed her hand and scowled. "Nae, not like that," he muttered, gripping her hand and yanking her into his arms. He lowered his head and captured her mouth in a kiss both hard and tender, bitter and sweet. Tears fell freely from her eyes by the time the train whistle sounded a final warning and Nick released her, then stepped away.

She thought she might have seen a sheen of tears in his own eyes as he gently cupped her cheek. "Good-bye, lass."

She could do no more than whisper, "God's speed, Nick."

He turned away and headed for the door. Halfway there, he stopped and looked back. "We could have had a fine family. I'll never forget you, Sarah."

Choking back the tears, she trailed him to the depot door and watched him cross the platform. Then, when she watched him hand not one, but two tickets to the conductor, Sarah's heart, already cracked, shattered.

Nick did not leave Fort Worth alone. His hand resting on the woman's waist, Nick guided Susan Harris up the train steps. That woman was leaving town with Nick.

Filled with both anger and an overpowering sense of loss, Sarah sank onto a bench and wept.

*It's bad luck for a bride to make drapes from the
same fabric as her wedding gown.*

~4~

*July 1877
Hunterbourne Manor, Surrey*

Dear Lady Innsbruck,
    *Please be advised that any correspondence
requiring my personal notice should be sent to
the attention of Mr. Nicholas Ross via the* New
York Herald *for the foreseeable future. Please
be advised that you should anticipate a substantial passage of time before receipt of a
reply. However, rest assured that I will do
everything in my power to see that a reply is
forthcoming.*

                                                    Innsbruck

*October 1877
Galveston, Texas*

Dear Nick,
    *I recently received a letter I assume was from
you although I must admit I found both the tone
and the message of the missive rather ambigu-
ous. Not to mention stuffy. I wonder how it is*

you have gone from traveling to England to assume a title and reunite with your father, to being a reporter for an American newspaper. However, I do not intend to worry about it as I am busy seeing to my own arrangements.

To avoid lingering public humiliation in the wake of your desertion, my mother and I have removed ourselves to a place where my aunt and uncle's social prominence will help us overcome the hurtful tongues of gossip.

You should be advised that any correspondence should be sent to me at 42 Main Street here in Galveston.

Your maligned wife, Sarah Ross

April 1878
Galveston, Texas

Dear Nick,

I have been reading your accounts of the Russo-Turkish War in the New York Herald. At first I didn't believe that you and the newspaper correspondent were one and the same, but when you wrote the story about the puppy in the Turkish village and compared it to the beloved spaniel of your childhood I knew it had to be you. I am filled with curiosity about how and why you have this new occupation. However, your talent for the work is undeniable. I have found your portrayal of the events surrounding the Great Assault and the Siege of Plevna haunting. Others with whom I have spoken about your work agree.

The prayers of the American public, mine in particular, are with you, Nick. Despite our differences, I *find the idea of you being in danger quite worri-some.*

Sarah

May 1878
Galveston, Texas

Dear Mother,

I hope you are enjoying your honeymoon trip and that Doctor Morrell is proving to be a considerate husband.

I have news. Following my success with the arrangements for your wedding, I have been approached by two affianced brides about designing a plan for their upcoming nuptials. After much thought, I approached Uncle Michael about helping me establish myself as a professional wedding consultant. I decided to use the unfortunate incident with Nick to my benefit, and as of this morning, Weddings by Lady Innsbruck is officially in business. That sounds rather fine, don't you think? I am quite excited about the entire process, and I trust you will be happy for me.

Speaking of my erstwhile husband, I have another bit of news to pass along. I believe we have finally come to understand why Nick Ross has become a foreign correspondent for the Herald, why he is portraying himself as an American journalist when in fact he is a British lord. Uncle Michael made a few discreet inquiries of a journalist friend and thus figured it out.

Mother, we think my husband is a spy.

It makes good sense. While Nick is a very

gifted writer, and his accounts of events in Asia are in my opinion superior to those of his fellow correspondent, Mr. MacGahan, I know for a fact that despite his years in our country, he considered himself British, not American. His family's circumstances being what they were, it is easy to believe he is working at the direction of his father. Uncle Michael larned that Nick's father is a confidant of Prime Minister Disraeli.

In light of these suspicions, I face the troublesome question of my own patriotic duty, and whether or not I should report my impressions to government authorities.

I am interested in your opinion, Mother. I admit to being torn. Despite the pain he caused me, I do not wish to cause Nick any harm. Also, Uncle Michael says that since Nick is still legally my husband, this could reflect poorly upon our family. You and my uncle and aunt have done so much for me during this difficult period in my life, and I cringe at the notion of bringing you any more grief.

I understand that pursuing an annulment might eradicate that problem. However, I am loath to give up my title. You see, brides adore having the Countess of Innsbruck arrange their weddings, and, selfishly, I want my business to succeed.

On that note, I will close. Please give my regards to Doctor Morrell.

> Your loving daughter,
> Sarah

September 3, 1879
Kabul, Afghanistan

Dear Sarah,

I understand you have not yet sought to have our marriage annulled. It appears you have made a financially rewarding decision. It is just past dawn here in Kabul, and Heratis rioters are outside the Residency compound, demanding the blood of those within. I believe it likely you will be a widow before noon.

If this note should someday make its way to you, know I thought of you fondly on this long, bloody morn.

Nick

December 1879
Galveston, Texas

Dear Abigail,

Merry Christmas. I hope you and your family are doing well. I'm still hoping to get to California for a visit soon. I'm so anxious to meet your darling twins. Also, please convey my congratulations to Jerry in regard to his promotion. The railroad is lucky to have him.

In reply to your latest letter, yes, I was quite relieved to see Nicholas Ross's byline in the New York Herald *last week. These past weeks have been difficult, as I found myself beset with worry over his safety. It is good to know that our prayers for his continued good health have been answered.*

It is also good to have such a dear friend as you with whom to share the burden of this secret about my husband's occupation that I have chosen to keep. Know that I recognize the blessing of your friendship.

Having received the good news, my heart is once again in my work. In regard to that, I am enclosing newspaper clippings of the most recent Weddings by Lady Innsbruck. Notice the last line in the Garrison-Miller nuptials. "Once again, Lady Innsbruck has proven that Galveston brides can always count on a countess." I laughed with delight to see it.

More notes about the weddings on the enclosed pages. I hope to see you soon.

Love,
Sarah

January 1881
Fort Worth, Texas

Dear Nick,

As I sit down to write, I find myself wondering in what corner of our world this letter will reach you. Wherever it is, I hope it finds you well.

I received a packet of your letters to me via the Herald *yesterday, and I read them with great pleasure. Such a life of adventure you are leading! Your story about the goats and the village children in Kashmir made me laugh out loud.*

Nick, I was gladdened to read that you find my own letters to be a comfort. It amazes me, in truth, as my notes are filled with little more than inconsequential tidbits of my life in Texas. After much consideration, I concluded that reading my letters about the place that was for a short time your home might be similar to wrapping oneself in an old, familiar quilt on a snowy afternoon.

I also find it a little bit amazing that we've managed to develop a friendship of sorts through our letters. Who would have thought three years ago it could be so? Obviously, in our case distance has made the heart grow fonder.

Now, on to "old quilt" business. I am pleased to announce a change of address. I have recently formed a partnership with two fine ladies of excellent reputation and talent and have returned to Fort Worth. Do you remember Trace McBride and his three mischievous girls? Trace's brother Tye moved to town and both men have married. Trace's wife, Jenny, has made quite a name for herself designing wedding gowns. Tye's wife Claire is a baker of extraordinary talent whose wedding cakes are in great demand by brides in Texas. The three of us compliment one another's specialties quite nicely.

I am excited about this venture, which we are calling Lucky in Love Weddings. Coming home to Fort Worth proved to be a pleasure, and I do so adore the McBride family. Someday I'll tell you the stories surrounding the romance between Trace and Jenny and Tye and Claire. They're quite humorous tales involving a Bad Luck Wedding Dress and a Bad Luck Wedding Cake. I find it somewhat ironic that despite the success of our ceremony and the "bad luck" label their weddings endured, their marriages have turned out exceptionally happy while ours ... well ... enough said.

I must draw this letter to a close as I have an appointment pending. I promise to write again within the week and tell you what Wilhemina Peters has been saying in her "Talk About Town" column for the Daily Democrat. As a fellow newspaperman, you no doubt share a professional interest. That will give you enough "old quilt" news to keep you warm for a month!

Before I close, I'd like to ask a question. In one of your articles in the Herald last summer you mentioned the beautiful silks available for sale in a remote Asian bazaar. Since my friend Jenny (the dressmaker) is forever on the lookout for quality silks, we wondered if fabric similar to what you described is available in any markets accessible to foreign trade. Do you have any information about this?

Take care, Nick. You remain, as always, in my prayers

Sarah

Winter 1882
Tashilhunpo, Tibet

Dear Madam Sarah,
Within the trunk that accompanies this letter you will find bolts of silk, China satin, a collection of precious curiosities, and three Tartar carpets. Please accept them as tokens of my esteem for the Babu Nicholas Ross, whose timely supply of smallpox vaccine saved many lives among my people.

Losan Palden, Senchen Lama
Chief Minister to Panchen Lama

Spring 1883
Hunterbourne Manor

Dear Sarah,

It is with no great regret that I write to inform
you of the death of my father, the Third Marquess
of Weston. I have returned to England and
presently reside at Hunterbourne, where I have
assumed responsibility for my three sisters. Any
correspondence that requires my signature may
safely be dispatched at this time.

Weston

Spring 1883
Fort Worth, Texas

Dear Nick,

I would offer my condolences, but I believe I
know you well enough to predict you do not
want them.

So, you are Weston now and no longer
Innsbruck? I swear I do not understand this
entire title protocol. All I know is that you have
changed names more often than any other man
of my acquaintance. I, however, have no wish at
this time to change mine.

Sarah

Summer 1884
London

Dear Sarah,

I write to you adrift from the treacherous
waters of the ton. Please accept my apology if
my latest letter offended. However, I fear this

one may be no better. During the year since my return to England, my acclimation to what is referred to as "Polite Society" has been less than polite, and, I fear, reflected in my correspondence.

I am in the process of seeing my oldest sister, Charlotte, launched into Society. The marriage mart is an ugly business and somewhat reminiscent of the slave markets of Calcutta. I see no end to it in sight, either, because waiting in the wings for their turn at a Season are my sisters Melanie and Aurora.

Please continue to pray for me, Sarah. I do believe I'd prefer a nice, violent Afghan war to this ordeal.

Weston

Summer 1885
Fort Worth, Texas

Dear Mother,
That man is up to his tricks again. I pity his sisters. I've lost track of the number of offers he's refused for his sister Charlotte's hand. How could the same man who scaled the Himalayas fail so miserably at brokering a marriage for his sibling?

In his latest letter, he asks for my advice. I intend to give it. I suspect he won't like what I have to say.

Your loving daughter,
Sarah

Fall 1885
Hunterbourne Manor

Dear Sarah,

I have given your letters of the past few months a substantial amount of thought, and I have decided to relax some—not all—of my standards concerning the men who court my sisters. I am persuaded not only by your arguments, but also because Charlotte is threatening fratricide should I scare off another beau, and Melanie tells me that if I ruin her debut the way I spoiled Charlotte's she'll find a way to make my time in the Khan's rat pit resemble a holiday.

Weston

January 1886
Hunterbourne Manor

Dear Sarah,

I trust this finds you well and that the McBride Monsters have not caused an inordinate amount of havoc in the city since your last letter.

The wedding gown arrived safely. Charlotte declared the McBride design far superior to a Worth gown. She looks like a princess wearing it. My compliments and sincere gratitude to your partner.

Weston

Spring 1886
Fort Worth, Texas

Dear Nick,

Regarding your letter of March 11ᵗʰ. Have you completely lost your mind?

I can only imagine Charlotte's humiliation. She has my most heartfelt sympathies for various reasons. Having you for a brother numbers first among them.

Nick, I understand why you had her fiancé investigated. Obviously it needed to be done. However, I cannot fathom how a man of your experience managed to hire such an incompetent detective. Any man worth his salt would have discovered something as significant as the groom's predilection for dressing in women's clothing long before the wedding day itself. Then, for you to stand up at the church and publicly withdraw your consent for the marriage in front of half of London. Poor Charlotte. I wouldn't speak to you either.

Really, Nick. Couldn't you have found a more subtle way to accomplish your goal? Hasn't subtlety been your stock in trade for years now?

What were you thinking?

Sarah

Spring 1886
Rowanclere Castle, Scotland

Dear Sarah,

What was I thinking, you ask? At the time, I was still reeling from a startling piece of news.

Shortly before the investigator arrived with

his report on the morning of Charlotte's aborted wedding, I received word that Flora and Gillian Ross—the sisters of my heart if not my blood—are alive. They were not with their parents at the time of the carriage accident. They, along with another younger sister of whose birth I was unaware, are living a day's journey from the Highland village where we grew up.

My father, the villain, either knowingly lied or simply didn't care that my foster sisters were left mostly to fend for themselves.

My mind was still reeling with this news when I learned that Charlotte's groom liked wearing garters. I traveled immediately to Scotland, where I am enjoying a joyous visit with Gillian, Flora, and young Robyn. One good thing, both Gillian and Flora are already married, so I'm only responsible for marrying off four sisters.

Four sisters. Four fiancés. Lord, help me.

Yes, I handled the situation with Charlotte poorly. I hired an inept detective, which resulted in my breaking the cardinal rule of Society: Thou shalt not make a scandal.

A thought occurs to me, Sarah. A quality wedding consultant would have stepped in and diffused the situation. It seems like I hired badly all the way around.

Next time I must do better.

Weston

Summer 1886
Glencoltran Castle, Scotland

Dear Lord Pratt,

I was glad to learn you enjoyed a safe return to London from your holiday in the Scottish Highlands. In answer to the questions you posed in your letter, I, too, was pleased to make your acquaintance during your visit, and you are certainly welcome to call at Weston House upon our return to London from our stay here at my brother's Highland retreat. In fact, my brother tells me he intends to respond affirmatively to your request to pay me suit. You should know I am quite pleased with his decision.

Alas, I cannot tell you when to expect us. Not only is my brother renewing his relationship with my new sisters, Flora, Gillian, and Robyn, but he appears to have formed an attachment with another visitor from England, Lady Steele.

My lord, I have a great favor to ask of you. Under ordinary circumstances, I would never think to make such an indiscreet request, but I am so very worried, and I've no one else to ask. Besides, as you mentioned in your letter, I also feel as if you and I have known each other forever.

The boon I seek from you is whatever information you are able to provide about Lady Steele. She seems to have quite an interest in my brother, but my sisters and I are less than enthusiastic about their relationship.

> Your friend,
> Lady Charlotte Ross

Summer 1886
London

Dear Lady Charlotte,
    I was thrilled to receive your most recent letters. I count the days until your return.
    In regard to your inquiry concerning Lady S_____, I will be happy to offer the information I have been able to gather at my club during the past week.
    Lady S_____ is the widow of the seventh Viscount S_____. She has three children, all boys now away at school, the oldest of whom was eight years of age when he inherited the title upon his father's death. The lady's name is without scandal, although she is said to be actively husband-hunting.
    The state of her finances is not widely known. Acquaintances say she gets along better with men than with women, and she is admired for her beauty and wit. However, I suspect you and your sisters' reaction to Lady S_____ is on the mark since I also learned that upon occasion she has been referred to as the Ice Queen. One gentleman told me she can freeze a person with only a look.
    That is a summary of the information I have uncovered to this point in my investigation. I admit to having enjoyed the effort thus far.
    Please convey my greetings to your sisters. I remain your servant.

                                            Pratt

Summer 1886
Glencoltran Castle, Scotland

Dear Mr. Franklin,

I will be returning to London within the week, and I require your legal advice. I would be pleased if you would call upon me at Weston House to discuss a most delicate matter. In preparation, you might research the legal particulars surrounding marriages made abroad.

Weston

Summer 1886
Hunterbourne Manor

Dear Sarah,

I take up my pen to formally request you visit England at your earliest convenience. Charlotte has formed yet another attachment, and the subject of a wedding is being bandied about. I require your professional help.

Enclosed please find information involving travel options and accommodations. Arrangements will, of course, be at my expense.

You will like England in summertime, Sarah. I recall what Texas is like in August.

Weston

Summer 1886
Fort Worth, Texas

Dear Nick,

While I appreciate the superior accommodations you arranged, I must respectfully decline your invitation to visit. I have weddings booked *throughout the summer and into the fall. I cannot possibly get away.*

I am enclosing a list of questions you should ask the wedding designers you interview on Charlotte's behalf. They should help you make your hiring decision.

I hope this will not interfere with our exchanges of letters. I value the friendship we have developed over the years.

Sarah

Summer 1886
Hunterbourne Manor

Dear Sarah,
You'll be pleased to learn that the questions you sent proved useful during my interviews of prospective wedding planners. I have hired a talented consultant, and she should be arriving in Fort Worth shortly to fill in for you while you are away.

Also, Mrs. Rollingsworth will arrive with a special bolt of fabric, a gift for the McBride ladies as a token of my thanks for allowing you this leave of absence from your business. Lest you find yourself envious, you should know I have stored over a dozen bolts of similarly fine fabrics from the Orient. You may have your pick of them when you visit.

I look forward to seeing you again.

Weston

Summer 1886
Fort Worth

Dear Nick,

Mrs. Rollingsworth arrived in Fort Worth safely. However, her services are not required. I told you I must refuse your invitation to visit.

Under the circumstances, Jenny and Claire McBride must regretfully refuse your most lovely gift. Their personal notes accompany this letter.

However, we are interested in purchasing this bolt of fabric and any others you would be willing to furnish. The cloth is quite fine, Nick. We are willing to pay a fair price.

Sarah

Summer 1886
Hunterbourne Manor

Dear Sarah,

You misunderstood. That was not an invitation, rather a directive. I am your husband and I require your presence. Wedding plans continue here, plus we have other matters to discuss. You will come to England. Consider the fabric part of your professional fee.

Weston

Fall 1886
Fort Worth, Texas

No.

Sarah

Fall 1886
Hunterbourne Manor

Sarah,
  *This letter is to introduce you to Mr. Rand
Jenkins. He will escort you to Scotland, where
we will meet at Rowanclere Castle the second
week of December. Failure to accompany him
will have dire consequences for you and your
precious business.*
  *I am quite serious, Sarah. It is in your best
interests to cooperate.*
                                        Nick

It's bad luck to have an odd number of wedding guests.

~5~

January 1888
Glencoltran Castle
Scottish Highlands

𝒩icholas, Lord Weston, eyed the drawing room door and grimaced. He'd rather walk the Khyber Pass barefoot in January than join in the evening's coming festivities. His sister Charlotte's prospective mother-in-law was slated to sing. His sister Charlotte's prospective mother-in-law sounded like a yak in season when she attempted an aria.

Nick thought longingly of the privacy of his study and began to turn away.

"Gweeshtens," came his Scots sister Gillian's amused voice. "Is that the stench of retreat I'm smelling, Nicholas?"

Nick folded his arms and glowered. "Oh hush. What is it about the females in my family anyway? Always sneaking about. You and Aurora are particularly talented."

"Dinna worry." Gillian patted his arm. "She'll not be sneaking out of Glencoltran without your ken."

"Only because we have four feet of new snow on

63

the ground. Aurora is a determined girl. Fancies herself in love and she's little more than a child." Then, as rarely occurred any longer, the Scots of his youth rolled off his tongue. "He's nothing but a back-jaw, ill-deedit limmer out to ruin her, Gilly. I'll not have it. I'll keep her here in the Highlands till she's auld and gray afore I'll stand for her sneaking out to run off with the likes of Willie Hart."

Gillian shook her head and clucked her tongue. "I missed ye sorely, Nicholas, but I do believe some parts of my life were easier without my overprotective older brother around."

As his scowl deepened, she laughed and hooked her arm through his. "Enough worry over Aurora tonight. She'll nae be going anywhere anytime soon. Tonight your presence is required in the drawing room, where you need to be charming to Charlotte's future guid-mither."

"I know," Nick replied, feeling as well as sounding like a petulant young boy. "But I warn you, Gillian. That woman cannot sing. It's torture to put ourselves through this. I would do everyone a favor if I rushed into that room and yelled 'fire.' "

His Scots sister put her hands on her hips, leaned forward, and studied him keenly. "You heard the rude comments Lady Pratt made about Charlotte."

He nodded. "I don't like them. I believe Charlotte is destined for unhappiness if she marries into that family."

"She loves him."

"She's eighteen. She's too young to know what love is. Believe me, I know about that."

Gillian rapped his shin with her shoe. "You said you liked him, Nicholas. You gave them your blessing."

"That was before I met his mother. She is a dragon in disguise. Charlotte's not strong enough to withstand her."

"I hope you're wrong, but Charlotte is a sweet, gentle girl. Melanie and Aurora say she is much like your mother."

"And look what my father did to *her*."

"Aha, there's the difference, brother. Your *father* destroyed your mother's will. It wasn't her guidmother who did it. I like Charlotte's beau. It took a strong man to convince his mother to travel north in winter. I believe Lord Pratt will defend his bride to her. Mark my words."

"I hope you are right. Otherwise, he'll have me to answer to."

A warm sparkle filled her brilliant blue eyes, and her face glowed with love. "So fierce and protective. You make me think of one of those Bengal tigers you and my Jake saw on your travels. You are a credit to your title, Lord Weston. A credit to your family— both the English and the Scottish ones."

"Thank you, Two."

She snorted, just as he had expected. Gillian didn't appreciate Nick's recent jest of numbering his sisters by birth order. That, of course, made him use the term more often. Leaning over, he kissed her cheek, then offered her his arm. "Now, as much as I dread the hour to come, I imagine we've skulked out here in the hallway long enough. I know that bruiser of a husband of yours is waiting for you within. May I escort you to the musicale?"

At that point Lady Pratt warmed up her voice by singing a scale. Gillian winced. "Ach, upon reflection, I do believe Jake can wait. I find I am suffering a maternal craving."

Immediately Nick grew concerned, and his gaze dropped to her blossoming waistline. "What do you need, love? Milk? A piece of chicken? An Arbroath smokie?"

"Nae, I canna abide fish this week. Not like last." She jerked her head toward the sitting room and said, "What I need now is peace."

"Then why are we standing here?"

Twenty minutes later they were hidden away in the library. Nick refilled his sister's water glass, then took a seat beside her on a brocade upholstered settee with a glass of his favorite Rowanclere malt. She eyed his whisky and sighed. Having grown up on excellent whisky, Gillian Delaney ordinarily could drink the Russian tsar under the table, but her pregnancy had soured her on the taste of spirits. Because she constantly bemoaned the fact, Nick particularly enjoyed partaking in front of her.

Such meanness, after all, was what brothers were for.

As she grumbled at him, he chuckled into his drink. His thoughts returned to Gillian's comment that he was a credit to his family. He was glad she believed it so. His own father certainly hadn't shared that point of view, and it was because of him that Nick had spent years believing this beloved sister had died. "If he wasn't already dead, I'd shoot him."

Gillian lowered her water glass. "Brooding about your father again, Nick?"

"Aye." The old bastard was winning from the grave. Nick had thought the game was over when word reached him in Calcutta that the Third Marquess of Weston had cocked up his toes. He should have known the blackguard wouldn't let such a minor thing as death defeat him in his vendetta against his son.

The so-called Great Game, the clandestine struggle between Britain and Russia for mastery of Central Asia wasn't the only competition—or even the primary one—for Nick's attention during the years he'd spent in Asia. His personal Great Game had been the battle to stay alive and thereby thwart his father's plans.

It was an ugly truth he'd learned after leaving Fort Worth and traveling to England in response to his father's summons. Nick hadn't been called home and welcomed into the bosom of his family, not by a long shot. He'd been the third marquess's designated sacrificial lamb.

Nick's father had been a political animal, with a special interest in foreign affairs, particularly those of India. Rumor had it that he'd lobbied to be named viceroy before Lord Lytton was named to the job, but his level of dedication had been doubted. Wracked by grief over the loss of his heir and second son and still unwilling to recognize the legitimacy of his third son's birth, Nick's father had sought to prove the naysayers wrong by suggesting to old friends from the Political and Secret Department of the India Office in London that his surviving son would make an effective British agent.

What better way for a man to prove his patriotism than to sacrifice his only son and heir to the secret service? the old marquess had said almost a decade ago.

Nick had decided then and there to play the game and win. As Nicholas Ross, American journalist, he had become one of the most useful and influential British spies of his time. He then used that power to strip his father of influence in foreign policy. When the old man died, Nick had thought the victory was his.

Then he returned to England and proceeded to learn that the corpse still had a trick up his sleeve. Three of them, to be exact. Charlotte, Melanie, and Aurora. Nick's English family. His sisters. His responsibility. His joy.

"How could such a bastard sire such lovely daughters?"

"The credit rests with their nanny," Gillian replied. "She's a fine woman."

"I thought so, too, until she abandoned me."

His sister sighed. "She retired, Nicholas. She's auld and tired. She's earned her rest."

When her brother simply continued to mutter into his drink, Gillian changed the subject. "Speaking of tired women, I wonder if your wife has rested from her journey by now. I dinna imagine she was too pleased to finally arrive at your country house only to find you'd returned to Scotland."

"It's her own fault," Nick defended himself. "If she'd come when I told her to come, she wouldn't have missed me first at Rowanclere and then at Hunterbourne."

Gillian rolled her tongue around her mouth. "Come when you 'told her to come'? How long have you been married, brither?"

"Depending on how you choose to look at it, either a day or a decade."

"Even in a day ye should have learned better."

Nick lifted his glass up to the lamplight and stared at the amber liquid within. Since leaving Fort Worth, he couldn't take a drink of whisky without recalling the color of Sarah's eyes. He bet wherever she was at the moment, her caramel-colored eyes were snapping with temper.

"It's her fault," he repeated.

Nick had waited for his wife at Gillian's Highland home until the week before Christmas, when he'd had to return to England to spend the holidays with the girls. Then, when Aurora pulled her nonsense of attempting to elope with that damned Willie Hart, he'd had little choice but to put some distance between the pair by removing the entire family to his own Scottish property, the remote Glencoltran Castle.

Upon arriving and contacting Gillian with news of his change of plans, he'd learned that Sarah had finally arrived at Rowanclere on December twenty-seventh and proceeded on to his country estate in England, Hunterbourne Manor, after New Year's Day. Chances were they had passed one another on their respective journeys.

"It's not her fault," Gillian declared, siding, as females were wont to do in battles between the sexes, with her own gender. "Ye dinna tell a woman what to do, Nicholas. Not a woman like Sarah."

A woman like Sarah. "Tell me about her, Gilly."

Gillian wrinkled her nose. "What can I tell you? She's *your* wife."

He scowled. She sniffed, then sighed. "She was at Rowanclere for only a week, and I confess I wasn't overly friendly to her at first. After all, you had waited on her for weeks, and at the time, I didn't ken all the particulars of your marriage." Slyly, she added, "I still don't."

Ever the strategist, Nick waited her out.

Gillian grinned. "She's beautiful, if that's what you're asking. Friendly in the way I've come to expect from those who hail from Texas. Warmer than that Lady Steele woman who has her claws into you."

"Gilly," Nick warned.

She replied with a wrinkle of her nose. "She speaks in the same slow way as my Jake, and she became quite protective of his friend Rand when she thought Annie Munro was working her witchy ways on the man who'd provided her escort from Texas."

"Jake told me how our own Annie bewitched his former business partner, that they married and he took her back to Texas."

"Aye. It was the most cheerisome thing I've ever seen. Dinna ask me how she did it, but after a visit to her home, he suddenly had cats following him everywhere. And the puir wee things made the mon itch and sneeze. It was awful. Your Sarah bickered with him constantly, but when she honestly thought Annie had caused him harm, she reacted like a tigress protecting her cub." After a significant pause she added, "Similar to how you act with your sisters."

"I'm just trying to keep them out of trouble. Otherwise, my English girls might turn out like a certain Scottish lass."

She stuck her tongue out at him and he grinned. When she tossed a small square pillow at him, he laughed aloud, then spoke with a gentle burr. "Ach, ye are still a pleasure to tease, Gillian Delaney. I have missed that."

"I don't see how. Ye tease the others constantly."

"True. But they do not appreciate it the way you do."

"That's because I dinna embarrass easily. You embarrass your English sisters, Nicholas."

"I know," he glumly replied. "Gillian, explain

something to me. I am fluent in five languages and numerous dialects. I know how to survive a Himalayan winter, an Indian monsoon, and an Afghan desert. I've debated religious theory with a Tibetan monk, talked my way out of a Khan's ravenous rat pit, and lost gracefully to the tsar of Russia during a night of vodka and cards. I'm a capable man. So why do I struggle so in English high society?"

His sister set down her glass. "It is a puzzle, I'll admit. Ye obviously have an exceptional mind, so the problem isna an inability to learn, and you have certainly proven your ability to gain acceptance in a wide variety of societies throughout the world. So why *are* you having trouble in London? I have my suspicions."

Nick waited. "And they are . . . ?"

"For one thing, you weren't trained from childhood to be a peer of the realm. Mama and Papa didn't go out in society. They didn't send you off to Eton or Harrow."

"They hired an excellent tutor for us," Nick pointed out.

"Obviously. But a young man learns more at school than how to speak Russian. The interaction with other young bloods teaches him the nuances and unstated shadings of his station. Of course, considering you had two older brothers, no one expected you would ever need to know such things. However, in my opinion, childhood experiences, or a lack thereof, contribute in only a minor way to your troubles."

"Oh?"

"Aye. Your primary problem, Nicholas, is that you are a rebel at heart. You love to stir things up, and you hate to follow rules. I have no doubt that were it not for all of us—your sisters—you'd take great pleasure in telling society to sod it."

"Why, Gillian Ross Delaney," Nick drawled, amused. "What language!"

"Can you deny it? Honestly, who else but a rebel would announce at his sister's coming-out ball that he hoped the Prince of Wales wouldn't attend because he disapproved of the man's morals? Charlotte told me all about it, Nick."

"I didn't name the prince. I referred to the entire Marlborough House set, and I stand by my conviction. That group sets a very poor example for married life, and I don't want them near my family. It's the wrong message to send to impressionable young ladies."

"Which brings me to my next point. What of the message you're sending by courting Lady Steele so openly?"

Nick grimaced. "That's different. Nobody knows I'm married."

Gillian's eyes rounded. "Ye haven't told the girls? Still? And Sarah already arrived?"

"I didn't know that until you told me, now did I?"

"Nicholas!" Gillian rolled her eyes. "You sent for her. You knew she was coming."

"Aye, but she was to go to Rowanclere and stay with you until we settled the legalities. I thought she'd wait until I returned. I didn't expect her to take it upon herself to hie off for Hunterbourne on the first clear day."

"It's a good thing Aurora gave you a bit of trouble then, isn't it? I can just see Sarah Ross waltzing into your country house announcing Lady Weston had arrived, and your sisters ken nothing of her. And the Ice Queen, what if she'd been there?"

Nick winced at the picture she painted, and Gillian added, "Oh, Nick, surely you've told *her* that you are married."

"I'm not well and truly married. It is a technicality, one that will be dealt with as soon as Sarah and I sign the papers my solicitor has prepared. And, Two, I'd appreciate it if you would cease to refer to Helen by that unflattering name. She is a fine woman."

Gillian snorted. "Robyn said she kicked Scooter."

"It was an accident," he defended, shifting uncomfortably. "Helen didn't see your husband's dog."

"What if you want to keep her?"

Nick sighed. "I'll make certain she does not hurt Scooter again."

"Not Helen. Sarah. What if once you see her again, you decide you want her for your wife?"

Nick felt a pang in his chest. The thought had occurred to him, too. He'd actually spent quite a bit of time considering the idea. "No, that will not happen. I asked Sarah to leave Texas for me once. I'll not do it again."

"Well now, isna yer back sore all the time from toting so much pride around, Lord Weston?"

"That's not what I meant." He dragged his fingers through his hair. "I don't know how much she told you, but Sarah and I have corresponded regularly over the years and have developed a friendship of sorts."

"She did not mention that. She was too busy swearing at you. I have to admit, I rather liked the woman."

Nick's lips flirted with a grin at that. In his mind's eye he could easily picture Sarah and Gillian tearing him apart like Scooter with a juicy bone. He cleared his throat. "She is well established in Fort Worth. She has a comfortable home, good friends, and a successful business. It took all my powers of persuasion to get her to visit Britain. She'd never agree to live here, and I cannot live there."

"Because of us. Your sisters."

"Aye. I went too many years without you. I'll not give up any more. Yet, in five years you'll likely all be married and moved away. I don't want to live alone, Gilly. I want a wife. Children. A handful of boys to add some balance to the family."

"Lady Steele bred boys," his sister said with a sneer.

"Aye." Nick shrugged. "Can you blame me? I'm up to my ears in petticoats and lace. It would be good to hear a belch or two at the dinner table or find a frog in my bed from time to time."

"Robyn can do that. Ye need not marry the dog kicker."

"Oh, stop sulking." Nick drained his glass, then stood. "It could be worse. I could fall for Charlotte's widowed guid-mither and you'd have to listen to her singing for life."

Horror creased her brow. "Dinna even tease about such a heinous thing, Nicholas."

Grinning, he offered her his arm. "Shall we adjourn to the drawing room and Lady Pratt's recital?"

"One must do one's duty, I suppose," Gillian said with a heavy sigh. "Lead on, brother mine. Perhaps we'll be in luck and she will have cut the program short."

To Nick's dismay, Lady Pratt not only sang the entire program, she also launched into an unrequested encore. By the time she had cracked the last note, Nick found himself looking at his sister

Charlotte in a new light. She was more than a bride-to-be. Damned if her willingness to marry into that family of her own free will didn't make his sister a saint.

His sisters and Jake Delaney broke into generous applause. Nick suspected their enthusiasm had more to do with the fact that the so-called entertainment was concluded than with their appreciation of the performance. Playing his part, he joined the accolade and rose to his feet to offer a standing ovation.

It was then that he felt a prickle at the back of his neck, the same sensation that had saved his life on a number of occasions over the years. Glencoltran Castle's blue drawing room suddenly had become a dangerous place.

He was a target.

Silently, Nick cursed his lack of a weapon even as a dozen different thoughts shot like bullets through his brain. *Pinpoint the girls' locations in the room. Their safety is the first priority. Draw any fire away from them. Who is it? Which of his enemies would brave an attack here in his home?*

"Madam, you dinna want to go in there," came a footman's voice.

Time slowed to a crawl as Nick turned toward the drawing room doorway. He spied the bedraggled figure coming toward him and his heart stopped. The world narrowed to the two of them, sound was reduced to the rush of blood in his ears. Nick stood frozen, a target without defense.

And the villain took the advantage.

Crack. The blow was no mere slap, but a true right hook to the jaw. Nick's head snapped back. His sisters gasped.

Her hair a mess, her hem mud-stained and torn,

her feet bare as the day she was born, Sarah, Lady Weston, glared up at him and said, "For three months now I've traveled through dust storms, rainstorms, hailstorms, sleet storms, and snowstorms. I've ridden trains, ships, boats, coaches, wagons, horses, two mules, and even a sled pulled by a two-legged dog. Damn you, Nick, you didn't even bother to stay put. You make me mad enough to chew barbed wire. This is a helluva way to run a reunion."

Knuckles throbbing, Sarah stared up at her husband, truly seeing him for the first time as the red haze of rage dissipated.

Oh my. He's such a ... man.

A decade's worth of hardships and adventures had hardened her husband's features. Angles appeared sharper, the height and breadth of him seemed bigger, larger. The thin lines reaching outward from the corners of his icy blue eyes were new; the air of confidence and danger slightly familiar, but greatly intensified.

She licked her lips, swallowed hard. His nostrils flared, and Sarah felt like dinner. His dinner.

She never should have hit him.

If not for the ache in her hand, she might not believe she'd actually done it. Sarah had imagined her reunion with Nick a thousand different times and never—*never!*—had it happened like this. She rarely lost her temper. It was a trait that served her well in her professional life.

It was a good thing she was on a holiday.

Long, silent seconds marched inexorably by. She vaguely considered moving her feet, but they seemed to be frozen in place. Slowly, Sarah grew aware of the finely dressed crowd occupying the drawing room.

Ladies and gentlemen. Lords and ladies. Sarah felt a blush steal up her cheeks. She looked like a ragamuffin, had cursed like a fishwife, and had kissed his eye-teeth with her knuckles.

Oh my stars. She was horrified. Mortified. Humiliated.

But hanged if she'd let anybody see it.

She squared her shoulders, lifted her chin, and spoke in a regal tone. "Perhaps a servant could show me to my room?"

A strange light lit her husband's eyes, a combined twinkle of amusement and promise of retribution. Sarah wished the floor would open right up and swallow her.

Nick—Lord Weston—looked past her and nodded.

Finally released from the prison of his gaze, Sarah turned around and spied the wide-eyed footman shifting uneasily in the doorway. She swept from the room, infinitely aware that stunned silence reigned in her wake.

From the hallway she heard the never-forgotten rumble of Nick Ross's laughter. "The woman always did know how to stage an entrance."

Right now what she'd love to do was practice an exit. From the castle.

Led through a maze of richly appointed hallways, Sarah dazedly followed the servant. Finally alone in a beautiful bedchamber decorated in tones of blue, gold, and white, she asked herself, "What just happened? Why did it happen? Why in the world did you hit him?"

She spied her bags and realized they'd been emptied, her things put away. Her brush and comb lay upon a marble-topped mahogany dressing table. Taking a seat, she stared into the mirror at her red-faced reflection and tugged a hairbrush through the windblown, tangled nest that was her hair. "You know why."

She'd been embarrassed and afraid. Embarrassed at walking into a room full of well-dressed people looking like a hag. Afraid because . . . well . . . just because. Who wouldn't be at least a little afraid under the circumstances?

Curse the man. It was all his fault. He was the one who forced her to make this trip, then wasn't where he'd said he'd be. *Twice.* Riding up to that fairy-tale fortress called Rowanclere Castle had been difficult enough. Arriving at Hunterbourne with its imposing Palladian facade, painted ceilings, marble statues, and maze of hallways that seemed to go on forever had been the most intimidating moment of her life. And had he been there to greet her?

Oh, no, he had not. He'd gone back to the snowy north.

She'd never been treated so rudely in her life. It's no wonder her dander got up. And then, upon seeing Nick Ross dressed like lord of the castle and looking so at ease in that gilded drawing room, so devastatingly handsome and masculine and . . . grown-up . . . Sarah's knees had turned to water. It had taken every remnant of her questionable courage not to turn tail and run. That weakness spiked her fury, and as a result, she'd let fly her fist.

"Better you had run away," she said, flexing her sore knuckles. Then she gripped the brush hard, gave it another mighty tug, and winced as strands of hair pulled loose from the roots. The tears that glistened in her eyes had nothing to do with the tangle. She'd acted like a termagant in front of Jake and Gillian Ross, in front of the pretty young women who must be his other sisters. Of course, they could have been princesses for all she knew. Heaven knows the surroundings were opulent enough for royalty.

Sarah set down her hairbrush, then buried her face in her hands. *How will I ever face any of those people again? How can I ever face Nick?*

She'd intended to be poised and self-possessed and as presentable as any debutante in London. She had come so close to making it happen, too. All she'd needed to do was to follow the footman past that open doorway and on to her guestroom. She could have washed away the travel stains and donned one of her stylish dresses. Then, having gathered her composure, she could have waited to find him alone.

"But no, you couldn't do that, could you?" she said, lifting her head and glaring into the mirror. "You took one look at the man and lost your composure. That's some impression you made. Some entrance."

She hadn't been this embarrassed since her wedding night.

Knock knock knock. "Sarah? May I come in?"

Nicholas. Lovely. Just lovely. Shades of nightmares past. "No."

He waited a moment, then said, "I will not have this conversation through a door."

She didn't want to have this conversation at all. "Go away. I'm sulking."

His chuckle drifted toward her, the sound so surprisingly familiar that she smiled upon hearing it. But the smile died when she saw the knob turn as he tried the door. "It's locked, Nick. Go away. I'll speak with you later."

"Locked?"

She heard the snick of metal releasing, then her audacious husband sauntered right into her room. "You shouldn't be so high-handed, Sarah. I own this castle. I own the key to this door. Legally, some would say I even own you."

"Only if they don't have the sense God gave an armadillo," she fired back, pushing to her feet. "Nick, I require privacy. I'm changing my clothes."

He waited a moment before saying, "Lass, that's not precisely a deterrent."

Sarah's eyes went wide. Despite the fact that she was still completely clothed, she snatched up the dressing gown that lay draped over a nearby chair and held it up against her like a suit of armor. "I'll meet you downstairs in an hour."

"Half an hour. The muniment room would be convenient, but under the circumstances probably not a good choice. Let's try the study, shall we? I'll send someone to escort you so you aren't late."

She nodded, then held her breath as he turned and left. When the door shut behind him, she sank back into her chair with a soft moan. The man was devastatingly handsome. Why in the world had she failed to prepare herself for that possibility?

What she needed was a fortifying cup of chocolate. Men might prefer brandy, but for Sarah and most of the women she knew, nothing hit the spot quite like chocolate.

She nearly jumped out of her chair when the bedroom door creaked open once again. Nick stuck his head inside, flashed a wicked grin and said, "Just as I suspected. You still have all your clothes on. Best get moving. You have half an hour. Don't be late."

The shoe she flung just missed his nose.

*It's bad luck for a bride to wear black shoes
to her wedding.*

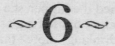

*T*wenty-five minutes later, the Marchioness of
Weston glided into Nick's study like a princess on a
rose-petaled path.

The Marquess of Weston's mouth went dry as
dust. She'd been a beautiful girl. Now a woman, she
was exquisite.

She wore her spun-gold hair piled artlessly on top
of her head. Wisps of curls escaped the pins and
called attention to her thickly lashed amber eyes that
gleamed with intelligence, confidence, and just
enough spirit to make a man take note—once he
made it past the lushness of her figure.

As his gaze skimmed her from head to toe, Nick
knew a bittersweet regret at having missed watching
her bloom.

The cut of her emerald silk gown was just different enough from current fashion to catch his style-
conscious sisters' interest and make them green
with envy. The luscious curves caressed by the silk

81

were bound to attract the notice of every man in the castle.

The surge of possessiveness that raged through him at the thought caught Nick off guard. He offered her a drink and a seat in a wingback chair placed before the fire. Having declined the former, she accepted the latter while Nick poured himself a glass of Rowanclere malt. He was drinking more than usual today. Women—this woman in particular—often had that effect on a man.

Claiming the chair beside her, he studied her pensively, then said, "Sarah, you are captivating."

She bowed her head regally, as though the compliment were her due.

Accustomed to praise, was she? He wondered just how many men had told her she was lovely during the past ten years. Dozens? Hundreds? Gruffly he added, "And you're five minutes early. I'm surprised."

"I despise tardiness."

He arched a brow. "Coming from you, that is quite amusing. Were you not due in Scotland weeks before you arrived?"

"According to your timetable, perhaps, not mine."

Her slow, Southern accent dripped like a warm and sultry night. Hearing it took his thoughts back to their disastrous wedding night, and his mood darkened considerably. Funny how that memory still had the ability to chafe. "Welcome to Glencoltran Castle."

She fluttered her lashes, her smile patently false. "Is that where I am? I fear I've quite lost track."

Little witch. "How was your trip?"

"I believe I covered that topic earlier."

"Ah, yes." Nick rubbed his hand across his jaw. "What happened to your escort? My footman said you arrived alone. Surely someone traveled with you from Hunterbourne."

Her smile didn't reach her eyes. "No. I'm quite accustomed to traveling alone. I noticed your sister Gillian in the drawing room. I assume she told you my kidnapper—that is, my escort, Mr. Jenkins—found something more appealing to do than continuing on to England?"

Dryly Nick said, "I understand he is on his honeymoon, and that he hired an escort to accompany you and your maid from Rowanclere to Hunterbourne."

"His honeymoon? That's welcome news. I trust he and Annie will be very happy together."

"But what of the escort he hired?"

Dainty shoulders shrugged. "We didn't suit."

He waited, but she added no more and he decided not to press the issue. Sarah was safe and apparently sound. Later he would make certain she understood things were different here than in Texas. Ladies went nowhere unescorted. They especially didn't travel without a companion.

Good Lord, what's the matter with you? She's here. Sarah is finally here. You have much larger problems to concern you than what happened to her maid.

Damnation. He hadn't felt this uncomfortable since he gave that bed of nails in Tibet a try.

An awkward silence fell between them. To fill it, Nick rose, lifted a tool, and tended the fire. Red sparks flew up the chimney as the log rolled.

Sarah shifted in her seat. "So. I believe you have something you wish to discuss?"

Nick scowled down at the flickering flames. Annoyed, he spoke in a tone that was sharper than necessary. "The manner of your arrival has complicated matters."

She blinked. "Excuse me? I believe *you* sent for *me*. Blackmailed me into coming. Basically had me kidnapped."

"Yes." He waved a hand in dismissal. "But you were supposed to meet me at Rowanclere so no one would know."

"No one would know what?"

"What we're doing," he snapped.

"Planning Charlotte's wedding? Why, is it a secret?"

"Not the wedding." He jabbed a burning log and sent it tumbling from the grate. Wonderful. Just wonderful. Ashes scattered as he grabbed the tongs and wrestled the log back into place and explained, "I had intended to keep our . . . relationship . . . quiet. However, Charlotte's fiancé and future mother-in-law were in the drawing room when you arrived. She's one of the biggest gossips in all of England."

Her drawl was a rattlesnake stuck in molasses—slow, but with a killer bite. "Well isn't it handy, then, that we're in Scotland."

His grip on the tongs turned his knuckles white. Amazed at the strength of the reaction she roused within him, he drew a deep, calming breath, then gently replaced the tool in the stand. He braced his hands on his hips and faced his wife. "Lady Pratt is a problem. You must help me here, Sarah. You owe me."

"What?" She shoved herself to her feet, inadvertently flashing him a show of ankle. "I owe you? Did you just say I owe you? Of all the nerve."

As she took a step toward him, he dragged his gaze away from her hem and held up one hand. "Do not attempt to hit me again."

"Oh, I won't hit you. I'll kill you."

Damned if he didn't want to smile, but he managed to muffle it. "You owe me because you used my title. 'Weddings by Lady Innsbruck.' Remember?"

She gave an unfeminine snort. "Did you take to wearing skirts in the years we were apart, Nick? I do believe the word 'Lady' refers to me. It is my title, not yours, and I'm not even using it anymore since I've gone into business with the McBrides."

"Actually, you're Lady Weston now, and in the past you have benefited from the use of my name. You admitted as much in your letters."

At his reference to the letters, their gazes met and held. A sense of warmth stole through Nick as a silent message was exchanged. Her letters had meant the world to him. Every time he spied her handwriting in the packets forwarded to him by the newspaper, he'd been both wary and elated. Wary because each time he expected to find annulment papers and elated because her letters never failed to lift his spirits. Sarah's letters had been a welcome taste of normalcy in the midst of the chaotic life of a British agent.

"Thank you for that, by the way. I always enjoyed your letters."

His words visibly took the starch out of her spine. Sarah smoothed a wrinkle on her gown, then resumed her seat. "I enjoyed yours, too. And also your articles in the *Herald*. You were an asset to the newspaper, Nick."

He laughed. "Purely by accident, I assure you. I never expected to enjoy the writing."

"You *were* a spy, weren't you?"

This time he blinked. "What makes you think that? What an absurd idea."

She spoke of her uncle and how they'd reached

their startling conclusion, and for the most part got it all right. She ended the recitation with a question. "How did it happen? You left Fort Worth with Miss Harris to go to England. How did you end up a secret agent in Afghanistan?"

Nick didn't know how to respond. Should he tell her how much he'd longed to return to Fort Worth—to her—after learning what his father wanted of him? What would she say if he told her how often he'd imagined their lives had he not left her following that debacle of a wedding night? Would it hurt or help to confess that he'd quickly come to realize he'd made the wrong choice?

That's water down the brae, Nick. Why bring it up? The minute he saw the betrayal in her eyes as she watched him board the train with Susan Harris, he'd known there was no going back.

So what did he say now? A part of him wanted her to know the truth, he realized. Wanted her respect. To that end he should explain Susan's place in his life, both then and today. But since he'd promised Susan his silence, he would ask her permission to speak before addressing that situation with Sarah. On the other hand, since his participation in the Great Game was done, he didn't see what it would hurt to confirm his wife's suspicions about his profession. "My father had ties to the government. He arranged it."

"I knew it."

The smug sparkle in her eyes nearly took his breath away. Nick cleared his throat. "I trust I can count on your discretion. You are one of only a handful of people who know the truth. In fact, you're the only person I know of outside of those directly involved who guessed that the American reporter Nick Ross is now the Marquess of Weston."

"I, and Uncle Michael," she corrected. "But Nick, don't people ask where you've been all these years?"

Nick's mouth lifted in a grin. "I tell them I was a chuck wagon cookie on cattle drives up the Chisholm Trail."

"A chuck wagon cookie? You? And they believe that?"

"Not necessarily. But few people ever ask a second time." In a more serious vein, he asked, "So, Sarah, will you continue to keep my secret?"

She measured him with her stare. "Do you operate against American interests?"

"No. I haven't and I won't. My days in the service are done. I've hung up my cloak and dagger."

"So why is discretion required? I would think being known as a former secret service agent would enhance your reputation."

He chose his words carefully. "It is remotely possible that others might come to harm should the truth come out. That in itself is enough, but also, I don't wish to deal with the inevitable questions. People are ghoulish, and their curiosity tends to focus on the ugly, bloody side of times I'd prefer to forget. They wouldn't ask me about a village boy and his dog. They'd ask about the body count of the massacre at Plevna." As Sarah nodded her understanding, he added, "My focus is on the future, now. Not the past."

"If that is the case, then why blackmail me into coming here? I'm part of the past."

Nick winced at the sharpness of her tone. "I don't know that blackmail is the proper word."

"You prefer extortion? Either one fits. However, why the need for secrecy?"

"It's complicated."

"Weddings usually are," she responded, her lips

twisting wryly. Then she sighed. "What's going on, Nick? You wouldn't go to this much trouble simply to secure my professional services in helping Charlotte plan her wedding. I am very good at my work, but as I explained in my letters, I feel certain England has some excellent wedding consultants available for hire."

"True. But I want only the best for my sisters."

She nodded, acknowledging the compliment before posing the question, "And since when has a Brit ever considered an American better at anything?"

Her eyes were the same warm amber as the Rowanclere malt, Nick decided, and ten times more intoxicating. "Times are changing."

"They haven't changed that much," she drawled. "Now, one of your letters mentioned that other matters require my attention. May I ask what they are?"

Nick set his whisky glass atop the gray marble mantel. He adjusted the fire screen, then stepped away from the fireplace. He wasn't at all anxious to get into this. "Would you like a tour of the castle?"

"No, thank you."

Nick began to pace. Damnation, the words weren't coming. He didn't know what to say. He couldn't lie to her; she'd see right through him. The Sarah he'd met and married in Fort Worth always was quick-witted. Young and naive and very nervous, but definitely intelligent.

She didn't appear overly nervous now. A slight bit, perhaps, but not nearly as nervous as he. No, the woman seated in his study bristled with confidence. And annoyance.

Sarah, Lady Weston, was indulging in a pout. She was also the most alluring, intriguing creature he'd encountered in many a year.

In that moment, Nick admitted he had a problem. He had doubts about his planned course of action, and he'd had them since the moment her knuckles connected with his jaw. Because Nicholas, Lord Weston, had needed no more than one look at his mussed and muddied and mettlesome wife to understand one thing.

He wanted her.

Badly.

That hasn't changed in the past ten years.

He'd never forget their first meeting. While purchasing a new knife in the Fort Worth mercantile, he had spied the advertisement for the Literary Society meeting. Part of the program was to be a reading from the poetry of Robert Burns. Homesickness had taken hold of him, and he'd been the first person to arrive. Sarah had been the second.

She'd walked into the room eating a peach—ripe and red and luscious—and his tongue had ached to lick the juice from her lips. When the program began, he wrangled a seat beside her, and three months later they were engaged to be married.

He'd never looked at a peach the same way since.

He refused to let himself think about cherries.

Nick cleared his throat, but words refused to come. He simply didn't know what to say—an unusual circumstance for him. During his years in the secret service, Nick had mastered the fine art of dissembling, honing his instincts on the hot sands of the Taklamakan Desert and the bitter slopes of the Himalayas. Right now those instincts were telling him to step carefully. He didn't want to say or do anything here tonight that couldn't be changed or undone.

Perhaps he didn't want this annulment after all.

Nick ran his tongue over his teeth. Judas, where had that come from? Of course he wanted the annulment.

Didn't he?

He couldn't remember the last time he'd been this indecisive. Or this needy. Were these doubts of his real? Or, was this a case of his good sense being overpowered by the baser instincts that had loaded his pistol the moment she walked through the drawing room door?

Perhaps he should take some time to figure it out.

It was foolish, really. He'd had ten years to decide what he wanted from Sarah. And it wasn't as if she had popped in unexpectedly now. Why wasn't he prepared? This wasn't like him. Not at all. He didn't like it one bit.

Deciding to proceed with caution, Nick softened his pace into a saunter and crossed the study to his desk. He propped his hip on one corner, folded his arms, and lazily swung his leg. His foot brushed the rich hues of the fine Persian carpet once, twice, three times. Then he took a deep breath and bought himself some time. "It's my sister Aurora. I'm at wit's end with her. She attempted an elopement. With a snatch-purse."

As always when he thought about Willie Hart, anger and frustration filled his tone, and thus Nick sounded quite convincing. "Thank God I caught up with them before the deed was done, but she is furious with me—and with her sisters for telling on her. She's a poor motherless girl, and she needs a woman's guidance. In your letters you wrote you served as confidant to the daughters of your business partners—the McBride Marauders."

"Menaces. The McBride Menaces."

"Aye. Well, Aurora needs similar counsel. I'm asking for your assistance, Sarah. Your help. I hope that while you work with Charlotte planning her wedding, you can befriend her sisters."

As Nick talked, he warmed up to the idea, considered it inspired. "The boy she ran off with is a true scoundrel. He's a worthless thief who thinks to steal a young girl's heart and make himself a rich man. She's sixteen. She's in love. Willie Hart makes me look like the pope."

"Oh, Nick."

"Aye, it is hard to believe, but it is the truth."

She sputtered a laugh, and he sensed he'd achieved his goal. "So, can I count on you? Will you help me? Help us?"

"Oh, all right," she said with a sigh. "I'll try. I can assist with Charlotte's wedding plans, and I'll see what I can do for Aurora. I'll do my best, but if Aurora is anything like Emma or Maribeth McBride, it may take more time than I'll have with her to gain her trust."

"Let's take each day as it comes, shall we? Not concern ourselves with time?"

When she nodded, he took her hands in his. The scent of peaches wafted up, stole into his senses, and reminded him of something. "I guess we'll have to tell the girls we're married. I hate to think about that."

"Well, thank you very much," she drawled.

When he responded with a laugh, Sarah gazed up into the sapphire gleam of her husband's eyes, her thoughts swirling like a springtime tornado. More was going on here than she knew at the moment. He was leading her in a direction she wasn't certain she wanted to go. "Why would we hide the truth?"

The devil laughed. "We have a complicated relationship. Counting both families, I have six sisters. Do you have any idea the speculation and interference we'll be inviting by giving them the facts? It'll be like living in a war zone, and in truth, I've had my fill of that."

Sarah could see his point. They would ask questions for which she didn't have answers. On the trip from Texas, Sarah had done quite a bit of soul-searching on the status of her marriage to the Marquess of Weston. She suspected he wanted to change the status quo, and darned if she knew what she wanted, providing that were the case. "Your sisters are inquisitive?"

"Nosy. And bossy. They'll not leave us alone."

"Very well." She nodded, surrendering to his argument. "Why don't we simply say I'm the wedding expert you hired, the old friend from Texas who sent the lovely wedding gown Charlotte wore last year."

"That might work. I'll think it through, then tell them in the morning."

"What happened to it, by the way? The wedding gown."

"I'm not certain, but I think they gave it away. They said the dress was unlucky."

Sarah glanced up at him and smiled. "A Bad Luck Wedding Dress? Another one?"

"I don't understand."

Sarah relayed a condensed version of the tale about the Bad Luck Wedding Dress. Eight years ago Jenny McBride had made a wedding gown for a wealthy ranching family whose three daughters married within months of one another. Each girl wore the gown at her wedding, and each girl suffered unpleasant and unusual accidents a short time later. The superstitious people of Fort Worth had declared the dress bad luck. In order to save her dressmaking business, Jenny wore the dress when she married Trace McBride, and despite a rocky beginning, by the time the story was done, everyone in town referred to the gown as the Good Luck Wedding Dress.

A sardonic smile accompanied his words as he muttered, "I'd hate to hear what the townspeople called your wedding gown." Then, before she could decide how to reply to that, he reached for her hand and tugged her toward the door. "Enough wedding talk. Let's walk, shall we? Since we've settled the immediate business, I'd like to visit with you a bit. Let's take a stroll beside the loch. It's a mild evening, and the moon is near full. I remember how you enjoyed the reflection of moonlight off the water when we walked along the Trinity River. Wait until you see its silvery shine upon the loch."

He guided her through a maze of staircases and corridors to an arched wooden doorway, pausing to remove his jacket and place it about her shoulders. "Welcome to Glencoltran, Sarah," he said softly before he leaned over to press a friendly kiss against first one cheek, then the other. "I should have a bouquet of flowers to present to you, but I fear 'tis the wrong season for such. I recall you had a fondness for flowers. Remember how Wilhemina Peters sneezed all the way through our wedding?"

"Roses," Sarah absently replied, shocked by the slow spread of pleasure from the spot where his lips brushed her skin. "Roses caused Mrs. Peters to sneeze. Brides in Fort Worth have abandoned the more fragrant varieties because of her susceptibility."

"Does she still shoulder her way into the front pew?"

"Right next to the bride's mother every time."

He chuckled. "Some things never change."

Like Nick leading her down the garden path, she thought as he escorted her out of the castle and into a crisp, moonlit world.

Sarah snuggled into the protection of his jacket, still warm from his body and perfumed with a woodsy, masculine scent that teased at her memory. They strolled without speaking along a garden path, the only sounds the scrunch of gravel beneath their feet and the whisper of an intermittent breeze through the evergreens. When the path opened out onto a rocky shore where moonlight painted a silver swath across a midnight lake, Sarah couldn't help but smile. "How lovely."

"This is one of my favorite spots on earth. Glencoltran is a tenth the size of Hunterbourne and has little of the gilt and glamor. But for me, it's home." He held her hand and helped her climb over a shadowy boulder, then asked, "So, tell me about your home, lass. Tell me about your life in Fort Worth."

The sound of his nickname for her sent a nostalgic chord singing through her and she sighed. "I have a good life in Texas, Nick. That hasn't changed. I have a lovely home on the south end of town, an occupation I enjoy, and dear friends."

His hand gripped hers a fraction tighter. "A lover?"

"No." Heavens no. She shuddered at the notion. Then, because a woman did have her pride, she added, "Not at the moment."

He must have thought she was cold, because he

slipped his arm around her and pulled her close. Casually he asked, "What about children? As I recall, you wanted to have a houseful."

Children. Leave it to Nick to hone in on her greatest regret. But to get children, she'd have to be intimate with a man, and she'd yet to meet anyone she trusted enough to do that.

Oh, she'd tried to move on after Nick left. She'd been up-front and honest about her marital status and for the most part circumspect in her actions. Because Fort Worth was a frontier town and populated mostly by men, she had never suffered a shortage of gentlemen callers. Why, she'd received four marriage proposals in the past year alone. She'd lost track of how many she received in the years since she and Nick had parted ways.

On three separate occasions she'd come close to accepting. Twice she'd gone so far as to have the annulment papers prepared. But when the time came for her to fix her signature to the page, she'd never quite managed to find the heart to do it. It was easier to stay married to an absent husband. Safer. Because not only did she not trust the men, she didn't trust herself.

She'd loved Nick. It had been a young love, true, but love nonetheless. She'd believed in him, and he'd left town with another woman the day following their wedding. After that, how could she trust her own judgment in matters of the heart?

Their stroll had taken them toward a small wooden boathouse built along the water's edge. Nick released the latch on a pair of broad wooden doors, and they creaked open to block the gentle but chilly breeze. Sarah stood inside, lost in thoughts of the past, barely noting the faint, fishy scent that hung on the air.

Moments later, lamplight flickered. One, two, then three lamps glowed, chasing away the shadows, revealing not the skiff and fishing supplies she had expected, but a cozy table and a quartet of chairs. "What's this?"

"Too many females in the house. A man needs a place to call his own, and I like to listen to the lap of waves upon the shore when I play cards."

Then the confounded man went and picked up the conversation where it had left off. "Sarah, don't you still want that houseful of children?"

She tossed him a look of annoyance, then shrugged. "My friends the McBrides have children to spare when I am plagued by maternal feelings."

"Seems like a poor substitute."

"The McBride children are special. I've told you stories about them over the years. The girls had a reputation for trouble when they were younger, but the boys . . ." She made a mock shudder. "They have far surpassed their sisters. I love them all dearly, but an hour spent with any of them goes a long way toward reminding one of the challenges of parenting."

He lifted a deck of cards from the center of the table and shuffled them. Fanning them out, he held the cards out to her, saying, "You run from challenges now, lass?"

"Hardly." She chose a card. The trey of clubs. "I'm here, aren't I?"

Nick laughed at that, then chose his own card. The queen of hearts. "Curse it all, I lost."

"Lost? What sort of card games do they play in Scotland? In my part of the world, a queen of hearts beats a trey of clubs handily."

"Aye, it's the same here. But you see, it was all in

the terms of the bet. I told myself if you won, I wouldn't do this."

Before she quite knew what had happened, she found herself backed against a support post. As his gaze fixed on her mouth, memories flooded her mind and she was suddenly sixteen again. She recalled stolen kisses at the Literary Society meetings. Those moonlit walks beside the Trinity River.

Lost in the pleasure of the past, Sarah swallowed hard. His arms encircled her waist, and the glitter in his eyes took on a dangerous tint as he lowered his mouth to hers.

At the first touch of his lips, Sarah was sixteen no longer. She was here, in a lamp-lit hideaway beside a Highland loch being kissed by the man who had haunted her dreams for a decade. Only now she wasn't sixteen, and his kiss was so much more. *He* was so much more.

Nick had always made her go soft inside. This time he made her melt. The scent of him. The taste of him. The rough rasp of his tongue against hers. The fluttery sensation low in her stomach that his kisses brought to life. Her knees went weak, but he pressed his lower body against her, supporting her, holding her in place. The proof of his desire was hard against her.

Sarah whimpered even as heat roared through her. What was happening to her? What was he doing?

His teeth nipped at her bottom lip and she gasped. In response, Nick made a noise, a growl, deep in his throat, and the sound of it skittered through her blood like a current.

A yawning ache opened up inside her, centered in her loins. Its intensity frightened her and gave her the will to push against him. "No," she said. "Stop this. Stop it, Nick. I didn't come to Glencoltran for this."

He murmured a protest against her mouth, then slowly stepped away, his arms falling to his sides. His eyes gleamed warm and unrepentant as he shoved his hands into his pockets and rocked back on his heels. "Actually, I suspect you did. I suspect this might be exactly why you've come to me."

Emotions stampeded through her like cattle. Need and regret and yearning. Fear. Pulsing, numbing, heartbreaking fear. She'd trusted him before, and he'd broken her heart.

This time he could destroy her.

Her voice was shrill and tremulous as she scooted away from him. "This is a mistake. You never should have made me come here."

"Sarah ..."

The fragrance in the air now struck her as fishy, and her stomach took a roll. She had turned to flee both the building and her husband when she heard him call, "Think about it. I would give you bonny children."

Sarah ran from the loch as if chased by a monster of the deep. Back in her room, she buried her face in his jacket, in his scent, and fought back tears she didn't understand. When hours later she finally got to sleep, she dreamed of a fairy-tale castle filled with the happy laughter of bonny, blue-eyed children.

It's bad luck for a bride to laugh on her wedding day.

"**W**ell? Who is she?" Lady Charlotte Ross asked when Nick strolled into the family sitting room the following morning in search of a strong cup of coffee. He'd asked his family to assemble here in private to hear his explanation about Sarah, a tangle of truth and lies he'd put together during the long, mostly sleepless night.

He felt like one of the ancient suits of armor his youngest Scots sister Robyn used in her mock battles—old and battered and beaten. The few minutes he'd slept had been filled with dreams of Sarah, hot, erotic dreams that left him needy and aching. Twice the urges had propelled him from his bed and sent him toward Sarah's, determined to turn fantasy into reality. Thank God for cold stone floors and bare feet. The combination cleared his thinking enough for him to realize the folly of his intent.

"You look awful, Nicholas." Lady Melanie Ross set down her cup of chocolate with a clatter and a spill. "Is it her fault? Aurora thinks she's your mistress and that you invited her to Glencoltran, only she was supposed to meet you in the hunting lodge, not the castle."

"Melanie!" Lady Aurora Ross protested. "You weren't supposed to tell him. I'm not supposed to know about mistresses."

"None of you are supposed to know about mistresses," Nick groused, scowling as he poured coffee into an oversized teacup. "Be quiet. One thing you girls must learn if you're to make successful marriages is that you don't bring up forbidden subjects and pepper a man with questions before he's had his morning coffee. Now, sit and be still."

They didn't obey him, but then, his sisters seldom obeyed him. What they did was ask one another questions, leaving him out of it, yet letting him know exactly what information they wanted. In addition to being the most loving, caring creatures on earth, his sisters were ultimately female—bright, scheming, and manipulative. In some ways he pitied the men who would finally win them.

Nick downed his first cup of coffee quickly, then sipped at the second more slowly. At that point, Melanie decided it was safe to speak to him. "We don't know much except that mistresses are wicked, Nick. Is this woman wicked? If so, why did you bring her to your home?"

"You are completely mistaken," Nick declared. "Sarah is not a wicked woman."

Aurora pinned him with a look. "Sarah? That's her name? And who is she?"

"As soon as the rest of your sisters arrive, I'll tell you all of it. This is an explanation I want to go through only once."

The trio nodded, then Charlotte asked. "We'll be

done by noon, won't we, Nicholas? I'm to meet Rodney and Lady Pratt in the drawing room then. She has yet to give her blessing to the match, and I'm hopeful she'll do it before they leave this afternoon."

"The Dragon Lady." Aurora shuddered dramatically. "You know, Charlotte, it occurs to me that Rodney is lucky she spent last Season in Paris. If you'd met her early on, I'll bet you'd have thought twice about falling in love with her son."

"She's the reason Flora and Alasdair cut their visit to Glencoltran short," Melanie said, referring to Nick's other Scottish sister, Gillian's twin Flora, and her husband. "Every time Dragon Lady Pratt looked at Flora's babies, she made them cry."

"That's not true," Nick countered. "Flora and Alasdair never intended to stay longer at Glencoltran. They had other commitments at home at Laichmoray."

Charlotte sipped at her chocolate and said, "I cannot get over how much alike Flora and Gillian look. How did you ever tell them apart when they were young?"

"I was the nice one," Gillian said, sweeping into the room along with Nick's youngest Scottish sister, fourteen-year-old Robyn.

Nick choked on his coffee. Robyn said, "That's a lie. Flora always has been the good twin. I, of course, take after her."

As Nick started coughing, the young girl added, "You haven't told them who Sarah is yet, have you, Nick? I was afraid I'd miss it. Jake said to go ahead without him. He's taking Scooter for a walk."

Nick grimaced, knowing what would come next. Leave it to the baby of the family to spill the beans.

"What about Sarah?" demanded Melanie. "Do you know who she is? How do you know about her?"

Aurora threw him a green-eyed glare. "You told your Scots sisters but not your English ones?"

"Girls, please," Nick said, wishing he had a splash of whisky to add to his coffee. He should have anticipated that Robyn would know about his wife. Robyn would have learned the detail from Jake or Gillian, and while they could keep their lips fastened, Robyn was another kettle of fish.

Charlotte set down her cup abruptly. "You know, I don't appreciate your speaking poorly about Lady Pratt. She is to be my mother-in-law soon, and that makes her my family. One shouldn't speak so about family."

Melanie rolled her eyes. "Charlotte, keep up. We're talking about Nicholas's mystery woman now."

"I'm not. I'm talking about my fiancé's mother. I want you to stop being mean about Rodney's mother," she continued, her voice growing a bit shrill. "I'll be happy at Breadsall Manor. Lady Pratt will learn to accept my place in the household. Rodney has promised."

The other sisters all shared a look, then Robyn reached over and patted her knee. "Of course he will, Char. I like Rodney. He tells funny jokes."

Melanie muttered, "Living with the Dragon Lady, he needs a good sense of humor."

Gillian shot the others a chastising look. "Rodney is a good man. We all think so. He'll do right by Charlotte. Otherwise, he'll answer to Nicholas. Won't he, Nicholas?"

Nick simply sighed. Not for the first time, he wondered if he wanted children of his own, after all. *Maybe if I just have boys it'll be all right. Quieter, certainly.*

"Your sister isn't marrying Dragon Lady Pratt, she's marrying the Dragon Lady's son," he said. "Lord Pratt is a good man. Young, true. But he'll learn. He and Charlotte will learn together—if they give themselves the time to adjust. That's the only interfering I plan to do—to make certain they have a nice, long honeymoon. Just the two of them, with no interruptions. Every marriage deserves that."

"I quite agree," Aurora declared, shooting her brother a blistering glare. "No one should have their honeymoon interrupted. I know how horrible that is."

"You weren't on your honeymoon, Aurora," Gillian pointed out. "Nicholas caught up with you and Willie Hart before you married."

Aurora gave a dismissive wave. "A minor detail."

"Not in the least," Nick inserted. Anxious to change the subject, he said, "So, do you wish to hear about Sarah?"

Breathing a sigh of relief at the sudden quiet, he drained his coffee, then set down his cup. Five feminine faces gazed at him with varying degrees of expectancy. Warmth filled his chest. This was his family: Charlotte, Melanie, and Aurora. Gillian and Robyn. Only Flora and her bairns were missing.

And Sarah. Despite everything, he'd always thought of her as family.

"Yes we do, brother," Melanie said. "Who is she, and why is she here?"

Gillian gave him an encouraging smile. Robyn giggled softly. The pretty speech Nick had spent half the night composing flew right out of his mind. So he spoke the only sentence he had left. "Sarah is my wife."

For a long moment, silence reigned like a queen. Then Aurora asked, "You *are* referring to the woman who punched you? The muddy one?"

Robyn piped up. "She was supposed to meet Nicholas at Rowanclere before Christmas, but she was late."

"That's why you went to Rowanclere in December?" Melanie asked, her eyes flashing. "To bring home a wife? And it slipped your mind to tell us about it?"

Charlotte nibbled worriedly at her lower lip. "Rodney's mother was quite upset last night. She asked why a harpy came to call at Glencoltran Castle."

"Harpy?" Gillian snorted. " 'Tis the pot calling the kettle black, that is. Lady Pratt canna see past the nose on her face. The girl is Quality through and through. Tell them, Nicholas."

"Quality?" Melanie repeated. "She wasn't dressed properly, and she didn't act mannerly. I guess she might be pretty enough beneath the muss and mud, but I cannot picture her at one of the queen's drawing rooms."

Aurora spoke up. "She does have courage, though. She punched Nicholas right in the mouth in front of people who were strangers to her. I always admire courage. For me, personally, that's a sign of Quality."

Charlotte asked, "Who is she, Nicholas? When did you marry? Why haven't you mentioned her? How soon do we get to meet her?"

Nick made a show of clearing his voice. "If you ladies will button your lips for a few minutes, I'll answer your questions. Most of them, anyway."

Like a teacher signaling the class to quiet, he folded his arms and waited. When finally he had their complete attention, he began. "I know that you know pieces of this story from others, but you've never heard it from me."

He spoke briefly of learning of his true parentage and the subsequent visit to Hunterbourne. "I saw you playing in the garden that day, Charlotte, but he refused to let me meet any of his other children."

The girls shared a look of pain but remained quiet. Nick continued with the marquess's offer to pay Nick a regular remittance if he'd leave the country and stay away. "It seemed like a good idea at the time. I was angry at the Rosses for hiding the truth from me and had nowhere else to go."

He told them how he'd made his way to Texas, and about the note that arrived from their father telling him that the entire Ross family had been killed.

"Why did Father lie about that, Nicholas?" Aurora asked, tears glistening in her eyes.

He had no answer for her, and he refused to state his own bitter conclusions. The third marquess had shown a different side of himself to his daughters, and Nick didn't want to destroy their illusions. He wouldn't lie to them, but he wouldn't tell them everything, either. So he answered that he didn't know and continued his story with how he happened to meet Miss Sarah Simpson at a Literary Society meeting in Fort Worth, Texas.

"I was lonely and grieving for my family," he told them. "Sarah made me laugh. She was pretty and fun and good-hearted. She made me feel that I belonged. I needed that. I liked it."

He'd also liked the way she made him feel randy, but that wasn't something he'd tell his sisters. "Fort

Worth seemed like a good place to live, and I asked Sarah to settle down with me."

"That sounds very dry," said Melanie with a sniff. "I hope your actual proposal was more romantic?"

Actually, to be technical about it, Sarah had proposed to him, the reason being something about an unusually large number of upcoming weddings and the need to book the church in advance. Nick grinned at the memory. She'd been so seductively coy about the entire thing. He'd agreed without a second thought.

"Our wedding was the very picture of romance," he replied, sidestepping his sister's question. "You'd have approved. In fact, you'd have been envious. Sarah has a talent for planning such events and has made a successful business of it. It's one of the reasons I invited her here. I'm hoping she'll help with your arrangements, Charlotte."

Charlotte's brows arched. "Oh?"

"I like that," Melanie said, nodding. "That Wilhoit woman who helped with the last one was adequate enough, but she has no imagination. And remember Viscount Hollis's daughter's wedding? Why, the flowers were wilted and the—"

"Melanie, please," Aurora protested. "We want to hear more about Nicholas's wife. What happened after the wedding? Did *her* brother come and steal *her* away before the honeymoon, too?"

He scowled at his rebellious younger sister, the one for whom his heart had a soft spot because she was so very much like him. "Sarah and I did not attempt elopement. We had a beautiful church wedding. Her uncle walked her down the aisle, and her mother cried into her handkerchief in the front pew."

As for what happened after that, he'd take up vol-

untary residence in a Khan's rat pit before he'd give
them too many details. Nor did he wish to dampen the
mood of the day by speaking of the riding accident that
killed their other brothers, so he chose his words carefully. "A message from your father arrived. He offered
me a place in the family, and I wanted to accept. Sarah
understandably didn't wish to leave her home and widowed mother, so we parted ways."

Melanie and Aurora shared a considering look.
Charlotte studied him like a bug beneath a micro-
scope. "So all this time you've been married to this
Sarah, but you haven't lived together? What kind of
a marriage is that?"

"Not much of one, I will admit."

Aurora wrinkled her nose. "Do you mean she's
spent all these years waiting for you? No wonder she
hit you the first time she saw you again."

"I think she used great restraint limiting her
weapon to only a fist," Gillian added.

All five females nodded at that. Nick glared at
them, while Charlotte asked, "Why is she here now?
You said helping with my wedding was only one reason."

"Oh, Nicholas," Melanie breathed. "Does Lady
Steele know this tidbit of truth?"

Aurora piped up. "Does your wife know about
Lady Steele?"

Avoiding a direct response, Nick sought Gillian's
eyes for support. "I sent for Sarah so we could legally
dissolve the marriage."

Charlotte gasped, then rose to her feet. "No, Nick.
You don't mean ... divorce!"

"Divorce!" his sisters exclaimed as one. Gillian
grimaced, Robyn frowned, Aurora gasped, and
Melanie groaned.

Charlotte looked as though she might lose her breakfast. "The scandal. Lady Pratt. Oh, my."

He closed his eyes. He couldn't worry them this way. It wasn't fair. Sharply, he said, "No divorce. It won't require a divorce."

As his sisters shared looks of confusion, Nick felt heat steal up his neck. Ach, this had become entirely too personal. What man wanted to admit he hadn't managed to make love to his bride on their wedding night—to his sisters, no less? Grimly he said, "We will have the marriage annulled and avoid a huge scandal, and that's all I'm going to say on the topic."

He set down his coffee cup, propped his elbows on his knees, and leaned forward earnestly. "However, to ensure it works out that way, I need your help, girls. Sarah doesn't know why I asked her to come here. In fact, she believes she is here mainly to help Charlotte plan her nuptials. I am asking you not to mention anything about what I've said to you here this morning."

"Why?" Aurora, ever the troublemaker, asked. "Do you want to keep her?"

Nick ground his teeth together. Be damned if he'd answer that question. Be damned if he *had* an answer to that question. He rose to his feet, scowling. "My reasons are my own, and I'll thank you to remember that. I'm asking for the support of my family. Do I have it? Can you keep your tattie-traps shut for just a few days while I set things aright? Will you all give me your word on it?"

The women shared a look and, in the way of females, carried on an entire conversation without voicing a word. Then Charlotte turned to Gillian. "You've met her?"

"Aye."

"What do you think?"

Gillian lifted her shoulders. "She's nae icy like the other."

Now the sisters' gazes turned speculative, and Nick could almost hear the wheels turning in their heads. Aurora finally folded her arms and voiced the thought so obviously on all of their minds. "So, brother, what of Lady Steele?"

"I beg your pardon? When were you ordained as inquisition priests?"

" 'Tis a fair question, Nick," Gillian observed.

He sent her a glare that shouted, *Traitor.* "Leave Helen out of this."

Charlotte licked her lips. "But isn't Lady Steele central to the question? She *is* the reason why you are addressing this issue now, isn't she? You want to annul your marriage to the American and marry Lady Steele?"

"The Ice Queen," Robyn observed.

Nick's temper flared. He braced his hands on his hips and snapped, "Lady Steele is no ice queen. Believe me, I know. I have personal experience with the queen of the ice queens. The woman gave me frostbite on my tossel. So what if I want to marry Lady Steele? She will enjoy sharing a bed with me. She wants to give me children!"

As the echo of his voice died away, even before his sisters' eyes shifted past his shoulders and rounded with horror, even before the sound of the teacup shattering against the marble floor reached his ears, Nick knew. Turning around only confirmed it. "Sarah."

She'd gone pale as a snowcapped mountain. "Excuse me. One of the servants directed me this way. I apologize for the intrusion."

As his wife turned and fled, Nick muttered a string of Afghan curses blue enough to make his sisters faint had they been able to understand them.

Gillian stood and raked him with a contemptuous gaze. "Well, brither, I hope you brought another pair of boots with ye. I do believe ye have stepped in the gullion now."

He finally tracked her down in the muniment room. Standing in the doorway, watching her test the weight of an ancient broadsword, he wondered if he'd be smarter to wait a bit and allow her to calm down before he approached her. He took too long to decide.

She turned to him with a smile. "So," she said brightly, "you intend to annul the marriage?"

Cautiously Nick stepped into the room. "We've left it to drift along for a decade."

"So we have."

After waiting for her to elaborate, then realizing she had no intention of doing so, he observed, "I always expected you to pursue the annulment. Why didn't you?"

Nick wanted an answer to this question. It was an issue he'd pondered long and hard over the years. He understood why *he* had not pursued the dissolution of their marriage up to now. For one thing, he'd always assumed he'd die in some remote spot in Asia, so he saw no reason to bother with it. He had other reasons, too, more complicated than that, some of them still just a jumble in his mind. They had to do with the letters they'd exchanged, his belief in the honor of his word, and the shadow of a dream dearly held and never completely forgotten.

But what was Sarah's excuse?

"Oh, I did pursue it," she said, figuratively knocking his feet right out from under him. As his brows winged up, she flashed a mocking smile. "Once or twice. I never went through with it, though. I realized I was content with the situation as it stood."

"Why?"

Her shoulders lifted, then fell in a gentle shrug. "I'm happy, Nick. I'm sorry you are not."

"It's not that," he said, scowling. He waited, allowing the silence to lengthen. When she finally met his gaze, he laid it out like a prayer rug. "It's time I had a wife."

Had he not been watching closely, he would not have seen her flinch. Ruthlessly he pressed on. "One with whom I share a continent. A house. A bed."

"Oh." She looked as if she'd sucked on a lemon. "I see."

Somehow he doubted it. "Do you?"

"I'm not stupid, Nick." She shrugged. "You have a lover. Now you want to formalize the relationship."

Damnation. How could she be so blasé about it? Annoyance flared in his gut like a match. Were the situation reversed, he certainly wouldn't be. The thought of Sarah rolling on a bed naked with another man made his stomach turn. But then, *she* was probably accustomed to the idea. "You convicted me of that sin ten years ago, didn't you?"

Sarah schooled her features into a perplexed frown. "Pardon me?"

"Actually, no pardon is involved. I think I've held this against you all these years. Susan Harris, Sarah. I'm certain you remember her. Poor, miserable, *pregnant* Susan Harris."

"Oh, yes. Now I remember."

He'd bet the entire contents of Hunterbourne's

library that she'd never forgotten. "Just so you know, I've said all I intend to say on that subject. Not only have I given Susan my word I'll never reveal the truth about her child, I also told you on our wedding night that I wasn't the father of that baby. I gave you my word—one of the few things of value I owned at that point in my life—and you threw it back in my face with your lack of faith. You didn't believe me, believe *in* me. Not enough, anyway."

Caught off guard by the burn of resentment fired by the memory, Nick addressed the question of a lover with less than perfect honesty or diplomacy. "When you eavesdropped this morning upon a private conversation between me and my sisters, you misinterpreted what was said. I have no intention of elevating a mistress to wife. That is not the way to win over the *ton,* and I assure you I will do nothing more to harm my sisters' chances of making the matches they desire."

"Of course. Your sisters." Though her tone dripped sugar, the look in her eyes had turned exceedingly sour.

"My *family,*" Nick warned, meaning every word. "Believe this. I protect my own. I will freely use the power of my name and of my fortune to secure their safety and their happiness. I will guard them like the precious jewels they are. Once they find worthy men and their hearts are decided, I'll do my utmost to make their dreams come true—even to the point of blackmailing a wedding planner into crossing an ocean to help make my sister's day perfect."

"You have made your point. I understand."

"No, I truly don't believe you do. I love my sisters, and I'm thrilled to call them family. But I want more. You see, Sarah, I've spent the majority of the past decade roaming the world. My feet are tired. I'm ready to have a home. My own home and my own family. I want children."

"The heir. Of course. You have a duty to your line."

She smiled at him again, which made him a bit crazy. He marched across the room and loomed above her. He wanted to snatch up that broadsword and break it across his knee. "I have a duty to myself. Yes, I'd like a son. I have six sisters. I'm surrounded by petticoats and perfume. A bit of balance would be nice, but I would joyfully welcome a daughter, too. However, in order to have that son or daughter—a *legitimate* son or daughter—I need a wife."

She patted his arm. "I am certain Lady Iron is a fine choice."

Nick looked down at her hand. Then he lifted his gaze back to her face. His pulse thrummed in his veins. "Steele. Lady Steele."

"Yes. A good fit for you, then."

Nick stared deep into her eyes and saw nothing but sincerity. Dammit, she looked as if she meant it. Didn't she care?

He wanted her to care.

He wanted her to refuse the annulment.

How foolish is that, anyway?

"Well now, I'm glad you told me, Nick. I'm glad it's settled." She idly ran a finger down the hilt of a thirteenth-century dagger. "How long will the annulment process take? Do you truly want me to help with Charlotte's wedding and befriend Aurora, or were those only excuses?"

Her ready acceptance of the ending of their marriage left him feeling thoroughly annoyed. "No, I would appreciate your help while you are here."

"Very well. Why don't you set up a meeting with your attorney as soon as possible?" Her tone was slightly chastising as she added, "And, Nick, you didn't need to go to such lengths. I have no desire to stand in your way."

She excused herself and left him alone in the muniment room. Nick lifted the jewel-encrusted dagger she'd fondled moments before and tested it for its balance. "A nice weapon," he murmured. He tested the blade, felt its bite. "Still sharp."

Not nearly as sharp, however, as the weapon Sarah wielded every time she opened her mouth. The woman had a tongue to slice a man to ribbons. "What a shame."

Nick could think of a dozen different ways to put her tongue to better use.

Emeralds in an engagement ring bring bad luck.

Sarah dressed for luncheon as though she were going to war.

After the humiliating encounter at breakfast, it had taken all her thespian talents to act nonchalant when Nick trailed her to the room full of swords and armor. Immediately afterward she'd retreated to her bedchamber, where she indulged in a quiet temper tantrum interspersed with a bout of tears.

She felt like such a fool. She'd known that someday this day would come. She had even suspected this might be the reason why Nick had summoned her to Scotland to begin with. So why had it upset her so to hear him talk about marrying another woman?

It wasn't fair for her to act the offended wife. Except for a few brief hours, they'd never had a true marriage. It wouldn't be right of her to sit here now and pretend they had more between them than a legal entanglement, one which she herself had considered ending on more than one occasion. So why the upset? Why the tears? Why the anger?

Why the kiss?

For a little while last night, he'd turned back the clock with his kiss. All the feelings she'd once harbored for him had been reborn with the touch of his lips against hers. She'd always been susceptible to his kisses, and—hang the man—that hadn't changed. It had taken her months to forget how his kisses made her feel. Years. And now she'd have to go and fight that fight all over again.

The louse. If he wanted an annulment, fine. She'd be happy to do whatever was necessary. But he shouldn't have touched her, should never have kissed her. Especially when he had plans to marry another woman. "The cad."

Sarah's pride wouldn't allow her to hide in her room any longer, so she mustered her defenses. First she donned her mental armor by recalling the hurt of his betrayal and desertion. She even went so far as to brush upon painful memories she ordinarily left locked away tight—those of her horrible wedding night.

Thus fortified, she called for a maid to help her slip into the second layer of protection, an attractive Fortune's Design day dress cut in the popular and appropriate military style. Gazing at her reflection in a mirror, she reached up to straighten the gold braid trim and muttered, "If he tries to touch me again, I'll pull out a gun and shoot him."

Of course, first she'd have to find a gun. Maybe she should detour back to that weapons room and grab one of those wicked-looking daggers. She'd show him if he tried anything funny.

"But that's just it," she grumbled to herself. "He

isn't going to try anything funny. 'It's time I had a wife,' he said. 'One with whom I share a continent. A house. A bed.' It's not *you* he wants, Sarah, it's Lady Brass."

Reminding herself that was a good thing, she took a deep, bracing breath, then exited her room.

Downstairs, she followed the scent of roasted chicken to the dining room. As she approached, she heard the unmistakable sounds of an argument taking place inside. Sarah's steps slowed as she sought to survey the lay of the land before committing herself.

"Rodney, it is just as I suspected. Lady Charlotte is not worthy of you. One marries more than a person, one marries a family. I'll not see you linked with a family the likes of this one."

Sarah scowled as she stepped closer to hear better. Rodney and Lady Charlotte. Theirs was the wedding Nick had wanted her to plan.

"Now wait one moment, Mother."

Mother plowed on without pause. "I share some responsibility, I'll admit, for remaining abroad so long and not being here to put a stop to this nonsense sooner. However, all is not lost. We can find an honorable way out of this mess. It is a lucky thing you insisted we make this trip north to spend time with Lord Weston's family. Normal social occasions fail to provide the level of intimacy required to sufficiently judge a prospective spouse. However, after spending almost a week with these people, culminating in the arrival last night of a female I can only assume is Weston's paramour, it is clear that Lady Charlotte is a totally inappropriate choice as your wife."

"I do not agree," the young man insisted. "Charlotte will make a lovely wife. I quite adore her. I love her."

The harridan sniffed loudly. "Love has little enough to do with marriage. No, we shall find someone more suitable. Someone whose guardian is not so peculiar as Weston. The man might be a marquess, but I don't trust him. He's not like us."

And that, Sarah thought, was the first kind thing she'd heard the old battle-ax say.

Rodney's mother continued, "In fact, after seeing the way this household is run, the way those girls are allowed such liberties, I feel I should give my circle fair warning to keep their sons away from all these girls. Beauty cannot overcome bad blood."

"And ugliness in the mind is so much more hideous than unattractive features," Sarah murmured. She had heard enough. People like this truly got her back up, and since she was properly dressed for battle and in just the right mood, she decided to launch her own attack. Squaring her shoulders, she swept into the room. "Good morning. Isn't it a most beautiful day? Crisp and clear and clean. Don't you adore the way the sun shines off the snowcapped mountains?"

Rodney's mother puffed out her enormous bosom and glared. "You!"

"Mother," protested the handsome young man.

Sarah warmed the smile she turned his way. "I would imagine the day looks especially bright to you, sir, since you'll spend at least part of it with such a sweet and lovely young woman as Lady Charlotte."

Rodney blinked hard, obviously taken aback. Then his expression melted to something soft and wistful. "Um, yes. It is a glorious day for that reason alone."

Sarah decided she liked the fellow in that instant. His mother, however, was a different kettle of chili. The harridan's eyes rounded and her mouth gaped. In a stiff, brittle tone she asked, "Have we met?"

Sarah took a moment to lay another sin at Nick's door. They'd never decided on a story. He'd spent the time kissing her instead, and now she didn't have a clue as to how she should introduce herself.

She decided to keep her reply vague—and maybe help out the young lovers while she was about it. "Possibly. You do look familiar. Of course, I've done so many weddings of late, and I've met so very many people. It's a failing of mine, I'm afraid. I can remember details about flowers and gowns and breakfast menus for every wedding I've planned for the past five years, but I'm a dreadful failure when it comes to names. Mrs. Astor completely lost her patience with me when I forgot Senator Hollingsworth's name, and I won't even mention the faux pas concerning President Cleveland at the Hilliard-Landsdowne wedding. You are the mother of the groom in this wedding, are you not? Mrs. . . ." She snapped her fingers. "Mrs. Bratts."

"Lady Pratt."

"Yes. That's right. Lady Pratt. It's these English titles. They constantly trip me up. I apologize for the mistake, especially considering the compliments Lord Weston has paid you in my presence."

"Compliments?"

"He told me you would be a great help to me in discovering the best local suppliers. I know where to buy the freshest flowers in Washington and who is the most talented chef in Boston, and as far as New York goes, well I know *everyone* in New York. I'll import whatever I feel is necessary, but I always like to include some local sources. I'm excited about expanding my consultancy to London, and I intend for my first wedding here to be the grandest ever seen. Why, Society will be pea green on both sides of the Atlantic by the time Lord Pratt and Lady Charlotte depart for their honeymoon. This will be the most talked-about wedding of the Season. Of a decade of Seasons. A century of Seasons!"

Interest lit the harridan's eyes. "Who did you say you are?"

"Oh, I'm sorry." She gave a good imitation of an embarrassed laugh. "I am Sarah of Lucky in Love Weddings, of course. Lord Weston lured me away from America because he wants every detail to be perfect for your son's wedding to his sister. At the risk of sounding boastful, I am the best woman for the job."

Then, smiling sweetly, Sarah played her trump card. "And you, Lady Pratt, will be the envy of every mama in Town."

"How lovely!" The sour face beamed.

Sarah took a seat at the table, snapped open her napkin, and spread it across her lap. *I'd like to see Nick's Lady Lead do any better.*

Out in the hallway, a wide-eyed Charlotte turned to her brother and whispered, "Is any of that true?"

Nick rolled his tongue around his mouth. "The part about you being sweet and lovely is true. As for the rest . . ."

He finished with a shrug.

Her murmur brimming with admiration, Gillian said, "She won the Dragon Lady over."

Aurora nodded. "Played her like a violin."

Melanie clicked her tongue, then glanced at her brother. "You intend to rid yourself of this wife so you can have Lady Steele? Nicholas, did you bring home one of those special pipes from the Orient?"

"What special pipes?" Robyn asked.

"She's teasing, Robbie," Nick said, sending Melanie a scolding glare. He motioned his sisters to proceed him into the dining room. He made quick work of formally introducing Sarah to the Pratts, and soon the conversation bubbled with talk of guest lists, gowns, and party favors. During the middle of it, Gillian's husband, Jake Delaney, wandered into the room. After perusing the buffet and pouring himself a cup of coffee, he ruffled Robyn's hair before taking a seat beside Gillian. He pressed a quick kiss to his wife's cheek, then winked at Sarah and observed, "You're becoming quite the traveler, gal."

The next half hour proved illuminating. In the time it took to consume a light luncheon, Nick watched the females in his family get to know his wife. They made friends over salads, cold meat, and sliced bread, then bonded over dessert. By the time the last crumb of chocolate cake was consumed, his sisters and his wife were bosom buddies, in a manner of speaking.

He found the development more than a little disconcerting. When women put their heads together, a man never knew what sort of mischief they might cook up.

They had certainly won the day where Lady Pratt was concerned. On a dining table battlefield, dressed in gold buttons and braid, Sarah marshaled her troops against Charlotte's prospective mother-in-law like a female Napoleon with a Texas drawl. She led her women in a war of words that used Society names as bullets and wedding plans for cannonballs. When conversation worked its way around to Lady Pratt's mother-of-the-groom attire, Nick knew victory was won. The old battle-ax all but waved a lace-trimmed handkerchief in defeat.

Observing the satisfied pleasure in his sisters' expressions and basking in the glow of Rodney and Charlotte's mutual devotion, Nick felt a niggling sense of concern.

He was fairly certain Sarah had lied about her social ties. She might be well connected in Texas and elsewhere in the South, but he didn't think she'd actually had dealings with the president of the United States. Surely she'd have mentioned that sort of detail in her letters. So why had Sarah jumped to Charlotte's defense that way? She'd never met the girl. What were her motives?

Did the cute little general think to muster his family against him?

His wife wouldn't meet his gaze. Oh, she'd speak to him, smile at him, and include him in the conversation—in a brother-of-the-bride manner. Never once did she refer to him as her husband, brushing off the Dragon Lady's veiled question about her arrival at Glencoltran Castle with a chagrined smile and an apologetic "travel-weary temper" explanation. Nick didn't know whether to be pleased or annoyed about her reticence.

He was halfway tempted to spill the news himself just to witness her reaction. But that would create a whole set of problems he was ill-prepared to deal with at the moment.

No, he'd keep to his original plan. They'd stay in Scotland until the marriage was legally ended, and Society need never know he'd been married to the beautiful baggage.

She'd called herself Sarah of Lucky in Love Weddings, but she would still need an identity to go with the name. She couldn't be Lady Innsbruck, because that would raise too many questions. He didn't care what name she used in Texas. In fact, he wondered if there was a way she could legitimately keep that minor title following the annulment. He seemed to remember that in the case of divorce, such a boon could be granted a former wife.

His lips quirked with a self-deprecating smile as the thought occurred that if not for the certain scandal and its reflection upon his sisters, he wouldn't mind going the route of divorce over annulment.

He'd love to take the opportunity to consummate the marriage, to put to use the training he'd received during his visits to the sultan's seraglio. The need to redeem himself for his wedding night had eaten at him since the day he left Fort Worth.

At that point, Nick's thoughts turned distinctly sexual. While the women talked about possible wedding dates and bridal bouquets, he mentally divested the general of her uniform, substituting a harem dancer's veils in its place.

Leaning one shoulder against the dining room wall, his arms folded, his legs crossed casually at the ankles, Nick sank into the fantasy. Instead of the lingering aroma of roasted chicken, he smelled the sweet bite of incense on the air. Rather than the chatter of feminine voices, he heard the beat of drums and chink of finger cymbals. He imagined a soft rug beneath him, a cup of wine, and a plate filled with pomegranates and grapes at his side. In front of him, her body veiled in such a way that it revealed more than it concealed, Sarah danced.

Her long, golden hair hung free, swinging with the

sensuality of her movement. Through the gauzy silk that draped her body, he could see the round, dusky shadows that tipped her high, full breasts. His stare slid lower, drinking in the vision of her undulating torso, pausing to put a jewel—a sapphire; no, a brilliant ruby—in her navel. His mouth grew dry as his gaze found her hips, adorned with a belt of clinking gold coins, beckoning with slow figure eights that gradually increased in speed, moving faster and faster and ...

"Nicholas? Nicholas!"

Charlotte's insistent voice broke through his daydream and Nick stood up straight to find a whole roomful of women staring expectantly his way. Thank God they appeared to be keeping their gazes above his waist. A flush of embarrassment stole up his neck, and he glowered at Rodney—just because it felt like the thing to do—before addressing his sister. "What?"

Charlotte gestured toward the mantel clock. "We lost track of the time, and Lady Pratt is concerned she might miss her train."

Now *that* would be disaster.

Nick checked his pocket watch, calculated the time required to transport the Dragon Lady to the railway station in Nairn, then heaved a mental sigh of relief and smiled at his guests. "I believe you have sufficient time left, Lady Pratt. I'll call for my fastest coach to take you to the station. If you will excuse me, I shall see to the arrangements now."

A short time later his family gathered in front of the castle to see Rodney and the Dragon Lady off. Nick tried not to notice that Melanie, Robyn, and Aurora ran interference with the old shrew to allow Charlotte and Rodney time for a private good-bye. He knew a few kisses weren't inappropriate at this point, but that didn't mean he had to like it.

When the coach bearing Lady Pratt finally clattered away from Glencoltran, Nick joined his sisters in a round of relieved applause.

"Charlotte, I hope Rodney appreciates the depths of your love," Nick said as they turned back toward the castle.

Buoyed by her fiancé's promise to visit her immediately upon the family's return to London or Hunterbourne, whichever came first, Charlotte threw her arms around her brother and offered a squeeze of a hug. "He is not blind to his mother's faults. Not at all. In fact, he has a plan for dealing with her."

"What's that?"

The sparkle in her eyes brought a smile to Nick's face as she said, "He's matchmaking. He is promoting a romance with an old acquaintance of Lady Pratt's—a widower—who lives in Ireland."

Nick's smile broadened into laughter. "Ah, posy, I think your man Rodney is growing on me."

"I think I like Sarah," Melanie said as she hurried into Aurora's bedchamber late that night. "Isn't she beautiful?"

"I adore her," Charlotte declared as she followed her younger sister. "The way she won over Lady Pratt was incredible."

"Shush." Aurora held her finger up to her mouth as she waved Robyn in behind the others. "When I sneaked into the kitchen for biscuits and milk, Nicholas was prowling around downstairs. We don't want him to hear any noise and come check on us."

"I still say we should have had this meeting in my room," Melanie said. She kicked off her slippers and sat cross-legged on her sister's bed. "If Nicholas checks on anyone, it will be you, since you're the wicked sister."

"That's not fair!" Robyn exclaimed. "That's what I want to be."

"You're not old enough, Robbie. I'll turn over the mantle to you in a few years."

"Don't tease her," Melanie scolded.

Aurora joined Melanie on the bed. She chose a gingersnap from the plate of sweets, took a dainty bite, and said, "You're just jealous that I won the coin toss and got to pretend to be in love with Willie Hart."

Melanie wrinkled her nose. "I'm not jealous. I was glad you won. I wouldn't want to kiss Willie Hart no matter how pretty he is."

Aurora's look went sly. "You would if you knew how well he kissed."

"Oh, yuck." Robyn grimaced and put her fingers in her ears. "I dinna want to hear about that. I canna get away from it. At Rowanclere, I am forever catching Jake and Gillian kissing."

Melanie snorted. "Believe me, you wouldn't have wanted to see Aurora and Willie. I spied on them and wished I hadn't. She let him put his tongue in her mouth."

"Aurora!" Charlotte exclaimed, sinking into a pink brocade chair. "You didn't."

The younger girl shrugged and said, "I thought that as long as I was being wicked, I might as well be very wicked."

Charlotte shook her head in wide-eyed wonder. "It's amazing Nicholas didn't kill Willie when he caught up with the two of you."

"It was a close thing. If we'd been farther than ten minutes away from Hunterbourne Manor, he might have. As it was, I was beginning to think I'd have to cosh Willie on the head myself. The moment we left Nicholas's lands, Willie started behaving as though the elopement was more than simply an act. I'll admit I was pleased to see our brother riding to the rescue."

"I still shudder to think of what could have happened," Charlotte said with a sigh. "You should have told me before—"

Melanie shook her head. "We couldn't tell you, Charlotte. You'd have given the game away right off. You're terrible at telling lies."

Primly, Charlotte said, "Some would consider that a good trait."

"Nevertheless, we succeeded in separating Nicholas and Lady Steele. I just knew she wouldn't visit the Highlands in the middle of winter."

"One would think someone that icy would take to cold better."

The girls paused a moment to ponder that thought, then nodded. Robyn asked, "So what happens next? How does his having a wife change your plans?"

Melanie and Aurora reached for the same short-bread cookie. The younger girl won, and triumphantly replied, "It doesn't. We didn't have a plan short of getting him away from Lady Steele. That's the purpose of this meeting tonight. We need to create one."

"Our strategy appears obvious to me," Charlotte said. "I liked what I saw of Sarah today. If Nicholas is set on having a wife, then Sarah strikes me as a much better choice than Horrible Helen. What we should do is convince him to keep her."

Robyn pursed her lips. "How do we do that?"

"We need ideas. Find a piece of paper and let's make a list."

While Aurora rummaged for writing supplies, Melanie stretched her feet out in front of her and wiggled her toes. "He must have liked her well enough at one time back when they both lived in Texas. He married her, didn't he?"

"Yes, but we don't know why. It would help if we knew that."

Aurora snorted. "According to Willie, there's only one reason a man wants to marry a woman. Bedding."

"You talked about the Sport of Venus with Willie?" Scandal shimmered in Melanie's voice.

Charlotte reached over to cover Robyn's ears. "Aurora!" she said. "Please. Robyn is too young to hear such talk."

"No, I'm not," Robyn said, tugging away from her sister's touch. "I know about bedding, and I know about swiving and Nick and Sarah. They didn't do it."

"What!"

"That's what Gillian believes. I heard her talking to Jake when Sarah was at Rowanclere. Gilly said Nick couldn't annul the marriage if he'd bedded her. Jake said Nick wouldn't let a prime woman like Sarah get away from him without taking a run at her first. Then Gilly said maybe Nick was ill and couldn't do it, and Jake said that wasn't the case because Nick had told him a story about sneaking into a Turkish sultan's harem."

"Oh, my." Charlotte dropped her cookie. Melanie and Aurora shared a look of scandalized interest, then each took a thoughtful sip of milk.

Robyn continued, "Then Gilly said it was none of their business, and they shouldn't be speculating. Jake said all the talk about bedding had made him hot so Gilly had to do something about it. Then he started tickling her and she giggled and he chased her up to their tower love nest."

"Tower love nest?" Aurora asked, leaning forward.

"It's a room they have at Rowanclere where they go to do it."

"Let's change the subject, please," Charlotte said, her complexion red as the Ross tartan.

Melanie reached over and patted her elder sister's knee. "There, there, Charlotte. Don't be embarrassed. I swear, I don't know how you'll manage as a wife. You've got to get over this reticence of yours."

"Besides," Aurora said, tapping her lips with a finger. "We can't change the subject. I think this is central to the problem and must be discussed."

"For heaven's sake, why?" Charlotte begged. "It's not proper. It simply isn't done."

Robyn piped up. "By us it is. We're the Ross girls. We'll do anything."

Aurora nodded and continued, "I think Gillian is right. Nick is obviously a virile man, so of course he wanted to bed a beautiful woman like Sarah, and if he didn't, that must mean it was her fault. Now, that was a long time ago, so chances are, whatever her problem was, she no longer has it. But what if it hasn't been fixed? Then they still won't be able to play the Sport of Venus, and he will still annul the marriage, and then we're back to worrying about Horrible Helen all over again."

Melanie nodded sagely. "We have to find out what the problem was and fix it if need be."

Charlotte flung up her hands. "How are we supposed to do that? We're four unmarried virgins. What do we know?"

"Maybe we should bring Gillian in on the plan. Maybe even Flora," Aurora suggested.

"No." Robyn shook her head. "That would ruin everything. Flora has always been rather stuffy, and now Gillian sometimes acts the same way. It's best they dinna ken a thing about this."

Aurora sniffed. "A woman who giggles her way up to her love nest for bed sport doesn't sound stuffy to me, but you know her better than we do. We'll handle this on our own. I think the first step is to discover what is wrong. We should be able to do that despite the handicap of our virginity."

"Handicap of virginity." Charlotte closed her eyes and moaned softly.

"Let's think, sisters. What could it be? Maybe Sarah is not attracted to Nicholas."

They considered the notion for a moment, then each girl shook her head. Melanie said what they all were thinking. *"Every* woman is attracted to Nicholas."

"All right." Aurora pursed her lips. "Maybe it's a physical problem. That could be troublesome, because she might still have the condition."

Four faces settled into frowns. Melanie said, "What sort of physical problem could it be? I don't know enough about it. Charlotte, it's too bad you're not already married, because then you could tell us."

"I won't be telling you such things!"

Aurora sniffed with disdain. "If you don't loosen up some, you're liable to end up like Nicholas's wife and not be *doing* such things, much less talking about them."

Charlotte lifted her chin. "I'll have you know I'm plenty loose with Rodney!"

"You are?" Melanie asked, surprise in her voice.

Aurora leaned forward, her eyes bright with interest. "Tell us."

Charlotte lifted her face toward the ceiling and sighed.

Melanie scooted off the bed and began to pace the room, thinking. "Look, we can guess all night and we'll never know for sure. The only way I see for us to obtain this information is to convince her to tell us."

Aurora shook her head. "She won't just tell us. We'll have to trick it out of her. I'm certain of that."

"I love to play tricks," Robyn said happily.

Melanie chewed at her thumbnail and mused, "How do we do it?"

Aurora nudged Melanie with a bare foot as her pacing took her within reach, then tapped Robyn on the shoulder. Having gained her sisters' attention, she cocked her head toward their elder sister.

Melanie grinned. "*We're* not going to do it. Charlotte, you are. You're the one getting married. It's only natural for you to ask Sarah about sex."

*It's bad luck to remove your engagement ring before
your wedding day.*

Other than at mealtime when the family dined
together, Sarah managed to avoid her husband for
the next few days. She divided her time between two
primary activities: meeting with Nick's sisters to discuss Charlotte's wedding preparations and searching
the castle storerooms for the fabric Nick had sent
home from foreign bazaars along the old Silk Road.

She wanted to find the fabric he had stored.
Badly. She'd never seen such fine silk as that which
Nick had sent to Fort Worth, and since she'd promised Lady Pratt the finest wedding of the century, she
intended to produce just that. The girls needed
bridesmaid's dresses, and if fine cloth was available
for them, she wanted to use it.

She realized the bolts could be stored in any number of places. The man had at least three homes,
maybe more, and for all she knew he kept such treasures in a warehouse. Glencoltran wasn't a huge
abode, but with four centuries worth of additions to

the old keep, it had plenty of nooks and crannies to keep her searching—and hidden—for days on end. She felt certain Nick would hand it over if she asked, but that would mean having to talk to her husband. Since avoiding him was her main reason for searching for the silk to begin with, seeking him out to ask him where it was would defeat her purpose.

"After I find it, perhaps I'll simply steal it and head for home," she grumbled.

Not that taking the fabric would truly be stealing. To her way of thinking, his crimes canceled out any wrongdoing on her part. He'd had her kidnapped, after all.

Kidnapped? her conscience questioned. Is that actually true?

"Oh, maybe not," she grumbled as she raised the lid of a dust covered trunk. To be perfectly honest, Rand Jenkins could not have made her go anywhere she didn't want to go. She'd made the trip under protest, but of her own free will.

Upon identifying the contents of the wooden box as men's clothing, she released the trunk lid to close with a bang, then immediately turned her attention to yet another trunk.

This chest was filled with toys—balls and wooden ships and pretty baby dolls that distracted her from her purpose. Lifting one of the dolls, she fussed with the frilly skirt, idly wondering if it had belonged to one of Nick's sisters.

Sarah enjoyed the time she spent with the girls. Witty, spirited, full of laughter and real affection, they reminded her so much of Trace and Jenny McBride's Menaces. She'd grown fond of them quickly.

If only they didn't ask such personal questions.

She was running from those questions now. Half an hour earlier, while discussing wedding gown designs with the Ross girls in a drawing room downstairs, Charlotte—sweet, relatively timid Charlotte—had asked what sort of nightgown Sarah wore for her wedding night with Nick.

Sarah had fumbled her teacup and spilled the steaming liquid all over her dress. She excused herself to change, then suggested they take a break from making wedding plans for the rest of the day, but the girls wouldn't hear of it. Encouraged by a sharp look from Aurora, Charlotte insisted they resume their discussion following an hour-long break. "I've important questions to ask you, Sarah," she had said. "They simply cannot wait any longer."

Now kneeling on the floor in the tower storeroom, Sarah returned the doll to the trunk, then reached for a child-sized tambourine. She thumped the skin in a slow, steady rhythm, which caused the tin disks to jangle. "They're up to something," she murmured. Sarah had seen that look on the McBride Menaces' faces more times than she could count.

She'd managed to flee the drawing room without agreeing to answer any questions, then after quickly changing into her oldest dress, Sarah had hurried to hide herself in the tower. She couldn't think of a better time to search for that fabric.

She shut the lid of the toy chest and studied the other possibilities open to her. Some boxes were too small, others an unlikely shape. Then she spied a long, narrow trunk that had a promising appearance. She opened the lid and spied an engraved jewel case inside. Intrigued, she stretched out a hand to investigate the contents.

Nick spoke from behind her. "Have you taken to thieving in the years we've been apart, lass?"

Startled, she allowed the trunk lid to slip from her grasp. It slammed shut, pinching her fingers. She squealed and brought her hand up to her mouth.

"Ach, throbbing, isn't it?" Behind a wince, blue eyes gleamed wickedly. "Sucking on it is certainly one of my favorite ways to make a hurt feel better."

She eyed him suspiciously but uncertainly. Sexual innuendo was not her forte, and she wasn't certain he was trying to be risqué. However, Sarah didn't have time to debate the issue with herself. Summoning her best "I'm offended" tone, she rose to her feet and said, "I'm not stealing. I'm doing my job."

"Hmm . . ." He strode over to the chest, flipped back the lid, and shook his head. Though he kept his manner casual, she sensed an energy about him, a tension that set her own senses on alert. "Explain to me, Sarah, what use a wedding planner has with costumes for a masquerade?"

She glanced back at the trunk and spied the black dominoes. *Costumes, yes. Of course.* However, something told her now was not the time to tell the truth. Searching for a plausible lie, she shrugged. "At Lucky in Love Weddings we sometimes use personal items in our decorating theme. I was seeing what is available."

"I see." He slammed the trunk lid closed. "Speaking of Charlotte's wedding, can I assume that you still intend to help?"

What has him in such a lather? "Of course I do. We've been discussing the event each day. I thought I made that clear the other night. When I give my word, I keep it."

"Oh really?" he arched a sardonic brow. "I wasn't

aware of that. I seem to remember something about 'Whither thou goest, I will go.' "

Sarah's mouth gaped at his nerve as her own anger stirred. *How dare he?* "You're quoting the Bible, Nick, not our wedding vows."

"Are you certain that wasn't mentioned in the ceremony somewhere? I do know of another one I am certain you said. How about the promise to obey? Seems to me you broke that one from the first."

The venom in his tone all but took her breath away. Heart pounding, she rose and brushed the dust from her skirt. "Nick, what has gotten into you? Look, I apologize for snooping in your storeroom, if that is what has you bothered. However, I truly do not believe you want to take the conversation in the direction of wedding vows."

"Why not? Perhaps we should talk about them. Love and honor and promises that didn't last a night. What of—"

Now her temper exploded. "What of 'forsaking all others and keeping only unto her'?" Sarah quoted, stepping forward and stabbing his chest with her index finger. "I distinctly recall that one. Shall we talk about that?"

He winced, then his mouth twisted as he made a show of looking himself over. "Do you sharpen those fingernails with a whetstone, wife?"

"Trying to change the subject, Lord Weston? Now why might that be?"

He folded his arms. "You want to talk about my sexual experience during the past decade? Fine. I'll tell you all you wish to know. But you will not be laying all the blame at my feet. Be fair, Sarah, you must admit it takes an awfully long pair of arms to hold a woman from an ocean away. Whither thou goest . . ."

She poked him again. "That wasn't in the vows!"

He stared down at her finger, pursed his lips, and said, "Did you know that in Kualistan when a woman pokes a man like that she's asking him to make love to her?"

Even as her finger surged forward for a third assault, she froze. "I . . . uh . . . it's not that way in Texas."

"Aye, I remember how it was in Texas," he said, the sound of Scotland thick on his tongue, the heat of a Texas August in his eyes. "Vividly."

Sarah swallowed hard, uncertain how to take that, how to respond. She chose to brazen it out. "Me, too," she replied, her chin going up. She flashed a smile full of teeth and added, "Which is why the notion of your arms holding another woman doesn't bother me in the least. Now if you'll excuse me, your sisters and I have more wedding plans to make."

She sailed courageously past him toward the doorway leading from the tower room. Just when she thought she might safely escape, he reached out and grabbed her sleeve, pulling her to a halt.

He spoke in a low tone as sharp as ice shards. "You are a staggeringly beautiful woman, Sarah, but when you smile that particular way at me, you bring to mind the grin of a Louisiana swamp gator."

Shocked by the turn in the conversation, she jerked her gaze up to meet his, but his had drifted downward, lingering on her bosom, then trailing a leisurely path to the curve of her hip.

"I do not doubt," he continued, "that one delicious swish of your tail could bring me to my knees. It was that way ten years ago and it does not appear to have changed. Lord knows I would love to wrestle with you here and now."

"Nick," she began. "I don't understand. What is happening here?"

"Happening? A warning, I guess. Our past is a murky swamp of hurts and troubles, but you should understand I'll have your hide for boots afore I'll let you chew me up and spit me out again. You think about that before you try it."

Now she was totally confused. What had stuck the burr in his backside? Not her foray into snooping in his storeroom, surely. Not unless he was hiding dead bodies or something up here. The place would smell bad if that were the case.

And what was he trying to say with this ridiculous alligator talk?

"Nick, what is it? What's wrong?"

Abruptly, he released her arm and stepped away. "We're needed downstairs. We've a guest waiting to speak with us."

"A guest?"

"Aye. The advocate is waiting in the library."

"Advocate? What's an advocate?"

"Solicitor. Attorney. It's Mr. Franklin. He's my damned lawyer, and he's here with the damned papers for us to sign."

Lawyer. Papers. The annulment.

Was this the reason for Nick's foul mood? If so, why? He was the one pursuing the darned thing. She was the one who should be upset, and maybe she was.

She'd be hanged if she'd let him see it, however. Sarah lifted her chin and gave her head a proud toss. "In that case, after you, Lord Weston. Let's not keep the gentleman waiting."

Nick sat behind a huge, carved mahogany desk and watched his wife pace the width of the room, back and forth, studiously ignoring the set of papers ready for her signature and his. Opposite Nick, his solicitor twisted in his leather seat to keep an eye on the action taking place behind him. Bright man, Nick's solicitor. He had reason to be cautious. Nick put the odds at fifty-fifty that Sarah would surrender to her obvious desire to fling a few leather-bound tomes at Mr. Franklin.

Unaccountably, Sarah's bad temper had served to improve his own.

This was the younger Mr. Franklin. His father had suffered a seizure six weeks ago and had turned all legal work over to his son and younger partner. Concerned about doing a good job for his richest and most powerful client, Franklin Jr. had reviewed Nick's records with a keen eye and discovered three different instances in which he disagreed with his father's legal position.

One of those was the subject of Lord Weston's marriage.

Sarah stalked to the empty chair beside the solicitor and took a seat. Her gaze settled on the desk's brass paperweight, then shifted to Nick, then returned to the brass bust of Aristotle. Also a cautious man, Nick moved it beyond her reach.

She folded her hands in her lap, then turned to Mr. Franklin and spoke in a calm, level voice that belied the temper snapping in her eyes. "What do you mean my word is not enough?"

The solicitor had the grace to look embarrassed. He cleared his throat and said, "You must understand, Lady Weston, that the dissolution of a marriage is taken quite seriously in Great Britain. Much more seriously than in America. Proof must be presented."

She glared at Franklin for a long, long minute. Nick winced. If his wife were a witch, the poor advocate would now be a pile of ashes.

Then she smiled, which was truly frightening. "Very well, we will get the annulment in America."

Mr. Franklin removed his handkerchief from his pocket and patted his damp brow. "But that dissolution wouldn't be recognized in Britain. Were he to remarry, Lord Weston would be guilty of bigamy."

Now she fired a glare his way. Nick shrugged and defended himself. "I want children, and I will not father bastards. My children will not be forced to deal with that sort of insecurity."

She rose to her feet and resumed her pacing. Nick gave himself the pleasure of watching the graceful swing of her hips. His wife was one ripe, bonny lass.

She whirled to face him, caught him lusting, and bared her teeth at him. Nick choked back a startled laugh. Sarah folded her arms. "In light of your background, Nick," she said, "I understand your viewpoint about this. However, I don't appreciate the position your British citizenship has put me in."

In that case, chances are she won't care at all for the position I want to have her in.

The solicitor's complexion went a bit pasty as he continued, "Also, Lady Weston, you must be aware that should the physical examination prove . . . um . . ."

Nick whistled in a breath and braced for violence as she approached Franklin's chair, her hands on her hips, fury in her eyes. A red flush stained Franklin's cheeks, and he cleared his throat. "Should the condition of *virgo intacta* be proven, it is still possible the court might refuse you an annulment."

Nick's elbow slipped off his armrest. Sarah froze

where she stood. "What!" they exclaimed simultaneously.

Mr. Franklin nodded. "It's true."

"That's ridiculous," Sarah shouted.

Nick dragged his hand along his jaw. "I don't understand. Nonconsummation is legal grounds for annulment, is it not?"

"It is, but I'm afraid your situation is not that simple."

"Certainly it is."

"I'm sorry, Lady Weston, but the extenuating circumstances in your particular case move your case into the gray area of the law, and thus the courts."

"What extenuating circumstances?" Nick asked, his mind racing to consider the possibilities this new information presented.

Mr. Franklin opened his file and reviewed a sheet of paper therein. "According to what you told my father, Lord Weston, you and Lady Weston exchanged vows, then spent your wedding night together."

Sarah shook a finger at the lawyer. "But not together in a literal sense."

"Um, yes, so I understand." By now Franklin was as crimson as the queen's coronation robes. "However, during the intervening years you portrayed yourself as wife and publicly used his title. In researching this case, I uncovered instances where the courts refused an annulment for less reason than that."

Nicholas swiveled his desk chair to one side, picked up a pencil, and began to tap it repeatedly on the desktop beside the legal documents. Mr. Franklin shifted uncomfortably in his seat, and then continued, "Take the case of Hopkins versus

Ralston. The bride and groom were forced into marriage by their families when they were little more than children, twelve and thirteen, I believe. Following the wedding, the bride and groom shared the same home, though never a bed. Settlements were spent. She identified herself as his wife and vice versa. The court agreed."

Sarah shook her head at the story. "I repeat, that's ridiculous."

"I must agree with you on that one," said Nick, switching to a double-tap rhythm of the pencil.

Sarah reached over the desk and yanked the pencil from his hand. As Nick's brows winged up, she snapped, "You don't appear nearly as concerned about this as you should be."

Turning her angry attention back to Mr. Franklin, she added, "Or maybe Lord Weston appears unconcerned because he realizes you are overstating your case, sir. Aren't you being rather pessimistic? Isn't it possible, and in fact probable, that Lord Weston would be quietly granted an annulment based on our sworn statements?"

Franklin shook his head. "No, Lady Weston. I can give you no guarantee of that, especially in light of the recent mood of the court. May I speak frankly, Lady Weston?"

Sarah nodded.

"If you wish your marriage annulled, you must prove your virginity through a physical examination. Then, unless Lord Weston is prepared to swear to a condition of impotence—"

"That will not happen," Nick quickly interjected, sitting up straight.

Sarah glanced at him and absently agreed. "No one would believe it, anyway."

Nick squared his shoulders, preening a bit at that.

Franklin continued. "You must prepare your-selves for a thorough and public inquiry into your lives, beginning with the events of your wedding night and through the very day you testify in court. You arrived here at Glencoltran Castle within the last few days, correct?"

"Yes."

"Did you sleep alone?"

Her spine snapped straight. "Of course I did!"

"But under the same roof as your husband."

"It's a fairly large roof, Mr. Franklin," Nick drawled.

"That is not the point. Depending on what view the court takes, one night beneath the same roof might well be enough."

Mouth agape, Sarah shook her head. "Now that's truly ridiculous. We are well chaperoned. His sisters are in residence."

"Unless they shared your room, it may not mat-ter."

She glared at Nick. "You knew about this?"

He glanced down to make sure his clothes weren't blazing. "Honestly, no. It never occurred to me that our staying in this rambling old fortress could com-plicate the issue. It does seem rather nonsensical."

That observation offended the solicitor. "Such rules are necessary when people refuse to obey the law."

"It's a stupid law," Sarah grumbled.

His tone defensive, Mr. Franklin said, "I beg to differ, Lady Weston. Despite the reform of marriage laws in Britain during the past thirty years, both law and society continue to hold the view that marriage should be preserved at all costs."

Sarah looked to Nick, a plea in her eyes.

"There must be another way to do this." She looked toward her husband for assistance. "Another option."

His tone helpful, Mr. Franklin said, "You could divorce."

"No," Nick said flatly, coldly. "Sarah, if you wish to proceed with that particular solution, I will not cooperate. I believe my family's reputation can weather an annulment, but I will not subject my sisters to the inevitable scandal caused by divorce."

She winced. "I don't relish a scandal any more than you, Nick, but neither will I be dictated to. Why would I need your cooperation? I can hire a lawyer of my own."

"Hire anyone you wish. He won't find grounds." Nick pushed to his feet, placed his hands on his desk, and leaned forward. "I will not admit to adultery, nor will you find anyone who will testify to such. Divorce is not an option for you, Sarah. Accept it."

She stood up, placed her hands on the desk, and leaned toward him until they stood nose to nose. "One of Lady Pewter's servants might be persuaded to testify."

"Lady Steele!"

At the mention of Helen's name, Mr. Franklin groaned softly. Nick would have cursed his sisters' big mouths, but he was too busy debating whether or not to close the distance and kiss his wife. He finally decided against it, since he was fairly certain she'd bite him given half a chance. "Any testimony by Lady *Steele's* servants would only support my cause."

Sarah's eyes narrowed. "Then I'll find someone else who will testify against you."

"No, you won't."

Taut silence stretched between them. Nick's gaze dropped to her lips and when she snarled at him again, lust's jagged teeth sank into him and grabbed hold. *A little nip now and then could be rather pleasant.* "Mr. Franklin, would you excuse us for a moment? I'd like to speak with my wife in private."

Nick never looked away from Sarah as the advocate hurried to exit the room. When the door thudded shut behind him, she started and skidded away from the desk. Nick stalked her like prey and moments later had her backed against the bookshelves.

Like most wild things, when finding herself trapped Sarah came out fighting. "I know about England's divorce law. I can charge you with adultery and desertion and win."

"No, lass. You do not want to take it in that direction."

"Are you trying to claim you've not taken a woman to your bed in ten years? I wouldn't believe that even if you talked of conversion and wore a Catholic priest's collar."

Nick's voice deepened. "All I claim is a hunger for you that has never gone away."

When her eyes widened, he softened his tone. "It's always been there, Sarah, no matter where I was or who I was with. I wanted you the first time I saw you, standing in that empty meeting room eating your peach. I wanted you the night we wed when youth and inexperience worked against us. I ached for you the morning you stood in the train depot and handed me my freedom when all I wanted was for you to take my hand and join me. I bought a ticket for you. I honestly thought you'd change your mind and come with me."

She closed her eyes, swayed on her feet. She spoke softly, sadly. "I almost went with you. Oh, Nick, I almost did. I loved you so much I was almost ready to run after you. But when I saw you board the train with her . . ."

"You did not trust me." He drew his finger across the silk of her cheek and smiled sadly. "I held it against you, you understand, and took the freedom you offered me. But only to a point and not as often as you probably think. Because you haunted me, lass. On a Tibetan mountain slope and in a sultan's palace. In an English ballroom. Especially in an English ballroom. Do you have any clue of how perfectly you would fit amongst the glitter and glamour of that place?"

He moved even closer, and her fresh, familiar fragrance stirred his soul. "I've dreamed of having my turn with you, Sarah lass. I was cheated of it. We were cheated of it."

"No, we chose, Nick. I chose by staying. You chose by leaving."

She was right, and the fact of it combined with the ache in his loins annoyed him. "Aren't you the least bit curious about what I've learned during the time we've been apart?"

"It's not my business. You spoke the truth when you said I gave you your freedom, just as you gave me mine."

That last comment gave him pause. Nick's annoyance deepened into irritation as the picture of her rolling in a haystack with some quick-draw cowboy flashed through his mind. His voice cooled. "Have I misinterpreted the situation? Did you refuse a physical examination because you have—shall we say—taken advantage of your freedom?"

Fire flashed in her eyes, born of anger and annoyance and . . . hurt? She placed her palms against his chest, pushed hard, then ducked beneath his arms and slipped away. She crossed the room to the desk, then turned to face him. "No, Lord Weston, that's not the reason. The reason is I don't want to be poked at. Not by a physician. Not by a blasted lawyer. And certainly not by you. My word—our word—should be enough, and I'll tell that to any and every officer of the court. However, if in the end, that's what it takes to end this farce of a marriage, I'll do it. You were right. It's time for dreams to die and for us to move on with our lives. The sooner the better."

She grabbed up the pen, then with a flourish, signed her name on the annulment petition. "Your turn."

Nick didn't move. He stood staring at the desk and the papers lying atop it as she spoke of locating the lawyer before fleeing the room. He was still standing and staring a good five minutes later when Mr. Franklin returned.

"Lady Weston said you wished to see me, my lord. She said you have reached an agreement and are ready to proceed with the annulment petition."

Nick sucked a breath of air past his teeth. *Stubborn wench. Damnation. She's signed the papers. Stubborn, obstinate, hardheaded wench.*

Standing at the desk, Franklin cleared his throat. "If you will be so kind as to add your signature to Lady Weston's, I shall set this matter in motion at once."

Slowly, Nick approached the desk. He reached for the pen. It felt cold in his grip. His gaze lit on Sarah's signature. Bold, he thought, like the woman—except for that particular time when she'd been the very definition of timid.

He found the appropriate line on the document for his own signature, set his teeth, and grimly signed his name.

"Very good, my lord," said Franklin. "I shall depart for London in the morning and file it immediately upon my return. A caution, however, one I perhaps should have mentioned in Lady Weston's presence. You should not expect a swift resolution in this matter. Because of the unusual nature of your circumstances, I fear the legal process will be a protracted one."

"Protracted?"

"Yes, it might very well take months. Lady Weston will need to remain in Britain because the court will no doubt wish to hear her testimony. Also, once the decree is issued, I'll have more documents requiring her signature."

"Months." With that, Nick's thoughts began to race. Months. She'd be with him for months.

He'd never be able to keep his hands off her for months.

He heard the echo of her voice in his mind. *I loved you so much. I almost went with you. It's time for dreams to die.*

Or, Nick thought, time for dreams to be reborn.

She'd almost come with him. She'd almost left her life in Texas once. She'd loved him once. Could she feel that way again?

Did he want her to feel that way again?

Aye, he did. He couldn't lie to himself. Hadn't this been in the back of his mind all along? Wasn't this the reason why he'd sent for her, forced her to come to him? He could settle for Helen or a woman like her, but he didn't want her. Not the way he wanted his wife. Sarah of the sunshine hair and saucy smile. Sarah of the letters that had warmed his heart on a snowy mountainside. This was why he'd brought her to Britain, even if he hadn't realized it at the time. He'd wanted one more chance with her before settling for someone else.

He still had feelings for her. Not love, he couldn't say that. It was more a sense of unfinished business, of missed opportunities. Missed possibilities. He'd been eighteen years old, lonely and looking for his place in the world when he married her. If he'd loved her the way a man should love his wife, he never would have left her. Although, he had since wondered if their disaster of a wedding night hadn't made his strings easier for his father to pull.

He did know he honestly liked the woman whose letters had followed him halfway around the world. She was warm and witty, caring, intelligent. Spirited. Intriguing. God knows she was desirable.

Nick had a gut feeling about her that was more than simply sexual. His years as an agent had taught him to trust his instincts, and right now those instincts were screaming at him.

He could love this woman. He could love Sarah the way his foster father had loved his foster mother. The way a man should love his wife. And Sarah, this grown-up version of the bright-eyed girl he had married, could love him back. Truly and deeply and forever.

Now it appeared that forever depended on the next few months. Thanks to a protracted legal process, he had time to win her heart. Time to win her trust.

Wasn't it handy that the wheels of justice turned slowly?

Nick handed the document to the solicitor and looked him straight in the eyes. "Time is not a problem. Just the opposite. Return to London at your leisure, Franklin, and do not rush to do the paperwork once you get there. You have my permission— no, my instruction—to put this task at the very bottom of your list."

The solicitor frowned. "I'm confused. I was under the impression you wished this matter concluded as soon as possible. Was I mistaken?"

"No, I was." With his mind on his lady rather than on minding his tongue, he spoke frankly. "As I mentioned earlier, impotence is not a problem. I've wanted that woman for a third of my life. Thinking about her kept me warm when I was trapped on a mountain pass in the middle of a Himalayan winter. Proceed with all possible delay, sir. I've decided I don't want an annulment."

"I shall be a tortoise, sir."

"Good. I do believe with time I can convince the lady to agree with me." He flashed an irreverent grin and added, "You see, Mr. Franklin, while you're being a tortoise, I am going to be a bull."

Sarah ran up the stairs to her room as if a herd of cattle stampeded at her back. An annulment. She'd signed the petition seeking a marriage annulment.

She thought she might lose her breakfast.

Once in her chamber, Sarah took refuge in her bed, pulling rich floral brocade curtains shut, enclosing herself in a private sanctuary where no one could question the tears that threatened to spill.

It was silly, really. She shouldn't be so upset. She herself had told her husband to send for his attorney. "My husband," she whispered as the first tear slipped from her eye to roll slowly down her cheek. Her husband for a little while yet. After that, she'd no longer be a married lady. She'd be a what? A spinster? Was there a term for a woman whose marriage had been anulled after a decade?

Yes. The word was *fool*. Sarah's lips twisted in a rueful smile. *Fool* certainly fit. It's what people would say, anyway. Who else but a fool would have been content with a phantom husband all these years?

Not that anyone would know. She couldn't let that happen. The citizens of Texas—Fort Worth in particular—set great store by the vagaries of luck. Years ago, someone had questioned if hiring a wedding planner whose own marriage was unhappy might prove unlucky for a bride. Sarah had seen no option but to create a few stories about her life with Nick— all right, they were lies—so now she could not possibly go home and announce her marriage had been annulled. An annulment would be as bad for her business as a divorce.

"Maybe I'll say he died," she mumbled into her pillow. He died and she married someone else. "I'll be Lady Liesalot."

The tears began to flow faster then as a dozen different emotions bubbled inside her—sadness, confusion, and an odd sense of relief among them. She didn't understand why she felt as she did. She wished she had a friend here to talk with, to help her make sense of all that had happened. Someone like Abigail or Jenny and Claire McBride. As desperate as she felt right now, maybe even her mother.

Under other circumstances, she'd write a letter to Nick Ross.

She'd miss his letters.

She'd miss Nick.

"Don't be stupid," she muttered, sitting up and digging in her pocket for a handkerchief. How could she miss Nick? The man had been out of her life for a decade. He'd been on the other side of the world, for goodness' sake.

On the other side of the world, true, but always in her heart.

While for him, thoughts of her apparently had been centered somewhat lower. *I have a hunger for you,* he'd said. *Aren't you curious about what I've learned?*

He'd frightened her. So intent. Almost violent with it. He'd have taken her where they stood, she believed. Right there against the bookshelves, between Milton and Wordsworth. What had stunned her even more was the part of her that wanted to tell him, *Yes, show me.*

The repercussions of such a move were enormous. Ridding her of her virginity would also do away with any possibility of annulment. Plus, Nick had made it perfectly clear he would protest a divorce. Why, if she'd gone along with the man today, the lawyer could have gone home empty-handed. Without an annulment or divorce, their situation would have to remain the same.

Their situation would have to remain the same.

The handkerchief slipped from Sarah's hand. Her heart began to pound. If Nick bedded her, he'd have an awfully difficult time getting rid of her.

"And what would that get you?"

Marriage to a man who, despite professing a hunger for her, had taken his own sweet time coming to claim her. And then he didn't even come himself, but sent an escort. "Probably too busy sampling the hors d'oeuvre trays across Asia and Europe to drag himself away."

Groaning, she buried her head in her pillows. With

her eyes closed, she saw a mental picture of the way he'd looked, the intensity in his expression when he'd professed his desire for her.

It made her shudder. It made her ache in a way she'd never ached before. It made her wonder.

What if she did give him what he wanted? What if she gave up her home, her friends, her livelihood to live as Lady Weston? What if she let herself love him again?

"I can't."

Nick would break her heart. Again. She couldn't trust him not to. Ten years ago he'd vowed to love, honor, and cherish her until death, and what had he done? He'd left her the very next day. Rode off into the sunset—actually to Dallas—with another woman.

Today, all he'd claimed was desire, and even if he said he loved her, she wouldn't believe him. He couldn't love her. He didn't know the woman she'd become. She loved her home. Loved her friends. Loved her work. It was her life, and she was happy enough with it.

She wouldn't give up her life for a man.

Sarah sat up, scrounged for the handkerchief she'd dropped, then wiped away her tears. It was right, what she'd done. Annulling the marriage was the only choice.

Nick Ross could just go hungry.

It's bad luck to wear a green wedding gown.

~10~

Like any good spy, Nick knew the value of information. As a result, daylight the following morning found him skulking in the corridor near Sarah's room, waiting for her to make her way downstairs, where every morning she invaded the kitchen and charmed a cup of coffee from the cook.

Today, he waited longer than expected for his wife to leave her room, causing him to wonder if she'd overslept. Had she had as much trouble sleeping as he last night? Was she as plagued by thoughts of him as he was of her? Nick took some comfort in the notion.

Finally, just when he'd begun to wonder if he'd have to send someone in to shake her awake, she exited her room with an annoying spring in her step. As soon as she disappeared from sight, Nick ducked into her room.

His search was methodical, thorough, and distinctly contrary to the rules of hospitality. He searched her wardrobe, studied the dresses, and scrutinized the shoes, seeking clues to the woman she'd become from her choice in buttons and bows. He might have dawdled over her lingerie and allowed his mind to wander a bit, but for the most part, he remained at his task.

His search proved fruitful. He found she kept a small hoard of chocolate, was reminded that she liked the color yellow, and learned she had an admiration for silly love sonnets—all pertinent information he could possibly use. It was only when he looked in the round candy tin that he had second thoughts about what he was about.

He recognized the collection of a dozen or so small stones inside. He'd given her each one of them during the short months of their courtship. The first evening they'd walked out, needing something to do to keep his hands busy and off her, he'd scooped up a handful of rocks to peg, one at a time, at the trunk of the cottonwood tree in her front yard. When she'd admired a smooth, amber-colored stone, he'd given it to her. She'd exclaimed with delight, then leaned over to kiss his cheek. Nick, always a quick thinker, had turned his head so that she missed his cheek and hit his lips.

From then on he'd kept a sharp eye for rocks with unusual shapes or colors to give to her. Years later, he was still picking up rocks for her. That was part of the reason he'd returned from Afghanistan with a fortune in uncut rubies.

"She kept the rocks," he murmured. All this time she had kept the rocks. And, she'd brought them with her from Texas. What did that mean? He had an idea or two, but he needed to take some time to think it through. Like any good spy, Nick knew that information analysis was just as important as information retrieval.

He had just returned the tin of rocks to her dressing table drawer when he heard the murmur of approaching voices. Damnation. Sarah would be furious if she caught him at his work. He saw no need to analyze that.

He ducked behind a heavy velvet window drape just as the door swung open and Sarah and three of his sisters stepped inside. His wife was speaking. ". . . a stunning design, not at all similar to the other gown. It would be perfect for you, Charlotte."

Silently Nick adjusted the drapery so that he could see through a slit. When Aurora and Melanie tugged back the bed curtains and climbed up to sit cross-legged on Sarah's mattress, he was glad he'd chosen the window as his hiding place. He could only imagine what they'd have to say if they found him in his wife's bedchamber.

Charlotte placed the tea tray she carried on the small fireside table, then proceeded to pour chocolate for herself and his wife, his younger sisters having declined their sister's offer of a cup. Sarah removed an emerald-green dress from her wardrobe and a sketch from a file of papers he'd shuffled through moments before, and the women settled in and started talking weddings.

Lovely. Just lovely. They were liable to be at this for hours.

Silently, Nick sighed. He was prepared to listen to wedding plans. It was part of his plot to get closer to Sarah, in fact. He intended to stand in as father of the bride and develop an interest—a detailed interest—in the arrangements his wife made for his sister. He was prepared to dither about dates, languish over lace, and vacillate over veils until his eyes rolled back in his head. He just didn't want to do it while skulking behind a window drape.

Nor was he prepared to seethe about sex.

But a few minutes later, that's exactly what he was doing.

The conversation began innocently enough with Melanie saying, "I think we should remove ourselves to Berkeley Square. It would be ever so much easier for Sarah to contact merchants and suppliers if we were in London rather than Scotland."

"You just want to shop for shoes," Charlotte accused.

Melanie's grin was fast and guiltless. "Of course. A lady can never have too many pairs of shoes."

"Or gentlemen callers," Aurora said casually. "When we're in London we always get gentlemen callers, no matter what time of year. You might like that, Sarah. Since you don't want our brother, maybe we could go to London and help you find someone you *do* like."

That little tidbit told Nick three things as he peeked around the drapery. One, Sarah had told them about the annulment. Two, he hadn't been paying enough attention to the girls during their London visits—the younger two weren't even out yet; they shouldn't be having gentlemen callers. And three, he didn't at all like hearing that his wife didn't want him.

"I like Nick," Sarah protested, taking a seat at the table and sipping her chocolate. "I just don't want to be married to him."

The sisters exchanged glances, then Charlotte asked, "Why not?"

Yeah, why not? Nick silently echoed.

Sarah winced. "It's complicated. Besides, we're supposed to be making a decision on the wedding gown."

Melanie plumped up the bed pillows and leaned back against them. "We have all afternoon. Let's talk about Nicholas a little first. We think he'd make an excellent husband. Maybe there are some things you should know about him that you don't, Sarah. For instance, our brother is strong and courageous. Has he told you about the time a rock slide buried him alive and he had to dig his way out?"

Charlotte stirred her chocolate with a silver spoon. "He's so intelligent, too. Do you know he speaks five different languages—or is it seven? I forget."

"And our Nicholas is kind and generous," Aurora added. "One of the first things he did as marquess was to give all his employees, from stableboy to estate manager, a substantial raise in wages."

"If Robyn were here instead of helping Gillian pack for the trip back to Rowanclere, she'd tell you he's talented, too," Melanie added, her eyes twinkling as she stretched out on the bed. "She's very impressed that our brother can touch the tip of his nose with his tongue."

Nick's mouth twisted in a grin at that. He'd known a woman or two who, for different reasons, was impressed with his talent with his tongue.

Charlotte continued, "And of course he's handsome and gallant and quite magnificent all in all. A girl couldn't ask for more in a brother, and frankly, I don't see how a woman could want more in a husband."

That remark put Sarah on the defensive. "A number of qualities pop to my mind. Honesty, for one.

Steadfastness is another. Gentleness a third. A husband should be faithful and friendly and ..."

"You make him sound like a dog," Aurora protested.

"A dog often makes a better companion," Sarah snapped back.

"Well I think Nicholas is all those things," Charlotte said. "Honestly, Sarah, Nicholas is a fine man. I don't understand why you want to end your marriage to him."

Sarah set down her cup with a clatter and her voice sounded just a bit shrill when she said, "That's not what I want. I'm happy with matters the way they are. It's your brother who wants to change everything. Nick is the one who is forcing the issue, not me."

She attempted to stand, but Charlotte outmaneuvered her by passing a basket of fruit. "Apple?"

"No, thank you."

She made a motion to move, and again Charlotte blocked her way. "Why?"

"I'm not hungry."

"Not the apple, the man. Why are you content with being married to my brother but residing an ocean away from him? You can't possibly find him physically unattractive."

"No."

"Dull?"

"No."

"Parsimonious? Critical? Quarrelsome?"

"No, none of those. Well, quarrelsome does fit him at times."

"That's true," Aurora agreed.

"Maybe she doesn't like the way he smells," Melanie offered. "My friend Miss Anna Lawrence has a particularly sensitive nose, and she says that even if they bathe regularly, some women and some men can be olfactorily incompatible."

Charlotte sniffed. "Oh, that Anna Lawrence, don't believe her. She's always making things up. Is that even a word? Olifactorily?"

Nick didn't know about the word itself, but damned if the condition existed. Not with him and Sarah. Quite the opposite, in fact. Her fragrance called to him, made him want to sink into it, into her, like a warm bath on a cold morning, and he had no reason to think Sarah felt differently. Back in Texas when they'd been necking, he distinctly remembered her telling him she loved the way he smelled.

Now she said, "Your brother's scent is pleasing to me."

Nick nodded decisively and relaxed.

"Thank heavens," Aurora said, sighing with relief. "That might be a problem that is difficult to overcome. So what is wrong with Nicholas, Sarah? Is it because he cannot dance? I know he's terrible at it, but we are trying to teach him."

Sarah gaped at Nick's sisters, whose expressions glowed with curiosity and determination, and wondered aloud, "How does Nick manage you? Counting his Scots sisters, there are six of you. With that many females around the house at one time or another, why does the man want a wife?"

Again his sisters shared a look. Charlotte blushed, but Aurora's eyes developed a wicked twinkle. "I should imagine it's sex."

Nick jerked back his head and banged it on a metal bolt that supported the drapery hardware. As pain radiated through his scalp, he watched Sarah almost slip out of her seat. "Um . . . well . . . oh."

His scandal of a sister continued, "That's just a guess, mind you. Nicholas doesn't talk about it. I don't think he beds Lady Steele, and he pretends mistresses don't exist. If he has one himself, he's very discreet and he doesn't visit her often. He watches over us too closely for that."

"Hush, Aurora," Melanie said. "You're not helping."

"But it's true. He's the most overprotective brother you can imagine. Why, he doesn't want us to know a thing about mistresses or sexual relations. Not until we're getting married, anyway."

Shyly, Charlotte added, "And even then he didn't have much to say."

Aurora snickered. "You should have seen him the night before Charlotte's first wedding, Sarah. He paced and drank and paced some more. He went to her room twice before he managed to knock on the door and ask to speak with her. We tried to eavesdrop, of course, but he made certain the balcony doors were shut tight. Anyway, he was white as a wedding gown when he came out, and all he'd say to us was that women should know what they're getting into, but not too soon."

Sarah wrinkled her nose. "Yes, I have to agree with your brother in that respect. If women knew ahead of time what would happen on their wedding night, I could never make a living doing what I do. One out of every two weddings surely would be canceled."

Aurora and Melanie shared a knowing look as Charlotte gasped. "Is it that bad?"

Sarah shut her eyes and rubbed her forehead. "I'm not going to speak about this. It's not my place."

That's the damned truth, Nick thought, fuming.

"But you must, Sarah. Charlotte needs to know. She has been trying to work up the courage to ask you, but she is unaccountably shy."

The young woman nodded. "That's true. I am."

"Then ask Gillian or her twin. They're both married. They're better ones for you to discuss this with than I."

Melanie shook her head. "We can't ask Gilly or Flora about their marriage beds. That's private."

Incredulously, Sarah said, "But you'll ask me?"

"You're a wedding planner. Wedding nights are part of your job."

Sarah drew back, her expression appalled. "No, they're not."

I need to put a stop to this, Nick told himself. But he couldn't seem to make his feet move.

Aurora lifted her chin. "They certainly should be. After all, I would think that in the long run, the success of one's wedding night has greater impact upon a person than how good one's wedding cake tastes."

Sarah cocked her head, her lips pursed in thought.

Hidden behind the drapery, Nick silently moaned.

Charlotte's teeth tugged at her lower lip. "I would appreciate the benefit of your experience, Sarah. I was a bit concerned following Nicholas's, um, talk, but I didn't have time then to dwell on it. Now . . . well . . ."

"Tell her what he said, Charlotte," Aurora said. "That way she'll know—"

Sarah attempted to interrupt. "I don't think we need to go into much detail."

"I can't go into much detail because Nicholas didn't," Charlotte insisted. "Mainly, he said the best thing to do was to relax and trust my husband."

"He said what?" Sarah asked with a squeak in her voice.

Nick mouthed the words along with Charlotte. "To relax and trust my husband."

Sarah, curse her black soul, snorted and said, "The *best* thing to do is to get good and tipsy so you can get through it."

Good and tipsy? Outrage erupted like a geyser in Nick.

His dear wife continued, "The good part is it only lasts five minutes, so at least it's over with quickly."

Everything within Nick froze. Surely he hadn't heard that right.

"I thought it took longer than five minutes," Aurora commented.

"No. From my experience, five minutes takes care of it."

Nick's throat felt as if the drapery cord were wrapped around his neck like a hangman's noose. His jaw dropped and his mouth worked uselessly. He seriously wondered if his eyes might pop out of his head.

Five minutes. Good and tipsy and five goddamned minutes! To my sisters, no less. My sisters!

He dragged his hand slowly down his face. His gaze slid to the floor, where he imagined his masculine pride lay tattered, beaten, sliced to shreds.

Meanwhile Sarah, having apparently warmed up to the idea of spreading the word about how poor a lover her husband was, continued, "Now that I think about it, you do have a point, Aurora. Perhaps I do have a duty to my brides. Not all of them have mothers as I did who can prepare a girl for what happens on her honeymoon."

"That's right." Melanie started thrumming her fingers on the table. "We don't have a mother, and we really should know what to expect. I think it's beyond silly to keep girls in the dark about such matters. What if we get the wrong idea about such things?"

"Melanie is right." Aurora nodded. "For instance, I thought sexual intercourse was something to look forward to. Am I wrong?"

Nick's eyes rolled back in his head, and he slumped against the cool window glass.

"I mean, it can't be all that bad, or women wouldn't cooperate. Look at Gillian. I think it's safe to say she likes it."

Melanie said, "I agree. Sometimes the way she looks at Jake almost sets the carpet afire."

"If that's the case, I suspect Mr. Delaney is especially gifted in that area," Sarah observed. "Aurora, you have hit upon an important point. Some women must find marital relations pleasant. Otherwise, women like my friends Jenny and Claire McBride wouldn't light up like candles whenever their husbands happen into the shop."

"But not every woman finds it pleasant?"

"Frankly, no."

"But every man does?"

"I believe so, yes."

"Hmm . . ." Melanie frowned. "I don't understand. Why do some women enjoy it and others don't?"

Sarah sighed. "Honestly, I'm not certain, although I suspect it has something to do with a man's talent."

"Did you like it, Sarah?"

Nick swallowed a moan.

After a long moment of hesitation, Sarah said, "I'll answer your other questions, but I'll not discuss any particulars about your brother or what happened between us."

"But how do we—"

"Girls, what do you know about the mechanics of lovemaking?"

Nick knew he should interrupt this now. He should have interrupted it five minutes ago. He should have locked his sisters in a convent and thrown away the key.

And he never, ever, should have left his marriage bed until he'd made his wife see heaven.

Braving another look into the room, he saw that Charlotte's skin was as red as the Texas chili Gillian was learning to make. Melanie wore a sheepish smile, and Aurora looked intrigued. She said, "I know it has something to do with getting naked and touching, and I suspect it makes a woman feel as if she's being sunburned, only on the inside. I think that because sometimes when I'm being kissed I get so feverish. So hot."

Nick felt a groan well up in his throat, and he swallowed hard against it.

Aurora questioned her sisters. "Do you know what I mean?"

"Yes, I do," Melanie offered. "And it does seem to depend upon the man kissing you, doesn't it? Remember Lord Wesley? His kisses made me burn, whereas Mr. Starling's left me wanting to brush my teeth. Why is that? Sarah, do you know?"

"A woman definitely reacts differently with different men. For instance, with Nick's kisses . . ."

His sisters—even Charlotte—leaned forward and spoke simultaneously. "Yes?"

Sarah shook her head. "No, I'll not be indiscreet."

Too late now, dinna ye think?

"Although I will say his kisses fell toward the fiery end of things rather than the teeth brushing."

"Well, I should damned well hope so," he muttered beneath his breath as he squared his shoulders, preparing to betray his presence.

"So am I right, Sarah?" asked Aurora. "Is it like a sunburn?"

"I think it's like a rash," Charlotte said, surprising everyone. "I get itchy just thinking about it."

"We've gone a bit off track. I'm not referring to the sensations, but the physical mechanics. As in who puts what where. Do you girls know those details?"

Not surprisingly, Aurora spoke for them all. "No."

"Very well. I think a visual aide might come in handy for this. Hmm . . ." She glanced around the room and lifted a bud vase from her dressing table. "Imagine this is the female. And the male . . ."

As his wife moved toward the fireplace, Nick's gaze went unerringly to the tall, thick cylindrical candle that sat on the fireplace mantel. But Sarah's hand passed right over it. Instead, the damned woman picked up a taper lying on its side.

A thin, little four-inch taper.

With that, Nick reached the end of his wick.

The figure lunged from behind the window drapery, snarling and snapping like a rabid coyote. Sarah dropped the bud vase. It banged against an andiron and shattered into a dozen pieces.

The three sisters shrieked, then Charlotte said, "Nicholas?"

"I will not have it!" he roared. He scorched the girls with a glare and declared, "You will each go to your rooms and pack a bag. I am sending you to Our Lady of Mercy convent today. And you . . ." He jerked his head around and leveled his glower on Sarah. "You have more nerve than a broken toe. How dare you speak of such things to my sisters."

"Me? Me!" Sarah braced her hands on her hips and stepped forward. "You were the one playing Peeping Tom in my bedchamber. For shame, Nick. What sort of man hides in a woman's room and spies on her? Were you content with only that, or did you search through my things, too? My underwear, perhaps?"

The tiniest flicker in his eyes betrayed him, and she gasped. "You did! Why, Lord Weston, you are a pervert."

"I'm no pervert. If I were, I'd have entered your room during the night and watched you sleep, watched you dress. Instead I waited until you left to do my job."

"And what job, pray tell, is that?"

He put his hands on his hips and stepped forward, too, until they stood but a foot apart. "Though I am no longer active, I am still an agent in Her Majesty's secret service. I'm a spy. Part of a spy's job is to search for clues and information, and that's exactly what I was doing!"

"Searching for clues and information. Uh-huh. And what state secret did you expect to find in my corsets?"

"I thought to find something in your handkerchiefs. The corsets were a personal bonus."

"Pervert!"

"I'm a man, Sarah. Your husband."

She lifted her chin, a matador waving her red cape. "Not for long."

"Maybe not." Each of Nick's senses was heightened, on full alert. He stood on the verge of battle, the precipice of war. And adrenaline pounded through his veins. "Girls, go to your rooms and pack. I intend for us to leave before noon."

"Leave!" Melanie exclaimed. "We're not leaving. You are not going to send us to any silly convent just for asking a few questions we need answered. We've discussed this in the past. It isn't fair of men to keep women in the dark about—"

"Haud yer wheest, Melanie," Nick said, slipping into Scots, his gaze never leaving Sarah's. "We'll debate this later. Now leave us. I've business with your guid-sister."

"But—"

Aurora grabbed her sister's arm and pulled her toward the door, murmuring in the other girl's ear. Nick overheard some of it. "Look at them, Melanie. That is the picture of passion. This is what we want."

Sarah's cheeks flushed. Either she'd heard them, too, and was embarrassed, or else her temper was ready to blow. The question seemed to be, who would explode first? Waiting for his sisters to make themselves scarce, Nick considered it even odds.

The moment the door shut behind the girls, both Sarah and Nick started talking. She said, "Just because some legal paper somewhere says we are married doesn't give you the right to paw through—"

"You had no business talking about sex with my sisters. They are young, impressionable girls, and you don't know what the hell you are talking about. If you feel the need to impart your so-called wisdom, then at least respect them enough to get it right."

"—my things. Privacy is a basic . . . What did you say?"

"I said you shouldn't try to be a teacher unless you've gone to school yourself. And, Sarah," he added, reaching for the hand that still held the taper, "while you're there, pay extra attention to measurement skills. They are obviously sadly lacking."

He yanked the taper from her hand and threw it over his shoulder, then tugged her against him and took her mouth in a long, demanding, make-her-toes-tingle kiss. Finally, breathless, he lifted his head and murmured, "Just call me Professor Nick."

Sarah, the wench, grabbed a fistful of his shirt and pulled him back to her, saying, "You think you're the only one who has studied? See what you think of my lecture."

This time Sarah took Nick in a kiss that was part challenge, part dare, and totally consuming. She took control, nipping at his lips, stroking him with her tongue, breathing need—fierce, hot, and aching—into every inch of his body.

He needed her skin. Craved to have her skin, soft and smooth, against him. So sleek and silky around him. Driven by instinct rather than intellect, he rather desperately tugged her skirts up in search of the prize.

At the first brush of his hand against her thigh, she broke away. "Sarah," he groaned softly, his gaze dropping to the rapid rise and fall of her bosom as she struggled to catch her breath.

"So, do you still say I don't know what I'm talking about?"

He exhaled a sigh, then dragged his gaze upward once more. "Lass, I'll cede you this. While you do need lessons in taking a man's measure, if kissing were a discipline of study, Oxford would be happy to have you."

She wrinkled her nose and sniffed but couldn't hide the smugness in her expression. When she added pursed lips to the look, she drew his attention back to her ripe and kiss-swollen lips. *Damnation, every man at Oxford would be happy to have her, period.*

Nick groaned again, stepped toward her again, and asked, "Teach me some more, Sarah, please?"

Now she scowled. "No. You are just trying to distract me. I want to know why you invaded my privacy, Nick, and I want to know now."

Her prissy demand was almost enough to push him into pushing her further, but now that distance had allowed some of the blood to flow back to his brain, Nick recognized it wasn't the proper time for further lessons. However, he did take a moment to make himself a quiet, simple promise. One way or another before they were done, he was going to give Sarah, Lady Weston, a close and very personal demonstration of how the right candle can light up a bud vase.

"You want to know why I searched your things? All right, I'll tell you. I was looking for love letters."

She blinked. "Is that how you thought of them?"

It took him a moment to realize she referred to the letters the two of them had exchanged. So Sarah connected their letters with love letters, did she? Nick filed away that piece of information to consider later.

Warming up to the story he was creating on the spot, he clarified, "I meant love letters from other men."

"What?"

"Letters from your lover. I was going to read them."

She folded her arms, her expression mutinous. "You're not going to read my letters."

Wait a minute. She *did* have love letters from another man? Nick's temper reignited in a flash. "You claimed not to have a lover."

"Then why were you looking for his letters?"

"Are you telling me you lied?"

"Are you calling me a liar?"

"Damnation, woman. You are as prickly as a thistle." He dragged his fingers through his hair and started over. "I was simply reassuring myself that nothing unexpected would appear to interfere with the annulment."

"Unexpected as in a beau?"

"You were rather insistent about avoiding a physical examination. You can't blame me for wondering . . ."

She sighed, and shook her head. "You are such a man, Nick."

"Considering your choice in candles, I am pleased you noticed," he grumbled.

She smirked. "I meant this display of possessive jealousy. It's quite unattractive. You don't want me, but you don't want anyone else to have me, either."

"No, I never said I don't want you. I happen to want you rather desperately, which you must have noticed a few minutes ago. In any case, it's been my experience that women like being the object of a man's jealous feelings."

"Oh?" Her Texas drawl dripped sugar. "And I suppose you are a man of substantial experience on the subject?"

Nick bit the inside of his mouth to hold back a laugh. Still, he couldn't help but say, "What's the matter, lass? Jealous?"

But his wife gave as good as she got. With a nonchalant shrug of her shoulders, she said, "Hardly. Lady Brass is welcome to you. I have my share of unattractive characteristics, but jealousy is not among them."

Marginally annoyed with her reply, Nick nodded

toward her shoulders. "I explained the significance of poking at a chest in Kualistan. Care to guess what a shrug means?"

"Nothing I want to hear, I'm certain." In a tone as dry as the ink on their marriage license, Sarah suggested, "Try to remember you're supposed to be a gentleman. That would solve a myriad of faults."

Now he did laugh. "I've missed you, lass."

To Nick's surprise, his comment appeared to sober her. She gave him a bittersweet smile. "You haven't missed me, Nick. You don't know me. You know a memory, not the woman I've become."

She was right and he knew it. That's what had brought him to her room this morning in the first place. He needed to know this woman standing before him today so he could woo *her*, not the girl he'd married. And so, like any good secret agent, Nick spiced his lie with the truth.

"I know the woman who writes me letters, Sarah. I like having that woman in my life, and I don't like the thought of losing her to an annulment or another man."

"What?"

"It's true. That's why I searched your things. After yesterday, I discovered I need a little reassurance. The next man in your life won't like you writing to your ex-husband. I find I am in no rush for this connection between us to end."

It was only after he'd said it that Nick realized every word was the truth. He hadn't needed to act the cad and rifle through her things to learn that she had a liking for lace on her drawers. All the time he thought he was lying to her, he'd actually been lying to himself.

His accidental honesty served him well, because

Sarah's pique melted right before his eyes. "Oh, Nick. Your letters have been a joy in my life. I have no intention of stopping them, and if in the future any man in my life tries to make me, well, I'll just tell him to go suck a lemon."

He grinned at that and stuck his hands in his pockets. It was either that or reach for her.

"Your letters are . . . well . . ." She shrugged, then said, "I don't know how to describe it other than to say they steal into a place deep down inside of me. I treasure them. I'd be lost without them."

Her vehemence took him aback, and Nick knew nothing more to say than, "Thank you, Sarah."

"No, thank you. You know, Nick, your profession as a reporter might have been only a cover for clandestine activities, but the fact remains you have a true talent for the written word. Much better, I daresay, than with spoken communication. Your letters never make me angry or frighten me or upset me, even when you deal with unsettling events. So be assured that once I've returned to Texas, I'll be making regular trips to the post office to look for letters from Britain. I won't let anyone interfere with my exchanging letters with you, and I hope you will say the same."

"Um, certainly. Yes. Of course." Nick drew his hands from his pockets and glanced down at them, halfway expecting to see them holding a silver platter. Could it be this easy? Had she just handed him the secret to her seduction?

Aye, she had.

It was all he could do not to grab her up there and then and plant a kiss on her. That would be a strategic mistake. From now on, all important matters would be introduced on paper, not in person.

Well, except for this one detail he thought needed addressing right away. "I am pleased that's settled. I feel much better. There is one more issue here, however."

"Yes?"

"About the girls. I don't mind you telling them about sex. In fact, upon reflection I think it's probably best they have a decent understanding of the mechanics of it heading into marriage. However, I would appreciate it if in the future, you used more thought in your choice of visual aides. You see, lass, men tend to be sensitive about the size of their . . . candle, so to speak. Considering your knowledge in this area arrives from but a single source—me—I'd appreciate it if you would choose a visual aide a bit closer to actual size than that little bitty taper you used earlier."

"All right. I don't mind doing that. What would you like me to use?"

"Well, I don't know." Nick gazed around the room, a vague sense of embarrassment inhibiting his choice. "You choose."

Sarah gave him a long look, then pursed her lips, clasped her hands behind her back, and made a studious circle around the room. She flipped up the lid on the humidor and studied the short, stumpy cigars inside before rejecting them in favor of a pencil, which she lifted and ran her fingers across. Nick almost growled. She was killing him.

Finally, she paused in front of the mantel and considered the tall cylindrical candle Nick had previously noted. She glanced from the candle to him, then back to the candle again. Finally, she lifted it down and turned to him. "Will this do?"

His mouth broke out in a wide smile. "It's your decision, but I think that's a fair representation."

He took his leave of her then, and the sound of her soft laughter followed him down the hallway. He almost tripped on a rug when he heard her say, "In some ways men are so easy to please."

Willie Hart arrived at Glencoltran Castle at mid-morning. The only reason Nick didn't kill the young man upon learning the news was the fact that he hadn't come alone. "He showed up at Hunterbourne looking for you," the young rogue said. "Said it was important he speak with you. Old Tom at the stables said Lord Kimball was an important man, that he works for the government. When I heard him asking directions to Glencoltran Castle, I thought it my proper place to show him the way, seeing as how I've been here before and knew the way. I was doing my duty as a good citizen, I was."

Nick eyed the young man's broad shoulders and the light in his eyes and wondered if he'd be forced to kill him yet. "So where is Lord Kimball now?"

"That's the strange part of me story," Hart said, scratching his cheek. "Once we got close enough to see the castle, he started looking for a place to stop. I left him at the old ruins sittin' atop the great rock that stretches out into the loch. He told me to tell my story to nobody but you and to give you this." He handed over an envelope.

Nick broke the seal and quickly scanned the contents of the note. Looking up, he pinned Willie Hart with his most deadly glare. "Stop by the kitchen and tell the cook I said to feed you, then report to the stables. Go near Aurora and I'll cut off your balls and feed them to my gamekeeper's wolfhounds. Any questions?"

The stable hand went pale, but managed a protest. "But my lord, I love her. I want her for my wife."

"Then I'll cut off your cock and feed that to my sister Robyn's pet snake."

The second threat drained all trace of color from young Hart's face, and he nodded. "I'll be straight for the stables, my lord. My appetite will hold till lunch."

"I'm assuming you are referring to your appetite for food, and that all other appetites will disappear for as long as you remain at Glencoltran. Am I correct?"

"Yes, my lord. Right as rain, my lord. Nothing but a growling stomach out of me."

Nick nodded, waited, and finally made a shooing motion with his hand. The trouble-making young pretty-boy scuttled away in retreat. Nick left the house almost immediately himself, pausing only long enough to grab a coat. The morning air had a bite to it yet, though judging by the sunshine the chill would burn away by afternoon.

Nick made his way quickly toward the promontory and the crumbling ruins of the first Glencoltran Castle, his mind torn between worry over that young bounder's proximity to his sister and concern as to what trouble had brought his former colleague all the way to Scotland.

Neither one boded well for his peace of mind.

Lord Kimball was the heir to the Duke of Halford and had been Nick's immediate superior for the first years of his sojourn overseas. More recently, Kimball had joined the Special Irish Branch of the Metropolitan Police where, Nick understood, he was in charge of coordinating anti-Fenian operations in the capital.

Nick both liked and respected Kimball, who served his country out of a deep and genuine sense of patriotism that Nick as a Scot-turned-Texan-turned-Englishman-pretending-to-be-American and so forth never managed to match. Kimball could also be one of the coldest, meanest, most dangerous men Nick had ever encountered, and that company included some of his old friends, the Khans.

"So what brings him to the Highlands on a sunny winter day?" Nick murmured aloud when he spied the Englishman standing on the shore, tossing gray rocks into the sapphire water. Had the so-called dynamite war waged by Irish terrorists against British cities moved northward?

More likely, Kimball wanted to lure Nick back into service in some fashion. If that was the case, his old friend was doomed to disappointment. Nick's focus was now centered on his family, and he intended to keep it that way.

"I should shoot you and throw your carcass in the loch," he called out as he approached. "Did you know you were bringing the horned serpent into our midst, or was that just lucky coincidence?"

The hesitation in Kimball's throw was so slight Nick almost missed it. "Your grievance against young Hart is for the most part unfounded," the former spymaster said.

"The little bastard attempted to run off with my sister."

"Yes. And Miss Aurora paid him one hundred guineas for his trouble. The price of a new Worth ball gown, I believe. The canceled order called for a frilly confection in ice blue with gold trim."

Nick didn't waste their time questioning the accuracy of Kimball's information. Instead, his mind started clicking. "Why, that little witch. What was she up ... oh. Helen. This had something to do with Helen, didn't it?"

"Mr. Hart is under the impression that your sisters thought you would benefit from having some distance from Lady Steele. They anticipated you would move to separate Miss Aurora from Hart following the elopement."

Nick nodded. "Melanie suggested Scotland."

A hint of a smile played about Kimball's mouth. "I should keep them in mind for future recruitment."

"Sod it, Kimball," Nick grumbled.

The spymaster laughed, his grin rare enough that Nick did a double take.

"Damnation, I forget how pretty you are when you smile. I hope you'll refrain from doing much of that around my sisters, or they'll be offering *you* money to elope, and this time they'll mean it. Then I'd have to kill you, of course."

"Of course. And after I've come all this way, too."

"Speaking of which, what brings you north, Lord Kimball?"

"Trouble."

Nick sighed. "I was afraid of that. Where? Afghanistan? India? Tibet?"

"Texas."

"Texas!"

Kimball nodded. "Pull up a rock, Nicholas, and let me ask you a few questions."

Nick gazed out over the water and shoved his hands in his pockets. "It's a cool morning, and I have a fine bottle of Rowanclere malt in my study."

"A bit early for me, I'm afraid, but I hope to sample it soon. But I understand that along with your potent Scotch whisky you also have a bit of Texas spice tucked away in your castle."

Texas spice? Nick blinked. "Sarah? This is about Sarah?"

"Sarah Simpson Ross, also known as Lady Innsbruck, also known as Lady Weston."

"Wait just one minute. Are you trying to claim that my Sarah is involved in some sort of espionage?"

"In a manner of speaking." Lord Kimball leveled a hard, narrowed-eye gaze on Nick and flatly said, "Your Sarah is suspected of being marginally involved in a plot to assassinate the queen."

It's bad luck for a bride's father to cry at her wedding.

~11~

If anyone other than Kimball had made the charge, Nick would pop him a right cross to the jaw and knock him in the loch. Since it *was* Kimball, the man in charge of political crime at Scotland Yard, he obeyed his suddenly weak knees and sat down. He dragged a hand down his bristled jaw, feeling as ancient as the stone wall beneath him. "Tell me."

"In Fort Worth, your wife socializes with a group that includes four gentlemen with ties to the British aristocracy."

Four? Damnation. No wonder she didn't want the physical examination.

Almost as soon as the thought burst into his brain, Nick discounted it. He was willing to accept that Sarah could have fooled him to a point, but not to that degree. He might have a blind spot or two where Sarah was concerned, but he wasn't stupid. "Is she in danger?"

"Honestly, I don't know. It depends on her level of involvement with these men."

"Who are they?" he demanded even as a series of possibilities streamed through his mind. "Did she plan their weddings? Do they attend the same church? Are they in a literary club together?"

The slightest widening of Kimball's eyes betrayed his surprise. "A perceptive guess, Weston, but not precisely accurate. Your wife is a member of the Folio Society of Fort Worth."

Casting his thoughts back to his time in Fort Worth, Nick couldn't recall a Folio Society. "What is it?"

"Each month the members of the group produce works based upon a chosen theme. The works are then bound in a leather portfolio and circulated for criticism. It's a mixture of drawings, watercolors, short stories, poetry—anything that falls under the auspices of art."

Nick thought a moment, considered what he knew of his wife, then said, "Sarah must write."

"Sometimes poetry and upon occasion an editorial."

"What of fiction?"

"Some."

Tension easing to an extent, Nick asked, "Is that what happened? Did Sarah write a fictional tale that involved the assassination of the queen? I can imagine the folio falling into the hands of one of your men and being taken as a threat. Assassination plots are not as rare as we'd like to think, are they?"

"This is the fourth my office has fielded in recent months, and I am afraid it is not as simple as you would hope. Your wife wrote no tale of political intrigue. In fact, her stories of late involve the antics of a group of young boys in Fort Worth known as the McBride Monsters. After reading her work, I don't doubt the youngsters capable of causing mischief. However, the ability to disrupt the Queen of England's golden jubilee is still a bit beyond them, I would think."

"The jubilee? That's what this is about?"

Kimball nodded. "I hope it will prove to be nothing more than a hoax. However, the information we have pieced together to this point is suspicious enough to warrant further investigation. Hence my visit to Glencoltran Castle."

"Why don't you start at the beginning?"

Kimball flung a stone across the water and watched it skip once, twice, three times. When it sank beneath the surface, he said, "My office received a letter from a judge in a little Texas town called Weather . . . something."

"Weatherford. It's west of Fort Worth."

"That's it. The judge had received an anonymous letter claiming knowledge of a particularly nefarious Fenian plot." Kimball skipped another stone, then said, "The plan, apparently, is to explode a bomb in Westminster Abbey during Queen Victoria's jubilee ceremony on June twenty-first."

Nick absorbed the information, then muttered a particularly vile curse.

"Precisely," said Kimball. "The judge wrote that he received the letter naming as the source of the information a man from Chicago—"

"A Fenian stronghold."

"Exactly. The anonymous letter claimed this man had come to Fort Worth to recruit the assistance of an Englishman who was an outspoken critic of the British system of primogeniture."

"A remittance man," Nick logically concluded.

"It would seem so. To complicate matters—and

give them a sense of credibility—the man from Chicago was found dead in his own bed, having been shot once through the forehead."

"Executed," Nick murmured.

"Two days after the judge received the tip and began making inquiries. I think it's safe to assume the fellow spoke out of turn about the plot and paid for it with his life."

"What of the Englishman? Was he successfully recruited?"

"That we do not know. His name died with the Fenian. However, the judge was sufficiently concerned to forward the names of any British citizens residing in Fort Worth at the time, along with their occupations and—"

"The clubs they belong to. My Sarah knows them."

"There were four names on the list. We believe she knows all of them and is particularly close to two of them."

"Particularly close?"

"One is Viscount Wexford, who, though he holds the title, has never actually lived in Britain. He is known in Fort Worth as Mr. Tye McBride."

"The McBrides are Sarah's business partners. I know something of the man. He may be an English viscount, but McBride considers himself American. He has no motive to commit such a crime. Who are the others?"

"Lord Trevor Chambers. He's the Marquess of Blakely's younger brother. He ... um ... called upon your wife for a time."

Energy flowed back into Nick's knees, and he rose quickly to his feet. Kicking at a stone, he sent it sailing into the loch with a plop.

Kimball waited a moment, then, when Nick failed to comment, continued. "The other two who concern me were also members of the Folio Society but are not as closely connected to your wife. Mr. Thomas Sheldon and Lord Robert Endicott."

"Sheldon?" Nick's head came up, and he dragged his thoughts away from his bride's beau. "Baron Yardley's son?"

Kimball nodded. "I believe he was in Texas at the same time as you?"

"I knew him," Nick said with a grim smile. Tom Sheldon had helped Susan Harris save Nick's life that rainy winter night so many years ago in Fort Worth. Tom had been the one to actually kill the man about to skewer Nick and, in doing so, earned from Nick a promise. Six months later, fulfilling it helped change the course of Nick's life. "I didn't know he'd returned to Fort Worth."

"Eight months ago, so I understand."

Eight months? Nick should have been told. Obviously, the investigator he'd been paying to find Tom Sheldon for the past year had not done his job. *Damnation, I hate incompetence.*

Nick's thoughts raced. Tom was back in town. What would he have heard? What would he have believed? Could Tom have become so bitter as to plot against his father? Against the Crown?

Perhaps.

Nick shut his eyes and swallowed a groan.

Kimball continued. "However, Sheldon is no longer in Texas. Nor are Chambers and Endicott, who is the second son of a Derbyshire viscount. Within the past six weeks all three men have returned to London."

After a moment's pause Nick observed, "Now that is not the best of news."

"An understatement, Lord Weston."

Nick scowled, shoved both hands in his pants pockets, and rocked back and forth on his heels. "I imagine you wish to interview Sarah."

"Yes."

Nick had no problem with that since he had some questions for her, too. Questions about this Chambers fellow and why she'd neglected to mention him. But before that happened, he wanted one thing perfectly clear. "I confided the circumstances of my marriage to you years ago. Can I assume that you are now aware that I sent for her, in effect forced her to make the trip? She is in Britain because of me and nothing else. She is in no way a suspect, correct?"

"Correct. I look to her simply as a source of information."

"Good." Nick kicked one more stone into the loch, then turned toward the castle. As the two men walked through the winter gloom, Nick asked, "By the way, Kimball, why did you bring that blackguard Willie Hart with you? You didn't need a guide, especially not one who has tried to ruin my sister."

"He might prove useful to me in the future," Kimball said, grinning. "He has quick hands."

"That better be all he has that's quick," Nick grumbled. "Anything else he'll lose to my knife."

Kimball chuckled, and Nick tossed him a glare. But as they walked toward the castle, his thoughts returned to the reason behind his old friend's visit. "Do you honestly believe there's anything to this rumored plot?"

Kimball shrugged. "Royalty and heads of state from all over the world will be in Westminster Abbey that day. Security plans for the event have been in the works for years. I would like to think this was no more than the fantasy of a bitter man who met his end for unrelated reasons. However, the circumstances of his death are troubling. Too, we are investigating every threat that comes our way. We cannot afford to do otherwise. All this, I might mention, leaves us short of manpower. I'm hoping you'll help, Weston."

Having anticipated the request, Nick had an excuse at the ready. He didn't use it. The moment Sarah's name had been mentioned, Nick Ross, intelligence agent in Her Majesty's secret service, had come out of retirement.

Sarah, after all, was family.

The fire flickered invitingly in the library's marble hearth as Nick introduced Sarah to a darkly handsome man whose steady, assessing stare proved unnerving. Something about Lord Kimball made her want to shudder, but she hid her reaction behind the handy facade of extreme politeness. Until Nick began telling her his story, that is.

Sarah sniffed with disdain and interrupted the tale. "Who is this judge who supposedly heard this nonsense?"

"Boyette. Judge A. P. Boyette of Weatherford," Kimball offered. "I believe he is prominent in the community."

"Maybe so, but that doesn't mean he can't be an idiot, which is exactly what he is if he thinks Tye McBride is involved in such a scheme. He couldn't care less about the queen. The only plotting he is apt to do is how to steal his wife away for private time together. You are fools if you think otherwise. And as for Trevor being a terrorist? That's almost as ludicrous. He is an upstanding man and a talented artist, I'll have you know. His drawings are outstanding."

Nick's crooked smile was more sneer than grin as he propped a hip on the edge of his desk and folded his arms. "All the better for copying floor plans."

Sarah shot him a look of disgust, then addressed Lord Kimball. "I should think Sheldon or Endicott are much more suited to such a thing. Sheldon in particular. He's been an absolute grouch since he returned to Fort Worth from the West. He made a fortune in California, but that doesn't seem to matter to him. He's a perfect example of how money doesn't buy happiness. If this plot does exist, I wouldn't be at all surprised if he was the culprit."

Kimball crossed the room and took the seat behind the desk. She was compelled to fidget, locked beneath the stares of two such imposing men, and it took a conscious effort on her part to remain still.

Especially when Kimball arched a brow and commented, "You were close to Lord Chambers?"

Sarah glanced at Nick. Accusation gleamed from his narrowed eyes. She thought of Lady Steele, gave her chin a toss, and said, "He wanted to marry me. Of course that couldn't happen because of this pesky little marriage Nick and I have."

"Pesky little marriage?" Nick repeated.

Kimball pursed his lips as if fighting a smile. "I see."

"He was quite sympathetic once I explained the situation."

Thrumming his fingers on the desk, Nick reiterated, "Pesky little marriage?"

"Yes, pesky little marriage," Sarah snapped back.

Kimball cleared his throat. "Did you and Lord Chambers part on good terms?"

"Yes, we did. Trevor was a gentleman about the entire matter."

Her husband snorted. "What a prince."

Kimball said something Sarah didn't catch, distracted as she was by her husband. She'd heard the expression, but she didn't think she'd ever seen a lip actually curl before.

"Lady Weston?" Kimball said, his voice raised.

"Hmm?"

"I asked what you can tell me of Endicott."

"Mr. Endicott?" Sara looked from one man to the other, spied the grim look in their eyes, and decided she'd best pay attention. Cautiously, she said, "He's only a casual acquaintance. I know he has a fine eye for horses and old family ties to horse racing in England."

Kimball waited a moment for her to continue, and when she said no more asked, "Do you know why he might have made a trip to England?"

"No."

"What of Lord Chambers and Mr. Sheldon? Do you know why they would have made the journey?"

Sarah shook her head and asked, "Are you saying they're all over here now?"

Kimball's gaze never left Sarah's face. "Sheldon, Chambers, and Endicott arrived on the same ship."

Sarah was surprised. "Really? I can understand Trevor and Mr. Endicott traveling together because they're friends of a sort. I imagine Mr. Sheldon being with them is coincidence. Is the fact they've come to England the reason why you give credence to this plot?"

Nodding, Kimball said, "In part. To be honest, Lady Weston, I don't know what to think. I was hoping you could provide information that would shed light on the situation, but . . ." He allowed the sentence to trail off.

"I am convinced Trevor is not a party to any plot, Lord Kimball," Sarah said, folding her arms. Then, ignoring the storm clouds gathering on her husband's face, she added, "But I'll be happy to ask him about it if you'd like."

"No!" Nick exclaimed.

"An excellent idea," Kimball said at the same time. "We wouldn't want you to ask him about the plot directly, but sounding him out wouldn't hurt. I will provide an appropriate list of questions for you to choose from and—"

"Kim!" Nick interrupted, bounding to his feet. He placed both hands on the desk and leaned forward. "Have you completely lost your mind? *I'm* the professional here. *I'll* ask any questions that need to be asked. I'll see to any investigating that needs doing. Leave my wife out of it."

Kimball flashed a smile that had Sarah blinking as if a photographer's light had just exploded in her face. My heavens, the man was handsome when he smiled. "Calm down, Weston. What I have in mind is relatively safe for everyone involved."

"Relatively?" Nick had a squeak in his voice. "Relatively!"

Lord Kimball ignored him, addressing Sarah instead. "I understand that along with your partners, Mesdames McBride, you facilitate the most spectacular weddings."

Sarah smiled with pleasure at the compliment and demurred, "My job is easy when Jenny's Good Luck Wedding Dress designs put Worth to shame, and Claire's Magical Wedding Cakes are divine."

Casually lacing his fingers over his stomach, Lord

Kimball shot another of those fabulous smiles. "I am confident your own contributions are quite exceptional. Lady Pratt certainly believes so. She has spread the word all over London that you've promised a wedding for her son and Nicholas's sister that Society will talk about for years to come. In May, I believe?"

"My." Sarah blinked. "You are quite well informed."

"Yes, Lady Weston. That is *my* job, you see."

Nick growled. "Quit flirting with my wife, Kimball. I won't allow her to become involved in this."

Sarah's brows winged up. "Allow me? Did you just say allow me?"

"Aye."

Idiot, she said silently. Aloud she said, "What do you want me to do, Lord Kimball?"

"I thought perhaps you might host a party in honor of your friends from Texas. Either that, or another social event to which each of them can be invited. Perhaps an engagement ball for Charlotte. I would find it useful to observe the interaction between the men. We cannot be certain this plot involves but a single man."

"You can't be certain this plot even exits!" Nick snapped. He moved to stand behind her, laying a hand upon each shoulder. "I know you have a job to do, Kimball, but so do I. Mine is to protect the women in my family. I'll not have an investigation of this assassination plot tied in any manner to my sister's wedding festivities. I must insist you find another way to approach the problem."

Kimball arched a brow, and as the two men stared at one another, Sarah was reminded of a clash of Titans. Finally, the spymaster said, "Very well. Do you have any ideas to offer, Lord Weston?"

"Actually, I do." Nick folded his arms. "First, I want you to take that pup Willie Hart away from Glencoltran immediately after luncheon. My family and I will leave for London tomorrow, where the women will plan Charlotte's nuptials and I will investigate the trio of suspects—without involving my family."

"That's silly," Sarah protested. "You should at least allow me to introduce Trevor and the others to you. You'll have an instant rapport with them that way. They all like me."

Nick frowned at her, scowled at her, and glowered at her.

"It would save time," Kimball suggested. "Perhaps by half."

"Oh, all right. But only an introduction. No dances or picnics or intimate walks in the garden. We'll arrange an introduction in a public place, then you will make yourself scarce. Understand?"

"I understand." Whether she agreed to and accepted his shortsighted demand was something else entirely.

Sarah could hardly suppress a laugh as, deep inside her, excitement sizzled. *Just call me Secret Agent Sarah.*

Luncheon conversation revealed that Gillian's husband, Jake, was slightly acquainted with one of the suspects, the one who'd wanted Sarah, Trevor Chambers. Since the Delaneys and Robyn were scheduled to return to Rowanclere that afternoon, Kimball decided to travel part of the way with them and interview Jake about the man Nick had mentally pegged as Lord Lovesick.

Nick would have liked to corner Jake himself and

quiz him about the bounder, but at the moment, he had a more important matter than a possible plot against the queen that needed his attention. Robyn needed him.

He'd never known anyone who had such a difficult time saying good-bye as that girl. Every time they parted, be it for days or weeks or the occasional month that went by between visits, he made a point of spending an hour or two with her in play and reassurance. Even so, as the coach pulled away from Glencoltran Castle, his youngest sister leaned out the window and waved wildly as tears rolled down her face.

He gritted his teeth against the lump of emotion in his throat, then turned back toward the castle and caught the sympathetic looks on the faces of his wife and other sisters. "What are ye doing standing around? Dinna ye have wedding menus to make or something?"

The females, for once, knew better than to comment.

Nick spent the rest of the afternoon involved in estate business while the women packed and planned. Then, rather than joining them for dinner, he sent for a tray in his library and spent a few minutes thinking about how he wanted to approach his investigation. The first step was obvious. He'd meet with Tom Sheldon and do a bit of bargaining. The man Nick had known ten years ago would have sacrificed his right arm for the information Nick was prepared to give him. Could he have changed that much?

"We will see," Nick muttered as he buttered a roll.

While Nick ate his meal, he considered, then discarded, a dozen different approaches to the problem that had been placed before him. By the time he finished, he'd settled on a method of work. That done, he turned to dessert and a much more intriguing mental exercise. As the taste of cherry pie exploded on his tongue, Nick contemplated the first move in his plan to seduce his wife.

Should he wait until they arrived in London as originally intended or should he begin tonight? After learning about Lord Lovesick, he was inclined to make his first move now. Despite improvements in transportation in recent years, the trip south was still long and tedious. Why not give her something to think about along the way?

With that, Nick opened the leather-bound journal and picked up his pen.

Sarah's mind whirled from the events of the day as she made her way up to her room that evening after a particularly cutthroat game of cards with Aurora that stretched long past the usual time to retire. She'd been in no hurry to go to bed; she doubted she'd get any sleep at all. To think she might be acquainted with a terrorist, one who wrote poetry or painted lovely landscapes. Or had kissed her.

"No," she murmured, refusing to believe it. Trevor wouldn't plan something so horrible. He wouldn't. Maybe he had spoken bitterly of his family a time or two, and he did upon occasion rail against the political system and inheritance laws of England, but she'd never sensed wickedness in the man. Lust, yes, but not evil. Never that.

Now, Mr. Sheldon was another matter. He'd been quite outspoken about his resentment of his father. And he'd been the singularly most unhappy man she'd ever encountered. She could almost see him sinking into such a black malaise that he'd contemplate such villainy, but to actually go through with it?

She shook her head. She simply couldn't see it. And what about Mr. Endicott? He was a quiet, pleasant man who composed clever musical ditties—not someone she'd suspect of harboring the kind of hate such an act would require.

Probably the entire thing was a hoax. She didn't recall a Judge Boyette from any social events in Fort Worth. The man likely didn't even exist.

Upon entering her room, she consciously dragged her thoughts away from plots and directed it toward plans. Charlotte had finally settled on a theme for the engagement ball—turtledoves and hearts—and Sarah wanted to think of a way to repeat it in the wedding events. It could be something as subtle as color, she thought. However, considering the promise she'd made to Lady Pratt, she thought boldness more in order.

Sarah was so busy mulling over possibilities as she prepared for bed that she didn't notice the book lying on her pillow until she went to crawl between the sheets. It was bound in rich burgundy leather and gilded with scrollwork. She found no sign of a title on either cover or spine.

Sitting cross-legged on her bed, Sarah rested the book in her lap. The leather was softer than on any book she'd ever held, and as she traced the golden loops and swirls with her finger, she was somewhat reluctant to open it. Not because she dreaded to discover what was inside, but because she sensed it was something special. Something to be savored. Something important.

Her touch was almost reverent as she slowly opened the book and turned to the title page. Even before she read the words, she recognized Nick's handwriting. Her pulse tripped faster as she read aloud, "Sarah's Pillow Book."

Pillow Book? What's a Pillow Book?

Wetting her suddenly dry lips, she flipped the page.

My dearest Sarah,

Amidst all the chaos of today, my mind has returned time and again to our morning conversation, and the fact that the letters we have exchanged over the years have apparently meant as much to you as they have to me. Despite our physical proximity, I feel distant from you now. I miss that sense of intimacy the act of sitting down to write you provided.

I want to be intimate with you, Sarah.

So I will write to you. Will you read what I have to say? Will you allow me into your mind? Will you open this journal each night and take my words inside you? I will be satisfied with that. For now.

I wish no letters in return. Indeed, if you write, I will not read. I intend to be selfish about it, you see. Nor will I discuss my letters with you. What I have to say is not for the light of day. These are words for nighttime, for candlelight. For dreaming.

Ah, dreams. Do you dream, my darling lass? As you lay your head upon your pillow and snuggle deep into the covers to ward off the winter's chill, of what do you dream? Is it of peppermints and parasols? Laughter in a schoolroom, or the tangy scent of cedar on a campfire on a starlit summer night?

I'll tell you of my dreams.

I dream of you.

Every night as I lay down, I close my eyes and think of you. It's true. It's always you, and it's always something different. You offer me such a delicious variety from which to choose.

Last night, I dreamed of your hair. Unbound. Soft as the finest silks of the Orient. Brilliant as a chest of old gold against a sunset on the sea of sand of a Persian desert. Thick as a sumptuous cloak that could keep a man warm forever.

I dreamed it was a waterfall flowing over my skin. My bare, naked flesh. I wanted to drown in it. I want to drown in you.

It was a captivating dream, Sarah. An alluring fantasy.

Tonight, I believe I'll dream of your eyes.

So, lass, what will you dream of this night? Will you tuck this book beneath your pillow and dream of me?

I hope so. Because I'll be dreaming of you.

Nick

Sarah realized her hands were trembling as she finished reading the letter. She snapped the book shut, then tossed it down as if it had burned her. But then, it *had* burned her, hadn't it? From the inside out?

"Oh my," she breathed. "Oh my oh my oh my."

She brought both hands to her face and felt the heat of her cheeks beneath her fingertips as she repeated, "Oh my oh my oh my."

The book—the Pillow Book, he'd called it—lay like a burgundy-and-gold serpent coiled on her bed. For a long minute she stared at it, her heart beating at double time. She licked her dry lips, then slowly reached out and, with finger and thumb, opened it once again.

I want to be intimate with you, Sarah.

She closed her eyes. Swallowed hard. Peeked through her lashes.

I want to drown in you.

Slammed the book shut.

"Oh my oh my oh my." What was the man trying to do?

"Oh, come now, Sarah," she muttered to herself. "That's obvious even to you, isn't it?"

The Pillow Book was a forthright declaration of intention on Nick's part, simple and not at all pure. He was out to seduce her, never mind the annulment. He wanted marriage. He'd said that before. He wanted marriage and children, a home and family.

Apparently, he wanted these things with her.

The woman in Sarah couldn't help but wrinkle her nose and sniff. "So there, Lady Steele."

But nothing had changed since she'd signed the petition. She still didn't want to give up her home, her friends, her comfortable life. Nick could just write letters until his hand cramped. It wouldn't make a difference. After all, she didn't even like sex!

She glared at the book. Darned if in her mind's eye she didn't see indigo ink on a parchment page.

...flowing over my skin. My bare, naked flesh.

At the precise moment she whimpered aloud, a knock sounded on the door. "Sarah?" Charlotte called. "Are you still awake? May I come in?"

Sarah lunged for the book, shoved it beneath her pillow, and propped herself against it. "Yes. All right. Come in."

The door cracked open and Nick's sister peered

around it. "Sarah? I've decided I don't like the turtle-dove theme for the engagement ball after all."

Sarah smiled brightly and tried to look comfortable. She didn't know how well she'd succeeded; any minute now her pillow was liable to start smoking. Thankfully, Charlotte didn't seem to notice, wrapped up in her thoughts and plans as she was.

"I'm so sorry, Sarah. I know I'm causing you a terrible amount of work by changing my mind what? Six times now?

"Seven."

"Seven, then." Charlotte crossed the room and sank onto the foot of the bed. Worry dimmed the sapphire eyes that Sarah found hauntingly similar to Nick's. "Maybe I shouldn't try to be so original with my wedding plans. After all, I certainly had an original wedding last time, didn't I? Maybe we should have a small, quiet ceremony and forget about Lady Pratt."

Sarah patted her knee. "Honey, I'm afraid forgetting Lady Pratt is not an option. Not unless you and Rodney decide to move to America or Australia or somewhere far away. In fact, that would no doubt be worse. She'd come to visit and stay six months."

Charlotte groaned and buried her face in her hands. "That would be horrible. You're right. We need a spectacular event. But not turtledoves, Sarah. Not my favorite colors or faraway places or any of the other things I chose before. Not parasols and peppermints, either."

Sarah choked and covered it with a cough. "Parasols and peppermints?"

Charlotte nodded. "Nick suggested it."

"Oh." At that, she'd have sworn she felt the book beneath her pillow vibrate. Sarah wriggled around a bit, trying to get comfortable again. "Well, parasols and peppermints sound nice, but another thought occurs to me. Recall that I told you about how superstitious the citizens of Fort Worth are and about how love transformed Jenny McBride's Bad Luck Wedding Dress into the Good Luck Wedding Dress? And how Claire McBride's Magical Wedding Cakes have the reputation of bringing good luck to marriages?"

"I remember."

"Well, since Jenny and Claire will certainly be here for your wedding, why don't we capitalize on that? Cultures all across the world have wedding customs and beliefs that symbolize good luck. That could be your theme. After all, you've told me you consider yourself the luckiest bride in the world to be marrying your Rodney, and from seeing the two of you together, I am certain he feels just as lucky."

"A Good Luck Wedding Day," Charlotte said. She thought about it a moment, then clapped her hands. "I love it! Oh, Sarah, I think this one is it. It's the first one that feels just right."

"I see one problem. If we use luck as our theme, you'll need to change the wedding date, because the saying goes: 'Marry in the month of May, You will surely rue the day.' We'll need to either move it forward to April and get to work fast, or push it back until after the jubilee."

"Oh. I don't want to wait. Besides, isn't April supposed to be a lucky month to marry?"

Sarah smiled and quoted, " 'Marry in April when you can, Joy for maiden and for man.' "

"April it is, then. What day in April?"

"We'll look at a calendar tomorrow, but I should think a Wednesday. That rhyme says 'Wed on Wednesday, luckiest day of all.' "

"A Wednesday in April. It sounds glorious." Then the ordinarily shy and demure Charlotte dove at Sarah, threw her arms around her, and gave her an exuberant hug. "It's perfect. Thank you. Oh, thank you so much."

Sarah couldn't help but smile. They launched into a discussion about good luck bridal tokens. They discussed Charlotte's wearing her grandmother's pearls and the possibility of using horseshoes in the decorations. The debate over which lucky floral choice to use—orange blossoms or ivy and white heather—lasted for quite some time. As a result, when Sarah reached back to plump her pillow, she forgot about the hot little bomb that lay beneath it and managed to scoot the Pillow Book right off the bed.

Charlotte reached down and picked it up, asking, "What's this? Is it your wedding design book?"

"No," Sarah replied, her smile going sickly as she firmly repossessed the book from her sister-in-law and tucked it back beneath her pillow. Her fingers almost burned to touch it, and when she turned back to Charlotte, her mind swirled with a nerve-wracking mixture of Nick, seduction, and good luck bridal tokens.

She blurted out. "We'll use orange blossoms *and* ivy and white heather. We'll get a white fur rug for you to stand on. We'll ask Rodney to wear odd socks for the ceremony and to pay the minister an odd amount of money for his fee. I'll make certain someone gives you a broom as a gift. And salt and pepper shakers. Lots of salt and pepper shakers. We'll have a hen ready to walk into the wedding breakfast and hope she cackles, and we'll drive a black cat in front of you as you leave the church. Another thing we can do—"

"Sarah?"

"—is ask all the wedding gifts to be wrapped in red and white."

"Sarah!"

"Yes?"

"Are you all right? What has you so flustered?"

Sarah tugged at her lower lip, then tried another smile. Judging by Charlotte's reaction, it was even less successful than the earlier one. "Bridal customs. Good luck tokens. That's what I'm thinking of. As your professional wedding designer, I think you should have as many good luck bridal tokens as we can manage during your bridal day."

She'd use anything and everything she could imagine that might help Charlotte avoid a Bad Luck Wedding Night.

It's bad luck to purchase a wedding ring on Friday.

~12~

London

Seated at his desk in his Berkeley Square townhouse study, Nick reviewed his correspondence. It was times like this that made him yearn for the old clandestine days. He truly despised paperwork. Over the course of two hours, he answered letters and authorized payments and handled a myriad of other details required of the Marquess of Weston. All the while, he listened with half an ear for sounds of the women's return.

On this, their first full day in London, Sarah and the girls spent the entire morning on a shopping expedition. Nick had not anticipated their early departure, and as a result, he'd missed the opportunity to see his wife that morning.

In truth, he missed her, period. He'd had little contact and absolutely no private time with her since leaving Glencoltran. Sarah, he had learned, was not a good traveler. The constant sway of coach and railcar gave the poor woman a severe case of motion sickness.

It was no wonder she so bitterly resented being forced to make the trip from Texas. The voyage, then the overland journey from Scotland, must have been pure hell for her. However, bastard that he was, Nick couldn't find it in himself to feel too sorry he'd made her suffer, since it had brought her to him. Also, the certainty of mal de mer would make it difficult for her to look forward to a return trip to Texas.

Grinning, Nick set down his pen, propped his feet on his desk, and laced his fingers behind his head. All in all, matters were falling into place. He had sent word around to the house in Tavistock Square that he would call later this afternoon. He'd received answers to his queries about where Tom Sheldon had rented rooms, and most delightful of all, he had Sarah right where he wanted her.

Well, closer to where he wanted her, anyway. She wasn't in his bed, but she was installed in the master suite at Weston House, and since her chamber at Glencoltran had been in an entirely different wing, he considered it a fine improvement.

Now his task was to convince her to take the next step and join him in his bed.

Mentally, he began to compose the second letter for her Pillow Book, the entry he intended to make this evening. Words for the next planned target of his attention—her eyes—came quickly, so before long he'd skipped to later entries. Number fourteen, he thought was particularly interesting.

So lost was he in his fantasy that he neglected to listen for the women. As a result, the knock at the door caught him by surprise, and he still had his feet on his desk when Sarah barged into the room without a by-your-leave.

"Working hard, I see," she observed.

Absorbed as he was in the moment, Nick couldn't help but allow his gaze to wander below her tiny waist and the inviting sway of her nicely rounded hips as she approached. Luckily, she didn't notice.

"Thank goodness you agreed to bring the girls to London before the beginning of the Season," she told him, taking a seat in the upholstered armchair on the opposite side of the desk. "One day in town and it is quite clear to me that I need a bit of education, or I'll end up hurting Charlotte instead of helping her. You know, Nick, I have dined with governors and senators and captains of industry without a misstep, but a morning at the milliner's is enough to show me I am out of my depth."

As Nick returned his feet to the floor and sat up straight in his chair, he decided the glow in those whisky eyes of hers was as intoxicating as a fine Speyside malt. *I'll have to remember that line for the Pillow Book,* he told himself before replying. "You out of your depth? I don't believe it. Not after seeing the magic you worked with Lady Pratt."

"Magic? Hardly. I'm afraid London's ladies definitely caught me without my wand today."

Nick chuckled at her dry tone. Sarah shook her head in amazement. "You should have seen it, Nick. We walked into Madame Valentine Meurice's pied-à-terre in Mount Street, and within a minute the gossips had swarmed like yellow jackets. I was shocked, and the girls were taken aback by it. Even Aurora."

After a moment's pause, during which her invitingly plump lips pursed, she got to the reason behind her invasion of his study. "A Mrs. Wallingford was most illuminating. She informed me that despite a few hints you have given in the past, most people in Society believed you to be a bachelor. Then Lady

Pratt came to town and spread the word of my existence and arrival at Glencoltran."

He nodded. "I expected she would do that."

Sarah visibly braced herself, then said, "I think you should know . . . well, the girls were standing there and I'm not much of a liar and . . . well . . . I told the truth to the London ladies."

"Which truth?"

She rolled her eyes in frustration. "About why I'm here."

"Charlotte's wedding?" he responded, choosing to be obtuse.

"The annulment!"

Keeping his manner offhand, he murmured, "Oh, that."

She stared at him, her lovely eyes wide, shocked into silence. Nick wished he had that kind of luck with his sisters.

Finally, she spoke in a strangled tone. *"Oh, that? Really, Lord Weston. Is the state of our marriage of such little consequence to you that it rates only an 'Oh, that?' "*

"You misunderstand." Standing, he extended his hand. "Come for a walk in the garden with me and allow me to explain, lass. The sun is shining, and I've a desire for fresh air after a morning at my desk."

"If that's the case, you'll need to go farther than your garden," she grumbled as she rose. "This is the smelliest city I've every visited."

Nick grabbed her hand, rolled a squeaky-caster chair out of the way, then tugged her toward the french window that led out into the small garden behind the townhouse. He kept her close as he turned the latch and pushed open the door.

Cool air brushed his face, but whether it smelled

or not he couldn't tell. His senses were wrapped up in Sarah's fresh, clean scent. He wanted to bury his face in her hair, to nuzzle her neck and other interesting places.

Patience, man, he told himself. In formulating his seduction plan, he'd decided to make at least five Pillow Book entries before attempting anything more than a casual touch.

Still, he couldn't quite stop himself from leaning closer and inhaling deeply. When she flicked her gaze up and caught him at it, he schooled his expression into one of perfect innocence. "You have a good point about London air."

She shot him a suspicious glower and Nick smothered a grin. Vexation looked good on his wife. It put sparkle in her eyes and a glow on her skin and starch in her spine that challenged a man, made him want to bend her to his will. Nick was smart enough to keep that particular observation to himself.

He led her past a sundial toward the gurgling marble fountain at the center of the garden. He dug in his pocket and pulled out a handful of coins. Offering her half of them, he took a seat on an iron-and-wood bench, motioned for her to join him, and began flicking the coins toward the fountain one by one. "Our annulment petition will be a matter of public record, Sarah. People are bound to find out about it. I never expected otherwise. However, the legal step we have put into motion is not a divorce. It won't be a social liability to either you or the girls, so I see no reason not to be up-front about it."

"Me, either," Sarah said, nodding in agreement even as suspicion filtered through her voice. "However, I'm surprised to hear you say it. Our marriage is our private business."

"We'd like to think so, but the truth is, nothing is private in Society." He showed her how to hold the coin to improve loft, then added, "Indeed, I'm tired of it, Sarah. For years my life was nothing but falsehoods, deceptions, and subterfuge. My patience for such business has worn thin. Therefore, unless I'm offered a compelling need for lies and secrecy—such as our investigation into this bombing plot—I intend to be truthful in both word and deed. In *all* aspects of my life." He paused until she met his gaze, then added, "You can trust me on that."

Sarah shot a shilling at the fish spewing water. "Can I?"

"Aye, lass. Believe it."

She offered him a smile that was part wistful, part chiding, then changed the subject. "Who is Mrs. Wallingford? Everyone at Madame Meurice's treated her with deference."

Nick silently debated whether to allow her the conversational escape, then decided to let her have her way. For now. "She's Clarence Wallingford's wife. He's an M.P. from Stockton who has Salisbury's ear. She's no wallpaper wife like many politicians' spouses, and her influence is undeniable."

"Political influence?"

"Yes." A coin pinged off the fountain rim and fell back into the grass. Nick frowned at the miss.

"That's difficult to imagine. When she wasn't occupied by grilling me, she was busy vacillating over a choice between stuffed birds or butterflies for her new hat."

He gave Sarah a sidelong glance. "She settled on the birds, didn't she?"

"How did you know?"

"Mrs. Wallingford always wears birds."

"That's why Aurora rolled her eyes when I recommended the butterflies," Sarah said with a grin as her guinea flew into the marble fish's mouth. "See, it's just like I told you earlier. I'd best get some guidance or I'll end up harming your sisters instead of helping them."

"It would be my pleasure to serve as your instructor in any number of areas, my dear."

She shot him a narrow, suspicious look.

The picture of innocence, he offered her another coin. She gave him a long, judgmental stare before accepting it. As she took aim, Nick guilelessly continued. "I should help you to understand the overlapping social circles of the fashionable world before you gad about town to any great extent. Certainly before you attend your first function. In the case of Prince Edward's set, it's imperative. You are exactly the sort of woman who will appeal to that group, Sarah. You are beautiful, witty, accomplished, and most important of all, already wed."

She'd begun to preen from his compliments, but the last comment put a look of confusion in her eyes. "What do you mean?"

"In the eyes of the Marlborough House set, being married makes you eligible to become a mistress."

Her eyes rounded with alarm. "What?"

"Ordinarily, the fact you've yet to give me an heir would protect you, but I have . . . oh, let's call it a history . . . with a few of those men, and they'd likely take an unholy pleasure in the prospect of providing the seed for the fifth Marquess of Weston."

Now she bristled. "Why, I wouldn't—"

"Of course not," he said soothingly, and sent the last of his coins sailing, spinning toward the fountain. "But they don't know that, and they'll most certainly make a run at you. You'll find the waters easier to navigate if you learn ahead of time who are the porpoises and who are the sharks."

"Oh, I can recognize sharks, Lord Weston," she drawled, then made a show of looking for a dorsal fin on his back. As Nick laughed, she added, "Speaking of which, upon our arrival yesterday you neglected to give me something. I didn't realize it until last night."

"Calling cards." He nodded. "They should be delivered this morning. I apologize for the oversight."

"I'm not referring to calling cards. I'm speaking of the key to the door between our rooms."

"Oh."

She waited expectantly. When he failed to elaborate, she tried again. "You'll note I didn't make a fuss over the proximity of our chambers. I understand this is a townhouse and not a sprawling country house or castle and that chambers must be at a premium with your sisters in residence. The room itself is lovely, as are the mistress's dressing room and the sitting room you and I are to share. However, I do require privacy, Nick, so I want that key."

Inwardly, he winced. She obviously had yet to learn the floor above the master suite contained fourteen guest rooms. Maybe he'd get lucky and be away when she discovered that little fact.

Nick had expected a protest from her yesterday when she learned which room she'd been given. He should have known she wouldn't let it go unchallenged.

This particular request both surprised and intrigued him. Did she truly believe a locked door could keep a man of his skills and experience out if he wanted in? Or was she sending a message to him about the Pillow Book? Was it a test of some sort? Was she throwing down the gauntlet, so to speak?

He eyed her thoughtfully, noted the determination in her gaze. *Ah, yes.* There *was* a message in this request. Sarah had taken up the game.

It was all Nick could do not to let out a gleeful chortle. This was exactly what he'd hoped would happen when he chose to seduce his wife with the written word. He'd suspected that an outright, open seduction might frighten his virginal virago. The privacy of the Pillow Book was just the right approach.

Taking her hand, he played the gallant and pressed a courtly kiss to the back of her hand. "Of course, lass. I'll see that you have the key before tea."

Never let it be said Nick Ross shied away from gauntlets.

Standing outside her bedroom door that night after dinner, Sarah took a deep, bracing breath. Her heart was racing and her palms were damp. She felt bold and brazen and more than a little bit wicked. This evening before going downstairs to dinner, she'd tucked Nick's book beneath her pillow.

Sarah tested the doorknob. Locked.

Her stomach took a dive. He had not invaded her room to write in the Pillow Book.

"Well, good," she told herself as she slid the key into the lock, turned it, and heard the bolt release with a crisp snick. Except, she didn't feel that it was good. She felt . . . well . . . disappointed. That shamed her.

Sarah despised women who told a man they wanted one thing when in truth they hoped for another. How many times had she watched women utilize such dishonest, manipulative tactics and sworn she'd never do the same? How was a man to know what a woman truly desired if she lied about those desires all the time?

"But I'm not lying," she murmured as she fled into her room. She was confused. That was different. She honestly didn't know what she wanted.

Then she glanced at the bed and her heart leapt. *Well, maybe I do know part of what I want, anyway.*

The book lay propped against her pillow.

Her mouth immediately went dry. Maybe Nick had two keys to the lock. Maybe he didn't need a key at all. After all, the man had been an espionage agent. And hadn't she known that when she'd asked for the key? *You challenged him, Sarah.*

"What sort of game are you playing?" she asked herself.

It's not a game. It's a war. What you must decide is whether you want to win or to lose.

With no idea of the answer to that question, Sarah licked her lips, then reached for the Pillow Book, a thrill of anticipation humming through her veins.

My dearest Sarah,

    As I take up my pen to write, I wonder what thoughts flow through your mind on this, your first night in London. Are you thinking of the plans you have set in motion for Charlotte's wedding? Are you remembering those silly biddies you encountered in the hat shop this morning?

    Dare I hope you are thinking of me?

    I am thinking of you.

    I am dreaming of you.

    Daydreams. Night dreams. Of late, I have dreamed of your eyes.

So beautiful. Amber with flecks of gold. Autumn eyes. Whisky eyes. Siren eyes. They call to a man, beckon him to submerge himself in their intoxicating depths. I go gladly.

I am swept away, held spellbound by the many emotions I see swirling around me. Humor and wit. Intelligence. Compassion. Passion.

Passion.

Passion.

My blood catches fire.

Look into your dreams, lass. See me. See how I want you. Close your eyes and feel the touch of my lips against your temple, your brow. Your long, sable-soft lashes brush my mouth. Do they tickle me? Tease me? Please me?

Please. Let me please you.

Tonight, I believe I'll dream of your mouth.

Until next time,
Nick

"Do *you* think they are engaging in the Sport of Venus?" Aurora asked Melanie the following afternoon, watching from the upstairs bedroom as their brother left the house, whistling. "I don't. Nicholas doesn't have that heavy-lidded, relaxed look that Jake Delaney so often has following a night with Gillian. Nicholas looks . . . tense."

"You may be right." Melanie turned away from the window and faced her sister. "I don't know what is wrong with him. Charlotte said she was up late last night and overheard him telling his valet he'd be at either Brooks or the Turf Club in case one of us needed him. Why, I ask you, is he playing at being a man-about-town instead of staying at home and wooing his wife?"

"It's a sad thing," Aurora agreed, answering a knock at her bedchamber door. Charlotte swept into the room and took a seat at the dressing table. Aurora continued, "I had such hopes when Nicholas installed Sarah in the master suite. But then she tells all of London that they're annulling the marriage, and as if that weren't enough, you'll never guess what Hermione Lassiter whispered in my ear at Madame Meurice's yesterday."

"What's that?" asked Charlotte as she set about experimenting with different hairstyles.

"She said she overheard her mother tell her father she saw Nicholas walking with Lady Steele along Rotten Row the day we arrived from Scotland."

Charlotte dropped her hairbrush. "No!"

"That's what she said."

Aurora tapped her lips with an index finger. "Maybe that's a good sign. Maybe he was telling Horrible Helen he couldn't see her anymore."

Melanie sank into a chair. "Or maybe he was telling her to be patient, that the annulment was in the works and that they could be together soon."

The three young women shared a sigh at that idea. Then Aurora said, "I don't believe that. Nicholas wants to keep Sarah. I know he feels desire for her. Some of the looks he gives her all but set the carpets afire."

"Then why hasn't he seduced her?"

"Maybe he has and they are being discreet. I've seen Sarah look his way a time or two, also. She's not immune to him, I tell you."

They mulled that over a few moments before Charlotte shook her head. "No, I don't think that's it. Melanie, you're not the only person who has heard some disturbing news. Yesterday, Sarah told me she still plans to return to Texas after my wedding."

"Oh, no," Aurora groaned. "I was afraid of that. And if she returns to Texas that means she won't stay married to Nicholas, and he won't seduce her because it would risk our being tainted by the scandal of divorce. It also means that walk with Lady Steele might have meant exactly what we're most afraid it meant."

Melanie winced. "I'll move to Texas with Sarah before I'll tolerate Horrible Helen as a sister-in-law."

"I'll go with you." Aurora shuddered.

"Well, I can't go because I'm marrying Rodney," Charlotte pointed out. "And since I don't want you two to go, we just need to come up with a different solution. We obviously cannot count on Nicholas to solve the problem properly."

For the next few minutes, the three sisters debated a dozen different responses to the day's revelations. They finally whittled the choices down to two. "Very well, then," Melanie said. "Which is it? Do we go to Sarah, tell her the whole sordid story, then enlist her help? Or, do we focus our attentions on Horrible Helen and do our best to convince her she would not be at all happy with us as sisters-in-law?"

"How would we do that?" Charlotte asked.

"Embarrass her." Aurora lifted a perfume bottle from the mirrored tray on Melanie's dressing table and sniffed. "Terribly. Publicly. Not something scandalous, but something prankish."

"Actually," Melanie said after pondering a moment. "I don't see why we can't do both. Sarah has told us she considers Nicholas her friend. Surely she'll want to protect him from the likes of Lady Steele. She may even have some fine ideas about an embarrassing joke to play."

"True." Aurora gestured toward a tortoiseshell

comb for Charlotte to try. "Although, I think I already have an idea about that. If you'd be willing to sacrifice for the cause, Charlotte, your engagement ball would be the perfect place to spawn a trick."

"You are right," Charlotte offered glumly. "Something in our own home would be much simpler to set in motion. However, I do not think we should take Sarah into our confidence. In telling her about Horrible Helen we run the risk that she will inform Nicholas what we're about."

Melanie shook her head. "I think that's a risk we must take. Here's what I think we should do. I think we should ask for Sarah's help in thwarting Nick's relationship with Lady Steele, but keep our idea about embarrassing the Ice Queen to ourselves. We have two weeks before the engagement ball. If Sarah can help us solve the problem by then, we won't need to do anything untoward at Charlotte's ball."

The sisters shared a look, then all three nodded. Aurora said, "It's settled then. Charlotte, why don't you address a ball invitation to Horrible Helen. I'll see if Sarah is willing to talk with us now."

"Now?" Charlotte grimaced. "This afternoon?"

"Why put it off? Besides, sister dear, as a bride-to-be you should keep in mind that old wedding superstition: Happy is the bride whose brother dumps his detested darling."

"Yes." Charlotte gave a madonna-like smile. "You know, I've always liked that one."

Nick had a bounce in his step and a song in his heart as he approached the tidy house in Tavistock Square. This was the second call he'd paid at the residence today, having been told by the housekeeper to return at this time because the party he'd come to call upon was out shopping.

He'd put the wait to good use, taking tea at his club and asking casual questions of fellow members about Sheldon, Endicott, and that rounder Trevor Chambers. Even the incident involving a clumsy, drunken baron, his gravy-laden plate, and Nick's trousers proved to be a boon. While he waited for the servant to return from Weston House with a change of clothes for him, Nick struck up a conversation with a baron who proved to be a player in the racing set. By the time Nick had donned clean trousers, he'd secured an invitation to watch an Arabian run during a racing club gathering the next week at the baron's country home. Other invited guests included Lord Robert Endicott.

All in all, it had been a good day's work, and now as he approached number 12, Tavistock Square, he looked forward to the reward he had dreamed of for years. Bounding up the front steps, he sounded the knocker. The housekeeper answered the door. "Hello again, Lord Weston."

"Is she home yet?" he asked.

"Yes, and she was delighted to learn you had come to call. She wanted to take advantage of the beautiful afternoon, so she is waiting for you in the park across the street. Do you have your key?"

"I do. Thank you, Mrs. Hansen." Then, after a moment's pause, he added, "I don't suppose you sent any of your scones with her?"

A smile wreathed the housekeeper's face. "Of course I did. I know you well enough by now after all these years, my lord. She has a basket with scones and your favorite strawberry jam."

Nick leaned over and kissed her cheek. "Mrs. Hansen, I love you. Run away with me."

She blushed and pushed familiarly at his shoulder. "Go on with you, scamp. They're waiting."

He chuckled all the way to the iron gate. Digging into his pocket, he removed his ring of keys and searched for the appropriate one. He didn't keep a key to her house, but he did have one for the park since they met there so often.

Metal groaned as the gate swung open, then shut with a clang, locking automatically behind him. He started down the graveled path, headed for the spot where they most often gathered. Soon, the music of children's laughter reached his ears. A smile broke across his face as a pair of towheaded youngsters ran shrieking across the path in front of him.

As usual, the boy was chasing the girl. The boy's height advantage worked against him as his sister darted under shrubs and around trees. Nick laughed softly as he watched young Millicent slow her flight just long enough to fling a bough in her brother's face. She reminded him so much of Aurora.

"That's it, Millie!" the boy shouted, increasing his speed. "Nothing will save you now."

Ever the knight in shining armor for ladies in distress, Nick cupped his hands over his mouth and called out, "I will save you, Millie."

The two children halted in their tracks. A wide grin split young Thomas's face, while Millie called out, "Papa Nick! Papa Nick! We've been waiting for you forever."

Nick knelt on one knee as they ran toward him, launching themselves into his arms. He hugged the children fiercely, then as Millicent started babbling in his ear about a recent spelling test score and Thomas reported on the collie pup that was the newest member of the family, Nick gazed over their shoulders and spied the dark-haired woman clucking her tongue in feigned exasperation. "Hello, love."

"Hello, Nick. We've missed you."

"And I've missed you, too," he said as he gave the children one more squeeze, then stood. Glancing down at the children, he said, "Mrs. Hansen told me she sent treats. Would you bring them to us at the park bench beside the fountain, please?"

"Sure, Papa Nick," the boy said.

"I'll race you, Thomas," Millicent added, taking off. "We'll be right back."

Nick waited until the children were out of earshot, then he took the woman's hands in his, leaned over, and placed a tender kiss upon her cheek. "I have news, sweetheart. Good news. Wonderful news, in fact."

Worry dimmed the beauty's eyes. "About your annulment? About Sarah?"

"Aye, I have tidings on that front, too, but that is not why I am here. Susan . . ." he cupped her face in his hands and stared deeply into her eyes, allowing her to see his pleasure in what he had to convey. Softly, he said, "I've found him, Susan. I've found Tom."

She went still, and her voice croaked. "Tom?"

"Aye. He is alive and well, and he has never married. And Susan, he's here. Here in London."

Susan Harris gasped and pulled from his grasp, taking an inadvertent step backward. She brought her hands up to her chest, clasped them. "Tom is in London?"

Nick nodded. "If you want, I'll send him to you tonight."

"Tonight? Oh, Nick. Tonight?"

His grin broke like sunshine after a storm. "The moment he arrives at his rooms."

"Oh, Nick. Thank you. Thank you. Oh, Nick!" Laughing, she threw herself into his arms. His laughter joined hers as he lifted off the ground and twirled her around. She placed grateful kisses on his brow, his cheeks, his lips. "You are so wonderful. So dear. I love you, love you, love you!"

"I love you, too, sweetheart," he replied as he set her feet back on the ground. "I love all of you, and I'm so happy to finally make this particular report."

At that point and in the incomprehensible way of females reacting to good news, Susan burst into tears. She threw herself into his arms and sobbed against his coat. Nick held her, smiling, shaking his head.

That's when he spied Sarah.

The number thirteen brings a bride bad luck.

~14~

"Papa Nick! Papa Nick!"

As the children's cries echoed on the warm, gentle breeze, Sarah felt her heart begin to break. She stood outside the garden gate and watched the pair of children greet Nick like a returning hero, a returning . . . father. Then Sarah heard her husband call Susan Harris "love."

She watched them touch, speak soft, intimate words, and embrace. She watched Nick lift Susan Harris and twirl her around. Laughing. She watched the other woman kiss Nick's mouth, then heard her declare her love.

Sarah swayed on her feet and grasped a cold iron fence rail for support when Nick voiced his love for Susan in return. It was more than she could bear. It was a nightmare. She'd had no idea he could hurt her this badly.

Again.

Then Nick looked around and saw her. Their gazes met and held.

Like Texas heat on an August afternoon, emotion rolled off her husband in waves. But where Sarah expected to see guilt, she spied frustration, indignation, righteousness. And expectation. Silently making demands upon her.

The children returned, carrying a basket and a blanket, and Nick released both his hold on Susan Harris and his lock on Sarah's gaze. Nick and Susan both turned their attention to the children. Obviously siblings, the pair shared blue eyes, a slender frame, and smiles that lit their faces. Judging from the difference in their height, Sarah guessed the boy to be only a year or so older than his sister. He'd be nine, she realized, this handsome child whom Susan had been carrying when she left Fort Worth. Idly, Sarah wondered if he'd been named for his father.

Her gaze shifted to the girl who now gazed worshipfully up at Nick. He reached down and pulled her braid and in doing so, tugged Sarah's heartstrings until they hurt. "Oh, Nick."

She tried to turn away, to flee, but her feet wouldn't move, not even when her husband spoke to the girl, gestured toward Sarah and then the garden gate. As if from a great distance, she watched the girl skip to the gate, turn the latch, and push it open.

"Please come in, ma'am," the girl called. "My Papa Nick says he wants to introduce us."

He wouldn't be so cruel, would he? Sarah looked up, found her husband staring at her, his blue eyes bright with challenge. She worked to find both her voice and the strength to move. "I can't," she said to the child, backing away from the fence. "I'm sorry, I can't." She turned around and started to hurry away. Away from the park, away from her husband, away from her past and unacknowledged dreams of the future.

Then he stopped her with a word. "Don't."

Her breath came shallow and fast as if she had run a mile. She remained frozen in place, even when she heard his footsteps approach.

Nick said, "You drive me crazy, woman. Worse than all my sisters—all six of them—lumped together. I want you to turn around and come meet the children and speak with Susan. She'll have some questions for you about Fort Worth."

Finally, she found her voice. "You want me to talk to her?"

"I *expect* you to talk to her. Have some faith in me, Sarah. I think it's about time."

Seconds dragged out and felt like minutes. Hours, even. And during that silent passage of time she heard the echo of his voice from long ago. *I'm not that baby's father.*

I believe him. She believed in him. In the very marrow of her bones, Sarah knew that Nick was not the father of those children, and as she closed her eyes and absorbed the truth, the ice around her heart cracked and slowly began to melt.

"Sarah?"

He was asking her to have faith in him. Faith in him as a man, a friend, a husband.

She turned around. He was tall and handsome and oh so annoyed. Fiercely annoyed.

It made her want to smile. In that moment, as the vise around her heart eased and the lump in her throat dissipated, she realized she'd *never* lost faith in him. Not on that awful wedding night, and not the following morning when he left her.

What Sarah had lost was her courage.

It was true. When the moment of truth arrived, she'd been afraid—of lovemaking, of leaving home and family and friends, of being a wife.

She'd been much better at being a bride.

"Sarah!"

She cleared her throat and said, "By all means, Lord Weston, introduce me to Susan's children. They appear to be quite delightful."

He shot her a hard look, then visibly relaxed, although the dare in his look didn't entirely fade. "Actually, they're scamps. Lovable, but constant trouble. They keep Susan busy from dawn till dusk."

He extended his elbow and waited for her to take it, then escorted her to the park bench where Susan Harris now sat making an obvious effort not to eavesdrop. "Sarah, you remember my friend Susan."

Sarah nodded. "I do. Hello, Miss Harris. It is nice to see you again."

"Welcome to England, Lady Weston. May I introduce you to my children, Thomas and Millicent Sheldon?"

"Hello Thomas, Millicent. It's very nice to meet yo . . ." Sarah's voice faltered as the import of Susan's words filtered through her brain. Sheldon. As in Tom Sheldon?

Nick watched her with a knowing look. "Their father is an old friend of mine."

"Oh, I see." But of course, she didn't.

Susan took pity on her and, after sending the children to the basket to get their treat, explained. "Tom and I married secretly shortly before he left Fort Worth. He signed on with a cattle drive with the intention of making enough to give us a start, and that was the last I saw of him. I thought he'd died."

She turned a luminous, grateful gaze upon Nick.

"Until a few moments ago, I still believed that. What I don't know is what happened to keep him away from us. It must have been something horrible."

Sarah recalled her reaction to Tom Sheldon upon his return to Fort Worth. He'd been a bear with a thorn in his paw—and money in his pockets. She hadn't liked him at all. Considering the uncomfortable questions he'd asked, it was a natural reaction on her part. She had a vivid recollection of the morning he'd knocked on her front door and made sharp inquiries about events Sarah had spent years trying to forget. "He asked about you."

"He did?"

Sarah nodded. "He'd heard you'd left town with my husband and he wanted details."

"What did you tell him?" Nick asked.

"Not much. All I knew was that Susan had boarded the train with Nick."

Nick's gaze followed the path of a sparrow flying from a lamppost to a winter-bare tree. "You never asked about her in your letters."

She looked away and admitted, "I didn't want to know. I didn't want to think about it."

"You didn't believe me when I said I wasn't her child's father."

"Children," Susan hastened to correct. "You're not my children's father, Lord Weston." To Sarah she said, "They're twins."

Twins. Oh, of course. That explained it. Sarah's gaze found the two youngsters now seated on a blanket chomping happily on scones. "Now I understand Mr. Sheldon's ire. He knew he'd lost his family."

"But why?" Bewilderment filled Susan's expression. "Where was he, and why didn't he come back to us?"

"I don't know, but I intend to find out. First, I need to be certain you want me to tell him how to find you. Do I have your permission?"

Susan nodded. "But I want to go with you, Nick. Now. I want to see him now."

"Let me approach him first," Nick said, taking his friend's hand and giving it a comforting squeeze. "It's important that I see his reaction."

"Why?"

Nick looked from Susan to the children, then back to their mother. "Trust me?"

"Of course."

Susan said it so quickly that Sarah knew a twinge of shame—until Nick shot her a smug look, that is. Then she reminded herself that whatever her own failings in the matter of their marriage, Nick was far from blameless. Her fear may have been the major stumbling block between them, but his pride had been a problem, too.

He could have told her the entire truth about Tom Sheldon and Susan Harris. Sarah still didn't understand why he'd played the hero for Susan without explaining the entire matter to his own wife.

Once Susan and the children retreated to their townhouse, leaving Sarah and Nick alone in the small park, Sarah posed the question. Nick answered with aplomb. "Ten years ago I was stupid. I expected blind faith from my bride."

"You still expect that."

"True. But you know me better now, so it's an educated blind faith."

The statement was so ridiculous that it startled a laugh from Sarah. Distracted, she was anything but prepared when he leaned over and kissed her.

The first one was quick and hard, an unconsidered

afterthought. But even as he drew back, Nick seemed to reevaluate. He leaned forward once again, a mesmerizing glint in his sapphire eyes. His breath fanned her lips, then he touched her mouth with his and gave her the gift of gentleness.

Satin-soft and sweet with the taste of Scottish scones, his kiss transported her from the winter-weary park to a world of rainbow colors, where sparkling sunshine heated tropical waters that slowed a woman's blood and caused her to sink into crystalline depths ruled by sensation.

Sarah's eyes drifted shut and her arms stole up to wrap around his neck. Her limbs felt heavy and pliant, and she was vaguely aware he'd backed her against a tree. She moaned faintly. He hummed a groan in reply, then escalated the intensity of the kiss.

Now came the passion, the heat. Her lips parted as his tongue swept inside her mouth, stroked and played and plundered. He made her forget her fear, his folly. Forget everything but the hot fire of passion now flowing like lava through her veins.

Until he fitted his body against hers and she felt the evidence of his need like a hot brand against her skin. The long-buried memory of her mother's voice on a day long ago speared through the haze of pleasure numbing her mind. *He has a Rod of Steel. A Rod of Steel.*

In a flash, she was sixteen again and her fear reignited. Sarah's eyes snapped open and she broke the kiss, wrenching her head away. Her heart pounded and her breasts ached and her womb wept with need, and Sarah considered screaming in frustration.

Nick stepped back, narrowed eyes drilling her, and she felt as if he could see into her soul. She waited for him to mock her, to chastise her. Instead, he simply held out his hand. "Would you accompany me to pay a call on Tom?"

She blinked. The question was almost as surprising as the kiss. Almost. What happened to his protests about it being too dangerous for her to assist in uncovering the bombing plot? Whatever the reason for his change of heart, she wasn't about to question it. "Yes, Nick, I'd like that."

"Very well. Let's stop by his rooms on the way home, shall we? Susan has waited for him for ten years, and I'm of the opinion that is long enough. Entirely long enough."

As he escorted her from the park, her lips still tingling from the force of his kiss, Sarah suspected he was talking about more than Susan Sheldon's wait.

Nick prowled his bedchamber that evening and wondered if a man could die from acute sexual frustration. Probably not, but it could at least make him ill. Especially when the condition was combined with frustration of a general sort, and at the moment, he was filled with that, too.

Tom Sheldon had disappeared from London a little over a week ago. Nick had learned that disturbing piece of news after speaking with the manager at the Savoy earlier that afternoon, though he'd been reassured to learn that Sheldon had indicated he'd return within two weeks. A subsequent search of his rooms supported the claim. The framed pencil sketch of Susan on the beside table suggested that Tom would, indeed, be pleased to learn the news Nick had to share. Still, Nick could kick himself for not confirming Tom's current whereabouts before sharing the news with Susan. He truly did hate to make her wait.

Waiting was hell on a man. It made him itchy. What he needed was some good, strenuous exercise.

What he needed was sex. A long, lusty bout of sex. With Sarah. Strenuous, sensuous sex with Sarah. *Now that would put some spring in my step.*

Unfortunately, it wasn't in the cards for that night. Unfortunately, his plans for his wife for that evening would no doubt only increase his frustration.

But his strategy was sound. He needed to remember that.

Every part of him needed to remember that.

With that admonition, Nick entered the sitting room he shared with Sarah. The firmness that lingered in his trousers melted away at the sound of feminine giggles coming from his wife's chamber.

Nick grimaced. He knew that particular noise well. That was the giggle that Aurora and Melanie made when they were up to something and dragging poor Charlotte right into trouble with them. Finding the girls in his wife's room, making that sound, worried Nick more than just a little. Had they pulled Sarah into one of their schemes? Had the Terrible Trio convinced his blushing bride to make it a Fearsome Foursome?

"That's all I need," Nick grumbled as he rapped lightly on the door in warning, then stuck his head inside. "Is it safe to come in?"

They sat in the center of her bed, surrounding a tray of sweets and wearing milk mustaches. Nick developed a sudden and severe craving for the dairy product he'd never particularly enjoyed. Had Sarah been alone, he couldn't have resisted the urge to lick it off her.

She looked adorable, sitting cross-legged on her bed, dressed in a voluminous cotton nightgown that didn't show so much as a hint of skin. The dance of laughter in her eyes faded as he entered the room, and she scooted backward on the bed. Against her pillow. Then she blushed.

Nick's mood lightened considerably at that. The Pillow Book was obviously doing its work.

Aurora scrambled down from the bed and greeted him with a hug and a kiss on the cheek. "Hello, Nicholas. We were just off to bed. Weren't we, sisters?"

"Yes, we were," Melanie agreed. Charlotte only nodded.

While Nick folded his arms and frowned at the females, Melanie scooted off the bed, then reached for the tray. At the same time, Charlotte handed Sarah a notebook and pencil along with a significant look. Adopting an air of nonchalance, Sarah slipped the notebook beneath her pillow, then busied herself brushing cookie crumbs off the bedclothes.

Nick's curiosity, already aroused, notched up another inch or ten at the delicious sight of his impish angel of a wife slipping secrets beneath her pillow. "What mischief have you girls been up to?"

Aurora faced him boldly. Melanie tried to hide a grin, but the twinkle in her eyes gave her away. Charlotte stared over his shoulders. "Charlotte?" he asked the sweet, weakest link.

For a split second, she met his gaze. Guilt. Now he knew he was in trouble. "Why do I suddenly suspect I'd have been better off sleeping at my club? What have the four of you done?"

"Oh, don't be silly," Melanie said as she brushed past him. "We've been busy making preparations for Charlotte's engagement ball. We have so much yet to do, but it's going to be such a wonderful event. I suspect that by the time the night is through, this good luck theme will have brought us all good luck. Don't you, sisters?"

"I do," said Aurora as she sailed out the door with a wave. "Good night."

"Um, I agree," said Charlotte as she stood on her tiptoes to give her brother a good-night kiss on the cheek. "See you in the morning, Sarah."

"Good night, everyone," Sarah called after them. "See you *all* in the morning."

Her hint for him to leave was broad and unmistakable. Nick chose to ignore it. Despite the fact that she'd used a napkin to wipe her mouth, he couldn't banish the fantasy of taking a taste of any tiny drops of milk that might have lingered.

He wanted her with a fierceness that nearly knocked him to his knees. So as she pulled her bedcovers up to her chin like a nervous virgin, Nick couldn't stop himself from shrugging out of his coat and tossing it over the back of the settee in front of the fireplace. Casually, he slipped the studs from his cuffs, tossed them atop the jacket, then rolled up his sleeves as he crossed the room to her bed. "So, Sarah, what's beneath your pillow?"

The woman went white as the sheet beneath her. She slapped back against her pillow, presenting more challenge than a secret service agent could resist. He slipped his hand behind her.

She pressed all of her weight against the pillow. "Excuse me, this is not your—"

He tugged from beneath her not the notepad she undoubtedly expected, but the true object of his search. The Pillow Book. "It's late and we both should be getting to sleep. Shall I read you a bedtime story, Sarah?"

Her gaze focused on the leather-bound volume in

his hand, her eyes wide and swimming with a combination of shock and . . . was it fascination? "You can't . . . you're not . . ."

Nick simply smiled.

She groaned and sank farther beneath her covers, the sheet pulled up to her chin. He tugged a chair up next to the bed, sat with the book in his lap, and pulled off his shoes. Then, propping his stocking feet at the foot of the mattress, he settled back against the chair, opened the book, and flipped through the pages to the last entry, the tenth. Some days he found himself inspired to write more than one.

Had she already read the letter he'd left her tonight, or had she saved it to read right before sleep? He suspected she saved it, but that didn't really matter. His letters were intended to be read over and over again.

His gaze skimmed over the words written on the page. He frowned slightly, then cleared his voice and began. "My dearest Sarah."

It's good luck for a bride to jump over a broom before entering her new home.

~15~

Sarah squeezed her eyes shut. She couldn't watch this. She couldn't believe this was happening, that he was actually *reading* those words, those secret, stirring words, aloud in his warm whisky voice. And since she had not read from the Pillow Book yet tonight, she didn't know what to expect.

Maybe he was just teasing. That was it. He would read the first line, just enough to worry her, then he would stop. It was just the sort of dirty trick Nick would like to play. He had to know she'd die of embarrassment, but he wouldn't care. Not Lord Weston. The man was not at all in her good graces at the moment.

Not since she'd learned from his sisters that she wasn't the only woman her husband had been romancing in a park of late.

She wondered if Lady Nickel had a Pillow Book, too. If so, Sarah thought she might cosh her husband over the head with hers.

"My dearest Sarah," he repeated, his voice a low, resonant rumble that skidded across her skin and made her shiver. "Do you realize how much I love to say your name? Sarah. My Sarah. It's a kiss to say. I hold it in my mouth, feel it on my tongue. Your name even tastes special—sweet and spicy, a flavor to crave."

Oh my. Sarah tried to hold onto her irritation, but she felt it give way to pure panic. He hadn't stopped after the first sentence. He was going to read the whole letter aloud. To her. And she was still flustered from the kiss in the park.

"I wonder, Sarah, is my name on your sweet, luscious lips also a kiss?"

She thought she might just burst into flames. Oh, my. She couldn't believe he'd do this.

"How does it taste?"

No, that wasn't true. She easily believed he'd do this. Nicholas, Lord Weston, would do anything he darn well pleased, and apparently tormenting her this way pleased him.

Maybe she'd be lucky. Last night he'd spent his entire letter on the sound of her laugh. If tonight's letter was all about her name, she might not melt away in embarrassment. Maybe. Perhaps.

"I have an idea. What I hope for, anyway. I want my name to be Rowanclere malt to you. I want it to flow over your tongue smooth and rich and full-bodied. I want it to light a fire deep within you, one that smolders, one that intoxicates."

It does. Heaven help me, it does. She tried to fight him, struggled to withstand this verbal assault as she waited on tenterhooks to hear what scandalous thing he'd say next.

Except, he didn't speak. Long, silent seconds

ticked by and the blasted man didn't say another word. Finally, unable to abide the wait a moment longer, she opened her eyes.

He was staring right at her. "I want to taste my name on your lips as you say it."

Trapped in the power of his gaze, the potency of his words, Sarah melted. She surrendered to the seductive warmth in his words and the knowing heat in his gaze. And as the last vestiges of resistance dissolved, a yearning like she'd never known before filled her. Bone deep and needy, it caught her unprepared. Frightened her.

She whipped the covers completely over her head.

He chuckled softly before continuing. "Your lips. I haven't told you this before, but I dream about your lips every night. I've been waiting to tell you, seeking the words. I fear I will never find ones to do them justice. I'm no poet, Sarah."

No poet? From her perspective, he could have taught Lord Byron a thing or two.

"I'm but a man with a man's needs and desires."

Sarah forced herself not to wriggle as she wanted to.

"I desire to have your mouth on mine. I need to feel the touch of your lips against my body. Everywhere. Long, lingering kisses. Soft, sweet suction. The nip of your teeth. The rough rasp of your tongue against my skin."

She clenched her teeth again a moan. She thought a whimper just might have slipped out. *Soft, sweet suction. Everywhere.* Heaven help her.

Yet she didn't want him to stop. She wanted to listen. Wanted to hear. It was exciting. Stimulating. It was oh, so wicked.

"So come to me and kiss me, Sarah. Come to me in my sleep, in my dreams. Night dreams. Daydreams. Any dreams. Come to me. Kiss me. Come to me."

Her mouth was as dry as week-old toast. Her heart pounded as she held her breath, waiting for him to continue, halfway expecting to feel his touch.

The moment dragged out. The room was silent. Nick was silent.

Sarah waited. And waited. And waited some more. Finally the anticipation grew too much. Stealthily she shifted the sheet and peeked. And blinked. She threw back the sheet and sat up.

Nick, the blighter, was gone. The Pillow Book lay on the empty seat of the chair. Sarah lunged for the volume and quickly stuffed it beneath her bedding. "Out of sight, out of mind," she told herself firmly.

She could have saved her breath. Nick's voice echoed through her mind, stirring her. Haunting her. Moments later, she pulled the book out and opened it. She wanted—no, she needed—to read this latest letter for herself. Maybe if she filled her eyes with the written word, she'd be able to banish the sound of his voice from her head.

She flipped to the last entry in the book and skimmed the first paragraph, expecting to read about her name. Instead, she blinked. Her mouth dropped open in shock.

Dearest Sarah,
Last night I dreamed of your breasts.

She dropped the book as if it had burned her and crossed her arms over her breasts. This was not the letter he'd just read. This wasn't about her name or his name.

Nick had written about her bosom.

"Oh my heavens." She covered her mouth with

her fingertips. Where was the other letter? Had he composed it in front of her?

I need to feel the touch of your lips. Come to me. Kiss me.

That's what he'd said. He'd written something else.

She felt the flush steal up her cheeks as her gaze stole to the Pillow Book. One particular sentence rose from the page like a beacon.

I want to take the rosy tip into my mouth and suckle it.

Vaguely Sarah heard herself moan. She didn't know what to do. She couldn't think. It was as if her mind had frozen, which was quite a paradox since her bedchamber had suddenly grown so *hot.*

She fanned herself with both hands as she stared down at the book. Once again, she heard the echo of his voice in her thoughts. *Come to me. Come to me. Come to me.*

Her hand darted out and flipped the Pillow Book shut in an attempt to quiet him. *Come to me. Come to me. Come to me.* Her pulse thrummed. Her breath came in shallow pants.

Her breasts ached.

"What are you doing to me, Nick?"

The answer came as clearly as if he had spoken it. *I'm seducing you.*

Sarah groaned, closed her eyes, and sank back onto her pillow. Seduction. Nick. Nick and seduction. Never mind that he had another woman on the string. Never mind that relations between them would ruin the possibility of annulment. Never mind that it would change her entire life. He wasn't letting the idea go away. Seduction. Nick. Sex.

Wasn't it just her bad luck that for the first time in

memory, Sarah wondered if she could bear giving sex a try.

Nick was lost in a steamily erotic dream when the cold bite of steel against his neck rudely yanked him from his slumber. "Sarah?" he asked groggily.

A rough male voice replied, "It says something about a man that his first thought upon realizing there's a knife at his neck is that a woman must be holding it."

Nick's thoughts cleared in an instant, and he tried to place the voice. It sounded faintly familiar, and he'd made plenty of enemies over the years. Who would be brazen enough, motivated enough, to break into the Marquess of Weston's home to assault him in his own bed?

The Afghan warlord Abdur Rahman came to mind, but the accent wasn't right. The accent was English, with an American twang.

"Where is she, you bloody bastard?"

In that moment he knew. Despite the fact that flexing his facial muscles caused the blade to slice thinly into his skin, he smiled. "Hello, Tom."

His old friend growled. "I've a fierce need to slit your throat, Nick Ross."

Nick imagined he did. He knew how he'd feel if Sarah left town with another man and disappeared from his life for a decade.

"But then maybe that's not the part I should be cutting on. Maybe I should slice off your balls instead."

"I'd rather you didn't. It's truly not necessary. If you'll step back and allow me a minute to light a lamp, I'll explain why and offer information I promise you will want to hear."

"Is it about my wife? Where is she? What have you—yeow!"

Whack. The knife fell away and clattered to the floor. *Whack whack whack . . . thud.*

As Tom Sheldon fell to the floor, Sarah's voice emerged from the darkness. "Nick, are you all right?"

"Sarah? What are you doing?"

"What does it look like I'm doing? I'm saving you from the burglar." She raised her voice to be heard over Tom's groan and added, "I heard him come in through the window. Get a rope or something so we can tie him. Hurry, Nick. We need light, too."

Nick was already reaching toward the bedside table, and seconds later the soft yellow glow of lamplight illuminated the room. Immediately, Sarah gasped. "Turn that off!"

"What?"

"You're naked!"

Nick sighed, then reached for his trousers. "I'm glad you noticed. What did you hit him with?"

"Oh, um, I just grabbed something handy," she said. Her hand nervously clutched at the neck of her dressing gown.

"A book," Tom Sheldon said from his seat on the floor where he nursed a lump on his head. "She pounded my head with a book."

Ah hah. The Pillow Book. Nick flashed his wife a grin. "Up late reading?"

She scowled at him as Nick extended a hand toward his old friend. "Get up, Tom, and properly greet my wife. Then I'll tell you of yours."

"Tom!" Sarah exclaimed, then took her first good look at her victim. "Mr. Sheldon! What were you doing sneaking into my bedroom?"

"Your bedroom? He went to yours first?" Nick shot a glare toward Sheldon. "You spied on my wife?"

"You ran off with mine." Sheldon made a fist and drew back his arm.

Nick released another heavy sigh, blocked Sheldon's punch, then knocked him back to the floor. "This is ridiculous. Get hold of yourself, man. You should be buying me a whisky rather than trying to lay me low. Now, Sarah and I are going into the sitting room and when you are prepared to listen quietly and speak calmly, you may join us."

Glancing toward his wife, he caught her staring at his chest. He considered donning a shirt, but quickly dismissed the idea. He'd learned to take advantage of situations presented him long ago. "After you, lass," he said graciously.

On the way out, she observed, "You spoke to him as if he were a child."

"It works on my sisters."

It worked on Tom Sheldon, too. More or less. He shuffled into the sitting room, then sat sullenly in a chair opposite the sofa where Sarah had taken a seat. Nick handed him a drink, eyed him closely and said, "So tell me about the bombing plot."

"What bombing plot?" Tom asked, scowling. Then his eyes widened and his brows winged up. "Is it Susan? Was she hurt? Is she all right?"

"She's fine," Sarah said, then to Nick added, "He *is* innocent, isn't he?"

"Aye. Of this plot, anyway."

"What plot, and what does it have to do with Susan?"

"Nothing." Then, finally having mercy on the man who had threatened his life a few short minutes ago,

Nick said, "Take a belt of whisky, Tom, and let me tell you about your twins."

All color drained from the man's face. "Twins?"

The exchange of stories took almost an hour and left Tom flabbergasted. Nick spoke first, relaying details of the scene in his honeymoon suite that long-ago morning, and how he'd escorted Susan to London and established her in a respectable home in a respectable neighborhood. He told Tom about the twins, about Susan's work as a contributor to women's presses, most recently the journal *Queen*, and how Susan never failed to ask if the investigator Nick had hired upon coming into his title and its wealth had discovered any news of her long-lost husband.

Tom had been ready to go to his wife then, but Nick had a few questions of his own before giving up the address of Susan's townhouse. At that point, Tom Sheldon admitted he'd spent most of the past ten years incarcerated in a Mexican prison. "Mexico?" Nick asked. "How did you set out for Kansas and end up in Mexico?"

It proved to be a long tale involving a fellow trail rider, the Mexican señorita he loved, the promise of financial reward for helping the star-crossed pair elope, and a powerful, vindictive father who solved the problem of his runaway daughter by concocting spurious charges and throwing Tom and his partner in jail.

"We rotted there for years until the old patrón died and the señorita's brother saw to our release. He gave us each gold—a lot of it—in order to soothe a guilty conscience, so I returned to Fort Worth a wealthy man." He paused a moment, then added in a voice ripe with pain, "I didn't expect Susan to wait for me all those years, not knowing if I was dead or alive. I hoped, but I didn't expect. When I learned that she'd left town with you so soon after I'd disappeared, I knew I had to find you."

"I've had people looking for you for a long time."

"What I don't understand is, why the lie? Why not tell her father we had secretly wed and that the child she carried was legitimate?"

Nick glanced at Sarah, then said, "Fear. She was young and afraid, and her father wanted a warm body to scream at. I was handy and I owed you both, so . . ." He shrugged. "Besides, your ceremony wasn't legal. I know Susan has always considered herself married to you, but she had no papers to prove it."

"She's my wife," Tom snapped. "We made vows to one another beside the Trinity River on the twenty-second of March in 1877. She's my wife!"

At that point Sarah, who had been quiet during the recitations, quoted, " 'Wed when March winds blow, joy and sorrow both you know.' Her house is in Tavistock Square. What number, Nick?"

Yes, she was right, Nick realized. Despite the early morning hour, the time had arrived for Tom to go to his family. In fact, this was an excellent time because the twins would sleep for a few hours yet, and Tom and Susan would have an opportunity for a private reunion.

They were the only married couple Nick knew who'd gone without sex longer than he and Sarah.

With that wry thought in mind, he stood. "Number twelve. Number twelve, Tavistock Square. Welcome home, Tom."

"Thank you." Distracted now, and obviously anxious, Tom shook Nick's hand and started for the door. Halfway there, he stopped and turned around.

"Thank you for taking care of them. You're a good man, Nick Ross."

Then Sarah looked at Nick with tears in her eyes. "You're a good man, Nick Ross. One of the best I've ever known."

Filled with the satisfaction of a job well done, Nick thought he'd see if he could extend his luck. "So do I get a reward?"

Cautiously she asked, "What do you want?"

As if you don't know. Nick was good at reading people, and what Sarah told him through her stance and expression was that he was in her good graces ... to a point. The long, lusty bout of lovemaking he craved wouldn't happen tonight. But maybe ...

"I want you beside me when I sleep. Just to sleep, nothing more. I promise. But I want to hold you, lass. Will you give me that gift?"

She eyed him suspiciously. "No monkey business?"

"I'll be a saint." When she sniffed and rolled her eyes, he quirked a grin. "All right, I'll promise to limit my sinning to thoughts alone. No actions. Trust me."

Though her mouth remained closed, her luminous eyes spoke volumes. She wanted to trust him, but she couldn't quite do it. Swallowing a sigh, he extended his hand. "Just tonight, Sarah. Trust me tonight."

Slowly she placed her hand in his.

A short time later, Nick drifted toward sleep with a smile on his face. Sarah lay spooned against him in his bed. Safely. Innocently. Chastely.

It led a man to wonder just what time tomorrow officially arrived.

He was gone when she awoke. The Pillow Book lay propped against his pillow in his place. Her heart began to beat faster even as the items lying beside it grabbed her attention.

Stones. He was giving her stones, just as he'd done before they were married. He'd remembered.

A slow smile stretched across Sarah's face. These were pretty rocks, too. Pink and crystalline, the five rocks ranged in size from large walnut down to acorn. Sarah lifted one up to the light and studied it. These were almost too pretty to be stored away with her others, she thought as she took the Pillow Book and flipped through it to the most recent entry.

My dearest Sarah,

I had the most wonderful dream last night. May I tell you about it?

In my dream, you were lying beside me in my bed, spooned against me. You were warm and so close that I could feel the rise and fall of your every breath and hear the little sigh of pleasure you made when you burrowed back against my heat. The scent of flowers clung to your skin— an exotic, spicy combination I could not place. I lay indulging in the fragrance, searching for the proper name for that particular, sultry scent.

I settled on Sarah.

Then, I dreamed you shifted in your sleep. You rolled over toward me. Your soft, unbound breasts pillowed against my naked chest and your legs entwined with mine. You sighed my name. The delight of it sucked the breath from my lungs.

My hands itched to touch you. They longed to stroke your satin skin, to play upon your body and bring it pleasure. My mouth yearned to taste you, to kiss and lick and suckle until you moaned from a need as great as my own. My loins ached to find you, to plunge into slick, tight heat, to stroke over and over and over until you cried out your satisfaction.

In my dream, I lay hurting with the need to make love to you until sunlight filtered through the draperies with the dawn of a new day.

Tonight was over. Tomorrow had arrived. Technically, time had run out on a promise made. I was tempted. Oh, so tempted.

But the spirit of my given word lingered. You lay next to me, lost in sleep, vulnerable. Trusting.

Trusting me.

It was a gift more valuable than gold, than diamonds, than uncut rubies plucked from the slope of an Afghan mountain in memory of a most special woman. I would never do anything to damage such a precious offering.

Remember that, Sarah. Never forget.

I leave you now with a small token of my thanks and a request. Look at the stones, lass. They are pretty as they are, but I want you to imagine the beauty that lies beneath the surface. Beauty and sparkle and fire. It's there, waiting for you.

You simply must be brave enough to make the first cut.

Nick

Nick learned that his wife's suitor, Lord Trevor Chambers, had taken to spending his afternoons wagering on his billiards skill at the Pelican Club, one of London's newest and most fashionable gentlemen's clubs. Word circling through the *ton* indicated that Chambers had forfeited his remittance by returning to England and that his brother, Lord Blakely, had refused to welcome his younger sibling back into the family fold upon his return to Britain. Apparently, billiards was what kept Lord Lovesick flush in the pockets.

'The aroma of roast beef and cigars greeted Nick as he strolled into the club during the afternoon rush. Immediately he was hailed by a foursome of card players and urged to join the game. He declined, but paused long enough to exchange opinions with the chairman of the boxing committee about a match scheduled for the following day. It took three more conversations and another ten minutes to make his way down the hallway past the trophy cases to the billiard room where the rhythmic crack of ivory ball against ball foretold the skill of the man holding the cue.

Lord Trevor Chambers. Nick despised him on principle. The man had courted Nick's wife.

Nick ordered a whisky and leaned casually against the linen-fold paneling as he observed the progress of the game. In the course of his study, Nick discovered his prey to be an affable fellow. Tall and wiry, Chambers exhibited a dry, ready wit, a keen intellect, and a true talent with a billiard stick. Over the course of the next hour, the fellow cheerily disposed of a series of challengers at the table and won a small fortune in the process.

The young man had been smiling when Nick engineered an introduction. The smile had died in an instant the moment a mutual acquaintance mentioned Nick's name. "You," he accused.

Nick gave him a rattlesnake's smile. "Yes, I am Sarah Ross's husband."

It wasn't at all what he'd intended to say. One

didn't threaten suspects while attempting to establish a rapport with them.

"Oh, I know who you are. The phantom husband. You're the man who abandoned the sweetest, most wonderful woman on the face of this earth. You, sir, are a scourge upon mankind." He punctuated his charge with a hard stroke of his billiard stick against the cue ball, which in turn sent the three ball flying across the felt-covered slate into the side pocket.

Nick smiled grimly as he wrapped his hand around a billiard stick hanging in the rack on the wall—as opposed to the young pup's throat—and said, "Care to put your money behind your mouth, Chambers?"

Lord Lovesick's victorious grin didn't bother Nick in the least. "Fifty pounds?"

"Make it a hundred."

"A hundred it is. I'll buy a gift for a lady friend with my windfall."

Even before the balls were racked for the new game, Nick was silently cursing himself. He'd done a better job striking up a dialogue with Nasrullah Quili Khan than he had with Lord Trevor Chambers.

But then the Khan hadn't tried to woo Nick's wife, had he?

"I understand Sarah has finally decided to end your farce of a marriage," Chambers observed. "Better late than never, as the saying goes. I don't know how you live with yourself, Weston, after deserting her as you did. Why, if not for her business talents, she might well have ended up destitute and on the streets."

It wasn't true. He'd provided funds for her every month of their marriage. Sarah had been too stubborn to use them. But Nick didn't intend to justify himself to Lord Lovesick, oh no. Instead, he'd whip his loud mouth in billiards.

Chambers broke to begin the game. As he sized up his shot, he continued. "The worst part of it was the children, of course. The ones she didn't have to mother." Addressing one of the flabbergasted observers, he said, "You should have seen the lady with the babies in town. The longing on her face made a man weep. She and I were both members of the Folio Society, and once she wrote a poem about children that had—"

"Quiet!" Nick demanded. "Take your shot or we'll still be at this game come the queen's jubilee."

Chambers smirked. Nick flexed his fingers and imagined knocking out the blackguard's teeth before making an effort to fulfill the duty that had brought him here. "I imagine you'll want to return to Texas before that. The jubilee is four months away yet."

"Oh, no," Chambers said, sinking his third ball. "I'll be here. I wouldn't miss it for the world. I hear that any number of exciting events are planned around the celebration of the fiftieth year of Queen Victoria's reign."

Nick's interest spiked, although he kept his expression casual. "I see. Is there any particular event you are especially anxious to attend?"

"Yes. Buffalo Bill is bringing his Indian show to town. I'm eager to see how Londoners react to the performances. The show came to Fort Worth a while back, did you know that? It was my good luck to be Sarah's escort that evening. Why, I'll never forget the way she held my hand during the stunt riders' death-defying feats. And then later, when she expressed her thanks for my care and concern . . . well . . . let's just say I'll treasure the memory until the day I die."

That's it. Nick would be damned before he'd listen to any more of this drivel. And so, for the first time Nick could recall, he allowed his personal considerations to outweigh his duty to his queen. Wielding the sword of his wit along with his superior talent at the game, Nick set about slaughtering Lord Trevor Chambers on the battlefield of the billiard table. When it was done, he was three hundred pounds richer and Lord Lovesick lay metaphorically, if not physically, bloodied and beaten on the Pelican Club's floor.

It should have left Nick in a good mood, but it didn't. He left the club feeling frustrated and angry and ready for a fight. Chambers's words hung around his mind like an unpleasant odor. *Abandoned the sweetest, most wonderful woman on the face of this earth. How do you live with yourself, Weston, after deserting her as you did? Sarah with the babies. Longing on her face.*

The pieces of truth in the accusations scraped him raw. He *had* abandoned her. *Had* deserted her. Had, in effect, denied her the children she apparently desired.

Right now, he felt like gutter slime.

He arrived back at Weston House to find a note from Sarah saying she and the girls had set off for the West End shops and expected to be gone all afternoon. Even though he had no intention of making another entry in the Pillow Book until after he saw her reaction to the one he'd left that morning, he found himself heading upstairs to retrieve the book.

Minutes later, he sat at the desk in his dressing room and picked up his pen.

Dear Sarah,

Do you have regrets about what happened between us in Fort Worth? Would your life have been better had we never married? Should I have stayed in town one day more and seen our marriage annulled at its beginning? You'd certainly be married again by now. You'd have children.

I find myself suddenly filled with doubts that sit uncomfortably on my shoulders. This is not a sensation I'm accustomed to feeling.

I have justifications galore for my actions, but at this moment, my thoughts are of you. Sarah, are the regrets too big to overcome?

Do you—in your heart of hearts—want me to let you go?

Nick

Ten minutes and a large whisky later, he added a postscript.

P.S. Not that I will, because I won't.

That night, Sarah gave him his answer in a most unexpected manner. When Nick adjourned to his bedchamber, he found his wife seated in one of two wing chairs pulled up in front of the fireplace. On the table between the chairs sat two glasses of milk and a plate of sweets.

"Hello, Nick," she said. "I think it's time we had a talk."

A bride should carry love letters from her groom to their wedding to ensure good luck.

~16~

Sarah held herself totally still as Nick approached the fireplace. Inside, she trembled like a willow in a gale.

"Good evening, Sarah." Nick loosened his necktie as he stepped toward the wardrobe against the far wall. His gaze landed somewhere over her shoulder as he added, "I appreciate the thought of refreshments, but I'm tired tonight. Maybe we could chat in the morning?"

"This isn't a chat, it's a talk," she insisted. "I want to have it now."

Grimacing, he muttered something that sounded like, "Wish someone had broken my fingers."

"Sit down and have a glass of milk."

Sulking like a boy, he stripped off his jacket, tugged off his tie, yanked out his cuff links, then sprawled in the chair. If he'd shouted his lack of desire to speak with her this evening, he couldn't have been more clear.

Silently, Sarah handed him his glass of milk. He slugged it back as if it were Rowanclere Malt, then stared glumly into the fire.

Sarah chose a shortbread cookie from the tray, took a dainty bite, then said, "I want to talk about the Pillow Book."

"I don't."

"You asked me questions, and I think it's time we answered them."

"No, Sarah, don't pay any attention to the last entry. I don't know what I was thinking. I was in a strange frame of mind."

She finished her cookie, sipped her milk, then said, "For weeks now, you have used those letters as tools of seduction, very effective tools, I might add. But tonight's letter is different, Nick. This one breaks my heart."

Though he remained slouched, she sensed a sudden tension in him. He didn't say anything, but still the question hovered in the air between them: *Why?*

"Because I honestly don't know the answers to the questions you asked me, Nick. I've never been so confused in my life."

Leaning forward, he propped his elbows on his knees and stared into the flickering flames. A weary sadness settled onto his face.

Sarah wanted to reach out, to brush the errant lock of hair off his brow. To comfort him because in doing so, she would find comfort herself. Instead, she sipped her milk and said, "You asked if my life would have been better had we never married. Who is to know the answer to that? I do know I'm happy with my life in Fort Worth. I love my work and I have wonderful friends."

After a moment of silence, Nick cleared his throat. "You're by yourself. You have no family."

A lump formed in Sarah's throat. She had to swallow it before she spoke. "Since Mother remarried, she lives elsewhere, so yes, I am alone quite often. I do regret not having a family of my own. I am envious of my friends who have a husband and children to fill their lives."

Nick kept his gaze on the fire. In a rough, soft voice, he asked, "So what stopped you from finding that for yourself? What stopped you from securing the annulment years ago? You could have had your husband and babies by now." He paused and shifted his feet. "I met Chambers today. He made it perfectly clear that he was a volunteer for the job."

Sarah took a long time to answer. "I didn't want Trevor, Nick. For a long time, I wanted you."

He closed his eyes as if absorbing a blow. "And now?"

Now, she wanted to avoid the answer. She gave a little laugh. "For the first five or six years, you were the perfect husband, Nick. You were absent. I was able to bill myself as Lady Innsbruck and build my business. Some potential clients didn't believe that an unhappily married woman could possibly arrange a brilliant wedding, so I created a fantasy life that you and I shared. You were a secret agent and I—"

"What?"

Now she laughed with true amusement. "At least twice a year I took a holiday and traveled to New Orleans. I shopped and dined and had an altogether lovely time. Then I returned home with stories of my romantic interlude with Lord Innsbruck who was on leave from his most recent mission."

"Why, you little liar," Nick said, one corner of his mouth lifting slightly in a faint grin.

"Yes, I'm quite good. I might publish a book of such stories some day."

The mood turned serious once more. "So is that what you want, Sarah? A fantasy husband?"

"No." She could say that with certainty. "I do want children."

Now, for the first time, he looked at her. "I would give you children."

"I know you would, Nick. And, to be honest, you're the only man in my life right now who I would want to give me babies. But that doesn't answer the question of whether you *should* be the father of my babies."

A hint of defense entered his tone. "I love children."

"I know you do. You're a wonderful family man." Troubled, Sarah searched for words to convey the feelings running through her. Her own confusion didn't make the task easier. "But Nick, your oldest son will be born an earl. Your children will be Englishmen. I am not at all certain that's what I want for my babies. I don't know that I'm ready to live in a place where a woman's main concern is whether to wear butterflies or a bird's nest on her hat."

He scowled and turned his attention back to the fire. "And women don't worry about such details in Texas?"

"Of course they do. But it's different here. *I'm* different here. I like the woman I am when I'm in Texas. I'm strong and confident and sure of myself. Here I'm ... not. With you, I'm not. I don't know who I am when I'm with you, Nick."

Silence stretched between them. He held himself

so still she could barely see him breathe. She tried again. "You identified the problem perfectly in this morning's letter. I *am* afraid. I know that. I don't know if that will ever change."

She inhaled a deep breath, then exhaled on a sigh. "What I don't know is whether or not I can make that cut you mentioned. I love the pretty pink stones. Do I really need a brilliant ruby?"

Then he moved, twisting his head sharply to shoot her a hard, glittering look. "Aye, you do. You shouldn't settle, Sarah. Whether it's with me or someone else, you damned well should reach for the jewel."

"Maybe so, but it needs to be the right jewel this time. I need to know it's right."

He held her gaze, his mouth set grimly. "Are you trying to say I'm not the right one? Shall I arrange passage home for you? Damnation, do you want me to book a spot for Lord Lovesick while I'm at it?"

Her chest hurt. "No, Nick. I'm asking for time."

"Time?" His brows rose, then he shut his eyes and let his head fall back against the chair as he gave a rueful groan. "Lass, I shared a bed with you last night and didn't touch you. If that's not giving you time, I don't know what is. What do you think I've been doing?"

"Seducing me."

Now he looked at her. Sarah continued, "Nick, when I read your letter tonight, I was ready to say forget the annulment, forget all my doubts, forget the life I have back home. It's lucky you stayed downstairs so long and gave me time to collect myself and figure out how to respond."

"Lucky isn't the word I'd use," he grumbled.

He was sounding sulky again, and she took that as

a good sign. "Nick, I can't answer your questions now because I don't have the answers myself. After tonight's letter, well . . . I'm asking you to allow me the time to decide what is right for me. In the meantime, you need to be certain about what's right for you. If we make a commitment to this marriage, I won't abide certain behaviors. For example, there will be no Lady Steeles."

He shot her a glare and opened his mouth, but she rushed on. "Please, Nick. This time, we've got to get it right."

With that, she stood and walked toward the bedroom door. Just before she exited the room, he stopped her with a question. "Why tonight's letter?"

"What do you mean?"

"The other letters have been much more . . . provocative. Why did this one compel you to confront me?"

Sarah took a deep breath, then said, "The others were letters about seduction. Whether you intended it this way or not, this letter, tonight's letter, spoke to me of love."

Nick departed Weston House the following morning, bound for the country and a meeting with a man about a horse. He drove a coach and four, grateful for the chance to expend some energy controlling the spirited beasts. Nick hadn't been this frustrated since the winter he spent in Siberia with only bearded, bad-tempered Cossacks for company.

Sarah had tossed that little word, the one with four letters and huge repercussions, between them like a bomb, then promptly retreated. He'd let her go, but it hadn't been easy. But then, it was so much easier for a man to concentrate on his physical desires for a woman than on the emotional ones. Trying to understand his own feelings was like tip-toeing across a frozen loch in stocking feet. It made him cold, off balance, and afraid he'd misstep and drown.

As the sounds of the city gave way to the bucolic music of the countryside, the questions that had plagued him throughout the night returned to torture him once more. Did he love her? The true, bone-deep, man-woman forever kind of love that she apparently wanted? Was he ready to answer the question with a yes, he did, beyond a shadow of a doubt?

One moment he thought he was. The next, he couldn't help but wonder.

He knew he cared for her more than any other woman who'd ever entered his life. She was his friend, his best friend, and he couldn't imagine his life without her in it. The very thought of it left him feeling queasy.

Then there was the question of other women. Since the moment he'd decided to send for Sarah last year, he had not taken another woman to his bed. He hadn't wanted any other woman. He wanted only his wife.

Sure, he'd gone through the public motions of courtship with Helen, but he suspected the reason for that lay with the unattainable Lady Steele's willingness to take him as a lover while denying every other man in town. Shallow fellow that he was, Nick liked the feeling of having come out on top. In a manner of speaking.

In that respect, escorting Helen about London had more to do with winning than anything else. It's what the lady herself had charged, anyway, when they met upon his return from Scotland and he told her he wouldn't be seeing her anymore.

So, what did all these truths tell him? Anything? Everything? Did he truly want to know?

Perhaps not. Perhaps in some ways, Nick was just as fearful as Sarah. Love had a way of knocking a bloke in the chops now and again, and from the moment he found out his parents weren't really his parents, Nick had begun building walls around his heart. Ten years ago Sarah breached the first line of his defenses, and in the years since then his sisters had certainly built a village there. But was he ready to admit anyone, even Sarah, to the innermost fortress?

Or was it a *fait accompli?* Was she there already in the deepest recesses of his heart? Was he in love with his wife?

Perhaps he didn't want to know. Perhaps he didn't want to risk that deep a look until she decided what she wanted.

Perhaps his walls were higher than he'd thought.

At that point, Nick decided he'd had enough of trying to peer into his own head or heart or whatever the proper body part was. At least he always knew what his loins were thinking. Around Sarah, he was always on point.

At that, his thoughts took a gratifying turn from the emotional toward the physical. On more familiar ground now, he spent the rest of his trip engaged in a fantasy involving him and his wife and veils made of silk he'd brought home with him from the Orient.

Silk he'd promised to give her. He'd forgotten all about it. "I should go ahead and give it to her now," he murmured as he made the turn onto Lord Cherryholm's estate. She'd like that, he knew. He had a whole stack of lovely gifts he intended to give her along with the Pillow Book entries, but those she'd view as blatant attempts at seduction. Which they were. The silk, however, she'd view as a promise upheld. It would be a subtle reminder of the man Nick was rather than another attempt at seduction.

Damnation. Seduction was the part of this relationship he especially liked, the part at which he excelled. But when she said she wanted time, he realized that meant she wanted his seduction efforts to cease.

Though it went against his inclinations, it made sense. She wanted to make her choice without undue influence or pressure. She didn't want to be seduced into staying. She wanted to make this decision with her mind, not her heart, which in abstract sounded smart.

In reality, the Sarah he had come to know would make her choice instinctively. Fear wouldn't cause her to leave him, nor would womanly desires compel her to stay. Sarah would stay with him if she trusted him. It was as simple and as complex as that.

So if Nick wanted to keep her, which he did, he needed to alter the course of his campaign. The goal was no longer to win her delicious little body, but instead to gain her trust.

All in all, he liked the first plan better. Lust was so much easier to achieve than trust.

He drove the coach and four to the apex of the circular drive in front of Cherryholm's manor house, and as he reined the horses to a halt, he settled on his new plan. He would give her the silk, but hold back the rest of the gifts until a more appropriate time. He'd quit flirting with her, teasing her, and sending her those silent, steamy, I-want-you-in-my-bed-right-now looks.

He would back away, prove he deserved her trust, and allow her to make her choice. Then, when she chose to stay with him, the victory would prove all the sweeter.

Besides, if she did something silly and made the wrong choice, he could always go back to writing letters about her breasts.

"Weston!" called Lord Cherryholm as he and another man exited the country house through the front door and made their way down sweeping stone steps. "Excellent timing. We're on our way to the stables now."

"Good morning, Cherryholm," Nick said, shaking the gentleman's hand, then turning his attention to the second man as his host added, "Do you know Endicott?"

"No," Nick responded with a social smile. "I haven't had the pleasure."

Endicott bowed. "Robert Endicott, Lord Weston. I believe you and I share a common interest."

"Horses?"

"Actually, I was referring to your wife."

Sarah and the girls left Weston House as women on a mission. Lady Pratt had sent word that one of her acquaintances had mentioned seeing a magnificent silver epergne that fit Charlotte's engagement ball theme to a tee. The silver centerpiece stood at least thirty inches tall, with four-leaf-clover filigree and hand-painted porcelain bowls, vases, and candleholders that repeated the lucky pattern, and it was available for purchase at a shop in Dover Street.

At least, Lady Pratt's friend thought the shop was in Dover Street. She wasn't entirely certain. The stores all ran together after a long day spent shopping, and it was possible she'd seen the epergne in Wigmore Street or Vere Street or maybe even Regent Street.

Despite the challenge of locating such a prize, Sarah and the girls agreed that a concerted effort be made to locate the item. Little touches such as this would set the tone for all the festivities surrounding what Sarah had promised to be the wedding of the Season.

As she gave their driver the address of their first planned destination, Sarah admitted she could have sent servants to track down the prize. Indeed, that's exactly what most women of her class would have done. But one never knew what treasures one might find among the bric-a-brac, so Sarah liked to do her shopping herself.

Besides, shopping in London was nothing like shopping in Fort Worth or New Orleans. If she ended up leaving Nick, shopping would be one of the many things she'd miss.

As the girls settled into their seats, Charlotte mentioned she'd decided on the design of the party favors for the wedding. Each guest who attended the wedding would be given a beautiful calling card case, and though she'd settled on the item itself while making their plans when still in Scotland, she had dithered over which good luck symbol to have engraved upon the silver case. Melanie had proposed horseshoes. Aurora wanted orange blossoms.

"I think the four-leaf clover is best because Rodney's title is Irish and it seems appropriate. If we find this epergne and it's as glorious as Lady Pratt claims, it will tie together nicely. Sarah, will we use the centerpiece at both the ball and the wedding breakfast?"

"That depends," Sarah answered, pondering the question. "I can't really say until I've seen it. We want to make a bold statement of our Good Luck Wedding theme at the engagement ball, keep it subtle and understated at the wedding, then display it in joyful abundance at the wedding breakfast. It's possible the epergne could form the centerpiece of the altar floral arrangements."

"Wait a moment," Aurora cautioned. "I thought you said green was considered an unlucky color for weddings."

"For the wedding *gown,* yes," said Melanie. "Not the decorations, correct?"

Sarah nodded. "Yes. In fact, green is a lucky color for the bride's headdress, although it's not at all in fashion."

They chatted about symbols of luck until they reached their first destination, Donegal House. Sarah hoped to find the epergne in this shop because Mrs. Earnest Hart carried a wonderful selection of Irish goods, and the porcelain on the centerpiece was apparently Belleek. However, Mrs. Hart wasn't aware of the piece, so they were forced to continue their search—after picking up some adorable hairpins decorated with four-leaf clovers for each of them to wear to Charlotte's ball.

Sarah and the girls then embarked on a shopping *flâneuse* through Piccadilly, Regent Street, and into Vere Street, when the girls took a peek at one of Marshall and Snelgroves's side windows, and paused for a moment at the mass of lovely silks on display. Then they walked north to Mmes Edmonds and Orr at 47 Wigmore Street because Aurora needed to get some of the special combination garments.

After consulting the *Journal* for an appropriate

restaurant, the ladies rested from their hunt with a luncheon at a tea shop in Regent Street. They resumed their search in Bruton Street and an hour later passed the plate-glass window of a whatnot shop just in time to see the shopkeeper hang a red "sold" tag around an arm of the object of their quest.

"That's it!" said Aurora.

"It's been sold!" cried Melanie.

"Oh, no," moaned Charlotte.

"It's perfect," murmured Sarah grimly as she imagined the epergne on the buffet table at the wedding. "We must have it."

"But it's been sold!" Charlotte's moan rose to a near wail.

Sarah squared her shoulders and lifted her chin. "Then it's time I tested the power of being a wealthy marchioness. Girls, let's go inside."

The chime on the door tinkled merrily to herald their entrance as Aurora led the way into the shop. She halted almost immediately, and her sisters and Sarah had to step quickly to keep from plowing into her back. At the same time Sarah noticed the tall, regal woman standing beside the shopkeeper's counter, she heard Aurora mutter, "Oh, wonderful."

The woman turned, and Sarah recognized her as the lady who'd taken a seat at the next table at the restaurant just as she and the girls were leaving. The girls' attention had been elsewhere, and they hadn't seemed to notice the woman. Sarah couldn't help but notice.

The woman was beautiful, with the kind of beauty that would make Helen of Troy look plain in comparison. Dark hair framed an aristocratic face. Her pale blue eyes, slim, straight nose, Cupid's-bow mouth, flawless complexion, and perfect figure were the kind of features that aroused lust in men and envy in other women. She wore a smart hat and a stylish dress, and carried herself in such a regal manner that even Queen Victoria could take lessons from her.

As Nick's sisters bristled visibly, Sarah assumed their reactions were the natural result of feminine jealousy. Then the woman spoke, and Sarah began to revise her conclusion.

"Oh, my, it's dear Nicholas's sisters. I'm caught. I've just purchased a little gift for you, and I intended to have it sent around to Weston House tomorrow. But since my surprise is discovered, perhaps you'd care to take it with you now? I've heard all about your plans for your engagement ball, and I believe you'll find my gift will come in useful." Then, meeting Sarah's gaze, she smiled politely and said, "And you must be Sarah Simpson. I recognize you from Nicholas's description."

A number of facts hit Sarah at once. She might be new to the scene when it came to proper British manners, but she knew it wasn't proper for this woman to refer to Nick by his first name unless she was family or, perhaps, an intimate friend. And not even in Texas, where formality was often relaxed, was it proper for one woman to refer to another by her first name *and maiden name* before being properly introduced. It was a veiled insult, and Sarah knew it.

She also realized this glorious woman's identity. If she hadn't figured it out on her own, the girls' reaction would have told her. Her stomach took a dive just as Melanie spoke up. "Allow me," the young woman said, laying a supportive hand on Sarah's arm. "Lady Steele, may I introduce my dear sister-in-law, Lady Weston."

The meeting deteriorated from there.

"I understand that back at your home in Texas you have a little wedding business."

Little wedding business? Sarah eyed the epergne the shopkeeper carried past and envisioned wrapping it around the other woman's neck.

"I think it's wonderful that you are able to work for Charlotte in a professional capacity during your visit to England," Lady Steele continued. "Nicholas tells me your efforts thus far are quite competent."

Competent? Sarah's eyes narrowed to slits, and she literally bit her tongue to keep from challenging the woman and embarrassing her sisters-in-law. As she searched her mind for exactly the right words with which to respond, the girls exchanged a peevish look with one another, something Sarah found somewhat mollifying.

Nick's paramour then had the temerity to laugh. "I must confess I wondered a bit at Nicholas's timing in pursuing the annulment now and stirring up talk before another of Charlotte's weddings. However, what man doesn't like to kill two birds with one stone, as the saying goes? He certainly couldn't hire the same wedding planner for this wedding as he used for the last. Why, that woman was terrible at her job. Anything would be an improvement."

All right. I've had it. Sarah pasted on a sugary smile and drawled, "My husband did mention something along those lines concerning available Englishwomen when he invited me to join him here in England. He found them totally inadequate. Now, if you'll excuse us, my sisters and I must be on our way. We are searching for the perfect centerpiece for Charlotte's bridal table, and . . ." She paused momentarily to glance at the beautiful epergne that she now wouldn't use under threat of death. "We simply haven't found anything tasteful yet."

With that, she turned and left, the girls following in her wake. Out in the street, Sarah thought she must be throwing off enough steam to power a ship. "He actually considered marrying that woman?"

The girls grimaced as one, then Charlotte nodded. "I don't know what he could have been thinking."

Sarah gave an unladylike snort. "I'll bet I know what he was thinking with, however."

And to think she'd always considered Nick to be more intelligent than the average man. "Now who is being foolish?"

"Foolish about what?" Melanie inquired.

Sarah sighed. "About the decorations for the ball. Charlotte, how would you feel if we didn't use that epergne after all?"

Smiling brightly, Charlotte clasped Sarah's hands and gave them a reassuring squeeze. "I'd be ever so relieved."

A grin played at Sarah's lips at the young woman's response. "It's petty of us. The centerpiece is beautiful. It's perfect."

"No, it's not," said Melanie.

"It was once, but not anymore," Aurora added with a sniff.

Sarah stopped in the middle of the sidewalk, heedless of the flow of people streaming around her, and met the gaze of each of Nick's sisters in turn. Emotion swelled within her. It was warm and tender and true and filled her heart to overflowing.

It was, she realized, love.

Sarah blinked back tears. Oh my, she'd miss this trio if she left. Now, after meeting That Woman, she found she had reached one decision, anyway. No matter how things turned out between her and Nick, before she left she'd make certain one way or another that Lady Steele would not become the next Lady Weston. She'd have it written into the annulment agreement if necessary.

In the meantime, there was shopping to be done.

Sarah linked her arms through Charlotte's and Melanie's, winked at Aurora, and said, "In that case, we'd best get to shopping. We've the perfect centerpiece to find, and I've the feeling it is sitting in a shop somewhere here in Bruton Street."

Half an hour later, they found a centerpiece that put the epergne to shame. Busy congratulating the girls for their wondrous find, Sarah literally ran into an old friend.

"Lady Weston," Lord Trevor Chambers said as he took her arm and prevented a fall. A wide smile wreathed his face. "I heard you were here in the West End buying up half of London. Is it true your coachman had to return to Weston House once already today to unload packages to make room for more?"

"Trev—I mean, Lord Chambers. How delightful to see you."

"Acting the proper lady, I see." He bowed over her hand. "When in London, as they say, and all that rot."

"My lord," she scolded. "Please."

Then, turning to the girls, she said, "Lord Chambers, may I present my sisters-in-law and dear friends, Lady Charlotte Ross, Lady Melanie Ross, and Lady Aurora Ross."

Charmer that he was, Trevor made a to-do over the girls. Like most females meeting Trevor for the first time, the three girls were immediately smitten.

At least, they were smitten until they grew suspicious. That happened the moment Trevor leaned over, pressed a kiss to Sarah's cheek, and said, "Did you young ladies know that Sarah and I were once informally engaged to wed? Now that I hear she's finally seeking an annulment, I hope to convince her to reconsider the question."

Being kissed by a chimney sweep on your wedding day brings good luck.

~17~

*L*ondon was abuzz with talk of the upcoming engagement ball at Weston House. In parlors and clubs all across the city, those recently returned to town in preparation for the opening of Parliament and the approaching social season speculated, surmised, and supposed about this, the first notable social event of the year.

The attractions of the topic were many. While the fourth Marquess of Weston had hosted a musical for Lady Charlotte's come-out the previous year and then a few small, low-key events before her doomed nuptials, he had never before given a ball. People were curious.

Lady Pratt did all she could to stir that particular soup, too. She dropped broad hints all over town about the food, the decorations, the guest list, and—what interested people most of all—the hostess.

The mysterious Lady Weston. Rumors about her abounded. She had yet to appear at any social functions, although those who had occasion to meet her at various shops about town spoke favorably of her. She was said to be beautiful, witty, and charming, and she apparently dealt quite well with the marquess's trio of sisters—no easy task.

With the approach of the ball, interest heightened as privately repeated hearsay claimed Lady Weston shared a past with at least one gentleman of the *ton* not her husband. Speculation ran rampant. By the time guests donned evening suits and ball gowns to attend the event, odds on a relationship having existed between the lady and Lord Chambers and between the lady and Lord Robert Endicott, both recently returned to England from the States, were evenly divided.

"Busybody peahens," Nick muttered, reflecting on the rumors while he waited in the grand entrance hall of his townhouse for the women in his life to join him downstairs to await their guests' arrival. He'd expected the volume of gossip—nothing like a bit of new blood in the mix to stir matters up. What he didn't anticipate was just how much that gossip would bother him.

Nick didn't appreciate the fact that those two men had courted his wife back in Texas. He especially didn't care for the idea that both Endicott and Chambers appeared to be taking advantage of the quite public annulment proceedings to renew their acquaintance with Sarah. Half a dozen times now he'd come home to find one or the other—and sometimes both—ensconced in his parlor, taking tea and indulging in flirtation.

The fact that his investigation into the bombing plot meant he couldn't throw them bodily out his front door made the situation all the more untenable. Never before had service to the Crown seemed quite so . . . nauseating, not even the time the Kualistanis had fed him goat's eyes for supper.

Oh, he'd done what he could to impede the bombing conspiracy suspects' progress, mostly by pretending to be their friend. Following his loss of professional demeanor with Chambers during that first meeting, he'd had to work to make that one appear believable, but he'd succeeded, using a mixture of lies and half-truths that appeared to satisfy Lord Lovesick. Nick suspected Chambers was happy to believe Nick represented no rival for the lady's affections, and thus failed to delve beneath the surface of their newfound "friendship."

Endicott hadn't proved as easy. While Chambers obviously lusted after Sarah, Nick believed Endicott wanted something else from Nick's wife. Much of an espionage agent's success depended upon his making an accurate judgment of a person's character, and that experience was telling Nick that Endicott was after more than romance. What he feared most was that it was somehow connected to the jubilee plot.

Nick wanted to pack his women off to Glencoltran or another safe spot even farther away while he uncovered the truth about the conspiracy, but they wouldn't hear of it. In hindsight, he should have left them in Scotland. Whatever made him think he could keep his family separate from this business when Sarah attracted men like bees to honey?

And after tonight, that would only get worse. Up until now, she knew only the men from Texas—and shopkeepers. Nick had never known a woman so enamored of the entire shopping process. But once the gentlemen of English society laid eyes on her at tonight's ball, his parlor was bound to be the most popular place in London.

"Add my sisters into the mix, and the problem grows exponentially," he grumbled, scowling at the portrait of a Weston ancestor hanging on the wall. He'd handled this marriage business poorly from the beginning, and now he was paying for it. If these hounds didn't know that the state of his marriage was less than perfect, they wouldn't be on the hunt. But when Nick had started down this particular path, he had expected his marriage *would* be perfect by now. He never would have guessed that after all these weeks Sarah would still be a virgin bride and the annulment would still be working its way through the legal system.

Slowly. Much more slowly than Sarah suspected. Nick felt a little more guilty about that every day. She had asked for time—well, she didn't have a clue about how much time the English court system was prepared to give her. Every time she asked, he dodged the question. If she discovered the truth before she decided to stay with him, he feared there would be hell to pay.

When he decided to make their marriage public, Nick never expected the seduction of Sarah, Lady Weston, would take place at a snail's pace. He never would have guessed he'd quit pursuing her, either. Not once he'd made the decision to make her his wife in all aspects of the word.

But he had quit chasing her outright. Since their night of milk and cookies, he'd stayed away from her chamber, away from the Pillow Book, and away from any behavior that could be perceived as flirtatious. He was trying his best to give her the power to make her own decision. As much power as the legal system would allow, anyway.

Still, no matter what the English courts said, Sarah

always had the option of returning to Texas and securing an annulment there. She'd be free.

He would not.

At this point, Nick didn't think that would matter. While he still wanted a home and children of his own, he now had a difficult time imagining living that dream with any woman but Sarah.

If he did something now to lose her, he deserved to lose the dream.

So tomorrow, in the spirit of her request, he would ignore the blackguards who would come to call on his wife. This evening, no matter how lovely she looked in her ball gown and how much he ached to waltz her into the garden and have his wicked way with her beneath the starlit sky, he would not do it.

Right now, however, before the guests began arriving, he should probably toss back a bracing whisky. Something told him he'd need fortifying tonight.

The prospect of making some progress toward uncovering the jubilee plot was the only part of the evening that Nick anticipated with any pleasure. Both Endicott and Chambers were expected to attend the ball, and Nick had plans for them that might eliminate one man as a suspect. The socializing part of the upcoming evening made him think fondly of remote Himalayan slopes.

To make matters worse, even after this he still had the wedding and Melanie's come-out to endure. And wouldn't it be just his luck for her to be a roaring success and wind up in love and wanting to marry? Later this year.

He shuddered at the thought. "I'll have to make it a condition of her debut," he murmured. "No wedding for at least a year."

It would be the best thing for her, anyway. In hindsight, he and Sarah had married too quickly. They didn't know each other well enough, so at the first sign of trouble, the marriage fell apart. If he had known her better before the wedding night, he'd have anticipated her ... reticence. If she'd known him better, she would have trusted him when Susan's father came pounding at their door.

She would trust him now.

Because of his own past mistakes, Nick could feel justified in demanding his younger sisters have long engagements. That way—

He broke off the thought abruptly. Younger sisters. Aurora. Right after Melanie came Aurora. He'd be going through this misery with two more sisters after Charlotte, and he'd been blocking that ugly truth from his mind.

That reality had him burying his head in his hands with a groan. Maybe he should give in to Aurora's whining and let her make her bow at the same time as Melanie. No matter her reasons, he had seen her kissing Willie Hart. Enthusiastically. He might be well served to marry her off while he still could.

But no, she was too young to marry. She was the same age as Sarah when the two of them had wed, and look at the trouble that had caused. She needed at least another two years.

If Nick was lucky, he might hold her back for one. He simply needed to stay on guard.

A sound from above him caught his attention, and as he turned his gaze toward the staircase, he completely lost the ability to breathe. "Aurora?"

She wore a white tulle dress trimmed with artificial snow drops. The fashionable cut of the gown clung to luscious curves he'd never before noticed she possessed. Her hair was up, her pearl earrings dangled. She looked beautiful and sophisticated and all grown up.

Nick's stomach sank. Even as the thought occurred to send her to change her dress, Melanie joined her younger sister on the staircase landing. Now Nick's neck constricted. Melanie's dress was sunset gold silk that clung like a second skin and had no shoulders. He'd no sooner managed a growl than those two were joined by the bride-to-be. Charlotte was dressed in a patterned gown of small four-leaf clovers against an ice-white background. The sparkle in her eyes reminded him of fire. She looked lush and lovely and . . . ready. His growl transformed to a groan. His sisters would start a riot.

Nick began to round toward the door, determined to lock his sisters in and the rogues of London out. Just as he turned his head, he caught a glimpse of movement next to Charlotte, a flash of golden temptation that kept him frozen in place.

"Sarah." He couldn't say anymore because his tongue was tied in a dozen different knots. He'd never seen such a glorious sight.

Dressed in a shimmering gown of sunshine-colored silk, his wife simply glowed. She was the sun, the moon, the stars wrapped up in a single package. She was every magnificent setting he'd seen in his worldwide travels tied up with a bow.

She was, in a word, stunning.

Nick wanted her with a fierceness that all but brought him to his knees.

His reaction had little to do with the outer trappings she sported, Nick knew. True, her gown was becoming, though cut too low. Also, the Weston jewels—a suite of emeralds and diamonds—added that rich, regal air. But Nick had always thought Sarah beautiful. On the day they met. Their wedding day. Even the day she arrived travel-stained and bedraggled at Glencoltran Castle. But tonight, as she stood at the top of the staircase and calmly met his stunned gaze, he saw something in his wife he'd never noticed before, at least not to this extent.

Confidence. Strength. Security in herself and her place in the world. All of this on the eve of diving into the shark-infested waters of London Society.

Nick crossed the entry hall to stand at the foot of the staircase. One after the other, his sisters gracefully descended. "Aurora, you are beautiful. If I had one bit of sense I would lock you in a nunnery," he said before leaning down to kiss her cheek.

To Melanie, he said, "I must assign bodyguards to protect you, love."

After kissing Charlotte's cheek, he said, "I hope your Rodney knows what a treasure he is getting. Enjoy your party. If anything or any person is not to your liking, let me know and I'll see it corrected."

When Charlotte moved off, Nick turned to his wife and dipped his head in a bow. In a formal tone, he said, "Lady Weston. You are exquisite. The jewels look right on you, though they pale in comparison to your beauty."

She smiled regally. "Thank you, my lord. I—" she broke off with a gasp, then completely destroyed the regal picture she presented by clapping her hands in delight, lifting her skirts up almost to her knees, and dashing across the entry hall, squealing, "Jenny! Claire! You're here!"

Nick turned to see his wife fly into the arms of a pair of unfamiliar beauties. An entire group of visitors flowed in behind the pair, and for the next few moments, chaos reigned.

Lady Pratt and Rodney quickly separated themselves from the group, she to stand aside patting her voluminous bosom as if to ward off a fainting spell while he made a beeline toward his bride-to-be.

"Oh my," breathed Melanie, standing beside Nick. "Look at the gowns on those girls. Who are they, Nick?"

Claire. Jenny. Memory clicked. McBride. He glanced over the trio of beautiful young women who appeared to be close in age to his own sisters and didn't know whether to feel heartened or despairing. And the McBride Menaces. His trouble just doubled. "I believe the McBrides have arrived from Fort Worth just in time for your engagement ball, Charlotte."

Aurora's mouth gaped. "Those girls are the McBride Menaces? The ones who set loose the mice and cats and dogs at their father's wedding?"

One of them, the youngest, Nick guessed, heard Aurora and flashed a grin their way. "That's us. But not to worry, we left our mischief years behind. The McBride Menaces are all grown up."

Then another sister added with a wry grin, "Don't feel too safe, though. Our brothers, the McBride Monsters, accompanied us on this trip."

Sarah had tears in her eyes as she watched Nick make the formal announcement of Lady Charlotte's engagement to Lord Pratt. Oh, what a lovely moment. Nick's love for his sister shone like a beacon from his eyes and dear Charlotte with tears in her eyes basked in the glow of love from the two most important men in her life.

Sarah sighed with delight and returned her attention to her duties as hostess. The evening was going splendidly. The food was wonderful, the music lovely, the crowd a crush that signified success. As the night wore on, compliments and comments about the good luck theme came to her in a steady stream, reassuring her of the success of the idea. That the majority of those kudos came from unmarried gentlemen didn't escape her notice, but Sarah received enough praise from the ladies to find it reassuring.

At one point in the evening she took the time to sneak upstairs for a short visit with Jenny and Claire. She still couldn't believe they were actually here. She hadn't expected them for at least another week. She'd tried to convince them to move into Weston House—the place had fourteen unused bedchambers on the floor above her own, Sarah had discovered—but her friends were settled in a townhouse that had come to Claire's husband Tye along with his title.

"We only arrived this morning, and the boys have already broken three vases," said Jenny with a sigh. "Be glad they are safely at home with the nanny we've hired for our time in London. Destroying their uncle's property is bad enough. I wouldn't dream of turning them loose in this place. It's a lovely home, Sarah, and you fit it so well. I'm not one bit surprised."

"Really?" She was shocked at her friend's observation. She'd never felt so out of place as she did right now. Despite the glamor of the evening, Sarah yearned for home. Seeing her dear friends again, hearing that familiar Texas twang for the first time in months, reminded her just how much she missed her life in Texas.

Claire nodded. "I know you called yourself Lady Innsbruck all those years because it helped professionally, but the title always suited you. And now that I've met your delicious Nick, I must say the man does, too."

"Claire!" Sarah protested. "What would Tye say? You are a happily married woman."

"She's married, not dead," Jenny pointed out. "Sarah, the talk is that the two of you are seeking an annulment. Lord Weston is a fine specimen of a man. Are you certain you don't want to keep him?"

"Mo-ther," Emma McBride, the eldest Menace said. Her sisters followed Melanie into the room, with Aurora bringing up the rear. "He's not a pet. You don't 'keep' a husband."

"My niece is right," Claire agreed. She gave a wicked grin, then brushed a finger across the jewels that dangled from Sarah's ears and added, "You let him 'keep' you. In grand style, I might add."

Sarah allowed the subject to drop because she couldn't say what she wanted to in front of the man's sisters. She stood and spread her arms. "Come here, you Menaces, and give me a hug."

"They're the Blessings," interjected Claire, stating an old argument with a smile. "Not Menaces."

As Emma, Maribeth, and Katrina McBride did as Sarah bade, their mother lifted a wry brow. "Can you believe she still calls them that? Despite the fact they've taken Claire's own trio of children under their wings and made them Menaces-in-training."

"We must pass the mantle to someone, Mother," Maribeth said. "And while our brothers show great promise, they're already being called the McBride Monsters. We don't want our legacy to die simply because we've grown up."

Sarah glanced from the twinkle-eyed Texans to an amused Melanie and Aurora, who watched the other girls with keen-eyed speculation. Homesickness swamped her. Heavens, she had missed these girls.

Aurora piped up. "Sarah has told us quite a bit about your families. I think we can be great friends."

Sarah couldn't help but wince a bit at that. She gazed at the five young beauties standing in front of her—Charlotte must have remained downstairs with her beloved Rodney—and imagined what sort of trouble they might attract. The possibilities were both staggering and endless. "It's like combining gunpowder with gas," she murmured. "Add one little spark and we're liable to have an explosion."

Shaking away the troublesome thoughts, she asked, "What are you girls doing upstairs?"

"Hiding," Melanie answered. "At least for the moment. I admit I enjoy a bit of masculine attention, but the gentlemen downstairs remind me of salivating dogs panting after a fresh piece of meat. I've danced my slippers off."

"Not me," Katrina McBride said glumly. "Papa won't let me dance at all. I don't know why you bothered to make me a gown, Mama. I might as well be dressed in a pinafore."

"Give him time to get accustomed to the idea, honey," Jenny advised. "The evening's young yet. You'll convince him to change his mind. I have complete faith in it."

"I hope so."

The youngest McBride daughter's downtrodden expression caused Sarah to offer a sympathetic grin before addressing the older girls. "So you came upstairs to give your feet a rest?"

"We're giving their father and uncle and Nicholas a rest," Aurora said with rueful sigh. "If the gentlemen of the *ton* are salivating dogs, our brother and the two Mr. McBrides are lions guarding their pride, ready to pounce if a threat comes too close."

"As well they should," Sarah stated. "You and Melanie are not out yet and wouldn't be dancing if this event were not in your home."

"If I lived in England, I'd have made my bow by now," Emma pointed out. "So would Mari. We're old enough to have beaus."

"Not English beaus," her mother said flatly. "It's too far away from home. Besides, once the newness wore off, you wouldn't like living here. British Society is old and set in its ways, and you girls are perfect examples of the brash, freedom-loving females of whom they love to disapprove."

Sarah gasped softly. Jenny had voiced her own problem so neatly.

Jenny continued, "Living here would crush your spirits, and as difficult as those spirits are at times for your father and me, it would break my heart to see that happen."

Aurora interjected. "With all respect, Mrs. McBride, I don't believe it necessarily has to be that way. I think if a girl finds the right British gentleman, he will want her to be herself and not a copy of all the other girls out in Society. The challenge is to find that correct gentleman."

Sarah nodded. Yes. Exactly.

Melanie grinned and fluttered her fan flirtatiously. "And to do that, we must dance with as many as we can, don't you see?"

Katrina McBride turned a frown in Sarah's direction. "Maybe you should be downstairs dancing, too, Miss Sarah. Aurora tells us you and her brother won't be married much longer. I saw two men from

Fort Worth downstairs. Maybe you should flirt with them and see if one won't suit."

"That's a good idea," Maribeth said. "Emma and Katie and I have long thought you should have something better than a long-distance marriage of convenience. Didn't Lord Chambers attempt to call on you for a time a few years ago?"

Sarah laughed softly. It was either that or cry. "You all have just managed to condense the troublesome questions facing me into a few short sentences."

Seven sets of eyebrows arched with curiosity. Seven posteriors found seats as the McBride and Ross women gave Sarah their devoted attention. Melanie spoke for them all. "Tell us all about it, Sarah. We'll help you decide what to do."

Sarah's rueful laugh transformed to a groan. How could she verbalize the feelings rumbling around inside her? How could she explain to these young women the agony of the choice she faced? She couldn't. No more than she could explain it to Nick. Dear, patient Nick who'd made a point of backing off like she had asked to give her the time and space she needed. She couldn't explain it to any of them because she still couldn't explain it to herself.

So she artfully dodged the question. "I love each of you dearly, but now is not the time. Lest you forget, I have hostess duties downstairs, and you, my friends, are missing a grand party."

Maribeth McBride wrinkled her nose. "You're trying to put us off."

"No, I *am* putting you off. Let's all go downstairs, shall we? Katie, as long as your mother doesn't object, I'll tell your father it's my ball and I want you to dance."

The young woman's face lit, and she bounced to her feet. But a tug on her skirt from Emma McBride had her sitting back down. "Y'all go on," the eldest sister said. "We'll follow in a few minutes. First, Melanie and Aurora are going to give us a bit of background on some of the gentlemen who have expressed interest in us."

"If we avoid the rakes and rogues on our own, that will give Papa and Uncle Tye less to worry about, right?" Maribeth added.

Claire eyed her nieces and said to their mother, "Jenny, your girls are up to something."

"Yes, I know," Jenny said, rising and heading for the door. "I want you to promise me you won't do anything to ruin Charlotte's night. Or your father's."

"We promise," chimed a quintet of voices.

"Does this door have a key?" Claire asked. "It might be safer to lock them in."

"Aunt Claire!" the McBride Menaces protested as Melanie and Aurora blinked in shocked surprise.

Sarah laughed. "They'll behave," she assured the McBride wives. "I trust them. Not because I don't think they're above a bit of mischief, even at their age, but because they all love me and they don't want to disappoint me, right, girls?"

"That's right, Sarah."

"Oh, you're good," commented Jenny McBride as she linked her arm with Sarah's and headed for the door. "On second thought, never mind what a fine specimen of manhood your Nick is. You must return to Texas."

"That's right," Claire agreed, following them out into the hall. "Our children need you. Imagine what trouble they might get into without your calming influence. I shudder to think about it."

At that moment, Sarah heard Aurora and Katrina burst into laughter and she caught her breath. The mingled music of British and Texan laughter ripped her heart in two.

"We have a plan to make Lady Steele shake in her shoes," Aurora told her new American friends.

"The three of you are our inspiration," Melanie added. "Sarah has entertained us with tales of your more imaginative antics."

Emma winced. "We've been living down our behavior at Papa and Mama's wedding for years. You must understand. We thought she was marrying someone else when we set all those animals loose in the church."

Katie grinned. "It's our little brothers' favorite bedtime story."

Maribeth shook her head. "Please tell me your plan for this evil woman doesn't include animals. I don't think our papa would ever forgive us."

"No, no animals. This plot actually combines a trick our Aunt Gillian played on our Uncle Jake and the one you three played on someone named Willfema."

Katrina pursed her lips. "Willfema?"

"Wilhemina," Maribeth deduced. "Mrs. Wilhemina Peters. The newspaper columnist."

"Oh, the music box story," Maribeth said. The three McBride Menaces smiled in fond memory.

"That's the one. We overheard Sarah telling our brother about it, and when we decided something must be done to convince Lady Steele to leave our brother alone, it seemed the perfect solution—with a little tweak from Gillian's ghost-playing days."

Melanie gave the McBrides the details of the evening's scheme, including a quick summary of

Aunt Gillian's romance with their Uncle Jake and her pretense at haunting Rowanclere Castle. "She rigged an almost invisible thread to a breadbasket, and when Jake reached for a roll, she tugged it out of reach. We're using the same concept with Lady Steele. It's an innocent prank, one that Sarah or even Charlotte would laugh off if we pulled on her tonight. Lady Steele will hate it."

"And you think she'll hate it so much that you'll scare her away?"

"No. We think she'll hate it—and us—so much that she'll decide Nicholas isn't worth fighting for any longer. We suspect he has tried to end things with her—we hope so, anyway—but the woman sticks like a burr. We're hoping this event will be enough to make her realize Nicholas will never forsake his sisters and show her how much she'd hate dealing with us for years to come. If our plan works, she'll turn her attention to some other gentleman this very night. You wait and see."

Emma McBride frowned. "I don't know. Though your plot sounds inspired, it does strike me as a bit childish. Are you certain you wish to take this approach?"

"We've tried being mature, but the woman won't take our hints. She is fiendish. You should have seen how catty she was to Gillian the day they were introduced. I can't help but think she is part of the reason Nicholas and Sarah act less than comfortable around each other these days. We may have begun our campaign against Lady Steele because we didn't want Nicholas to marry her, but now we're doing it for Sarah. We love Sarah and we think she's perfect for our brother. We cannot allow Lady Steele to ruin things. This is war."

"I love the idea," said Katrina McBride. "You have my full support. How can I help?"

The five young ladies spent the next ten minutes revising their scheme to include the assistance of their new American friends. When they finally made their way downstairs, they were united in their purpose.

Sarah had promised the *ton* a wedding they wouldn't soon forget. The newly self-christened Ross Rascals, united with the force of the McBride Menaces, were ready to make the prewedding festivities a fitting prelude.

Sarah had expected the curious whispers and murmurs of the guests that flowed around her as the ball went along. She'd even anticipated the undercurrent of tension that had swept through the ballroom with the arrival of Lady Steele. What had caught her by surprise, however, was how much she was enjoying her role as hostess of Lady Charlotte's ball. As a wedding planner, she'd been a part of many balls and parties over the years, but never before had she been so personally involved. It made the evening special.

She was honestly having a lovely time. She'd said as much to the Susan Sheldon as they waited for her happily attentive Tom to bring them a cup of punch. She'd repeated the sentiment to Lord Kimball during a dance right before the Queen's business called the spymaster away. All in all, she thoroughly enjoyed the first half of the evening.

Now, however, she had to survive supper.

Having circulated discreetly to assist the appropriate pairing off of guests for the supper dance, Sarah paused for a quick exchange with Nick in advance of the promenade into dinner. She felt as if a million butterflies had taken up residence in her stomach.

Until now the evening had gone as smooth as the promised silk Nick had finally delivered to her early last week, but this was the stickiest part of the evening, because of the attention paid to the order of precedence. Woe betide Sarah as a hostess if she mixed up a pair of dukes, giving honors to the peer of lesser rank.

On top of that concern, she'd begun to worry excessively about her menu. So much depended on how supper was received. What if these Britons didn't appreciate the subtlety of carrying her good luck theme to the supper table? With that worry momentarily uppermost in her mind, Sarah leaned toward her husband and murmured, "Do you think I went too far with the cornbread and black-eyed peas?"

The twinkle in his blue eyes made a lie of his serious frown. "Hmm . . . as long as you have sufficient quantities of more sophisticated foods like the lobster bisque and those little four-leaf clover meringues, then I wouldn't expect a problem. Unless the guests don't care for the shade of green you used."

"Nick, don't tease me about this!"

He chuckled. "Actually, I think it's a nice touch, especially since you incorporated an explanation of all the good luck traditions in the menu cards."

She beamed up at him as her stomach settled. "You're a good man, Nick Ross."

He flashed her a hot, heated look the likes of which she'd not seen from him since the night they shared milk and honesty in his bedchamber. "I am hoping you'll remember that."

Now the butterflies returned, but for a different reason entirely. Offering up a nervous smile, she said, "I think it's time we found our partners."

With that, Sarah made a graceful retreat in search of the Duke of Rollingsworth, the highest ranking gentleman at the ball and the hostess's traditional dinner partner. Exactly how she ended up approaching the table on the arm of Lord Endicott was something she couldn't quite fathom.

Even worse was the fact that her husband appeared to be escorting Sarah's nemesis, Lady Steele, to the table next to hers.

Her butterflies transformed to bitter pills of lead as she allowed Lord Endicott to seat her.

"Lady Weston," the gentleman said. "Allow me to compliment you on the ball. I suspect hostesses of upcoming events are gnashing their teeth in concern at this moment. You've set a standard that will be impossible to meet."

Sarah barely heard him, since she was busy biting her lower lip and scanning the room for the duke. Nobody was seated with their supper dance partners. What had happened here? "Lord Endicott, may I ask you a question?"

"Please, feel free."

"I hope you won't take this the wrong way, but as a fellow Texan of sorts, I feel that I can ask. I made every effort to follow the guidelines of proper etiquette with seating at this meal. How is it you are at my right rather than Lord Rollingsworth?"

Endicott flashed a bashful smile. "His Grace and I were at Eton together. I begged the boon, and though he protested, in the name of friendship he graciously conceded his spot and we switched place cards."

Place cards? Sarah hadn't used place cards at the tables. Where had these come from? She glanced at the other cards on her table and spied Tye McBride's name along with two of his daughters', and struggled to keep the frown from her face. That might explain Endicott's presence at her side, but not exactly why Nick was feeding the flames of gossip on Charlotte's night by escorting his paramour to the supper table rather than the Duchess of Rollingsworth! Her suspicions were tempered, however, by the fact that his too-innocent sisters Aurora and Melanie took seats at the same table as their brother. Noting the glint in their eyes, Sarah suspected whatever mischief the girls had planned was about to transpire.

For a moment, she considered trying to stop it. But then Lady Steele batted her lashes up at Nick, and Sarah wanted to pitch the contents of her water glass in the flirt's face.

"No, I'll mind my own business," she said beneath her breath. Whatever the jest, Charlotte obviously had agreed to it, and since this was her special night, that was all the approval Sarah needed. Besides, after meeting Lady Steele, Sarah found herself supportive of whatever plan the girls had in store for the waspish woman.

Endicott asked what foods she'd like him to bring her from the buffet. "You choose, please," she absently replied, her entire attention focused on the tableau at the other table.

At least Nick didn't appear happy. Sarah took some comfort in that, and as she watched him pull the chair out for Lady Steele, a sense of anticipation filled her. That woman had made a mistake in the way she treated Nick's sisters. Sarah knew in her bones that somehow, someway, the Ladies Ross were fixing to make her pay.

Lady Steele took her seat. Immediately, the tinkling notes of "God Save the Queen" drifted up from beneath her bustle. The Englishwoman stiffened and frowned in confusion while in Sarah's mind the American version of the song began to echo. *"My country 'tis of thee . . ."*

Lady Steele hopped from her chair like a frog, and abruptly the music stopped.

She sat back down.

Music played.

"Sweet land of liberty . . ."

Aurora and Melanie gasped loudly as Lady Steele vaulted from her chair. Ten tables away, Charlotte helped focus further attention by calling out, "What is that noise?"

Pink brushed Lady Steele's patrician cheeks. Her lips fluttered with a hesitant smile, then cautiously she sat down again.

Music tinkled.

"Of thee I sing."

Lady Steele jumped to her feet.

Every eye in the supper room turned toward her in fascinated interest. Gentlemen at the table next to her burst out in guffaws, quickly muffled. Astonishment colored half the faces; amusement, the rest. A combination of anger and embarrassment flashed across the Ice Queen's pale features, and icicles dripped from her voice as she demanded, "Footman, bring me another chair!"

Sarah sat back in her chair, cattily entertained as servants scurried to do Lady Steele's bidding. She rejected the first chair they brought her and demanded a second. Lifting her nose into the air, she regally took her seat.

Music saluted her again.

"Land where my fathers died . . ."

"Aawk!" she squawked, bounding up. She stood frozen, staring in fury at her chair.

Laughter bubbled, then swelled through the room like a wave racing toward shore. Seated at Lady Steele's right, Nick pursed his lips in an obvious and valiant attempt not to laugh. He managed to hold out until Aurora spoke in a girlishly excited voice, "Goodness, Lady Steele. Your dress is playing 'God Save the Queen.' You have a jubilee bustle."

"A jubilee bustle!" Melanie exclaimed. "I've heard a shop is selling them, but I didn't believe any lady would have nerve enough to wear one."

Aurora nodded. "Especially to this, the grandest event of the Season. What made you do such a thing?"

Melanie wrinkled her nose as if in defense of a displeasing odor. "I think it's rather tacky, myself. I know the jubilee is all the talk this spring, but one would think if you had to wear a musical bustle, you could have found a song in keeping with tonight's good luck theme. 'His Lucky Love Charm' would have been a perfect choice."

Maribeth McBride lifted her voice and called to her friends at the other table. "I thought that was an American song. You know, 'Land of the pilgrim's pride.' "

Her sister Katrina said, "For some reason, when I first heard the musical notes rising from her seat, I expected to hear the fanfare announcing a horse race."

"Really?" Maribeth asked. "Thoroughbreds or nags?"

A couple of gentlemen offered up, "Thoroughbreds."

Simultaneously, the majority of the ladies joined Maribeth in declaring, "Nags."

Lady Steele, stiff as an ice carving, glared at the Ladies Ross. As she drew in a breath, then exhaled it in a rush, Sarah could almost see the cracks forming in the woman's composure. *My oh my. This will certainly cause talk.*

"How dare you . . . you . . . menaces. I wish to speak with you in private, Lord Weston. Please, follow me."

"Menaces!" protested Emma McBride. "Hey, that's our nickname."

The amusement on Nick's face quickly transformed to annoyance at Lady Steele's summons, and seeing it lifted Sarah's spirits, as did witnessing the glare he shot his sisters. It told her he, too, suspected they were behind this quite entertaining prank. The quick grins and winks the Ross sisters shared with the McBride Menaces as their uncle followed his paramour out into the garden confirmed it.

Sarah wanted to lift her glass in a toast. Before she could, Trace McBride narrowed his eyes at his second oldest daughter and scolded, "You gave me your word."

"It wasn't us. I promise."

Katrina McBride agreed. "I know it's hard to believe, but we are totally innocent, Papa."

"You knew nothing about this?"

Maribeth winced. "Well, in the strictest interpretation of the question, Papa, we might have learned a detail or two beforehand. But we had no active role in the plan's conception or implementation."

Trace McBride's gaze swept around the nearby tables, pausing to light upon the sparkling countenances of Aurora and Melanie Ross. Addressing his daughters, he said, "You girls have made friends, haven't you?"

"We like Sarah's sisters-in-law very much."

The maligned father sighed and said, "We'll discuss this later."

Tye met Sarah's gaze. "You should have warned us, Sarah. Despite the fact they've passed on their mischief-making mantle to their younger brothers, the Menaces still know how to cause trouble. It looks as if they've found more of their kind in your husband's sisters. You must feel as if you've never left home."

"That's not true," Sarah protested as a wave of homesickness washed through her once more. "You know I love your Menaces and your Monsters and Claire and Tye's children, too. I've missed them desperately while I've been away. Why, look how much Katie has grown just in the months I've been gone."

Trace's mouth lifted in a wry grin. "You should see the changes that have happened in town during the last few months. You'd be shocked at the amount of construction going on. Three buildings I designed should reach completion this month."

"I can't wait to see them," Sarah said truthfully. Then, catching the two-fingered wave Aurora sent toward Charlotte, she felt a pang in her heart and once again felt torn in two. "Have you ever considered moving to England, Trace?"

"What?"

"Never mind. Here comes Lord Endicott with our supper."

Trace nodded. "Looks like he loaded up on the black-eyed peas. I wonder what he's needing to feel lucky about?"

"Maybe he simply likes black-eyed peas."

He shuddered and muttered, "Pig feed. Should never have made it to the supper table, if you ask me. And by the way, I know a person is supposed to eat black-eyed peas on New Year's to bring good luck in the coming year, but I didn't know the lucky aspect extended beyond the New Year."

"Don't be picky, McBride." She beamed a smile up at her supper partner and said, "Thank you, my lord. I suddenly find myself famished."

"Entertainment often does that, I understand," the man said, casting a wry glance toward the empty chairs recently occupied by Nick and Lady Steele.

Sarah smiled and took a bite of cold chicken. Trace McBride sent her a knowing look, then said, "Lady Weston and I were just talking about all the building taking place back home. Didn't I hear that you are involved in some of that?"

Lord Endicott hesitated slightly, then set down his fork. "I work for Daniel Waggoner at the Bar C Ranch. I'm in England to do a bit of horse trading on his behalf."

At that the conversation turned to horses, and while Sarah did share a Texan's natural interest in good horseflesh, her attention continued to wander to the french doors leading out into the garden. What was keeping Nick?

She picked at her food and exchanged small talk with the McBride girls until they excused themselves to join Nick's sisters in the ladies' retiring room. A few minutes later, Trace also left the table, stating a desire to check on Jenny and make certain she was eating right.

"Another child?" Sarah asked, delighted at the prospect.

Though Trace grinned sheepishly, nothing could

hide the sparkle of pride in his eyes. "Yes. After three boys in a row, we're all hoping for another girl to spoil."

"You do such a fine job at that," she teased, but inside her heart was aching. She wasn't certain exactly why it was aching, either. She was happy for Jenny and Trace. Thrilled for them. But at the same time, she couldn't help but feel a yearning for her own child.

The child Nick had offered to give her.

If she was brave enough to give up her home and the dearest friends on earth for a man who had left her once before.

She swallowed a groan.

"The meringues are delicious, aren't they?" Endicott commented, surprising Sarah until she looked down at her fork and saw that she'd taken a bite of the sweet dessert. "And I think baking them into the shape of a four-leaf clover was a clever idea. You do excel at entertaining, Lady Weston. London's ladies will be green with envy."

Something in his voice, some insistent note that had nothing to do with the words he'd said dragged her gaze from the garden door, her thoughts away from Nick and back to Lord Robert Endicott. The light in his eyes was determined, almost desperate, and suddenly she was forcibly reminded of Nick's suspicions about him. "What do you want of me, sir?"

The question took him aback. "Um, what do you mean?"

All the plans for the ball and wedding to follow had pushed concern over the alleged assassination plot to the back of Sarah's mind. She'd never honestly believed any truth to the rumor existed, but faced with Lord Endicott's obvious discomfort, she had to wonder. "Sir, may I speak frankly?"

"Please do."

"What is your interest in me? It's obviously not a romantic one. I'm not so foolish that I would miss that entirely. But I have seen more of you since my arrival in London than in months back home. Why is that?"

He sat back in his chair. She'd caught him unaware. Twice he opened his mouth to speak, then abruptly shut it. Finally, he said, "Would you care to take a walk in the garden, Lady Weston?"

Sarah licked her lips as uneasiness trickled through her. Nick suspected this man of being a killer. "No, I think it best we stay right here for the moment."

Among a crowd.

He nodded, looked away, then visibly gathered his forces. Sarah braced herself. Was he about to give her a clue about the plot to kill the queen? Was he going to ask something of her that would compromise her morals in regard to God and country? Would he tell her something that might threaten her life?

Lord Endicott said, "Lady Weston, I want to buy your house."

"Excuse me?" If he'd asked her to stand on the table and dance a jig she would not have been so surprised.

The Englishman leaned forward, his expression earnest. "Your house. I want to buy it. I'll pay a premium price for it. George Larsen at Fort Worth National Bank has promised financial backing for a project I am working on with Robert Cameron, the immigration agent for the Fort Worth and Denver Railway."

All right. He meant the house in Fort Worth, not one of Nick's properties. He meant the beautiful little house with the big front porch and the prettiest yellow rosebushes in town. It was the house she'd grown up in, the one her mother had given her after she'd remarried, and the only place she'd ever thought of as home. Lord Endicott was a fool to think she'd give it up.

She'd have to give it up if she stayed with Nick.

Sarah's voice betrayed a slight tremble as she asked, "You want to buy my home? Why?"

"For the Texas Spring Palace."

"A saloon!" she croaked.

"No, not at all. The Texas Spring Palace will be a magnificent agricultural exhibition hall displaying all the natural products of Texas under one roof. It will be a grand building, something out of a fantasy world, with wheat, cotton, and other Texas products covering the entire structure. I was excited to see Mr. McBride here tonight, in fact, because we hope to secure his architectural services to design the structure."

"What does this have to do with my house?"

Endicott didn't reply to that, but continued with his sales pitch. "Inside the exhibit hall, we want settlers and investors to be able to study samples of most grains, grasses, fruits, vegetables, and minerals produced in the state. Those interested in aesthetic pursuits will also be encouraged to tour floral, historic, scientific, and art exhibits."

As Endicott spoke, his enthusiasm grew and he reminded Sarah of some of these young Englishmen when they talked about acquiring their first coach and four.

"The Texas Spring Palace we intend to build will surpass the Sioux City Corn Palace and Toronto Ice

Palace in both novelty and artistic genius. It will serve as an educational, cultural, and entertainment center for Texas residents and guests. We expect to advertise the fair throughout the nation, and special trains will bring visitors to our fair city from as far away as Boston and Chicago. The plan is for the palace to attract settlers and investors to Texas."

"That sounds like quite an undertaking. What, may I ask again—and I trust you will answer this time—does my house have to do with it?"

"I'll explain just exactly what your home has to do with the project. You see, Lady Weston, I've quietly lined up Fort Worth's civic leaders and newspapers to support the plan. Local railroads have agreed to cosponsor the project. We'll have band concerts, vocal performances, political and religious orators, dances, and sporting events. It will be the grandest event Fort Worth has ever seen. And . . ."—he paused for effect—"it will enable Fort Worth to put Dallas to shame."

"My house, Lord Endicott. My house!"

He drew a deep breath, then exhaled in a rush. "Your home is on one of our proposed building sites, Lady Weston. I've been able to purchase or arrange to purchase every other piece of land we'll need. Our target for the opening of the Texas Spring Palace is June of 1889."

"You want to tear down my house?"

"If you'd like, we could attempt to move it."

"But I love my house. I love my roses. It's my home."

Endicott sighed. "So I understand. But think of all the good you'll be doing. Think of your civic duty."

"My mother planted those rosebushes."

"I'll transplant them myself."

Sarah sat back in her chair, her arms folded, her head tilted to one side as she studied her supper partner. Better to dwell upon this problem than worry about why Nick had yet to return from the garden with Lady Steele. "You truly care about this project, don't you?"

He nodded. "It's my life's goal."

"Buying that horse was only an excuse for you to follow me to Britain, wasn't it?"

"Yes."

Nick needs to be here to hear this. Where was he? She was having to do his job for him while he was off with another woman. "Do you harbor any deep-seated resentments against the inheritance laws of England and the aristocracy such a system has created?"

"No," he said slowly, frowning as if struggling to follow her train of thought. "Not to any great extent. I will admit to preferring the opportunities afforded a man in the American system, and while I have resented my status as a remittance man over the years, I now consider the day I sailed from England as being the luckiest day of my life."

I thought so. He has nothing to do with any assassination plot. He's too busy trying to build a seed pavilion.

That decided, Sarah still had a question or two. "But if you came all this way to convince me to sell you my property, why didn't you simply come out and ask? Why all the afternoons in my parlor pretending to court me?"

Wincing bashfully, he dragged a hand down his face. "That wasn't pretense, my lady. If you intend to end your association with Lord Weston, I would be very pleased for you to seriously consider my suit.

You are a lovely woman, inside and out, and I've come to admire you tremendously. I would be most pleased to become the gentleman in your life."

Sarah's mouth quirked. "But all in all, you'd rather buy my house."

He blinked, and his chin dropped in shock. But he recovered quickly, and for the first time since she'd known him, Robert Endicott cracked an honest grin. "Well, yes. Actually I would."

Now she laughed aloud and rose to her feet. "I think I'd like to take that stroll in the garden now, Mr. Endicott. While I am an independent woman accustomed to making my own decisions, in this particular case I insist you run your proposition past my husband. I suspect in this instance he'll be quite interested in hearing your plans for the Texas Spring Palace."

"Perhaps he would be interested in investing in the project. He does, after all, have ties to Texas."

"That he does, Mr. Endicott. For the moment, anyway."

Nick seriously considered tying Helen up and dumping her in the bushes. He was trying to be a gentleman about this, but how long did good manners require he stand there and allow the woman to chastise him?

She'd gone on for a good ten minutes, and a man could only take so much. He wouldn't have been this patient if she had said anything about his sisters that wasn't true, and he knew that much of her fury arose from an attempt to save face in the wake of his ending their burgeoning relationship.

"Helen," he said, attempting once more to interrupt her tirade. "Please. You're repeating yourself.

Besides, we can't be certain my sisters are the ones behind the prank."

"What I have to say bears repeating, and of course your sisters are the perpetrators of this vicious deed. Those girls are troublemakers, and they should be punished. They're vicious and wicked and cruel."

Now she'd crossed the line. "Enough," he said, a jagged edge to his voice. "Such talk is beneath you. You are welcome to deride me as much as you wish, but I cannot and will not allow you to denigrate my sisters. Mischievous acts aside, they are not at fault for what has transpired between us. I am sorry if I hurt you, Helen. It was never my intention."

"You made promises to me," she accused. "You purposely deceived me."

"No," he quietly defended himself. "That I never did. I spent time with you, provided you escort, but I never made you promises. I never took you to my bed."

"No, you didn't. You didn't, curse you. You didn't."

She raised her hand to slap him, but Nick grabbed her wrist. When she would have used the other hand, he grasped that one, too. Disturbed to see the Ice Queen lose her composure, Nick spoke in a conciliatory tone. "Helen, please."

"Do you know how many men have invited me to their beds since my husband died? Dozens. Do you know how many men have proposed marriage to me? Dozens. Do you know how many men I've wanted in my bed, wanted to marry? One. You, Lord Weston. You are the only one. You are the only man for me. I love you."

Damnation. Her confession left him at a loss for words. He'd known she admired him, desired him, but he never realized her feelings went this deep. He'd always believed she was more interested in being the Marchioness of Weston than his wife.

Then a tear spilled from her eye to trail slowly down her cheek, and Nick could stand no more. He wrapped her in his arms and gave her a comforting hug.

She caught him by surprise when she lifted her face, pulled his head down to hers, and trapped his mouth in a kiss.

Wasn't it just Nick's luck that at that particular moment, Sarah strolled down the garden path?

When a hen walks into a wedding reception and cackles, it brings good luck.

~18~

When Nick spied his wife standing in the muted glow of Chinese lanterns lighting the garden, his lips still damp from Helen's kiss, he felt like howling at the moon. Was this not the worst sort of cliché?

He immediately stepped away from Helen and toward Sarah, and that was when he noticed she was taking her garden stroll on the arm of a suspected assassin. His temper, already strained from his own situation, soared. "Sarah, what do you think you are doing?"

Even as he said it, he thought it quite likely the dumbest comment he'd ever made.

Apparently, Sarah agreed because she laughed. An honest, amused giggle. That, more than Helen's declaration of love, shocked Nick speechless. That was why he didn't say anything when she turned to Endicott and said, "I do believe I'm ready to bargain, Robert. You get that woman out of my garden and away from my party, and I'll reconsider selling you my house."

Endicott, curse his black soul, beamed a grin, then leaned down and kissed Sarah. Right on the mouth. "I make it a practice to always seal my bargains with a kiss."

Nick snarled and came close to baring his teeth as Endicott approached. As little as he wanted Helen clinging to him, his conscience troubled him at releasing her to this man. What if he was part of a plot to kill Queen Victoria?

He's not going to do it tonight in your garden, no more than in your drawing room on a weekday afternoon while he's calling on your wife.

"I'm losing my mind," Nick muttered.

"I'm not leaving," Helen snapped, her chin lifting

"Yes, you are." Endicott took her hand and tugged. "I have my heart set on that house." When she planted her feet and refused to budge, he lifted her up and carried her from the scene.

"Well," Nick said. "Alone at last."

Sarah folded her arms. "I wondered what was keeping you."

Distracted by the way her arms pillowed and pushed up her breasts, he fumbled for a response. "Sarah ... um ... it's not ... I didn't ... you arrived at an awkward time."

"Obviously."

"That's not what I ... oh, damnation." He raked his fingers through his hair, then made a stab at distracting her. "What is this about selling Endicott your house?"

Her brow arched pointedly. "All right, I'll start. But we will revisit the subject of Lady Steele."

Lovely.

"Mr. Endicott is not your assassin, Nick."

Grimly he replied, "From the appearance of things, he is *your* assassin, Sarah."

Her lips twitched. Nick wanted to bite them. "Are you jealous?"

"Yes, as a matter of fact I am."

"Good. That makes two of us."

So she was jealous? Well. Good. That *was* a positive sign, wasn't it?

As Nick mulled over that question, she launched into a tale of how Endicott came to be in England, and why she didn't consider him a candidate for the mastermind of a plot to kill the queen. Once Nick got past the idea that the man had followed Sarah all the way from Texas to London, he focused on what she was saying. When she had finished, he frowned. "Endicott's reported involvement in this project may be a cover story for his true reason for being in London—an assassination attempt."

"True, but I don't believe that. He spoke with such enthusiasm and conviction. It occurs to me that one way to prove his intentions would be to sell him my house and see if he leaves London."

Everything inside Nick froze. He wanted to ask her if that meant she'd made up her mind to stay in England. To stay with him. But a flash of emotion he saw in her eyes convinced him to choose his words with care. "You'd sell him your house?"

She shrugged. "He convinced me that the Texas Spring Palace is a good idea and important for the future of Fort Worth. He tells me it might be possible to move my house, and I could transplant Mother's rosebushes. I wouldn't mind being farther from downtown. It's quite noisy on Saturday nights."

Nick's stomach slid into a dive, and finally he lost his patience. "Damnation, Sarah. What are you saying? Have you decided to return to Fort Worth?"

She closed her eyes and spoke softly. "A vision

plays across my mind. It's my home with its yellow roses in bloom, the McBride Menaces pushing their little brothers and cousins in the swing hanging from the branch of an old oak tree. I see myself laughing with Jenny over silks and satins in Jenny's workroom and swiping a spoonful of chocolate icing from a bowl in Claire's bakery, then sharing it with her little ones. I picture sitting in my office sipping tea with my aunt and mother during their biannual trips to Fort Worth."

Then she looked at him, eyes gleaming in the moonlight. She was so lovely, almost ethereal in the soft, hazy light. Dressed in a gown of sunbeams and sparkling jewels, Sarah was a fairy princess stepped from the pages of a book.

However, the tale she told was worthy of the Brothers Grimm.

"The McBrides' arrival has brought it all back to me," she explained. "It's reminded me how much I love my home. For a while, I ached with the need to be there. We're different in that way, Nick. You're the adventurer, the wanderer, the world traveler. I'm a small-town homebody who builds a nest—with lots of frippery, true—but it's my space and that's where I belong. That was true on the day we wed and it's still true today."

"You've been happy here with us, with me," he told her.

"Yes. I have. Lady Steele reminded me of that tonight."

Nick drew back. How was it this woman always managed to surprise him? "She did?"

Nodding, she approached him, her hips swaying gracefully, an enigmatic glint in her eyes. "Your family has made a place for me. I love that. I love them.

The McBrides and Lord Endicott helped me remember all the good things about Texas. It's your turn, Nick. Seeing Lady Steele in your arms convinces me that you should remind me of why I like it here in England."

She completely robbed him of all conscious thought when she lifted her hand to his face, pulled him toward her, and said, "Nick, if you wanted to indulge in moonlit kisses, why didn't you ask me?"

Then Sarah, completely of her own volition, fused her mouth with his.

Nick was accustomed to the lust that slammed into him like a hot, greedy fist. What he didn't expect was the sense of coming home that flooded through him like a warm and gentle rain.

He wrapped his arms around her and gathered her against him, drowning in the sweet, luscious taste of her tender kiss. She felt like heaven in his arms. He'd missed her. Caught up in the strategy of winning her, of denying himself the pleasure of seduction, he hadn't realized how much he missed just holding her.

Nick groaned against her mouth and she stretched like a cat and purred in return. The sound shuddered through him. Unable to resist, he deepened the kiss.

His tongue delved into her mouth, stroked her sweet velvet softness. She answered him, played with him, tested the bounds of his control. Seconds passed and the need within him spiraled. Again and again and again he plundered her mouth, giving her the reminder she'd requested, stoking the desire that had hummed between them for so long. God, how he wanted this. Wanted her.

What would he do if she left him?

Fear struck like a bullet. *No. I won't let that happen. I won't let you go. You're mine, Sarah. Mine!*

In an instant, the tenor of his touch changed. She wanted reminding, did she? Fine. He was good at this, better than good, and it was time she allowed him to show her. She'd given him an opening, and Nick, by God, would take it.

He growled deep in his throat and yanked her against him. He crushed her mouth with his as his hands swept mercilessly over her, determined to arouse, to inflame, to bring her to the razor edge of need upon which he himself stood in balance.

She whimpered and wriggled and dropped her head back, offering herself. Nick felt the pounding of her pulse as his lips feasted on her neck. His nostrils flared as the scent of arousal perfumed the air, and it took every ounce of his willpower not to toss up her skirts and take her then and there.

Wild and feral, he half carried, half dragged her deeper into the shadows and there, in the darkness, he blessed the current fashion of ball gowns and made short work of baring her breasts.

Allowing her no time for fear or doubt, he drew one nipple into his hungry mouth while his hand kneaded the other breast. She gave a soft cry and tellingly clasped him to her. Ruthlessly his hands delved beneath her skirt, coaxed and stroked and pushed past the barriers of fine underclothes to find the softest silk of all.

She gasped out his name, and he groaned in reply. His mouth trailed hot hungry kisses against every inch of skin bared to him. She trembled in his arms. Shuddered. Nick's fingers played across that slick, heated skin, and he decided the time had come to show her what she was missing. To give her some of what he was aching to give her, dying to give her.

The weeks of slow seduction had taken their toll on

Nick. Lust was a living, fire-breathing animal inside him. He wanted to use his mouth on her, to give her the most intimate of kisses and feast upon her until she screamed. He wanted to rip off his trousers and take her, to bury himself in her tight, wet passage and pound away the months—the years—of frustrated desire he felt for this woman alone.

But Sarah, he remembered—just barely—was a virgin. His frightened little virgin bride. She deserved better than a tumble in a darkened garden while hundreds waltzed in the ballroom only a shout away. No matter how badly he wanted it, wanted her, he couldn't do this. Not here and now, maybe not ever.

He would allow her the choice, even if it killed him.

But in the meantime, he'd give her something to think about. He slipped a finger into her weeping sheath and his thumb found that little knot of nerves. Slowly, lovingly, he worked her.

"Nick?"

"Let go, lass. Don't fight it. Give us this. You said it was my turn to remind you. Let me give you something you'll never want to forget."

Nick closed his eyes and submersed himself in the sensations available to him. Slick, satiny heat. A salty taste on his tongue. Soft, needy whimpers and the musky scent of sex. Moments later, he sent her flying. Sarah cried out as release found her and she shook in his arms like a tree in a gale.

"Yes, lass. Yes," he murmured fiercely, her satisfaction his own.

When she finally calmed, Nick cradled her gently and tenderly kissed away the tears that had slipped from her eyes to spill silently down her cheeks.

The last walls guarding his heart shattered.

From out of the pieces came the words that pride and self-preservation had kept silent. *I love you, Sarah. I love you. Don't leave me.*

In the days following the engagement ball, the pace of life picked up considerably. Awnings went up on the grand flower-decked mansions of Belgravia as the gaiety of the Season shifted into full swing. Between the fashionable flower shows, luncheon engagements, appearances among the bustle of Rotten Row, visits to the theater, the opera, concerts, dinner parties, and balls, Sarah was busy with wedding preparations and trying to control Lady Pratt. The groom's mother was driving poor Charlotte to distraction.

Nick, on the other hand, was driving Sarah crazy.

After their exchange in the garden—which still had the power to bring a blush to Sarah's cheeks—the tone of their relationship had taken yet another turn. Her husband had resumed his Pillow Book entries, but rather than writing letters of seduction, he'd taken to telling her stories about his family. He wrote little snippets about his life either during his childhood or in the years since his return. Sarah enjoyed reading them, and she was happy for the view inside the family. It made her feel included.

But all in all, she rather missed the risqué letters, especially since she now had a clearer understanding of what he'd written.

Nick never referred to the incident in the garden, but then, she didn't see him all that much. His social calendar and hers seldom overlapped. Whether due to coincidence or his design, she couldn't say for certain, but she liked to think it was because of the differences in their individual pursuits. She was making wedding arrangements. He was tracking a suspected assassin—Lord Chambers.

Sarah still didn't believe Trevor had anything to do with a plot to kill the queen. The man didn't have a murderous bone in his body, despite the blood-thirsty looks he shot her husband whenever their paths had crossed since the night of Charlotte's ball. Trevor had caught her sneaking up to her room to tidy herself after her gambol in the garden with Nick, and her swollen lips and mussed appearance had left little doubt as to her activities. His pursuit of her had cooled since then, and he'd stopped paying his after-noon calls at Weston House, hence Nick's need to venture farther afield to keep track of his suspect.

Now if Sarah could do something to weed out the others who had taken his place in her parlor. What was it about these Britons anyway? Were there not enough women to go around? Why did so many feel compelled to pursue a woman whose annulment might yet take months to work its way through the legal system?

Yes, months. Perhaps even a year. After consulting with her attorney husband, Claire McBride had let Sarah in on that little fact. Sarah was still trying to fig-ure out how to feel about that revelation. Claire claimed her difficulty in making a decision about her future was, in fact, a decision in itself. Jenny had agreed with her sister-in-law, saying if Sarah truly wanted the annulment, she'd have taken up residence someplace other than the bedroom next to Nick's.

On those rare occasions when Sarah allowed her-self to think about it, she suspected they just might be right.

One of those moments when the annulment was

very much on her mind occurred as she dressed one morning just a week before the wedding. Her gaze kept straying to the Pillow Book on the table beside her bed. Finally, she broke down and picked it up to read yet again Nick's entry from the night before. This one dealt neither with family nor seduction, and it touched her heart differently than any of the others.

My Dearest Sarah,

I spent an hour this afternoon playing ball with the McBride boys in the garden at Weston House. At one point, when young Bobby McBride overthrew his brother and the ball landed beneath a yew bush, they called upon me to save the day—something about trousers and dirt and their mother's happiness—by retrieving it.

While down on my hands and knees reaching for the ball, my fingers brushed the round leather surface and I found myself contemplating the nature of a sphere.

At first glance, a sphere is but a single entity—a ball, an orange, the moon in the sky. On closer study, one will see that it is, in fact, made up of an infinite number of circles. In life, those circles are home, family, friends, career . . . the list goes on. What those circles share is a midpoint. A common center. A common core.

I closed my hand around the ball and dragged it from beneath the bush. I sat in the grass and stared at the ball in my hand and thought of you.

Many circles make up the sphere of my life, Sarah. They have but one core.

That core is you.

Nick

Sarah sighed as she gently closed the book and returned it to the table. What exactly was he trying to say with that letter? She had a suspicion, but she shied away from the little four-letter word. The ramifications were too great, and she didn't have time to deal with them right now. "I have a wedding to arrange," she murmured.

And at last night's dinner party she'd learned of a little shop on Oxford Street that carried white grosgrain ribbon decorated with green four-leaf clovers, and she simply had to have it. She'd think of a way to use it somewhere, she felt certain.

As she made her way downstairs, she heard the rumble of masculine speech coming from the dining room. She recognized Nick's voice, and the other sounded familiar, too, though she couldn't quite place it until she entered the room.

"Good morning, Sarah," Nick said, rising from his seat at the table. "You remember Lord Kimball, don't you?"

"Of course. Welcome to Weston House, Lord Kimball. I know my husband has been anxious to speak with you."

"It's my pleasure to be here, my lady. Very much so. My trip to Ireland was . . ."—he paused, and his mouth twisted in a wry grin—"less than pleasant. I understand Lady Charlotte's engagement ball proved quite eventful."

Alarmed, Sarah darted a glance toward Nick. Surely he wouldn't have told about their . . . encounter . . . in the garden.

Her husband calmly poured her a cup of coffee and gestured for her to join them at the table. "I've been telling Kimball about your supper talk with Endicott."

She all but sighed aloud in relief. "I signed my house over to him last week. He sailed for home on Monday."

"Excellent. That leaves us with Lord Chambers as our only suspect."

"If such a plot even exists," Sarah said, setting down her cup. "I truly don't believe Lord Chambers would be involved in something this wicked."

Lord Kimball nodded. "You may be right, Lady Weston. My office is investigating this rumor from other directions, and as of now, we have failed to discover any information that corroborates the letter from Texas. However, in the case of bomb threats, I will pursue every warning, rumor, and whisper in the wind to its end."

The conviction in his voice gave Sarah pause. Lord Kimball had a personal stake in the matter of bombings.

His next words proved her suspicions true. "Six years ago I was slow to believe a threat that came across my desk, and as a result, a seven-year-old boy died in a bombing outside Salford Barracks. While this particular Texas connection to the Fenians is suspect, others are quite real. My recent trip to Ireland netted two criminals who admitted to a frighteningly similar plan. A third man died of wounds suffered in a knife fight with one of my detectives, who was also fatally wounded in the struggle. Until Lord Chambers is exonerated or proven guilty, he will be kept under surveillance." Turning to Weston, he added, "I trust you've taken measures to see to this?"

Nick nodded. "I've hired the best private security available. Although, now that you're back, if you can spare a man or two of yours I'd be happier. I'm not confident in these men's ability."

While Nick and the spymaster discussed the surveillance operation, Sarah checked the time displayed on the ormolu mantel clock and waited for a pause in the conversation. "If you will excuse me, I've some wedding business that needs tending."

The men stood, and Nick walked her to the door. "What are your plans for this evening?"

She thought a moment. "Lady Pratt has asked me to attend the Wainscott musicale. A cousin of hers has come to town for the wedding, and she wants to introduce us. Is there something you needed?"

"You." He smiled ruefully and gave his head a shake. "I'd like to have dinner with you tonight if at all possible. A simple meal and pleasant conversation for just the two of us. I feel the need for one peaceful evening before all the wedding madness commences."

"That sounds lovely."

"Eight o'clock?"

"I'll be here."

Sarah floated all the way to Oxford Street. She found the ribbon and bought the shopkeeper's entire stock. Then, with her dinner appointment preempting the upcoming wedding in her mind, she recalled a perfumer she'd visited last week, and decided she could spare the time for one more call.

Halfway between the ribbon shop and the perfumers, she spied a familiar figure peering at the silks and plushes displayed in Marshall and Snelgrove's side windows. At least, she thought he was looking at the fabrics. The way he moved his head made her wonder if he were actually primping in his reflection in the plate-glass windows.

Trevor Chambers always had been rather vain about his appearance.

Though her natural inclination was to greet him and exchange pleasantries, Lord Kimball's warnings of the morning caused her to hesitate. She was glad she did when, seconds later, he turned sharply away from the window and bolted toward a nearby alley. "Well," she murmured aloud. "That was certainly odd."

His motives became clear when she realized a street vendor had hurried after him. Trevor had spotted Nick's surveillance person.

His reaction bothered Sarah. Why would an innocent man act in such a manner? Maybe he wasn't as innocent as she thought. However, he could be acting guilty for a reason other than involvement in a plan to kill the queen. Maybe he was seeing a married woman, and he thought her husband was on his trail.

Sarah could certainly attest to the fact that he didn't mind courting married women.

The urge to follow the men was strong, but Sarah recognized the foolishness of the idea. If by some chance Trevor were guilty of the nefarious plot, and spying the spy had tipped him off that his secret was revealed, her former beau could be dangerous. It would be better for her to turn around and hurry home and tell Nick what she'd seen.

But she truly did want that new perfume.

Nibbling at her bottom lip, Sarah decided she wouldn't follow them. She'd simply continue on her way to the perfume shop and maybe glance down the alley as she walked past. She probably wouldn't see a thing, since they'd probably be gone by the time she reached them.

Justifications in place, Sarah resumed her walk. She made it halfway across the opening of the alley when the crash of an ash can and a human yelp of pain drew her gaze like a magnet down the passageway's narrow, murky length. At first she spied nothing more then spilling shadows, then as her eyes adjusted to the gloom, what she saw made her gasp in shock.

Trevor and the man were wrestling on the ground. Over a knife. They rolled in the muck, both of them grunting with exertion, turning the air blue with their curses and the cobbles beneath them red with blood. Sarah couldn't tell which man was wounded. Maybe both were.

Her heart pounded. What to do? She opened her mouth to scream for help when suddenly the other man spotted her. "Lady Weston," he ground out. "Run."

After that, everything happened in a flash. Trevor's head whipped around, and the other man took advantage of his distraction and grabbed the knife. "Have you now, you blighter," the stranger growled. "I'll not—"

He suddenly gasped, groaned, and rolled off Trevor, his hand covering his privates as he curled into a ball. Trevor bounded to his feet and rushed toward Sarah. She backed away. "Help!" she cried, even as she turned to run.

He caught her from behind, one hand wrapping around her waist, the other muffling her mouth. She struggled, twisting and kicking and even trying to bite as he pulled her back into the shadows of the alley. The metallic scent of blood wafted up to assault her nostrils, and the harsh sound of his labored breaths against her ear sent shivers down her spine. She was frightened clear down to the bone.

"Hell, Sarah. Why did it have to be you?"

She spied the glint of the knife in his hand, then

something else. A small bottle. She renewed her struggles, and he shifted her in his arms. For a moment his hold on her eased, and she had the wild idea that she might just get away.

Then a handkerchief in Trevor's hand came toward Sarah's face, and suddenly she saw no more.

~19~

Nick had met Trace and Tye McBride at the Turf Club for lunch when a Weston House footman tracked him down to tell him of an emergency at home. The three men rushed back to find a Mr. Tom Parnell sitting in Nick's kitchen, his various scrapes, scratches, and one vicious-looking knife wound on his meaty arm being tended to by the housekeeper.

"A wily fox, that one was," he said, dabbing at the cut on his mouth with a damp rag. "Never expected him to ambush me like that. Still, I held my own until your lady showed up. I fell trying to protect her, I did. You shouldn't have let her go off on her own, milord. These modern ideas will lead a woman into trouble every time, if you ask me. Why—"

"Where is my wife?"

"That's what I came to tell you. He disappeared with her. There I was rolling on the ground, me nuts smashed all the way up to me throat, and me vision in a haze when I saw him grab her. Got up, I did, hardly able to move, but it was too late. She collapsed, went boneless as bread pudding, and he carried her off. By the time I hobbled meself to the street, they'd disappeared."

The old saying about killing the messenger had never sounded so good. Nick eyed a kitchen knife with the thought of finishing what Trevor Chambers had begun. It helped his temper not at all when his three worried sisters rushed into the kitchen, the three McBride Menaces and two McBride wives on their heels. He didn't need to deal with hand-wringing women right now.

A second look revealed that none of them were wringing their hands. Every last one of them held a weapon of one sort or another. "Aurora, where in the world did you get a bullwhip?"

"I bought it for your birthday gift, but I decided I might need it now."

Claire McBride expertly checked the chamber of a pistol, then tucked it in her skirt pocket. "What can we do to help, Lord Weston?"

His mind in a whirl, Nick glanced around at the people Sarah loved and admitted, "I don't know. I don't know where to start."

Fear was a living, breathing monster inside him, and only his training and experience kept him from surrendering to the beast. He turned to the McBride brothers. "Do you have any suggestions?"

Tye McBride rubbed the back of his neck, then suggested, "Well, first I'd send word to your friend Lord Kimball at the Special Branch. Then I think we should put men in every club Chambers is known to frequent."

Charlotte turned a worried gaze on Nick. "Loudon is a terribly big city. How can we hope to find her?"

"I'll find her," Nick said grimly. "I promise you, I'll find her if I have to search every building in London."

Having said it aloud, he suddenly believed it. He strode toward his office, gesturing for the others to follow. "Ladies, I appreciate your willingness to join the search, but what I need most at the moment is your penmanship. I need to send notes around to a number of different people, and the sooner they're written and dispatched, the sooner we'll be able to begin our search, and the sooner we'll bring Sarah home."

Five of the girls and the McBride wives headed immediately for Nick's office, but Charlotte hung behind. The teary guilt in her eyes stopped him. "What is it, love?" he asked.

"It's all my fault. She wouldn't have gone out today if Lady Pratt hadn't gone on and on about the ribbon. This wedding business has gotten entirely out of hand, and it's all my fault. I wanted a special wedding, and now Sarah is in danger because of it. Why didn't Rodney and I just elope! If something terrible happens to Sarah, I'll never forgive myself."

Nick gave his sister a quick, hard hug. "Nothing terrible is going to happen to Sarah. I won't allow it."

"But how are we going to find her?"

"I'm the Marquess of Weston, sweetheart, and I will use every bit of power and influence that position has to offer. I'll tear this town apart to find her."

She sniffled and wiped away a tear. "You must bring her home, Nicholas. I love her."

"I love her, too, Charlotte. I love her, too."

And by God, he'd tell her so himself before this day was done.

Sarah awoke with a pounding head and a queasy stomach. Slowly the events of the morning came trickling back, and alarm gave her the energy to lift her eyelids.

A set of beady black eyes stared back at her from a narrow, furry face, black but for the line of white running down the center.

Oh, my heavens. Is that a ... ?

Trevor Chambers spoke up. "You're awake."

"Skunk?"

"It's Trevor, Sarah."

"It's a skunk," she repeated.

He patted her face with a cool, damp cloth. "I know it may seem that way to you now, but you have to understand that I tried to protect you. That man had a knife."

She tore her gaze away from the animal pacing in a cage a short distance away and focused on the man she once considered her friend. He knelt on one knee in front of her in torn and bloodied shirtsleeves. "*You* had a knife."

"I took it away from him. After he cut me. Look." He pulled aside the tear in the white linen and showed her a long, oozing slice in his skin.

She shut her eyes, tried to concentrate and clear her head. "Where are we? What happened?"

"That man attacked me. He followed me and I caught him at it. I only thought to confront him. I never expected him to try to kill me."

Sarah struggled to sit up. Her head reeled and her stomach threatened to revolt, but she gritted her teeth and waited for the worst of it to pass. "You hit me."

"No, I did not!" His voice rang with offense. "I anesthetized you. The warehouse was on my itinerary for the day, so I was carrying a bottle of chloroform for the skunks."

So those spots before her eyes—or stripe, in this case—weren't a figment of her imagination. "The girls and I have talked about this. England doesn't have skunks."

Trevor's eyes twinkled wickedly, and he grinned. "They do now."

At that point, Sarah attempted to stand. She realized she was bound at both wrists and ankles, and she began to struggle. "What is this? Why am—"

"Wait. Be still. You're making her nervous. She's beginning to pace, and that's a warning sign."

He lifted Sarah into his arms and carried her away from the cage, which she now realized was one of two. The smaller of the two held one skunk; the larger a mama and six little babies. No fool, Sarah quit struggling until he attempted to set her down a good fifty feet from the cages. She wondered if it was far enough. "Where are we?"

"St. Katherine's Docks. I told the landlord I'm exporting antiques to Texas. There's a pleasing view of Tower Bridge I'll show you later if possible. First, though, I need to fix a bed for you. I wasn't expecting guests." He hesitated, frowned, and said, "I don't know quite what to do about all of this, Sarah. I never intended to involve you. What a piece of bad luck that you saw me. I should not have followed you, I know, but I saw you in Oxford Street and you looked so beautiful, so happy. It was quite a blow."

Incredulous, Sarah could do no more than stare at him.

He continued, "All these months, I have carried a

torch for you. I didn't want to believe that our relationship was over. I thought once your legal tangle was solved, you would turn to me once again. Then I watched you at Charlotte's engagement ball and saw how you sparkled with Weston and I began to doubt. Today when I saw you walking in the street, your happiness a beacon in your smile, the spring in your step, the glow about you, I finally realized I had lost. You're his. I was following you, realizing this, when I noted the man following me." He exhaled a heavy sigh and added, "And then you had to see us. What am I going to do now, Sarah?"

"Let me go."

"I cannot do that, I'm afraid. It would ruin everything."

"What's everything?"

His gaze traveled from her to the skunks and he smirked. "Just a little surprise I have planned for the jubilee."

She gasped. "Trevor, no. Nick was right. You're part of the Fenian dynamite war."

Trevor drew back. "The Fenians! I should say not. They're killers. You wouldn't believe the shocking information about them that came my way. Do you remember Shaun Gallagher who worked for the Triple C Ranch out toward Weatherford? His cousin from Chicago was part of that group. I met him one night in Hell's Half Acre. After we spent a few hours drinking and disparaging Britain, he approached me about joining his cause and told me about a truly ghastly scheme the Fenians were planning."

He shuddered at the memory, then continued, "I reported what I knew—anonymously, of course— and two days later Gallagher was found murdered in his bed. I think the Fenians killed him for speaking out of turn. The only reason I'm still alive is that I pretended to have been too drunk to recall meeting Gallagher, much less the plot. It's true that as an American I can sympathize with the Fenians' cause, but I don't condone killing."

Somewhat reassured, Sarah was also confused. "You are referring to the conspiracy to bomb Westminster Abbey during the queen's jubilee thanksgiving service?"

"That's the one."

"But if you're not involved in that, then why am I here? What's going on? Why am I tied up?"

"Well . . ." He stood and backed away from her, the ease in his manner fading. "The truth is, my darling, while I'm not involved in the Fenian conspiracy, I do have a bombing plot of my own."

Sarah's stomach dropped and rolled around some more. "Now I'm totally befuddled. Didn't you just say you don't condone killing?"

"Killing is not required to make a political statement, Sarah. The Fenians want to bring down a government. I want to get the government's attention. Times have changed, and the aristocracy refuses to change with it. Primogeniture is a barbaric system that has brought heartache and despair to many a family. Why should birth order determine the worthiness of a man, I ask? Why should younger sons be forced to leave their home, family, and country to seek their fortune?

"It's hard to leave one's home, Sarah. To go a stranger to a strange land, especially when one has been trained to idleness and sport, not the skills needed to work. Knowledge of Cicero and Caesar doesn't help a man survive a Montana blizzard. Knowing how to command a coach and four won't help bake a loaf of bread to keep yourself from starving."

"Oh, Trevor. What are you planning?"

"The inheritance laws in this country must be changed. Parliament is the only one who can change them. I intend to get Parliament's attention in such a manner they'll never forget. I have taken the Fenians' plan and given it my own special twist. It's quite clever, I must admit. Some might say diabolically clever. Imagine, if you will, Sarah, the scene in Westminster Abbey at the jubilee service. Every peer in the realm will be there. Every eldest son in his velvet and ermine coronation robes passed down through generations with their precious titles. Think of all the satins and silks." A maniacal light entered his eyes as his gaze slid toward the cages. A soft laugh escaped him.

Recognition of his intentions burst in Sarah's brain like a bomb. A particularly malodorous explosion.

Trevor Chambers intended to turn his skunks loose in Westminster Abbey during Queen Victoria's thanksgiving service.

"Oh my heavens."

"Yes. It will cause quite a stink, won't it?"

Within an hour, Nick had thirty men on the job with the prospect of twice that many more on the way. The plan was to begin in the West End at the spot of the abduction and stop every four-wheeler and hansom cab on the street. Drivers were asked whether they had either seen or transported a pair matching the description of Sarah or Lord Chambers. Men were assigned to search every spot Chambers had been known to visit since his return to

London. Others were charged with the task of interviewing every family member, friend, servant, and acquaintance in any way connected with Trevor Chambers. Word was put out on the street that the Marquess of Weston was offering a significant reward for information that led to the rescue of his wife.

Once the rush of making the initial arrangements had passed, time dragged like a slug for Nick. He paced his study, pausing to set the old, yellowed globe of the world slowly spinning as if that would make time pass faster. Seated around his desk, the McBride brothers spoke in low tones with the newly arrived Lord Kimball, informing him of the status of the search.

Suddenly Nick couldn't bear to stay at home and wait for news another moment. He slapped the surface of the globe, sending it whirling. "I'll be helping the men at the intersection of Regent and Bond. Send word to me there if you hear anything at all."

With that, he strode from the room and out of the house. He was descending the broad stone steps of the portico when he heard the sound of footsteps in pursuit. At the half landing, he glanced back to see his sisters with the McBride girls hot on their heels. "Can we come with you, Nicholas?" Melanie asked.

"Isn't there something we can do?" Maribeth McBride added.

"Pray," he told them. "Stay here where you're safe and where I needn't worry about you, and pray for Sarah's safety. Please?"

They protested mildly but agreed with his request. Nick then spent the next four hours stopping cabs, asking questions, then handing over a calling card for the drivers to display to signify they already had been questioned.

With each hour that passed, he grew just a little more desperate. Then finally, as church bells rang half past the hour of three, he heard a voice call his name. "Weston. Hurry. We have a lead."

Tied, gagged, propped against a wooden crate, and facing two occupied skunk cages, Sarah sat fuming. And praying that didn't prove to be a poor choice of words.

She was almost afraid to move. Before he'd left the warehouse, Trevor had given her a quick review of how to coexist peacefully with the little mammals. "You might know this already, since you're a Texas girl, but just in case, remember that skunks demand respect. They won't spray unless they're feeling threatened, so as long as you're quiet and still, you should not be bothered by them. If one of them should stomp his feet and turn his back to you, you're in trouble. By the time he raises his tail and glances back over his shoulder, it's too late."

Because Sarah had no intention of causing it to become "too late," she moved as little as possible while she was left alone. When sometime later a door opened, then banged shut, it was all she could do not to shush whoever came inside.

"Whoever" turned out to be Trevor, returned with a mattress, a dressing screen, a chamber pot, blankets, and a picnic basket. The blankets he draped over the cages as a measure of protection. According to Trevor, the skunks were less likely to spray if they didn't see the threat.

He arranged the items in a makeshift bedroom complete with a bud vase and a fragrant red rose which he placed atop a small crate beside the mattress. From the warehouse itself, he unearthed a rug, a pair of chairs, and a set of fine Irish bed linens. Finally, he resettled Sarah into a chair and, after cautioning her to quiet, removed the gag from her mouth and the bindings from her wrists and ankles. He added a further caution against attempting an escape. As soon as she had sipped the water he offered, she said, "Trevor, you cannot get away with this. You must release me."

He ignored her, saying, "I brought cold meats and cheeses for dinner. I know you missed lunch and must be quite hungry. I apologize for the accommodations, and I assure you that I'll do everything within my power to afford you comfort. You'll be pleased to know I've identified another place for us to sleep tonight. We will need to wait until dark to go there, however, but that shouldn't be a problem. The skunks are nocturnal, so they are not particularly active until those hours."

At this point, certain he wouldn't hurt her, Sarah was more angry than afraid. She tried again, "Nick will find me. He'll know that you are behind my disappearance, and he'll track us down. He was an intelligence agent, Trevor. He is already working with the head of a Special Branch of the Metropolitan Police, plus he has an unlimited source of funds. You'll never evade him for a month until the jubilee. Your plan will not work!"

He shoved his hands in his pockets, rocked back on his heels, and looked past her shoulder for a long moment. When finally he spoke, his voice was subdued. "I know."

She waited, allowing the silence between them to stretch out. He sighed heavily and sank down into one of the chairs. He sat with his elbows on his knees, his head down, and his chin against his chest. "I know it's over. I didn't want to face it. You know what this means."

"Nick may very well hurt you."

"He might kill me," Trevor said with a snort. "Although, hopefully I'll be gone before he finds me. I've booked passage on a ship that leaves with the morning tide. This will be my last night in England. I'll release you in the morning, Sarah."

The relief she felt was tempered by a twinge of sadness she felt on Trevor's behalf. "You love it here."

"England is my home. This is where I was born, where I went to school, where I came of age. This is where my mother and my brothers and sisters live, where the friends I've known my entire life make their homes. It's the scents of the countryside and the sounds of the city. Put yourself in my place, Sarah. You've been here what? Four months?"

"A bit longer."

"Long enough to have a glimpse of understanding, I would think. Imagine, if you will, going years on end without hearing that soft drawl native to a Texan's tongue or seeing a spectacular Texas sunset. Think of your Thanksgiving dinner without sweet potato pie or even . . ." He paused and laughed. "Or never smelling the particular fragrance in the air that announces when a cattle drive is headed through town."

With an inward grin, she made a show of sniffing the air. "Do you mean you actually miss the stink of the Thames, Trevor?"

"It's the stench of home, of the familiar. Believe it or not, I do miss it upon occasion. Not as often as I find myself missing steak and kidney pie, of course."

"Of course." She blew a strand of hair away from

her face. "But Trevor, as I remember, I introduced you to molasses cookies. You came to adore them. In the same vein, can you not adapt to your new home just as well? Can't you make new memories? New friends? A new family?"

"I tried. I tried with you, if you'll recall. It's been five years since I left home, and no matter what new friends I make, I always feel as if something is missing. There is a place inside me that has been empty all this time. Coming home filled that hole in my soul. It shouldn't be that way, I know. People leave their homes and family to make new lives in new places all the time. I should be able to do so, too. However, it hasn't worked that way for me. Life in England fits me like a comfortable old slipper. I've been walking barefoot over nettles in America."

Sarah shifted in her seat. His talk had made her uneasy because it struck so close to her own heart, her own fears. "So why did you ever leave?"

His smile was bittersweet. "When my father died, my brother inherited everything—title, estate, and, most important to me, control of my trust fund. He wanted me gone. I resisted, but all the power rested with him, and eventually he succeeded in forcing me to go. My first years in America were ... difficult. I kept my sanity by dreaming of revenge."

Shooting her a wry look, he added, "Believe me when I say my early schemes were much more violent than turning skunks loose during a church service."

Sarah bit back a grin. "I can just see Queen Victoria up on her throne, holding up her robes as Sally Skunk marches past with a line of babies following behind. Did you ever hear the story of when the McBride Menaces turned mice and cats and dogs loose in First Methodist during Trace and Jenny's wedding?"

He nodded. "That's what gave me the idea."

Laughter bubbled out at that. "The McBride Menaces strike again."

"I like those girls. They have spirit."

"Yes. They're a lot like Nick's sisters." The mention of her husband caused Sarah to sober. They must be frantic with worry by now. "Trevor, why don't you let me go now. You haven't committed a crime yet, I don't believe. Unless importing skunks is illegal, and I'm trying to forget they're over there."

"I kidnapped you."

"Well, yes. There is that. But I think I could explain it away to Nick. I certainly could try, I understand what you're going through, Trevor." She hesitated, licked her lips, then said, "I'm facing a similar situation myself. Nick would like me to stay here, but I'm afraid I feel about Texas the way you feel about England."

"Are you no more a marchioness than I am a cowboy?"

She smiled ruefully. "I'm afraid not. But then again, if I wear that proverbial new slipper long enough, I might break it in. It's all a jumble in my mind. I thought I'd have it figured out by now."

"Maybe you've been too busy with wedding preparations to give it sufficient thought."

"Possibly. It's been a busy time. And if one takes into account that Nick and I have been apart for a decade, I haven't taken an inordinate amount of time with the decision. Matters of the heart are too important to be rushed. Now, enough about me. Let's see if we can't come up with a solution for your problem."

The voice came from out of the warehouse shadows. "Oh, I have a solution. Lord Chambers here need not worry about any hole in his soul anymore."

Nick stepped into the light, a pistol in his hand. "He'll be too busy dealing with the hole in his head."

Crying on her wedding day brings a bride good luck.

~20~

The last time Nick had been this angry, a Kualistani Khan had just shot his dog. It was a blue-ice anger, cold clear to the bone. Menace dripped from his voice. "Get away from my wife."

He hadn't killed anyone in a long time and never in cold blood, but he was prepared to do so now. He'd just spent one of the most horrendous afternoons ever, and the thought of making the responsible person pay with his life seemed rather appropriate punishment.

Then Sarah, damn her, stepped in front of Chambers and said, "Now, Nick."

Immediately, he shifted his aim. *Now, Nick? Now, Nick!*

"There's no need for violence here. I'm fine."

"How pleasant for you. Move away from him."

"No, Nick."

Chambers proved once again what a fool he was by daring to speak. "I'm surprised you found us so soon. The warehouse is rented in an assumed name, and I was careful to lay a false trail."

Nick could have told him that he'd found a street vendor who'd spotted Chambers carrying a mattress, but the thought of a connection between a mattress, the kidnapping bastard, and Sarah made the red haze rise within him once more. "Move. Away. Sarah."

She took a pair of steps toward him, her hand out, her voice soothing as if trying to calm a wild animal. *A likely comparison*, the rational part of Nick admitted.

"You cannot shoot him."

"Yes, I can. He's an assassin."

"No, he's a stinker."

It was just strange enough to give Nick pause. "What?"

In quick, concise terms, Sarah provided a summary of Chambers' plot to "bomb" Westminster Abbey that left Nick incredulous. Lowering his gun, he addressed Chambers directly. "That has to be the most asinine, lunatic idea I've ever heard."

Chambers only shrugged.

Sarah said, "He's given up, Nick, and he's leaving England on the morning tide."

"No, I don't believe he is. He's a criminal and he's going to pay for his crimes."

"What crimes?"

"Kidnapping, for one."

Sarah's chin came up. "He didn't kidnap me. I went with him voluntarily."

Why, the bold-faced little liar. She *still* had a soft spot for this blackguard. Nick narrowed his eyes and snapped, "I have an entire list of others. Illegal importing of skunks. Conspiracy to commit . . . stink."

A burst of laughter escaped his bride. "I'd like to see you bring that one before a court. You'd have to arrest half of London."

"Damnation, Sarah."

"Oh, calm down, Lord Weston. Calm down and use your brain. Stop thinking like a man. We need to decide what we're going to do about Trevor, and you can't have him arrested for fouling London air."

Calm down? Stop thinking like a man? Fury pulsed through his veins. "I know what I'm going to do about Trevor. To use a Texas term, I intend to beat the tar out of him, then turn him over to Kimball and the Special Branch."

"You can't."

"Just watch me."

"Please, Nick. He has to leave England, and that is punishment enough. You know that. He swears he'll never set foot here ever again, right, Trevor?"

"That's right."

"You understand his frustration. You understand—"

Suddenly, Nick had had enough of old Trevor. "I understand I'm becoming exceptionally weary of your defense of that man. Chambers, sit down!"

The man recoiled from the menace in Nick's tone and did as he'd been bid. Nick picked up one of the fine bedsheets, tore at the edge with his teeth, then ripped it in two and again into quarters, which he used as ropes to tightly bind Chambers's wrists and ankles.

"Nick," Sarah protested. "There's a rope. . . ."

He shot her a glare. "Not. One. Word."

After testing his knots, he straightened and seriously debated the notion of clipping Lord Lovesick's jaw to knock him out. He decided he'd better not.

Rage boiled within him. He might accidentally strike a killing blow. Which might not be an accident at all.

He settled for leaning down and whispering ugly threats in the ear of the bastard who'd kidnapped his wife, and as Chambers sat shuddering in fear, Nick grabbed Sarah by the arm and tugged her to the far side of the warehouse to give them some privacy.

There, he braced his hands on his hips and demanded, "Why, Sarah? The man kidnapped you. He put me and my sisters and your friends through hell. Why are you defending him?"

For a long moment she held herself still as a stone. Then she drew a deep breath, exhaled in a rush, and said, "Because he reminds me of you, Nick."

"Excuse me?"

"It's true. Trevor is so much like you, the old you. The Nick Ross I married ten years ago. Remember him? He was the Nick who had lost his home and family. He was the young man so lonely, so hungry to replace what he had lost, so desperate to fill the emptiness inside him that he married a girl he didn't love."

The blow held twice the force as that which he'd loosed on Chambers. Nick dragged a hand down his jaw, licked his dry lips, and said gruffly, "I loved you."

"No, Nick, you didn't."

His heartbeat thumped. His frustration stirred. Chambers let out a groan, and Nick shoved his fingers through his hair. "Damnation, lass. Don't tell me how I felt. I loved you when I married you. Maybe not as much as I do now, but I did love you."

This time she was the one reeling from a verbal blow. "What? What did you say?"

"I said, don't tell me how I felt."

"Not that part. The other part. The *now* part."

Nick grimaced and attempted a retreat. "I don't think this is an appropriate time for this particular discussion. Your friends and my family followed me here determined to join the search. One of them is liable to check this warehouse any minute."

"I don't care if Queen Victoria arrives, I want to have this discussion here and now. You can't toss out something that profound and leave it lying between us like a . . . like a . . ."

"Skunk?"

She responded with a droll look and silence. He scowled. Surrendered. "Oh, all right. I love you, Sarah."

She took a step backward, slumped against a crate. Bewilderment painted her face. "You've never said it before."

Annoyance rippled through Nick. She didn't have to look so surprised. He exhaled a harsh, frustrated breath. "Maybe I was waiting for you to say it first. You're the one who is being stubborn about agreeing to make a go of this marriage. A man does have his pride, you know."

"Oh. Well."

" 'Oh. Well?' " He braced his hands on his hips and loomed over her. "That's all you have to say?"

Now she was the one licking dry lips. "I suppose you want to know how I feel about you."

"The thought did occur, yes."

Her complexion took on a greenish tint that stirred panic in Nick's soul. *Good, Lord. She doesn't . . .*

"I do."

He waited a beat. "Do what?"

"Love you." She swallowed hard. "I love you, too."

He froze like a stone. "Say it again."

Now a smile fluttered at her lips. "I love you, Nick."

Sunlight burst across the darkness of Nick's lonely soul. A smile began in his heart and worked its way slowly to his lips. "Thank God."

He pulled her into his arms and kissed her, long and lovingly. He kissed her with joy, with promise, and with passion. When they finally broke apart, he rested his forehead against hers, and said softly, "You won't be sorry, Sarah. We'll have a good life, I promise. You'll like it here in England."

She pulled away, gazed up at him with worry clouding her eyes, and Nick got a bad feeling in his stomach.

Sarah's stomach rolled and pitched so much she thought she might just throw up. Desire ran heavy and hot within her, and her woman's core felt empty and aching. But it was her heart that gave her the most trouble at the moment. The coppery sensation of fear had her heart firmly in its grip.

"Nick . . . about my staying. I'm not . . . I don't . . ."

He took a long step back. Cautiously, he asked, "You don't what?"

She fumbled for the words and ended up with a weak, "I need more time."

Frustration flashed in his eyes. "Damnation, Sarah! Why are you saying this? I don't understand. I love you. You love me. Shouldn't that take care of all the questions?"

"One would think so, yes. But love didn't exactly solve our problems last time, did it?"

"That was different." He exhaled loudly. "We were little more than children then. We didn't know how to make compromises. I was wrong to ask you to leave with me on such short notice, and I know seeing me with Susan Harris complicated matters. But if we'd been more honest with each other and compromised, been flexible, we could have made it work. Now we have a second chance. We can make our marriage work this time around."

Sarah wasn't so certain, and she fought to find the words to explain. "I don't know if I believe that love can overcome everything."

Again he raked his fingers through his hair in frustration. "We can work something out about where we live. I'm willing to spend time in Texas every year, although I'd prefer it not to be the summer. It's compromise, Sarah. That's all. Love and a willingness to compromise."

"Oh, Nick." Despair washed through her in waves. "The prospect of living in England isn't nearly as daunting as it once was. The McBrides' visit has proven to me that distance need not mean the end of special friendships. They may require a little extra care to maintain, but anything worthwhile deserves an investment of time. It's the rest of it. . . ."

He waited. When she didn't speak, he prodded, "Rest of what? Is it the title? Are you still afraid to take your place in Society as a marchioness?"

"No, I'm comfortable with that now, too. The wedding festivities have shown me I can hold my own in that particular shark pool."

"In that case, I don't see what is still holding you back. I have to tell you I find that both perplexing and annoying. Please explain yourself."

"I'm trying," she snapped.

"Try harder," he snarled back. "I'm a good man, Sarah, but I'm at the end of my patience."

She pushed past him and began to pace, trying to find the words to express the emotions in her heart. She didn't blame him for losing patience with her. She was fed up with herself.

"Sarah, I'm waiting. What's wrong? Is it me? Did I do—"

The challenge in his tone was enough to fan her temper and loosen her tongue. "It's not you. Nothing is wrong with you. You're perfect! That's the problem. You're a wonderful husband and a wonderful brother and I'm sure that someday you'll be a wonderful father. You're handsome and intelligent and kind and just wicked enough to be interesting. You're an excellent friend, a savvy spy, a loyal and dedicated servant of your queen. The only bad thing about you is, you have a tendency to be bossy, and that is something I can just ignore."

"Thank you, I think. So what, pray tell, is the problem here?"

"It's *me.*" Realization of the truth was a blow to the heart that shattered it into little pieces. "*I'm* the problem, Nick. I don't think I can be the wife you deserve."

"What nonsense is this?"

"It's not nonsense. It's the truth. Something is wrong with me as a woman. I don't . . . I don't like sexual relations, and you are too much a man to be content with a woman who doesn't enjoy the physical aspect of marriage. You'd never be happy with me, not in the long term. You'd find someone else who could give you what you need in that respect, and that would break my heart."

Nick turned his head away and muttered a dozen different invectives, each more colorful and more base than the last. But it was his final comment that offended her the most.

"If that's not by far the most idiotic, feeble-minded, insanely stupid thing I have ever heard a woman say. And I've heard plenty of women say plenty of ridiculous things."

She stiffened. "Well, pardon me."

"I damn well won't. Not as long as you are repeating such utter nonsense."

"It's not nonsense. I don't like sex."

"Liar." He braced his hands on his hips and leaned forward. "I seduced you with the Pillow Book and you liked it. You sure as hell liked what I did to you in the garden at Charlotte's ball."

"That wasn't sex."

"It wasn't?" He smacked his forehead with the palm of his hand. "Fancy that. Here I've gone all these years thinking I knew what sex was."

"You know what I mean."

He snapped his fingers. "Oh, you mean no ride up the cockloft. Of course. The expression of love doesn't count if a man doesn't dip his spoon and give his gravy."

"Don't be vulgar."

"You're the one being vulgar, Sarah. I made love with you, and by God, you liked it. You loved it. Saying you didn't is the lie."

"I'm not lying," she insisted, a sob in her voice. "I'm trying to tell you my deepest feelings, my deepest fears, and you aren't listening. You're laughing at me."

"That's because your fears and feelings are so damned insulting!" Fury blazed, but deep within himself, Nick felt a core of cold, bitter hurt. He halfway suspected if he looked down, he'd see a knife buried in his chest. "In saying you are not woman enough for me, you're telling me *I* am not man enough for *you.*"

"No, Nick."

"You don't trust me to be man enough to show you you're a woman. You claim to love me, but you don't believe in me."

"That's not true."

"Then prove it. I dare you. Here. Now. Lord Lovesick has graciously provided a mattress. Let's throw him and the skunks out of here and put it to use. I'll make you scream your pleasure, Lady Weston. Damned if I won't."

Tears spilled down her cheeks, and she wrapped her arms around herself. "No, Nick. Don't."

God, he felt like crying himself. His chest heaved with the force of the breaths he took. He clenched his jaw, glared at his wife. Felt ill.

"Come to think of it, perhaps you're right," he said, his voice furiously flat. "Perhaps you're not enough woman for me. A woman worthy of the love I am aching to give her would be willing to follow me into fire, much less the marriage bed. Perhaps you've been right all along. Perhaps we're not suited. Perhaps we should see this annulment done and you should just go back to Texas."

Unable to look at her any longer, he turned away and attempted to force his attention back to Lord Chambers and the problem he presented the Crown. He'd covered half the distance between where he'd left Sarah and where Chambers sat tied, when he heard the surprising sound of his sister Aurora's happy shout. "Here they are, Mrs. McBride. In here. Nick has found her!"

After that, chaos reigned.

The entire Texas contingent and Nick's sisters streamed into the warehouse. Shouts and screeches of joy echoed through the building as the females reunited with hugs and dances, laughter and giggles. Nick observed the exchange with a bittersweet ache in his heart and wondered about the circumstances that allowed the women to be here in the warehouse district rather than safely at home.

Charlotte ran to him, wrapped her arms around his waist, and gave him a big hug. "Thank you, Nick. We were all so scared. We love her so much."

"I know, sweetheart," he said, the words catching in his throat. "I know."

The McBride brothers approached and began firing questions like bullets. Sarah wandered over to provide some of the answers about what had happened to her since leaving Weston House that morning. With a brotherly arm draped around Charlotte's shoulders, and making a point not to look at his wife, Nick added some of the details Sarah skipped. As a result, he only vaguely listened when Aurora went courting calamity.

"Oh, look. Some awful person has caged this funny-looking cat and her kittens. Isn't that awful? I don't believe in caging animals, and a mama and her kittens . . . that just makes me so angry!"

From that moment on, time slowed to a crawl. His arms fell away from Charlotte as he turned in time to see his youngest sister throw back the blanket covering the skunk cage and kneel down. He heard Emma McBride shout, "No!" even as Aurora unlatched the door.

"Aurora, no! Get away!" Nick called, shoving his elder sister toward the McBride men and stepping forward as the mama skunk snapped at Aurora, who pulled her hand back just in time.

"Skunk!" Maribeth McBride yelled, darting for the exit.

"Oh, hell. You're getting married in a week," Tye McBride said as he pushed Charlotte out the warehouse door.

Nick stood at the doorway, his gaze on the skunk as he circled his hand in the air, motioning for the ladies to hurry. But Melanie and Aurora, unfamiliar with the ugliness that awaited them, were slow to follow the McBride females as they darted toward the exit.

"Aurora, Melanie! Run. Now!"

English ladies to the end, the girls walked briskly instead.

Sarah muttered something and started toward them, but Jenny grabbed her hand as she flew past, tugging her friend along with her. Trace McBride followed his wife outside.

Seconds passed like minutes as Nick, with a growing sense of doom, watched his sisters bring up the rear. Their hesitation had cost them. "It's too late," Nick muttered as the mama skunk stomped her feet.

The skunk's tail came up.

"Damnation."

She sprayed.

The acrid stink of skunk musk filled the air along with Aurora's and Melanie's screams.

Now they ran. They ran and screamed and choked and screamed some more until Aurora paused just long enough to bend over and vomit.

"Damnation," Nick repeated. "Today has not been my day."

He stepped back inside the warehouse to help his miserable, frightened sisters. Almost immediately his eyes began to burn. His skin tingled, and curses as nasty as stench in the air tumbled off his tongue.

This was all that cursed Chambers's fault. He

The Bad Luck Wedding Night

turned his head to glare at the cause of all this trouble, and despite his disgust with the man, Nick couldn't help but wince. Chambers was rolling on the floor, groaning. He'd caught a direct hit of the foamy yellow spray.

"Oh, my eyes hurt," Melanie moaned as Nick hurried her and Aurora outside. "They burn."

The others waiting outside took a big step back, then circled around Nick and the girls, taking position upwind. Aurora sniffled. "My eyes burn, too. And my skin. Am I going blind? Is my skin going to turn black as though it's been on fire?"

"No. You'll be all right in time," Nick said. "I promise."

"I think I'm going to be sick again," Aurora sobbed. "What was that animal?"

"They're skunks. That odor is their defense."

"It's all over me!" Melanie wailed, pulling away from Nick and brushing at her sleeves, her bodice, her skirt. "Get it off me. I need it off. I'm going to jump in the river."

"Yeew," observed Emma McBride, covering her mouth and nose. "Wouldn't that compound the problem?"

"I think it's in their hair." Maribeth McBride leaned toward her mother and lowered her voice. "They won't have to shave their heads, will they?"

Nick winced, and Aurora and Melanie gasped, their hands flying to their heads. "No!"

The howls rose another octave.

"No, you won't need to shave your heads," Sarah said, her face locked in a grimace as she stepped forward—just a little—and took charge. "We'll get you home and out of these clothes. I've heard a number of different treatments for skunk odor. We'll use

345

them all. Now, we'll need separate transportation home for those of us who were inside, and those who made it out. Trace, would you find us an open-air wagon? Buy it if you must. Jenny, if you and Claire would take the girls home in our coach and ask Mrs. Higgins to send someone for tomato juice—lots of it, carbolic soap, vinegar, ammonia. Can you think of anything else?"

Claire nodded. "I've also heard a mixture of hydrogen peroxide, baking soda, and soap is quite effective in neutralizing this particular odor. You apply it in a paste while it still bubbles."

Tye McBride squeezed his wife's shoulder, then called out to Melanie and Aurora as he left to retrieve the coach. "Don't worry, girls, we'll get rid of the smell. It simply takes a little time."

"How much time?" Melanie asked.

Trace offered a comforting smile as he, too, departed. "Oh, only a week or so."

"A week!" all the girls exclaimed. "It can't last a week. Charlotte's wedding is in a week."

Now even the clean-smelling females were wailing and moaning. Nick wanted to cover his ears with his hands. Instead, he tried to comfort his stinky sisters. Sarah, he was glad to see, looked after Charlotte.

In the midst of this turmoil, Jenny McBride motioned toward the warehouse and brought up another smelly subject. "Nick, you do realize we still have a bit of a problem in there, don't you?"

Nick did know, he'd simply been trying not to think about it.

Jenny continued, "What are you going to do about Lord Chambers?"

Overhearing the question, Sarah stiffened, and

her gaze whipped around to meet his. Damn her whisky eyes, he thought. Damned if she wasn't still pleading for the bastard. Nick's stomach took a nauseated roll that had nothing to do with the skunk spray.

Nick turned his face toward the wind in hopes of soothing the burning discomfort in his eyes. In the periphery of his vision, he saw Sarah give Charlotte one more hug before releasing her. She then turned toward Nick, swallowed hard, and squared her shoulders. "Nick? Please let Trevor go. I would say that under the circumstances, he has been justly punished."

"I'll cut him loose," Nick replied, grimly addressing Jenny McBride instead of his wife. He couldn't talk to her now. He just couldn't. "He can wait until after the girls are settled, though, and the warehouse has aired out a bit. He brought this trouble on himself."

"I won't argue that," Jenny said, her worried gaze shifting between Nick and Sarah.

Moments later, Tye McBride arrived with the coach. His family and Charlotte climbed inside. One foot on the step, Sarah turned to look at him, a dozen different questions in her sad and somber eyes.

Nick's answer was to turn away.

The stinging in his eyes grew worse and he blinked rapidly, blaming it on the skunk musk, as the coach rattled off. Turning his attention to a wretched Aurora and a miserable Melanie, he attempted to console them until Trace arrived with transportation.

"A refuse wagon?" Aurora wailed.

Melanie moaned. "If anyone sees us, I'll die!"

With three daughters of his own, Trace was well prepared. He tossed a pair of blankets from the front of the wagon into the back. "You can use these to hide yourself. No one will know it's you under there, and I won't let anyone stop us."

Aurora held the blanket like a lifeline until a worrisome thought occurred. "What if someone tries to dump trash in the wagon?"

"Trace will run them down," Nick assured her. "Right, McBride?"

"I'll squash them flat."

"Good," Melanie declared. Sniffing and releasing an occasional sob, the two girls climbed into the back of the wagon and pulled the blankets over their heads.

"Speaking of squashing flat," Trace said to Nick from a safe distance upwind. "What are you planning to do about Chambers?"

Nick closed his eyes and shook his head. "I have half of Scotland Yard out looking for him. I can't simply send them a note saying never mind. I expect Lord Kimball or one of his men to arrive at any moment now. I thought I'd turn Chambers over with a recommendation to give him a bar of carbolic soap and help him find his way aboard the *Hampstead*. It sails tonight." He paused a moment, then added, "Sarah was right. His punishment has been fitting."

The Texan nodded, then glanced toward the warehouse. "What about the skunks?"

Yet another subject he'd tried to avoid. Nick sighed wearily. "I can't leave them to run free, can I?"

"I shouldn't think so."

Skunk trapping was an exceptionally risky business. He wondered what his chances were of getting through the task unscathed. "At least I've become rather impervious to the odor."

"You're the only one," Trace McBride replied. "Let's hope one of those odor-removing remedies works, otherwise you'll be difficult to be around for awhile."

Nick shrugged. "That's all right. Sarah did promise a wedding London would never forget. Looks like we're off to an unforgettable start."

It's good luck to be the first man to kiss the bride.

~21~

May 1877
Buckingham Palace

My Lord Marquess,
In recognition of your recent service to the Crown, Her Majesty the Queen wishes to offer a boon. I have been instructed to ascertain any particular preferences you might have in regard to the nature of a Royal gift. Your reply is requested at least one hour prior to your private audience scheduled for two o'clock this afternoon.

> Lord Chancellor
> Appointment
> Secretary

May 1877
Weston House

My Lord,
The opportunity to serve my Queen was ample reward for my small efforts in regard to the events that transpired four days ago.

However, the Queen's support in a personal matter would prove quite advantageous at this time. Following a review of the summary of events enclosed forthwith, including medical evidence proving Lady Weston to be virgo intacta, *should Her Majesty feel inclined to forward a letter to the Court in support of my annulment petition and urging the expedition of its execution, my wife and I would consider it a boon of infinite magnitude.*

Regarding this afternoon's reception, might I suggest that the palace windows of the room in which I am to be received remain open?

Weston

Tuesday, 10 May 1877
Weston House

Dear Jenny and Claire,
On this, the eve of Lady Charlotte's wedding day, I wanted to take a moment to thank both of you not only for your efforts on this special young woman's behalf, but also for your years of invaluable friendship. I love you both dearly and without your support, I would have been lost during these last few difficult days.

Nick's attorney sent notice that he would deliver the annulment papers before the wedding tomorrow. I find it amazing how swift the tide of justice can run once a monarch waves her scepter over the proceedings.

I have secured passage to New York on the Manchester, *departing on the evening tide tomorrow. I look forward to our reunion in Fort Worth. Enjoy the rest of your holiday in Britain.*

I will pray that you and your families enjoy a safe trip home.

> All my love,
> Sarah

P.S. Keep your fingers crossed that all goes well tomorrow. Lady Pratt has been giving poor Charlotte a terrible time of it. I almost wish the boys hadn't convinced their father to have the scent glands removed from the skunks. I am just about ready to turn Stripe loose in Lady Pratt's bedchamber!

Tuesday, 10 May 1877
Weston House

Dear Sarah,
   Please read the enclosed note, then give it to my brother at a time you deem appropriate. I am afraid to do it.
   I love you. Please forgive me.

> Charlotte

Tuesday, 10 May 1877
Weston House

Dear Nicholas,
   This note is to inform you that I am a very wretched, ungrateful sister, but Rodney and I have reached the end of our patience with Lady Pratt. Tonight she insisted you, Aurora, and Melanie be barred from attending the wedding, despite the fact that Gillian, Flora, and Robyn all insisted that they could not detect skunk odor on you when their "fresh" noses arrived from

Scotland this morning. My future mother-in-law
threatened to make a scene, and I find I must
preempt her.

    Nicholas, Rodney and I have eloped. Please
make our excuses to our wedding guests.

Love,

Your wicked sister Charlotte

Sarah sat on her bed in her bedchamber, laughing, the letter from Charlotte in her hand. So much for the theme of a Good Luck Wedding. Then again, as long as Charlotte's wedding day was free of Dragon Lady Pratt, perhaps it would be a good luck wedding after all.

She glanced at the mantel clock. Seven A.M. She should probably take Nick the note immediately—she'd heard him go downstairs almost an hour ago now—but she couldn't bring herself to go to him. The doors between them had been shut both literally and figuratively for the past week.

And besides, his solicitor might be with him now. Walking in on that particular meeting would be far too humiliating.

She and her husband had barely spoken over the past week. For the first couple of days, he stayed away from Weston House entirely as he and Melanie and Aurora made the trip out to the country house for repeated odor-treatment baths and long days spent in pursuits involving fresh air and sunshine. When they returned for his appointment at the palace, the fragrance of skunk had faded from his skin, but the anger radiating from his body remained just as strong as ever.

It broke her heart. He'd never before been angry with her, not like this. As was so often the case, she hadn't realized how much she valued his admiration and respect until she'd lost it.

Knock knock knock. At the chamber separating her bedchamber from their shared sitting room, Nick spoke. "Sarah, would you join me in the sitting room, please?"

Her stomach sank. He sounded serious and grim. Maybe he'd already heard about Charlotte's running off. "I'll be right there."

She slipped on her dressing gown and tucked Charlotte's letter into her pocket. In the sitting room, Nick stood staring out the window into the garden. He didn't turn when she entered, only said, "The rain clouds are clearing. Charlotte will have a beautiful day for her wedding."

"Hmm," she responded as she said to herself, *Not necessarily.* Sarah suspected the young lovers had left London to marry. The farther away from Lady Pratt the better.

While Sarah searched for a way to break the news of Charlotte's elopement, Nick took the matter from her hands by introducing the subject she'd done her best to ignore. "The papers are on your desk awaiting your signature, Sarah."

Now he turned and met her gaze, his expression one of properly cool British detachment.

Sarah blinked. It took a concentrated effort not to fall backward a step. She'd seen him turn that chilly, dispassionate look on a number of people in the past, but never on herself. Never on her or the girls or anyone he cared about. Now, standing in the middle of the sitting room, faced with Nick's indifference, Sarah felt as if she'd been torn in half.

She'd lost him.

Blindly she turned toward the desk and the sheaf of

papers lying atop it. "Thank you," she said softly, the polite response automatic but having nothing to do with the emotions surging through her like a storm.

He nodded once. "I am told you plan to depart this evening."

"Yes. On the *Manchester.*"

"I'm familiar with the *Manchester.* It's a nice ship. Now, if you'll excuse me, I need to leave early for St. George's. I promised Lady Pratt I would speak with Reverend Tomlinson personally concerning the homily he has planned for the service. I understand you intend to see to Charlotte this morning?"

"Hmm . . ." she murmured, hoping he'd take it as an assent. She didn't want to lie to him, and she doubted she could say a word without bursting into tears.

"Very well, then. I will see you at the church." Nick then turned to leave, hesitating only when he reached the doorway. "I doubt we'll have the opportunity to speak privately again, Sarah. I want you to know . . ." He stopped and took a deep breath, visibly bracing himself. "I wish you a safe journey, lass. In your travels and in your life."

With that, Nicholas, Lord Weston, left her.

Sarah stumbled to the writing desk and sank into the chair. The annulment papers lay on the surface like a serpent waiting to strike. Cautiously she reached out and with her index finger shuffled aside the pages until she revealed the signature page. Lines indicated a space for her signature and that of her husband's. Both were blank.

He wanted her to sign first. Sarah's stomach rolled, got a hard knot in it. Her breaths came in shallow pants.

As she reached for a pen, she spied her treasure

tin and pictured the contents within. Her rock collection. The smooth, amber-colored stone that symbolized their first kiss. The milky piece of quartz he'd given her on their wedding day. The uncut rubies he'd gathered for her in the mountains of Afghanistan.

Sarah slowly pulled the box closer and gently lifted the lid. The stones inside were more beautiful to her than a chest full of glittering gems.

She removed one of the rubies and held it cradled in the palm of her hand. She stroked a finger across its rough pink ridges and recalled the words he had written in the Pillow Book:

> *You lay next to me, lost in sleep, vulnerable.*
> *Trusting.*
> *Trusting me.*
> *It was a gift more valuable than gold,*

She closed her hand, gripped the rock tightly.

> *I would never do anything to damage such a*
> *precious offering.*
> *Remember that, Sarah. Never forget.*

Sarah licked her lips. The sensation of standing on the edge of a precipice propelled her to her feet. Blindly she picked up the treasure tin and returned the stone. Then with the box in one hand and the annulment papers in the other, she carried them back to her bedroom. There, she tossed her burdens in the center of her bed. The rock tin spilled and stones tumbled out, the uncut rubies rolling to lie atop the annulment decree.

Sarah reached into the bedside table for the

leather-bound tome buried at the bottom of the drawer. She opened the Pillow Book and flipped the pages until she found the particular letter she sought. Nick's bold handwriting stretched across the parchment-colored page.

Look at the stones, lass. They are pretty as they are, but I want you to imagine the beauty that lies beneath the surface. Beauty and sparkle and fire. It's there, waiting for you.

You simply must be brave enough to make the first cut.

" 'It's there, waiting for you,' " she read again, aloud. " 'You simply must be brave enough to make the first cut.' "

Now her knees went a bit weak. Trust and courage. That's what he truly asked of her. Trust and courage.

Her gaze shifted to the legal decree and the promises of beauty lying atop it. She hugged the Pillow Book close to her chest and used her husband's favorite invective. "Damnation, Sarah. As they say in Texas, you have been dumb as a box of rocks."

Then Sarah, Lady Weston, whipped the annulment decree off the bed and ripped it over and over and over again, the tear of paper music to her ears. Laughing, she flung the tiny pieces into the air so that they drifted down around her like snowflakes.

Then, taking a pen, she climbed into the middle of her bed, sat cross-legged, opened the Pillow Book, and began to write.

*   *   *

Nick rode to the church in a foul humor. He'd had all he wanted of weddings and marriages and women in general. One woman in particular. One woman who was leaving him today.

Damnation, Sarah. How am I going to live without you?

At St. George's, Nick met with the vicar as promised, then pulled up a chair next to the tomb of a courtier of Elizabeth I, propped his feet on the stone effigy, and began a one-sided conversation about the perversity of women. He passed the time in this manner, regretting his lack of whisky, until Trace McBride sauntered up and nodded. "Morning, Weston. Jenny asked me to track you down and point out that wedding guests are beginning to arrive. They're waiting for you in the vicar's office."

"Hmmph." Nick dropped his feet from the tomb and rose. "Good. I'm ready to get this nonsense over with. I trust Charlotte's groom is here and ready?"

The Texan pursed his lips. "Lord Pratt is definitely ready to say his vows."

Nick nodded and made his way to the office, stopping to shake a hand or two with a wedding guest along the way. To his surprise, neither the vicar nor any of his sisters were in the room when he arrived. Nick frowned. He'd thought this was where he was to meet Charlotte to escort her down the aisle.

Glancing around the room, he spied a boutonniere—a cleverly constructed white rose and four-leaf clover affair—he assumed was meant for him. It was only when he went to affix it to his jacket that he realized just what the flower lay upon. A book, bound in burgundy leather with gold filigree.

The Pillow Book.

Nick's heart began to pound.

He sucked in a breath. Propping a hip against the vicar's desk, he picked up the Pillow Book and flipped through the pages. When he reached the final entry, he found a small blue velvet bag tucked between the pages. He opened the envelope and emptied its contents into the palm of his hand.

It was a teardrop of a ruby partially cut, half of it shining and brilliant and beautiful. The rest of the gem was rough and waiting. His heart was in his throat as he dropped his gaze to the Pillow Book and began to read.

My dearest Nick,

While lying in my bed—in my lonely bed—I had the most marvelous dream. May I tell you about it?

I was seated at a workbench in a lapidary's shop. Before me lay a rock—an untouched stone—and I had never seen another like it. My rock wasn't formed of solid minerals or crystals, but rather of a hard lump of fear born in the fires of misunderstanding, inexperience, and imagination.

It was an ugly rock, Nick. My gaze shied away from it time and time again as I worked with other, prettier stones. I was content to leave the unsightly rock on the bench just beyond my immediate sight.

Then one day you came into the shop and offered a kingdom of dreams in exchange for the finest ruby in the land. I looked at the ugly rock and sensed that something sparkling, beautiful, and alive was trapped inside it, waiting to be freed. I knew that all I needed to do was make that first cut and you would make all my dreams come true.

I was afraid. I was afraid to trust—not you, never you, but my own talent. I was afraid to pick up the chisel and put blade to stone.

You left, and I was alone with the sad little rock. I stared at it hard, for the first time in years, and I could see the dream within it.

Your voice whispered to me in my mind, my heart, my soul. You urged me, encouraged me. Breathed your strength into me.

I picked up the chisel, Nick, and I made the first cut. Now, I ask for your help to finish the work.

I know it's been slow in coming, but I have come to the realization that Pliny the Elder knew of what he spoke when he said, Home is where the heart is.

My heart has found a home here on this side of the Atlantic.

My heart has found a home with you. Will you allow me to stay? Will you take me to your bed and seal the promise between us? I'm ready, Nick. I'm finally ready.

> *With love,*
> *Sarah, your wife*

The Pillow Book slipped from Nick's fingers and fell to the floor with a thud. He stared at it numbly, his thoughts in a daze, then instinctively retrieved it and returned it gently to the desk.

Relief rolled over him in waves. He was fairly certain he would not have allowed her to board that ship, and while the thought of locking her in his bedchamber had a certain appeal, the battle would have been ugly.

A smile played at the corners of his mouth as the

gray fog of his mood lifted. While the two of them still had one particular hurdle to jump, Nick was confident in his lovemaking skills. In fact, he quite looked forward to putting them to the test.

He sank into a fantasy about Sarah and rubies and a bed the size of Loch Rowanclere. How long he was lost in the illusion he wasn't certain, but it seemed like just a few minutes before he realized Trace McBride stood in the doorway calling his name. "Weston? Weston!"

"Mmm?"

"They're waiting for you. It's time."

"Oh. All right." Damnation. Nick's brow knitted in a frown. He'd intended to take a private moment with Charlotte, to wish her well and verify this was what she truly wanted. Not that he had any doubts. Only a woman deeply in love would willingly take Lady Pratt on as her mother-in-law.

Before Nick had quite made it to the back of the church, Jenny McBride signaled the organist and Aurora, a vision in blue, started down the aisle. Nick expected Sarah to have performed that particular service, and he glanced around for his wife in confusion as he took his place beside the bride. Leaning over, he whispered, "Where's Sarah?"

When she didn't respond, he remembered his brotherly duty and added, "You look beautiful, love."

Not that he could tell too much with that veil covering her face. He did note the flattering cut of her wedding gown and wondered idly what tricks Jenny had used to give his sister a bosom. Then there was no more time. Claire McBride gave Nick a gentle push to start them down the aisle.

Almost immediately, the hair on the back of Nick's neck rose. Something was wrong. His gaze flicked around the church. "Good Lord," he murmured to Charlotte, "Lady Pratt is wearing chartreuse."

As unpleasant as that sight was, it wasn't the source of Nick's unease. He spied his Scottish sisters, Robyn, Flora, and Gillian, and their husbands. Robyn finger-waved, and he returned the acknowledgment. Then, spying a flash of black and white at the end of one church pew in front of them, his eyes rounded. *Oh, no. Not the skunk!*

He exhaled sharply when he passed and realized the perceived threat was simply a lady's fur jacket.

Like days of old when he'd scanned Kualistani mountain passes for potential trouble, Nick surveyed the wedding guests. Other than a few additional crimes of fashion, he saw nothing to justify his disquiet. Then his stare flickered to the front of the church and a dozen different curses fluttered through his brain. Rodney wasn't waiting. That bastard Lord Pratt was nowhere in sight.

Oh, Charlotte. Not again.

Damnation. What was it about Nick and weddings that brought such a run of bad luck? It must be a powerful evil spell to offset all the good luck charms Sarah had incorporated into this ceremony.

They were almost to the altar, and Nick knew Charlotte must have realized by now that her groom was missing. From the corner of his mouth, he said, "Don't panic, love. It'll be all right. I'll fix this. Somehow I'll fix it."

They halted at the altar steps. Nick gripped his sister's hands. She had yet to speak, and he assumed she must be in shock. "Love, what do you want me to do?"

The bride pulled away from him and grasped the

ends of her veil. Slowly, she raised it up, revealing Sarah's beaming, breathtaking, and beloved face. "Please, Nick. Will you marry me again?"

At that point the vicar's voice boomed, as did Nick's heart. "We are gathered here today to witness the renewal of wedding vows between the Most Honorable, the Marquess of Weston and his lady wife."

Bathed, powdered, and perfumed, Sarah awaited her husband in the master suite at Weston Abbey. They had made the journey to Nick's country house after the wedding breakfast and had spent the afternoon walking in the gardens, discussing family matters like Charlotte's elopement, Sarah's future as a wedding consultant in London, and the frequency of their visits to Texas, settling on three times a year. Nick had suggested four transatlantic trips, but since Sarah liked the idea of spending summers in Scotland, she didn't see how they'd have time to fit everything in.

As the day wore on, Sarah found herself anticipating the coming night with pleasure. To her great surprise, she wasn't in the least bit scared. It was a shame she couldn't say the same about Nick.

One would think he was the inexperienced near-virgin here tonight. For her part, Sarah would have been happy to retire to their suite shortly after their arrival at Weston Abbey. Nick had been the one to delay the matter. He'd been the one to seem skittish.

They'd shared an intimate dinner before a crackling fire in the sitting room upstairs, sipping champagne and eating strawberries. Finally, she'd excused herself and retreated to her bedroom to prepare for what was, in effect, her wedding night. She wore a clinging gown of crimson silk, something Jenny had stitched up for her while she was with the jewel cutter she'd rousted from his bed early that morning. She'd left her hair down and brushed it until in shimmered in the lamplight. Now all she needed was her groom.

The man was slow in arriving. Sarah waited and waited some more. Finally, the butterfly wings of nervousness made themselves known in her stomach, and she lost her patience. Crossing to his chamber door, she banged on the thick dark wood with her fist. "Nick, are we going to do this or not?"

"Come in, Sarah."

He stood by the window, still dressed. Mostly. His jacket and necktie were gone. His snowy white shirt was unbuttoned and hanging open to reveal a torso dusted with hair and rippling with muscles. His gaze made a slow journey from her head to her feet, then back up again. His eyes blazed, and Sarah's mouth went dry. But when the fire sank to a smoulder, she frowned. "Have I misunderstood how this works? I thought you were supposed to come to me."

He sipped from the glass in his hand. "I'm slow tonight."

Milk? He's drinking milk? "Should I be insulted?"

"Savored, Sarah. You should be savored."

His words sent a shiver streaking down her spine. Blue eyes glittered as he gestured toward a tray. "Would you care for some refreshment?"

She tore her gaze away from him. Milk and cookies. The smile began in her heart and flowed to her lips. "Yes, I would."

He made a move toward the food and drink, until her next words stopped him cold. "I'd like a kiss, please."

Nick closed his eyes.

"What's the matter, Nick?" she asked gently.

"You are a bold woman, Lady Weston."

"I'm trying."

"You're doing well."

"Kiss me, Nick."

"Damnation." He drew her into his arms and kissed her hard and quick.

Sarah melted against him. "I thought you were going to go slow?"

A reluctant chuckle escaped Nick, and this time when he kissed her, he took the time to do it right. His tongue delved into her mouth, stroked her, explored her, demanded. He tasted of milk and molasses cookies, a sweetness that flowed through her senses and made her moan. His scent was a mixture of man, magic, and moonlight that was deliciously Nick. Like always, the touch of his mouth on hers made Sarah's blood catch fire. This time, however, the restlessness inside her demanded daring. This time, her commitment to her marriage and her love for Nick demanded boldness.

He was her husband. Legally and morally. Resolved, she ignored the butterfly wings of nervousness and doubt fluttering inside her and brazenly reached toward his trousers to touch him.

He tore his mouth from hers. His eyes were hot, hungry, and a little wild. "Damnation, Sarah!"

An exhilarating sense of power swept over her, and she laughed. She fitted her hand against him as he had done to her that night in the garden, and when he groaned low in his throat, instinct and the driving force of passion swept every other thought from her mind.

She skimmed her hands beneath his shirt and over the rippling muscles of his back. Wildness streaked through her, and she arched against him, softness to steel. She ached. A hollow, glorious aching that shuddered through her bones.

As if sensing her need, Nick pressed his hand to her lower back and brought her against him. She gasped at the hard, heated length of him, at the zing of pleasure such pressure provoked.

And she wasn't afraid.

He bent her backward, trailing his lips downward to the sensitive skin at the base of her neck. A low moan, almost a growl, rumbled from Nick's throat and he nipped at her gently. Sarah shuddered. "Nick, take me to your bed. Make love to me. Now, please."

"Oh, lass," he said, the brogue of his youth thick in his voice. "I dinna want to rush you."

She offered him a wide, heartfelt smile. "Ten years is not exactly rushing, my love."

With that, he picked her up, carried her to his bed, and lay her gently upon his mattress. Then he stepped away, his eyes hungry as if feasting on the sight of her.

Sarah stretched sensuously against the sheets, once again feeling the force of a woman's power over a man. Was it different this time, or had she missed it the first? "Take off your clothes, Nick. I want to see you."

"You're a temptress, woman. A wicked siren," he said as he flung his shirt to the floor. Then he stripped off his trousers and rose above her on the bed. "I plan to thank God for it every day."

Her gaze locked on the proof of his desire, and she felt a frisson of nervousness. From out of long ago came her mother's words, and they spilled from Sarah's lips. "The Rod of Steel."

In the process of slipping the straps of her nightgown off her shoulders and revealing the full, round globes of her breasts, Nick froze. "What did you say?"

"My mother's instruction on lovemaking."

He frowned down at his erection. "Oh. Now I remember. No wonder you panicked."

"I'm still a little nervous. May I touch you and get accustomed to the feel?"

"Lass, if you don't touch me I think I'll probably die."

He was steel, but velvet, too. She ran her fingers over him, around him, learning him. The weight of him felt lovely in her hand, and the way he sucked his breath past clenched teeth created a rush of power and desire within her.

"Enough," he said in a raspy tone, closing his hand around her wrist and pulled her away from him. "I'm hanging on by a thread here."

She gave him a saucy look. "A thread. Hardly."

"Seductress." He grinned and lay down beside her. "This isn't what I anticipated from you, you know."

"I'm surprising myself, too. What's the difference, do you think?"

He lifted her hand and gently kissed her palm. "Love." Kissed her wrist. "Mature love." Kissed his way up her arm to her shoulder. "You and I are woman and man now. Not girl and boy like before. Our bodies were ready, but our minds still had some growing up to do."

"I'm all grown up now."

"You won't see me arguing." He leaned close to kiss that sensitive skin just below her ear.

She arched her neck to offer better access and purred. "What *will* I see you doing, Lord Weston?"

He lifted his head and stared at her. The teasing light in his eyes had died and was replaced with somber sincerity that she knew came straight from his heart. "You will see me love you, now, always, and forever. I won't lose you again, Sarah. You are my heart, my soulmate, my friend. I will cherish you and honor you all the days of my life."

These, too, she thought, were his marriage vows, as much as those he'd spoken in church that morning, and certainly those he'd repeated to her a decade ago. She lifted her hand to his face, stroked his cheek, gazed deeply into his eyes, and made a vow of her own. "I will go where you go, Nick. I will make a family with you, a home for you, and it will be filled with happiness and love. I offer you my heart, my body, my faith, my trust. I love you, Nick. Now, please, finally, make me your wife."

And so he did. Sweetly, tenderly, and gently—and finally—Nick breached her maidenhead with a minimum of pain. While her body adjusted to the novelty of being filled, he feasted on her breasts, kissing and licking and sucking until she felt the pull of desire deep in her loins and her inner muscles gripped him. "Mmmm . . ." he murmured against her. Then he moved inside her, and Sarah gasped with pleasure and once again caught fire.

Soon she whirled in a storm of sensation, the musky scent of arousal in the air, the salty taste of sweat on bare skin, the sound of one heart calling out to its mate.

A wild, primitive force took control of her, and Sarah met Nick thrust for thrust, her nails sinking into his back as she arched and drew him deeper. Ribbons of lightning sizzled along her nerves and tension coiled in her womb. His breathing was ragged, her own whimpering, aching, needy gasps.

It went on forever, but not nearly long enough.

The pressure within her built slowly, fiercely, hotter and hotter and higher until she wanted to scream. "I love you, Sarah," he said, repeating it in time with his strokes. "I love you . . . love you . . . love you."

She screamed. She shattered. A great quaking spilled from her womb, the inner tremors gripping Nick, milking Nick, until he gave a cry of his own and emptied his life force inside her.

They fell together back to earth. Nick collapsed, then rolled to his back, taking her with him. He tucked her head against his chest and held her, his hand gently stroking her hair. Contentment enveloped them like a cloud, and for a short few minutes they lay together without speaking, cherishing the moment and one another.

Then Sarah lifted her head and looked at him. "That was, by far, the most thrilling moment of my life. Can we do it again, please?"

"Now?"

"Right now."

Nick's Rod of Steel stirred against her stomach. "Damnation." He laughed, rolled her on her back, and settled himself between her legs. "Get ready, Lady Weston, tonight is your lucky night. Your Good Luck Wedding Night."

"Yours, too?"

"Mine, too. Because every night for the rest of my life, I will be sharing a bed with you."

He brought his mouth down to hers and gave her a swift, hard kiss. "That, my love, makes me the luckiest man on earth."

~Epilogue~

FORT WORTH DAILY DEMOCRAT
JUNE 2, 1888

The McBride/Tate Wedding
An EXCLUSIVE report

by Wilhemina Peters

Today I offer you, the citizens of Fort Worth, a follow-up to yesterday's column concerning the scandalous livestock parade through First Methodist Church during the wedding of Miss Emmaline McBride to Fort Worth rancher Mr. Casey Tate.

What had yet to become public knowledge at press time yesterday was the disturbing information that in addition to the "skunking" of their sister's wedding by the McBride Monsters, even more nefarious acts were taking place in the church pews.

As was reported by this correspondent prior to the wedding, Lady Weston, formerly known as Mrs. Sarah Ross in Fort Worth and now the Marchioness of Weston, served as the official wedding consultant to the bride's family despite being well-advanced with child. Lady Weston's family, including her handsome husband, Lord Weston, and three of his sisters, Lady Melanie Ross, Lady Aurora Ross, and Miss Robyn Ross—don't ask me to explain all the title folderol and why two of the girls are "Lady" while the other only a "Miss" because it's quite confusing and not necessary to the story—joined Lady Weston at First Methodist for the ceremony.

It was sometime during the McBride boys' skunk scare prank, when everyone was fleeing the church in fear of that pernicious perfume, that villainy struck.

Yesterday, at approximately two twenty-five in the afternoon, Lady Melanie Ross was abducted from First Methodist Church. A note, the contents of which remain private despite concerted efforts by this reporter, was left for the victim's brother, Lord Weston.

In light of past McBride family weddings, one cannot help but observe that in the congregation at First Methodist Church this past Saturday afternoon sat a Bad Luck Wedding Guest.

Watch for further developments on this story in forthcoming issues of this newspaper.

The End

Available from

GERALYN DAWSON

Simmer All Night

The Kissing Stars

The Bad Luck Wedding Cake

The Wedding Ransom

The Wedding Raffle

Sizzle All Day

Published by
POCKET BOOKS

2352–02